Joseph Ashby-Sterry

Tiny Travels

Joseph Ashby-Sterry

Tiny Travels

ISBN/EAN: 9783337212810

Printed in Europe, USA, Canada, Australia, Japan

Cover: Foto ©Andreas Hilbeck / pixelio.de

More available books at **www.hansebooks.com**

TINY TRAVELS.

BY

J. ASHBY-STERRY,

AUTHOR OF

'THE SHUTTLECOCK PAPERS,' 'BOUDOIR BALLADS,' ETC. ETC.

LONDON:

TINSLEY BROTHERS, 8, CATHERINE ST., STRAND.

1874.

TO

William Marshall—

IN MEMORY OF MANY PLEASANT TINY TRAVELS

IN HIS COMPANY, AT HOME AND ABROAD,—

THIS VOLUME IS INSCRIBED

BY HIS FRIEND

THE AUTHOR.

PREFACE.

My only excuse for troubling the public with the following reprints is, that my travels are very small. They are every-day travels, sometimes at home, sometimes abroad; occasionally trips without venturing outside my own door, and not infrequently rambles round my own brain—excursions which good-natured friends inform me must necessarily be of the most limited nature. The book may be briefly described as a *Snailway Guide*, in which, it is needless to say, no attempt has been made to rival in any respect the great guide-books of the day. In it will be found no mention of 'through routes' nor 'skeleton tours;' neither are the difficulties of luggage, the embarrassment of passports, nor the complications of coinage, treated of. I feel certain that in no case have I given the population of a town, however small, and sincerely trust that I have never so far forgotten myself as to insist upon my readers knowing how many feet any mountain, however short, is above the level of the sea. I can scarcely imagine my ' guide ' will furnish any substantial intellectual food for its readers, but I am not without hope that, as a light *soufflée*, it may not prove an unpalateable addition to the book-banquet of the hour. There may be times when even the most well-regulated tourist may become weary of the erudition of *Murray*, dazzled with the figures of *Bradshaw*, and jaded with the comprehensiveness of *Baedeker*. If such occasions ever occur, and this volume should act as a lullaby, and cause the traveller to forget for a while his severer studies, I shall feel it has not been written in vain.

J. ASHBY-STERRY.

TEMPLE,
  August, 1874.

CONTENTS.

CONTENTS.

TINY TRAVELS.

IN THE SILENT CITY.

TO City men the idea of silence being connected, in any way, with the City may appear in the highest degree ridiculous. They are so used to a perpetual excitement from the time they enter it to the time they leave it; they are so infected with the everlasting bustle, the eternal jingle of money, and the unceasing roar of the worshippers of the Golden Calf, that quiet to them would mean panic, and silence bankruptcy. City men never experience silence in the City. Its silence has been broken long before they arrive at their offices in the morning, and its hum continues long after they have left in the evening. The great cauldron of commerce is bubbling even before they commence their daily work, and it continues to simmer long after they have reached their mansions at South Kensington and Bayswater, or their suburban villas at Hampstead, Highgate, Lewisham, Camberwell, and Denmark Hill, or their river-side retreats, anywhere you please between Putney and Windsor. They know nothing whatever of the silence of the City. This knowledge is only given

1

to night policemen, to wakeful octogenarian City housekeepers, to bank watchmen, and to house-breakers. On second thoughts, perhaps the latter class know little of it; they seldom go anywhere unless there is business to be done, and although they know that there are plenty of cribs worth cracking in the City, the whole place is so watched that it renders their be-crackment a matter of considerable difficulty as well as danger.

The present writer, who is neither a night police-man, nor a wakeful octogenarian City housekeeper, nor a bank watchman, nor a housebreaker, recently went for a tour in the silent City. He had not been to an entertainment at the Mansion House; neither had he been banqueting with the Most Worshipful Company of Serene Stevedores; nor had he been dining with the captain of the guard at the Bank of England; nor was he on his way back from the Guards' mess at the Tower; nor had he arrived at some unreasonable hour by a tidal train at London Bridge. He had done none of these things, and yet there he was—no matter why—standing in front of the official residence of the Lord Mayor, just at that period when silence is beginning to steal over the City like a mist, and settle down on it like a dense fog—a fog which seems to muffle every voice, put india-rubber tires round all the wheels, tie up every knocker with white kid, shoe every horse with felt, and every passer-by with American goloshes.

I find I am particularly fortunate in the evening I have selected. There is no great civic festival going on, my meditations will not be broken by

the clatter of a hundred carriages, the vapid conversations of a myriad of powdered footmen, and
the flash of lights innumerable. A competitive
examination in clock-striking has just been held
by the various steeples in the neighbourhood.
Every one has struck twelve according to its own
time and its own tune; each in its turn strives to
impress upon the silence that its own is the only
right way of striking, and that it is the only regular and well-behaved clock in the neighbourhood. Such an impressive way have all the chimes
of doing this, that when a disgracefully laggard
clock, St Tympanum-by-the-Sideboard, rings out
twelve with querulous distinctness, at least a
quarter of an hour late, one is firmly convinced
that it must be the steadiest and most accurate
time-keeper in the City of London.

Your first thought, whilst standing upon the
kerb-stone of what is, in its normal condition, the
busiest centre of London, is—what can possibly
have become of all the omnibuses? Do they all
sleep out of town as well as the City merchants
and City clerks! Where, again, are all the
newspaper boys? Where are the disreputable,
dirty, ragged 'prisoner's friends' who always
hang about the pavement when the court is sitting
at the Mansion-house? Is anybody left in that
mysterious cell under the dock, from which the
prisoner emerges like a jack-in-the-box, and to
which he retires, also like a jack-in-the-box, when
the chief magistrate puts the lid down with a
sentence of six months' hard labour! Is any one
there, and if so, what is he thinking about? Is

he determining, in his own mind, to turn over a
new leaf, and so one day to become Lord Mayor
of London? The clocks are commencing another
competitive examination, and St Tympanum-by-
the-Sideboard, which, by the way, does not shine
at all in striking the quarters, is being run hard
by St Thomas Tiddlerius, and we have no time for
idle speculation; so take my arm, gentle reader,
and let us cross the road. In the daytime we
would not venture to do this unless we had pre-
viously insured our lives heavily in the Accidental,
but now we could roll about the road, or play
a game of hopscotch in it, if we forgot our dignity
in the darkness and stillness of the night. Let us
coast round the Bank, and dance gaily over the
heaps of treasure that are buried beneath our feet.
I wonder it has never occurred to some of those
energetic people who are always pulling up the
roadway under the excuse of gas, water, or paving,
to make a secret burrow under the Bank, hoist up
treasure in buckets of mud, and carry it away in
mud-carts, till the Governor and Company of the
Bank of England awakened some fine morning and
found themselves bullionless. I protest I should
like to wander about the interior of the Bank—
with no burglarious intention let it be distinctly
understood—and see the Temple of the Golden
Calf in its silence, when its high priests were
asleep. I should like to wander through the Three
per Cent office when all the books were closed,
when the brisk young clerks who are so particular
about signatures were asleep, and when the imbecile old ladies, with money in the funds, were

dreaming of the perils they had gone through in
being knocked about from beadle to clerk, and
from clerk to beadle, in the pursuit of dividend;
to see the Parlour with all the chairs tenantless,
the entrances beadleless, and the Rotunda silent
as the grave. Are there any clerks left in charge
all night? If so, I take it for granted that they
sleep upon mattresses of dividend warrants, and
lay their heads upon pillows of crisp bank-notes.
Possibly the wraith of Mr Matthew Marshall,
accompanied by a ghostly Bearer, rises now and
then to haunt these unfortunate watchers with
demands impossible to be satisfied. Who shall
say? It is certain that few things look more inscrutable and adamantine, and none less sympathetic, than the outer walls of the Bank of England in the dead of night.

Let us glance at the Grocers' Hall as we go by
—which looks like a well-endowed Dissenters'
chapel in the dim light, and as if excellent dinners
and superb wines had never been consumed within
its precincts—and turn down Lothbury. There is
not a soul stirring besides ourselves, and the stock-
brokers' cab-stand in Bartholomew-lane is untenanted. We turn up Capel-court: there is no
bellowing of bulls nor growling of bears now; our
footsteps re-echo with such startling distinctness
that we turn round sharply, thinking we are being
followed, and that there are other prowlers about
besides ourselves. The flags themselves look so
innocent of speculation and jobbery, so full of
good intentions, that they might serve as paving-
stones to that quarter, to which the descent, ac-

cording to classical authority, is so easy. As for the portals of the Stock Exchange itself, they appear to be closed so tightly that you wonder how it will be possible for them to be opened again at the proper time to-morrow morning. ' The House,' indeed, looks so serious, so dignified, so severely respectable, that it might be the Tomb of the Stocks, the sepulchre of shares, a mausoleum for bubble companies. One can hardly realize the fact that in a dozen hours' time these doors will be everlastingly on the swing; that a roaring, frantic, anxious crowd will be tearing up and down the worn steps; and that whatever there may be within the walls of our mausoleum will be galvanized into feverish and frantic life. As we turn to leave this dismal court we hear a species of Gregorian chant being dismally crooned, on a fourth-rate concertina, somewhere up on the top floor. What is the meaning of this? Is there an asylum for demented jobbers in this quarter, or is it the ' sweet little cherub who sits up aloft and keeps watch o'er the life of poor Stock,' who is giving this melancholy performance?

We take our way to the Royal Exchange, for we would fain see what goes on here at the witching hour of night. Do the merchants of long ago troop down here after twelve o'clock and whisper spectral quotations, and conclude phantom bargains? Does the ghost of Sir Thomas Gresham perambulate the French, American, Spanish, Portuguese, German, Greek, and Dutch walks, attended by sprites in the form of gigantic grasshoppers frisking and chirruping gleefully? We

pass in at the principal entrance. We notice the
doorway to Lloyd's closed hard and fast, as if
Lloyd were dead, and all the underwriters had
gone out of town to attend his funeral, or as if Mr
Plimsoll's agitation had made the insurance of
ships illegal, and Lloyd—who, by the way, is, or
was, Lloyd?—had closed his establishment in
despair. We peer through the ornate iron gate
at the entrance to the quadrangle. The whole
place is dark and deserted. There is not even a
beadle to break the monotony of the view ; we
can just catch a glimpse of the lights in front of
the Mansion House winking and glittering through
the western gate on the other side. A cold blast
comes whirling through the elaborate gates ; it
chills us—we walk briskly away across Cornhill
and enter Change-alley. We pause beneath the
shadow of Garraway's, and think how the neighbourhood must be haunted with the uneasy spirits
of the mad dabblers in the South Sea Bubble.
There is a light in the windows of a banking-
house giving on the alley. What is going on ?
Are fraudulent directors cooking accounts, or is it
merely a staff of hard-worked clerks 'on the
balance ' ? It is neither the one nor the other.
It is simply some men whitewashing the interior
of the office. You see time is so precious in the
City that they cannot afford to sacrifice even a
moment for cleanliness and beautification. Hence
bankers are compelled to do their work by day,
and their washing by night. The whitewashers
do not seem to like their job : they are depressed ;
they do not whistle blithely, and slap the ceiling

merrily after the usual fashion of healthy whitewashers. They do their work stealthily, as if
whitewashing were a capital offence, and they
were afraid of being discovered every moment.
We jump up and tap playfully at the window : the
whitewasher starts and peers anxiously in the
direction of the noise : he looks scared, and no
doubt thinks he has seen the ghost of Mr Secretary Craggs, Sir John Blunt, or any one of the
wild speculators who flourished a century and a
half ago. Out into Lombard-street—Lombard-
street, dark, sad, and silent. There are no
anxious crowds jostling one another, no doors
continually on the swing, like popular gin-shops
in a low neighbourhood, as happy mortals plunge
wildly in to drink of the Pactolean fount; no
rustle of bank-notes, no auriferous jingle of sove-
reigns, no pleasant song with the refrain of
'Owlyeravit.' This happy hunting-ground of
Thomas Tiddler might just as well be the Great
Desert of Sahara, for all the use it would be to me
at the present moment if I wanted to get a cheque
cashed. Why should banking operations be confined to the hours between nine A.M. and four P.M.,
and why should not bankers have a clerk for nocturnal duty, on the principle of the inn-keepers,
who have a porter up all night ? Supposing I
were to ring the bell and present a properly signed
cheque at one of these banks, is it likely that
some ancient housekeeper would come down with
a weird cloak thrown over her night-dress, and
give me the change ? I think it is far more likely
that the night watchman would awake suddenly

from his slumber, and that I should find myself
without delay in charge of the nearest policeman.

The silence increases. We can hear distinctly
the measured tread of the policeman at the other
end of the street, and we feel compelled to speak
in whispers, in order that he may not overhear
our conversation. There is no one about, there
are no roysterers and no revellers; the thunder of
late trains has entirely died away, and the thunder
of early ones has not commenced. In the whole
length of Fenchurch-street we encounter but one
person, and he is a stalwart Irish gentleman who
has charge of some works in connexion with pulling up the roadway, or illuminating an ancient
lantern, or keeping a very black cutty pipe in full
blast, we cannot tell exactly which. Mincing-
lane, gayest and most varied of the many retreats
of commerce, is the most deserted and dismal
quarter we have yet visited, and we shudder as we
see our faces reflected in ghostly fashion in the
vast plate glasses of the office windows, as we pass
by. The most curious part is that there is no
sign, no vestige of the vast business conducted
here, remaining. Who would ever dream of the
sales of every description that are going on in this
lane daily? Of rice, of sugar, of pepper, of nut-
megs, of cinnamon, of tea, of coffee, of indigo, of
hides, of ginger, of logwood, of shellac, of gum
benjamin, of myrabolams, of nutgalls, and a hundred other articles of which particulars are given
in catalogues which look like serious play-bills
run to seed. Not a sign of any of these things to
be seen. We can gaze right into some of the

offices, and see that they seem to be swept and cleared, as if they were going to be let to-morrow morning. The dismal passage by the Commercial Sale Rooms looks more dismal than ever, as we gaze through the iron gate and note the one lamp fitfully flickering in what appears to be the entrance to some third-rate baths.

We drift into Mark-lane, and find there the silence to be even more intense; we can distinctly hear the tick of a clock within a house as we pass by. We gaze through the windows of the Corn Exchange: it looks like a bankrupt railway station, about to be converted into a literary institution. The stands seem as if they were going to be transformed into reading-desks and newspaper slopes, and there is not so much as a grain of corn to be seen anywhere on the premises. We become objects of suspicion to a policeman, who evidently thinks we want to break into the Corn Exchange : we move on, and descend a somewhat steep and tortuous lane, and find ourselves in Thames-street. Here we are in a region of cellar-flaps, which groan dismally or wheeze asthmatically, in different keys, as we pass over them. We turn our faces westward and pass the Custom House. It looks as if the freest of free trade had been established; as if all duties, inwards and outwards, were entirely abolished, and the whole building converted into one vast crèche for poor children, in which all the inmates went to bed at seven o'clock. There are no lights to be seen except in a couple of windows on the top floor. Who is this burning the midnight gas, I wonder? Is it a surveyor-general, an inspector-general, a comptroller of accounts, a landing waiter, a searcher, or a jerquer? I have rather an idea that it must be a jerquer. I have not, of course, the least notion what a jerquer is; except that he must be something very mysterious, and, I should opine, more likely than any one else to carry on his operations at two in the morning.

We meet a dilapidated chiffonier, who is grubbing about amongst the rubbish heaps, and he is evidently very much scared at finding two tolerably respectable-looking individuals on his own ground so early in the morning. We pass through Billingsgate Market, we are too early, there is no one astir yet; but the bright light glimmering in the upper windows of a certain famous hostelry, close to the river, indicates that in an hour's time the place will be busy enough. In Darkhouse-lane we meet an individual, something between a decayed merman and a pinchbeck Diogenes, who is carrying a lantern, and talking to himself, and under the church of St Magnus we meet a misanthropic scavenger who is talking to his horses. These are the only persons we encounter. And yet, in a little while, this thoroughfare will be crammed with waggons, porter will jostle porter, and each vie with the other in the depth and variety of his objurgations. There will be shouting and screaming; there will be a loading and unloading of merchandise; warehouse doors will be thrown open; shops will display their wares, and the whirr and whiz of the crane will be heard without ceasing. And yet, at the present moment, it is as quiet and deserted as the back street of a

small cathedral town. There are noisome odours
as of decomposed fish, of decayed fruit, and of
bilge water. There is an irritating dust containing splinters of straw, which our friend the scavenger has distributed in the ardour of his occupation. Let us go up the steps on to London
Bridge, and see if we can get a breath of fresh air.

Up the dirty, greasy, disreputable steps we
pick our way gingerly. There we find one or two
poor creatures, one or two poor women in rags,
sleeping so soundly, enjoying a few hours' fitful
oblivion, only to wake up and find life more
wretched than ever. Tread softly, hush your
voice ; do not let us take away the small scrap of
comfort that oblivion alone can give. The bridge
is almost deserted, for the scavengers have finished
their work; there are no vehicles on it, so you
have every chance of crossing without seeing the
proverbial grey horse. There is a policeman on
one side of the way and a young lady in a red
shawl on the other, and one or two shapeless
masses—it is hard to say to which sex they belong—crouch on the stone seats here and there.
We find a seat that is untenanted, and we lean
over the parapet, and gaze down-stream at the
lights winking in the dark night, and glittering in
the black river as it hurries to the sea. Far away
down the Pool can we trace them; down past the
Tower, through the groves of masts and the tangle
of cordage, past the forest of Dockdom, the picturesque shores of Wapping, and as far as Lime-
house can we see the tiny glitter of lamps, like
fallen stars in the distance. Here and there

we notice a red or a green light, marking the
situation of some pier or station; there are no
busy boats about, no fussy penny steamers to
break the ceaseless swirl of the dark river as it
hurries away from the silent City. There is nothing to check the monotonous rush of its onward
course. Stay, what is that black mysterious boat
that is hovering about and shattering the long
lines of lamp reflections. Is it the police boat?
Or is it the craft of some aquatic burglar? What
is that they are towing astern? They break the
silence of the night by shouting. There is some
sign of life on board the Hull steamer at Fresh
Wharf; there is a clanking of chains, and a faint
steam issuing from her funnel; a heavy waggon
has just lumbered over the bridge towards the
Borough Market, and a couple of cabs have clat-
tered along in the opposite direction; there are
sounds as of the shunting of carriages and bump-
ing of turn-tables in the Cannon-street Station.

The spell is broken. Here comes an empty hansom. Let us jump into it, and drive home, for in
a little while the City will be no longer silent, but
will wake up to that feverish anxiety of speculation, to the everlasting fighting and struggling for
so much per cent., to trade, to barter, to profit and
to loss, which will last as long as Commerce lives,
and until Enterprise retires from business.

PANTING.

PANTING! Yes, literally panting!
I dare not move for fear I should faint, and
I am afraid to stir hand or foot, in case I should
throw myself into a violent perspiration. I am in a
very bad temper, and I would get in a rage only I
know I am not equal to the exertion. Bad plan to
lose your temper; it always punishes yourself more
than it does any one else, upsets your digestion,
brings on palpitation, makes you feel like a fool.
Besides, if you can only keep cool you can say
such aggravating things to your antagonist. To
lose your temper, to get in a rage—in short, to do
anything at all violent during this weather—would
be as bad as drinking three bottles of South African
port, or half-a-dozen of ball champagne. It would
throw you into such a heat that you would not get
over it for a fortnight. Why, bless your heart,
you would have prickly heat on the coats of the
stomach, whiskey in the hair, fireworks on the
brain, and all sorts of the most irritating and ex-
plosive complaints in two minutes. Therefore I
will not get in a rage. I should think not. If I
wink it throws me into a fever, which is only al-
layed by the cool breezelet which my falling eye-
lash flutters over my cheek. If I attempt to get
out my pocket-handkerchief to mop the beads of
perspiration off my heated brow, the exertion is so

great that I am unable to raise my hand to my face.
Why have I not a retinue of servants as they have
in India ? Why have I not a *khaunsaumaun* to
attend to my faintest wish, a *sais* waiting with my
steed to carry me wheresoever I list, a *punkahbadar*
to swing my punkah, and a *hookahbadar* to light
my pipe, and a *pocket-handkerchiefbadar*—it is
quite sufficient if I manufacture my own Hindoo-
stanee this weather—to mop my forehead.

I am just beginning to get a little cool, at least
I am not so hot as I was. I have been going
through a most aggravating evening. Friend dined
with me before starting for Paris. Dinner rather
hurried by reason of his wanting to catch his train.
Bad thing to hurry dinner this weather. As dinner proceeded I began to think I should like to go
with him. He used his persuasive powers after
every fresh glass of wine. He became quite eloquent at last, and finally I said I would go. On
consideration I recollected my old passport required
a *visa*, and so there was no help for it ; I must
stay behind. Very hot, indeed, all this made me
feel. I was about to get furious, but considering
the state of the weather I did nothing of the kind.
He was only just in time : half a minute more and
he would have missed the train. I wish he had.
We were bumped about and pummelled by hot
guards, perspiring porters, and incandescent cabmen. He made his way through a seething crowd
at the barrier, he had his ticket clipped, he looked
over the barrier, his hot hand clasped my hot
hand. There was a banging of doors, a ringing
of bells, a shrieking of whistles, the train slowly

forged out of the station, I saw red and green
lamps growing smaller in the distance, like the fag
end of a Cremorne firework, and I was left on the
platform, limp, lonely, and disconsolate.

I managed to crawl down to a certain club
that I wot of—a cosy, quiet, exclusive club, celebrated for the brilliancy of its wit and the lateness of its hours—a club that overlooks the
Thames, and where you can sit in the balcony
and enjoy the cool breezes wafted from the river.
I walk in, I shall surely find it cool. No, it
is nothing of the kind All the windows are
wide open—the gentleman who sets his face
steadily against draughts is away at Scarborough,
so the club is taking advantage of his temporary
absence by having every window and door in
the place agape—but the room is like an oven.
The red paper looks red hot, the frames of the
pictures are like unto molten gold, and the gas
burns fiercely. I lounge limply in. I nod to a
few members who are engaged in conversation.
It is too much exertion to open my mouth, and my
tongue is so dry that I am certain it would refuse
to form words. I drop on the first sofa I come to
and pant. The sofa feels exactly like a warm bed
in which the pan had been left till it scorched the
sheets. I feel it is burning me, but I have not
energy to get up. I think I will lie there and be
burned. I wonder how long it will take before
the heat will dry up the perspiration and actual
combustion of the cuticle take place. I cannot move. I remain on the sofa and hang my
tongue out of my mouth. I observe a highly

respected member of the club looking sternly at me. I am afraid he will bring me before the committee, under the 14th rule, something about 'ungentlemanly conduct.' I wish I could tell him that I am not putting my tongue out at him, but am only hanging it out to cool. My tongue is too dry to articulate. I try to pull it in. It is too dry to pull in. I take it by the tip—it feels like a kippered reindeer's tongue—and shove it back into my mouth and shut my lips fast. Severe member evidently thinks worse of me than he did before. I am afraid I shall be 'invited' to explain my conduct to the committee. By a superhuman exertion I manage to rise, I say something unintelligible to the waiter, which he will, doubtless, interpret as meaning a very cooling drink, and plenty of it. I stagger to an arm-chair, I pull it round to the balcony, I place my feet on the cool iron railing, and there I am where I was when I begun —panting.

I think I am getting a little better, the cool iron of the balcony rail is beginning to exercise a beneficial effect on my ankles. You know how foot-warmers in railway carriages warm the entire body, and I fancy there is no reason why foot-coolers should not have exactly the opposite effect. I can actually feel a current of cold passing up my legs and generally reducing my body in temperature. Why does not some clever speculator start foot-coolers? I am still panting but I am considerably better. I begin to feel tolerably happy as I watch the smoke wreathe up in blue curls above my head. I gaze across the

river, I seem to have left the club for awhile, and
it is only when some scraps of conversation or a
roar of laughter comes over my head that I am
conscious that I am still enrolled among its members. I gaze out upon the starlit night, I gaze up
into the deep blue vault, and I gaze down into the
swift running river. I trace the Embankment by
its row of lights, I count the lamps on Waterloo
Bridge, I note the coruscation of coloured lanterns
at the signal-box at Charing Cross, and I hear
some very late trains booming over the bridge.
I wonder what they are. Luggage, I dare say.
Luggage, by the pant and the snort of the engine.
It is quite delicious to find anything panting besides yourself this weather. Up in one of the shot
towers—which looks almost as grand as the tower
of St Mark in the still night—high up at the topmost window do I see a faint flickering light.
'How I wonder what you are!' you man with a
lantern or a candle. How deliciously cool you
must find it 'Up above the world so high.' Me!
What a glorious place it would be to pass the
night. I wonder if I were to present my compliments to the proprietors of either of the shot
towers whether they would allow me to pass the
night at such an elevation and make observations
therefrom.

There is a faint light at the dismantled 'Fox
under the Hill' that hovers about in some of the
upper windows in a weird fashion. Is it the wraith
of a stalwart bargee come back to dance a ghostly
'cellar-flap' on the roof, or to blow the spirit-
ual froth off a pot of spectral porter in the dead

of night ?   There is a dim lantern moving about
just below my balcony, there is a rattling of chains,
a stamping of horses, and a man who seems talking
to himself something about ' hullywoop ! '   Is it a
burglar, and is this some mysterious ' back slang ' ?
I am inclined to think it is nothing of the kind, but
merely a late carrier who has just got his horses
safely stabled and is going home.   There is the
clock at the Houses of Parliament still illuminated,
and looking like a property moon.   The House is
sitting late to-night.   There are mysterious lights
flitting about on the river, there are some that you
cannot account for over on the other side, and our
commonplace, work-a-day, unromantic London becomes a scene of wondrous beauty beneath the
mantle of the night.   There are weird reflections
cast across the water, and their ripple is just sufficient to give evidence of the swift, silent roll of the
stream.   Opposite is a mass of shadow, queer-
shapen roofs, odd chimneys, and scaffoldings,
broken here and there with a huge barge mast,
which, with its furled sail, looks more like the skeleton of an antediluvian bird of prey than anything
else.   The hot air wafts outwards from the club-room,
and singes the back of my neck, and the warm
breeze blows upon my face and scorches my nose,
and leaves me still gasping and panting.   I find the
cool iron railing is no longer cool.   I have begun
to warm it, and I fear if I keep my feet on it much
longer I shall make it red hot.   Of a truth my
plan for foot-coolers is a failure.

Without, all is a dead stillness, with the exception of the occasional bark of a dog, the clatter of

a hansom cab along the Embankment, and the
measured chiming of the clocks as they record the
fact that the large hours are gone, so are the very
small ones, and we are getting on towards the large
again. No matter. It is much too hot to go to
bed, and I see the House of Commons are still at
it as hard as they can be. From within do scraps
of conversation of the most tantalizing kind strike
upon my ear. A few men are talking over a tour.
Some of them are going, and others are not, but
are enjoying the keenest pleasure in fighting their
battles over again—in recommending various hotels
and devising particular routes. 'Whatever you
do, go to the Hotel du Parc and stay a few days.'
'If you are at Bellagio, don't forget to run over
to Varenna and lunch at the Albergo Marcionni.'
'Yes, if you stop at the Drei Mohren, at Augsburg,
you won't get away in a hurry, I'll promise you.'
'Go over to La Certosa, by all means.' 'O, you
could spend a week at Desenzano and enjoy yourself prodigiously.' 'Don't go to Venice till the
mosquitoes are gone, or you'll be driven mad.'
'Tumbled down a *crevasse,* and wasn't heard of for
two days.' 'Tremendous row with *vetturini,* fight
with waiters, turned out of the hotel.' All this
disjointed conversation comes to me in broken
scraps through the window, and I hear a scratch-
ing of pens, as some one is making a list of hotels
and pricking out a route for the benefit of some
one else. I wish they would not talk in this tantalizing fashion, for I am panting to be off somewhere, and I do not see any prospect of getting
away at present. Just a ghost of a cool breeze

at last. Ah! do not I see a faint glimmer of daylight, and is not the river actually beginning to look cold. The irrepressible tourists are tired of talking, they are putting on their hats and wishing one another good night. The clock at the House of Commons is out at last, the wearisome occupation of the members is over for to-night at any rate. It is quite time all reasonable people were asleep.

I retreat from my cool balcony, the blue daylight is streaming in—getting bluer and bluer every minute—to the morning room of the club; I find my hat, I lounge out into the street, and I walk home very slowly in the broad daylight, still panting.

PAPER PINIONS.

I PROPOSE, gentle reader, to soar upon paper pinions and go for a ramble amongst bills. Old bills, tattered bills, dusty, musty, fusty bills: bills unpaid, and bills that are receipted. I purpose to confine my investigation on this occasion principally to tradesmen's accounts, for I feel that to explore the uncertain labyrinth which is typified by certain long slips of blue paper, impressed with an embossed stamp and bearing a variety of curious autographs, though it might be profitable in its lessons, would scarcely be pleasing in its reminiscences. So I take my old file down. Its steel work is rusty with damp, and its brass work bronzed with age. The dust flies off as I flutter over its ancient memoranda of time and money misspent, and makes me cough and sneeze: it is a pungent, snuff-like kind of dust, and seems to enter a protest against being disturbed in so unceremonious a manner. Haphazard I run my hand in and pull out a dead leaf here and there, reminding one of bygone folly and pleasures that are no more.

Here are a little cluster of dead leaves all on one branch as it were. When I was staying down at Blankton—ah, never mind how long ago—when I was young and careless, and my cottage by the Thames was a paradise. Here are

brewer's bills: a good many eighteen gallon casks
of beer there seem to be. What capital beer he
used to brew, and how the boys used to pull away
at it out of the big tankard. There are a heap of
weekly accounts close to this, containing such items
as milk, sugar, eggs, candles, rent, &c., all made
out in the pretty writing of the daughter of my
landlady, Mrs Blackton. Mrs Blackton was a
paragon of a landlady; she was never put out of
the way if half-a-dozen men unexpectedly dropped
in to supper at twelve o'clock. You could smoke
in every room of the house, you might dance
breakdowns in the kitchen if you were so minded,
and your beer never ran short and your spirits were
rigorously respected. More leaves I turn over, all
bearing upon the same time. Here is one with a
badly lithographed heading supposed to picture
the aquatic delights of Blankton, with the legend
'———, Esq., to Robert Vast, Fisherman and
Boatman,' and then occurs a quantity of items
such as 'Hire of outrigger for season,' 'Punt and
day's fishing,' 'Baits, &c.,' 'Skiff,' 'Centre-board
on 14,' 'Excursion to Sedgeton,' 'Gig to Crownton
on 10,' 'Punt for bathing, at per morning,' and a
variety of other mysterious inscriptions, which all
awaken at a glance reminiscences of those jolly
days. Of the days when one rose at six o'clock
and took tremendous headers into the clear stream,
when one had such a tremendous appetite for
breakfast, and when one could pull an oar with any
one on the river. Pleasant times of lazy gudgeon-
fishing, which formed a capital excuse for a day's
dreaming in the sunshine, and a useful cold lunch-

eon. Luncheon! Why it was as good as a dinner. Do not I remember Mrs Blackton's marvellous beef-steak pie! Why, I protest it was something delicious, I do not believe they make such pies now-a-days. The hard-boiled eggs, the cold fowls, the sardines, the ham, the lobster salad, the sandwiches, the Stilton cheese, the jam puffs. Me! we could eat anything and everything in those days. And then the bottles of claret and sherry slung carefully in the well of the punt to keep cool, and, above all, that bacchanalian-looking little wooden keg, which appeared so small but yet held such a quantity of beer. This fisherman's account also awakens a whole host of pleasant recollections in connection with boating at the charming little river-side hamlet; of gay picnic parties; of glorious lounging beneath the overhanging willows, and gazing into bright eyes on a sunny day; dreams of sweet down-stream drifting in the moonlight, with the pleasant accompaniment of silvery girlish laughter, of

'Those dreamy August afternoons when in our skiff we lay,
To hear the current murmuring as slow it swirled away;
The plaintive hum of dragon-fly, the old weir's plash and roar,
While Some-one's gentle voice, too, seems whispering there once more.
Come back those days of love and trust, those times of hope and fear,
When girls were girls and hearts were hearts, about old Blankton Weir.'

All these pleasant pictures, however, vanish in a whiff of dust as I turn quickly over this bill and pass on to another.

I now drift on to a heap of tavern bills. How these come to be here I do not know. I hold that a man who keeps tavern bills is a fool. Nevertheless, they awaken some pleasant associations. Here is one bearing the title of ' Hotel et Pension Meyerhof, Hospenthal.' I have not been to Hospenthal for years; indeed, I had almost forgotten there was such a place; but this little slip of paper brings back to my mind the day when with three trusty companions I toiled over the St Gothard, knapsack on back. What a jolly little dinner we had at the Pension Meyerhof, and how superb the lake trout were, and how capitally cooked! Many years ago that is. The best man of that careless crew who climbed the pass on that sunny day will never shoulder a knapsack again; one of the party has become very serious, and nothing will tempt him out of England unless he could turn missionary; another when he travels always goes now *en grand seigneur*, and nothing would induce him to go ' out on the tramp' in the present day; and, as for me, if I undertook such rambles in the present day I fear I should want to turn back and look at the view oftener and rest longer at the Devil's Bridge than I did in the times to which I refer. Here are some more reminiscences. A bill from ' Guillaume Fils ' for a lot of Breton crockeryware I speculated in when sketching at Quimper years ago, when I fancied I was going to be a painter. A bill from the ' Albergo Reale,' at Desenzano, with the inscription *Situato in riva di Lago di Garda. Con omnibus tutti i giorni per Peschiera.* Do not I remember that very day the bill was made out, and what a

row we had with our *vetturini* who drove us in a
couple of broken-down chaises from Lonato? Cannot I recall the morning we spent on the field of
Solferino?   Do I not recollect sitting under the
vines, and gazing across the exquisite dazzling blue
of the Lago di Garda, and saying to one of my friends
how it reminded me of a picture by George Stanfield.   Do I not remember lazily plucking grapes
from a large purple cluster, smoking cigarettes,
and watching a pretty girl angling from an adjacent
balcony.   I cannot tear myself easily away from
this attractive group of bills.   Look here!   *Grand
Hôtel Vittoria, tenu par C. L. Borletti* and *A Bon a
Venise.*   I wonder whether handsome, white-headed, polite Signor Borletti is still there, and as
polite as ever to his guests.   Probably not, perhaps
he has retired from the hotel, for the time I allude
to was, it must be borne in mind, before the
Austrians quitted Venice.   Possibly he has retired
from the world altogether, and, like Thackeray's
famous Monsieur Terré, he has run his race—

> 'He's done with feasting and with drinking,
> With Burgundy and Bouillabaisse.'

How I recollect at this pleasant hotel some very
excellent *Lacryma Christi* of which we had sundry
bottles on one Sunday afternoon, and subsequently
scandalized an English clergyman by singing songs
of a somewhat secular nature in our bed-room afterwards.

Continental reminiscences, however, might be
multiplied to infinity, and it is a hard matter to
know where to begin, and when to leave off, and

what selection to make from a collection of bills
awakening so many pleasant trains of thought
as these I have just been turning over. Let us
look at something of a different kind, however.
Here is a small square of blue paper, with faint lines
on it, and appears to have emanated from the
establishment of a livery stable-keeper. It bears the
words ' To clarence to Barnes, 15s.; coachman, 2s.
6d.' Why could I not have gone to Barnes by the
ordinary railway or the common cab I wonder, and
why should I have been extravagant enough to
have chartered a clarence all to myself? When
hansoms are plentiful, surely it is as extravagant
for a man to hire a clarence as to bathe in a butt
of Malmsey. But then you see I did not mean
to ride all by myself. It was important to me in
those days that I should arrive at a certain evening
party in spotless patent leathers, with my hair unruffled, with my face unreddened by the cold, and
with my elaborate shirt-front unwrinkled. And
then I thought there was a chance—a poor chance,
but a possible one—of offering my clarence and
escort to Some-one and her sister on the return home.
So I went to my party; I did not make the *coup* I
expected. Somehow things went wrong; neither
my clarence, nor my escort, nor myself were accepted; I returned home by myself, and smoked persistently and savagely all the way to town, so that
the linings of the carriage must have stank for a
month. The bit of blue paper only remains as a
beacon of my youthful folly. I might just as well
have kept my mind at rest and the seventeen-and-
sixpence in my pocket. I am older now—and

wiser. Pleasanter than this is to turn to a bill of
luncheon at Skindle's, for the bright eyes that
sparkled over that banquet are yet as bright as
ever, and the rosy lips that were kissed by the up-
flying bead on that occasion are just as kissable as
heretofore. So it is with one of Ser Antonio's
bills of a choice little dinner at the Trattoria della
Luna at Florence. The good and true ones who
deigned to sit down with me on that occasion are
good and true still; they are yet merry and laughing. Every one is not false, neither is everything
altered for the worse.

But stay—here is another specimen. It is different to the others. It is neither a tradesman's
bill, nor a tavern bill, nor the account from a livery
stable-keeper. It is a very yellow, dirty piece of
paper: it is doubled across and across, it is nearly
torn in two, and is partly written and partly printed.
It has all the peculiar rough greasiness belonging to
continental paper, and all the most marked characteristics of cheap foreign typography. On unfold-
ing it I found it inscribed as follows :—

BERLINES DU MONT BLANC.

Grand Quai, 12.　　　Genève.　　　Grand Quai, 12.

Bureau de Genève.

———

Départ du *9 Octobre, 18*—à *7½* heures du *matin.*
Destination, *Chamouni.*
Nombres de places retenues, *deux.* Nos. *1, 3, 1re*
banquette.

Sous le nom de *Monsieur Brown*.

Somme payée. *Frs. 42.*

Laquelle sera acquise à l'Enterprise, faute par le
  Voyageur de se trouver au Bureau à l'heure
  fixée ci-dessus pour le départ.

Genève, le 8 Octobre, 18—

(Vois l'avis d'autre part.)   *Reichen.*

This official-looking document, which seems to
have all the importance of a title-deed to some
vast estate, is signed and stamped and counter-
signed, as if it were one of the most important of
state papers—indeed, the signature ' Reichen ' is
given with such a tremendous flourish, and is so
intensely illegible, that it is worthy a dozen cabinet
ministers at least. When I tell my readers that
the document in question was neither a warrant
for instant decapitation of the bearer, nor did it
represent a vast tract of landed property, but was
simply a receipt of fare for the morrow's ride in
the little *diligence* plying between Geneva and St
Martin, and that Reichen was neither a Fouché
nor a Robespierre, but simply one of the stupidest,
shabbiest, most garlic-scented, foreign clerks I
ever encountered, and that he persisted in smoking
the very worst cigars it was possible to procure,
perchance they will be somewhat disappointed.

How did this mysterious document come into
my possession ? Well it came about in this wise.
Late one autumn the present writer and his old
friend Brown found themselves in Geneva. We
had exhausted the amusements of this somewhat
uninteresting town, we had tried every wine in the

carte of the Hotel du Métropole, and Brown had
flirted with every girl he could find in that admirable hotel. The season was far advanced: it was getting autumnal, not to say wintry ; and yet we were
loth to return to London for a few weeks. Strolling through the Place des Bergues one day in search
of some good cigars we saw the well-known vermilion triangle, which is so much associated in the
British mind with Bass's pale ale. We looked
again, and found it was displayed in the window
of an English chemist. Brown, glancing at the
name over the door, declared that this individual
was a fellow-townsman of his, and he would go in
and ask him how he did. In we went. Mr English Chemist was delighted to see us, and we found
ourselves at once quite at home amongst the truly
British surroundings. There was Burgess's an-
chovy sauce, Lawrence's hair gloves, Maw's feed-
ing bottles, Windsor soap, Rowland's macassar oil,
tooth brushes, nail brushes, and hair brushes.
Here, too, might be found sponges, seltzer, soda,
and Saratoga waters, and Mrs Johnson's soothing
syrup, which history informs us is as great a comfort to mothers as Bass's pale ale is generally supposed to be to sons. Talking of Bass's pale ale
brings me back to the point I started from. Mr
English Chemist led us into a mysterious apartment which he called his surgery : here we expected
to see nothing but medical books and surgical
instruments, but were agreeably surprised to find
it a cheerful sort of warehouse. We took our seats
on tea-chests. Mr E. C. disappeared down a mysterious trap-door and presently returned with his

arms full of quart-bottles bearing the well-known
red label. He then retired to the shop and came
back laden with glasses and a box of very fine
Havannahs. He bade us sit down and make merry.
We sat down and were merry. We talked and
laughed so that some of the grave English dowagers, who came in to purchase tooth-powder, must
have wondered what on earth was going on, or
what could be the meaning of the festive expression on Mr E. C.'s face when he came into the
shop to talk to them. It was during this call that
we happened to hear from our entertainer that he
had just seen tourists from Chamouni, who reported the weather was deliciously fine there still.
This settled us, we determined to go to Chamouni,
we called at the Grand Quai, numero 12, and became possessed of the little document, of which a
copy is given above, we invited Mr English
Chemist to a farewell dinner at the Hotel du
Métropole, and the next morning found ourselves
seated in the *banquette* of the little *diligence* on our
way to St Martin.

We found the *conducteur* to be a very capital
fellow, pointing out every object of interest on the
road; the rest of the passengers were all natives,
jolly and communicative: there were no tourists
except a hideous old gentleman, in a travelling
cap, and two very stout old ladies, who were asleep
inside the *coupé*. The morning was bright and
clear, the air was brisk and bracing, and we soon
were capital friends with all our travelling companions, a friendship which we cemented by passing
round our tobacco pouches and our flask of *Kirsch-*

wasser. Through the little town of Chesne, and
past the village of Nangy, a little while after passing which you may if you please—for my own part
I do not care twopence about ruins—see the ruins
of the Castle of Faucigny. At Bonneville we
descend and go into the neat little inn, the Cou-
ronne : the morning air and our early breakfast
has made us fearfully hungry, so we lay to with a
will at some Gruyère cheese and some long crisp
loaves, and take a good pull at some sour wine.
Our driver is in a hurry to start again, so we rush
out, Brown with his mouth full, and about half a
yard of bread under his arm. We find our party
has been augmented by a young Swiss maiden—
really not bad-looking as Swiss maiden go—Brown
—sad man that Brown—manages to sit close, indeed, I may say quite close to her. He talks nonsense to her, she laughs prettily, but I am certain she cannot understand a word he says. Once
I detect him—for in those days he had all the confidence and iniquity of Miss Snevellicci's papa—
positively winking at the fair damsel. I turn my
head away and endeavour to improve my mind by
studying *Murray*. I am deep in one of this
author's superb passages running thus :—'On leaving Cluses, the road is carried through the defile
on the borders of the river, and beneath grand
Alpine precipices. The valley is very narrow nearly
all the way to Maglan, and in some places the
road is straitened in between the river and the
bases of the precipices which actually overhang the
traveller. The banks of the river are well wooded,
and the scenery is as beautiful as it is wild.'

When I hear the Swiss maiden give a cry of joy I look up, she is waving her hand gleefully. *Ah! le voila! Regardez donc! C'est Auguste!* she shouts, and her eyes sparkle with pleasure. I find we have arrived at St Martin, and, as the *diligence* approaches the Hotel du Mont Blanc, a brawny, red-faced, mustachioed individual in a blouse comes up to the vehicle with many frantic salutations and assists the maiden to dismount; he kisses her on both cheeks, and is evidently delighted to see her. Brown begins to look frightened and pretends to be intensely interested in the surrounding scenery —O, what a hypocrite was Brown in those days— but mademoiselle is not to be put off in this way. *Bon jour, Messieurs, bon jour!* she says prettily, waving her hand with the utmost *nonchalance* : her companion raises his cap, Brown looks relieved, we take off our wideawakes, and they are gone.

Here the little *diligence* comes to a stop, we must hire a trap of some kind to reach Chamouni, so we have plenty of time to look about us. We begin to feel hungry again and Brown suggests dinner. We turn into the Hotel du Mont Blanc and are shown into a comfortable up-stairs room; presently we have a very capital little dinner served up to us; we are waited upon by a motherly old lady who we fancy has cooked the dinner herself; we compliment her on her *cuisine*, whereat she seems to be greatly delighted; we consult her with regard to the wine, and she indicates which is the best, but by no means the most expensive on the *carte*. We find we have done well in this, for it is of very excellent quality, so excellent indeed that

Brown proposes to have another bottle. We have another bottle, and by the time it is finished Brown gets talkative, not to say garrulous; the reckless way in which he ventures into the depths of an unknown tongue is something astounding. I find him at last leaning over the wooden rails of the balcony 'chy-iking' natives on the other side of the way, and holding animated conversations with people in the street below. I see our carriage is being brought round, so I haul Brown in forcibly by the coat-tails and tell him it is time to start. We pay our bill, take an affectionate farewell of Madame —Brown had to be controlled, as he was getting very demonstrative—and we start with a tremendous cracking of whips and a jingling of bells.

Brown manifests a desire to take off his hat to every woman he meets, and has a general disposition in favour of nodding violently to everybody. However, he quiets down, and endeavours to appear interested when I point out to him the traces of the flood of 1852 along the valley of the Arve. I try to improve his mind by reading *Murray* aloud to him. I read 'The mountain above Servoz abounds in tertiary fossils.' Brown irreverently remarks 'Tertiary fossils, be hanged.' Brown, with all his faults, never was a geologist. It is very sad. I must give him up. At Servoz we come up with the uninteresting gentleman, who travelled with our *diligence* this morning. He is in a capital carriage, good horses, and going along well; his two stout ladies are all smiles and enthusiasm with regard to the scenery. The affable Brown takes off his hat as our carriage comes to a stand, and we walk up the hill with the gentleman. We

find him not to be such a bad sort after all, but he
has never been out of England before, whereat
Brown puts on the air of an old traveller who has
knocked about Europe all his life, and gives him
most startling information with regard to hotels
and the manners and customs of the Swiss people.
He presently rejoins his carriage, we bow once
more to the ladies, and they drive on. Our horses
are very shaky, so we find that hiring a carriage
to take us to Chamouni means—walking all the
way, helping to push the carriage over difficult
places, and treating the driver at every opportunity. It suited us well enough this loitering.
We walked on ahead, picked up walnuts, and then
sat down and cracked them till the carriage over-
took us; we looked in at the wayside cottages
and talked to the children, and we made ourselves
vastly popular by treating a lot of workmen to some
wine at a picturesque little *cabaret*. Perhaps this
part of the valley of Chamouni never looks so well
as in the middle of October. I think I never recollect seeing such vivid colours of every shade
from the palest orange to the deepest vermilion
that the autumnal foliage presented, backed up as
it was by the sombre pines.

Thus we loitered and lounged, we gossiped
and smoked; and our driver, who was not a bad
sort of fellow after all, was nothing loth to do as
we did. It was getting dusk when we reached the
village of Les Ouches, and it was nearly dark when
we sighted the glacier of Taconey. After this it
came on to rain, so we pulled up the head of the
carriage and got inside, and amused ourselves by
watching the many tumbling streams and torrents

passing beneath the road which we could just distinguish in the fading light. Long after it was pitch
dark Brown vowed several times he could see Mont
Blanc, and we were fast asleep when we passed
through the little village of Bossons. The constant
roaring of the stream and the tumbling of the torrents contributed not a little to lull us off to sleep.
We must have been asleep a tremendous time :
the torrents suddenly seem to stop altogether.
I think in my sleep that it has been turned off
at the main, and mumble some words from a song
that I have heard Mr Toole sing, something about
' nothing was left but an unpaid water-rate.' There
is a banging of doors, a letting down of steps, and
a flashing of lights. 'O, here we are,' says Brown
yawning. *Bon soir, messieurs!* says Madame.
' Anybody in the house ? ' say I to the Anglo-Swiss
waiter. 'Not much of the world,' he replies. ' An
English Monsieur and Madame *seulement.*' I wonder
who they can be. I had little idea then that they
would eventually be numbered among the best
friends I ever had in my life.

I could tell you a great deal more. My paper
pinions would carry me on a much longer flight. The
show is by no means over. Old yellow bills flutter
past, crisp blue bills, cream-laid bills, foreign thin'
paper bills, crumpled bills, and torn bills. The
dust of years flies from them, and the reminiscences
of times gone by are awakened. But enough, O
showman, close thy paper pinions, put up thy file
of bills : let the dust of years once more gather
on their withered leaves and help to bury the re-
cords of bright days long passed away.

FADED PHOTOGRAPHS.

DO not imagine that I am going deeply into the question of the permanence of photographs. Do not fancy I am about to give an account of the chemistry of the art, and to demonstrate that in a hundred -years' time the pictures which we prize so much will be nothing but sheets of blank paper. I have no intention of doing anything of the kind. I am inclined to think that the good photographs of the present do not fade, that they will remain in their present tint as long as the paper on which they are printed exists. All I can say is that photographs used to fade, and we all of us have a number of faded photographs in our possession. I know I have a goodly number—taken long before the art had been brought to its present perfection. I have many of these : they have turned yellow, the half-tones have entirely disappeared, and the shadows bleached. I have portraits of my intimate friends which I thought so excellent when they were taken, faded to boiled ghosts, and local habitations, which were true to a brick and a stone many years ago, faded to airy nothings. It is sad to gaze upon these wrecks, and try to call back features in the faint outline and to discover landmarks in the mist. It is heart-breaking work to

endeavour to fill up details; to peer into the fog
in the hope of discovering a trace of something substantial.   It is bad for the eyes, it is bad for the
temper, and it is a weariness to the mind, and,
therefore, I will have nothing to do with it.   I will
rather turn my attention to the particular object
of my paper, which is the faded photographs of
the brain.

Have we not, all of us, a vast collection of
these?   And do we not have a marvellous power
of developing them at will?   In this we have the
advantage over the actual photograph.   We can
fix them, we can think of them, and in a little
while the outline will become visible, the shadows
will deepen, the half-tones will return in all their
delicacy, and we shall see the whole picture stand
out with marvellous distinctness.   I do not know
how I came to think on this matter, unless it was
my seeing a lamplighter go along the street just
now to light the lamps.   This man was armed with
an instrument which looked something between a
gigantic billiard-cue and an *alpen-stock*, with a
brass top that gave it the appearance of a beadle's
staff that had outgrown its strength.   The lamplighter himself seemed to be a luxurious individual,
and he lighted his lamps from the pavement in a
lazy *nonchalant* manner.   He prodded them playfully, he tickled them in the ribs, so to speak, he
gave them a sort of ‘ *c-c-c-k-k-k!* ’ — like the
comic man always does to the pretty chambermaid
on the stage—and they suddenly became illuminated.   Where he got his light from I am unable

to say. I did not like to stop him and ask him, as lamplighters are apt to consider people of enquiring minds impertinent. He might have given me a cuff over the head or tilted savagely at me with his staff of office, he might have suddenly turned the light on and burnt my best coat. Besides, I did not care twopence how he lighted his lamps so long as my street was illuminated at the proper period. But this man brought forth a faded photograph in my mind which I proceeded at once to develop. How different he was to the lamplighter of my youth. What a marvel of activity and despatch was that individual! To 'run like a lamplighter' was a saying indicative of great speed many years ago. I recollect a certain nursery window from which the evolutions of this official used to be watched with breathless interest. I remember reserved seats used to be taken long before he could be expected, and sometimes there was considerable ebullition of temper and an occasional resort to fisticuffs concerning the retention of front places. It was then as in after-life. Might was right, the weakest went to the wall, the impudent and the selfish had the reward, the good-natured and obliging was hidden in some dark corner behind the curtain and saw nothing : the strong bully had the most comfortable place and witnessed the whole of the exhibition. That was how I managed to see the show so well, and am able so many years afterwards to report accurately upon it. I recollect how tiresome it used to be waiting, how cold the window-panes used to feel to chubby cheeks pressed against them, and how one used to get one's face fluted for the entire evening by pressing it against the warm window-sash by way of a change. I could draw at this very moment the pattern of the iron balcony outside the window, and know exactly the position of a few scrubby plants, that never flourished successfully on account of the researches I was everlastingly making in experimental horticulture. I know how it used to be a moment of breathless anxiety when the top of the ladder was seen coming round the corner of the street, and when the lamplighter himself appeared it was a signal for applause. How skilfully he carried the ladder, and with what ease did he swing his lantern. There was no hesitation about this man : he was as quick as he was skilful. The whole operation was over in two-two's, in the 'twinkling of a bedpost,' in the click of a hair trigger. Then was the time if you owed a grudge against any of your companions to get up a row : the worst of it was in preventing their participation in the entertainment, you generally lost your own share of the exhibition. I never did this till I became somewhat *blasé* and looked upon watching the lamplighter as a somewhat childish amusement. He was *so* quick was our lamplighter. He did not stay to see if he had placed his ladder securely, he knew to an inch the right position and never thought of testing its safety before he mounted. Bless your heart. He was round the corner, his ladder was placed, he was up, the lamp was lighted—he seemed to fly up and slide down—his ladder was on his shoulder

and he was at the next lamp-post before you could
say Jack Robinson.' We used to look upon this
lamplighter with awe and reverence, a man who
was clever, courageous, and a very great traveller
in unknown regions. My admiration for the great
African traveller Captain Burton is something
enormous, but it is nothing, absolutely nothing, to
the admiration and awe with which I looked upon
this lamplighter. He was a man, we were told,
who ran terrible risks to life and limb by reason
of his dangerous calling. I recollect a paper
being brought round at Christmas, a large paper
with printing in the middle and woodcuts down
either side. I do not recollect what the reading
was, my education being not sufficiently advanced
at that period, but I can call to mind one of the
woodcuts represented a lamplighter's ladder being
cut over by a very frisky looking horse and gig.
The lamplighter was depicted flying through the
air with his legs and arms extended and his hat
falling after him. The effect was very awful. We
somehow got hold of the idea that this man was the
elder brother of our own especial lamplighter, and
there was some talk of getting up a subscription
for him, but I do not think it came to much. I
rather fancy I constituted myself treasurer, and
when the subscription reached fourpence ceased
to believe in lamplighters and invested the money
on my own account.

Another faded photograph I see of about this
period. I recollect being carried out by my nurse,
being taken to a baker's shop, and buying a large
cake nearly as big as myself. We had not gone

half-a-dozen yards from the shop when I dropped
the cake, and a beggar picked it up and ate it.
Never shall I forget the utter helplessness of my
situation; my head and my hand with the cake in
it were over the nurse's shoulder, so she could not
see what had occurred. I was unable to speak, and
long before my howls of rage and disappointment
had aroused her to the nature of the catastrophe,
the beggar had disappeared. I do not know to
this day why I was not immediately supplied with
another cake. I think this must have been my
first idea that there was such a thing as injustice
in the world. I should be afraid to say how many
years ago this occurred, but I could give you an
exact picture of the baker's shop, the peculiar
kind of baskets in which he put his cakes, and
could describe nearly every variety of cake he
had in his window. I recollect the old rascal, with
his battered hat, his shambling legs, his three days'
grey beard, his red nose, and his generally greasy
and grimy appearance. I could depict even his
gnarled stick, with the bark stripped off half way
down, and with its unferruled ragged end. I could
show which of his coat-buttons were greasy, which
showed the metal, and which were gone altogether.
I could indicate which button-holes had been sewn
up with string, and which had gone into long slits,
so that it looked like the entrance to a breast-
pocket in the wrong place. I could sketch you an
accurate, full-length portrait of my nurse; a right
jolly, good soul she was, and I rather think she
must have paid for that unfortunate cake out of
her own pocket. I recollect she stood my friend

afterwards when I was about to be sent off to the saddler's to be measured for a muzzle, because I chose to try and bite a piece out of my sister's arm. It may seem to be absurd to write all these things. I dare say it is. But I select these from my bundle of faded photographs, haphazard, as they turn up.

I turn up suddenly, I do not know why or wherefore, a photograph of Vauxhall Gardens, and it gradually becomes more and more distinct as I gaze upon it. My recollections will not drift back so far as the days when Mr Pendennis and Miss Fanny, and Captain Costigan and Mrs Bolton, spent that merry evening there, which, if I remember rightly, ended in a row with Mr Hunter, but still I have some pleasant reminiscences connected with the place. I loved its leafy shade, its long, mysterious walks, its curious rooms, its winding staircases, which took you out on roofs before you knew where you were. I loved to moon about those walks and people the curious nooks and the covered alleys with ghosts of the past. I enjoyed to muse on the brave old times ' when the fine City ladies, in parties to Ranelagh went or Vauxhall,' and drift back in imagination half a century. You see I am giving you a faded photograph within a faded photograph, and if I do not take care I shall be giving you a third within the second. Let me hark back, then. I hold that a place that once exists in the country never entirely loses its rural smack. You may run railways close to it, you may surround it with hideous houses and filthy manufactories, but still it will never altogether lose its flavour of

rusticity. And this was true with regard to Vauxhall Gardens. It was a charming little oasis in the
midst of an unsavoury neighbourhood devoted to
bone-boiling and pottery. Directly you had paid
your money and entered through the mysterious
portal you began to breathe a different atmosphere.
The visitors became transformed into beings of a
superior order, and as for the waiters, you never in
the whole course of your life encountered anything
so superb as the Vauxhall waiters. The extraordinary part of the matter is this, you never saw them
anywhere else; you never met them at chop-
houses, or at evening parties, or at public dinners.
They always seemed to me like archdeacons, and
I invariably treated them with the most profound
respect. I have left Vauxhall Gardens very early
in the morning and never saw any waiters going
home. I have gone there very early in the afternoon and never seen any waiters arriving. My
belief is that they either slept in the little supper
boxes, or that they were accommodated with bed-
rooms by his Grace the Archbishop of Canterbury
in his palace of Lambeth hard by, or that they
were turned on with the gas in some mysterious
fashion. I was at these gardens the last night
they were ever open to the public, and I think I
enjoyed myself very much. I was young in those
days, and generally managed to get half-a-crown's
worth of enjoyment for my shilling. I recollect
that I felt very pastoral, directly I entered the ' royal
property.' I had a sort of suspicion that I was a
' shepherd swain.' I had a general disposition to
sing songs with an interminable refrain of ' fa-la-

la !' I encountered a charming, laughing, curly-headed Amaryllis who was disposed to foot it deftly on the green sward. It was not easy to dance on account of the vast crowd. We were jostled, and bumped, and pushed, and elbowed. At last I thought it would be more amusing 'to sport with Amaryllis in the shade,' and we wandered along the Italian Walk, down the Dark Walk, explored the gardens generally, and finally found ourselves —I do not know how we got there—on the top of a roof looking at the moon and gazing on the lamp-lit gardens below us. I do not know what my excellent friend the Countess of Grundy would say to all this. You see I was not acquainted with her in those days, and I had no intention of offering my hand and heart—or my hand without my heart —to one of her daughters. Besides, all this happened in that delightful period before I had arrived at years of discretion. But to resume. Amaryllis was mortal after all. She became tired of staring at the moon, and listening to the nonsense of Corydon, and on being asked the question, whether she was an hungred, she replied in the affirmative, and added, by way of a rider, 'and thirsty too.' We descended from the roof, we encountered Miss Amaryllis's sister and Miss Amaryllis's sister's young man. We had a snug little supper party, we had a goodly quantity of stout out of those peculiar brown mugs. I think we saw the young ladies home, and that I swore eternal friendship to Amaryllis's sister's young man at three o'clock on a fine summer morning in the Westminster Bridge Road, and that I promised to be his 'best man' on the occasion of his marriage. I have never seen Amaryllis, or her sister, or her sister's young man since that time. I attended the sale of the effects of Vauxhall Gardens, and I purchased a brown mug, which stands on my mantelpiece to the present day in memory of Amaryllis. I was strolling about the neighbourhood of Vauxhall the other day, and I could not discover a stick or stone which reminded me of the old place. There is scarcely a single landmark remaining by which you can trace where the pleasant gardens once stood. There is a church, a working man's college, a school of art, and a number of inferior houses built upon the site. Among these latter are two streets, which, in a degree, call back reminiscences of the neighbourhood in its palmy and leafy days —namely Gye Street and Italian Walk.

I have a large number of faded photographs which I am desirous of restoring and showing them to you in all their sharpness and distinctness. Indeed, my gallery of such pictures is almost without limit. The restoration of faded photographs of the brain is an art, to use the language of advertisers, 'within the reach of all.' Sometimes this work is very sad—in my present paper I have dwelt principally upon its more pleasant aspect—the revival of some recollections is but a melancholy pleasure. A long catalogue of failures, of ships that never came home, of friends that were untrue, and, worst of all, of girls that were false, crowds upon my brain as certain pictures occur to my mind. Alas and alas! there are many photographs of the brain that we would rather wish to fade away altogether, that they should become as blank as a sheet of white paper. How curious it is that these photographs are just the kind that never will fade, or, if they do so, persist in restoring themselves in the most vivid and elaborate manner at the very period when we are anxious to forget all about them !

SPRING SUNSHINE.

RIGHT away from London. Far away from town. Away from the roar of the Strand and the rumble of Pall Mall. Far removed from the gossip and scandal of Clubopolis do I take my first 'pull' of spring sunshine. And what a refreshing, invigorating draught it is! How everything bounds and sparkles! What spirit it gives you! How it pulls you together! How it knits your muscles up. How it makes you feel inclined to take the most violent exertion, to perform the greatest marvels of gymnastics, and to become the most muscular of Christians. How it makes you wish to row violently, to swim for a mile or two, and to walk for twenty! How it causes you to get up early in the morning, to accomplish unheard of things in the way of breakfasts, and to fancy the calling of farmer to be the most delightful of all callings, and a country life to be the most charming of all existences!

What have I been doing all the week? Well, nothing particular. I have been enjoying myself very much. I have been very happy. I have been 'pottering' to my heart's content. I have not been worried. I have been allowed to do pretty much as I pleased. The other morning I spent a dreamy morning at Blankton Weir—you know

Blankton Weir, an intimate friend of mine has
written some verses thereanent. Well, I spent
a very delicious morning up there. I did not
mean to go there exactly, but I lounged down
to the boat-house, and feeling unusually energetic
I got into a canoe and thought I would go for
a vigorous paddle as far as the weir. When I
got some way on I bethought me that I would
turn down some of the backwaters—backwaters of
which I knew nearly every stone and each individual reed in the old time—and see if they still
remained as formerly. Then it came to pass that
I slackened my speed. I meandered about. I
paddled round islands and paused or drifted by
well-remembered corners. After all, this is the
great use of a canoe. I scarcely fancy I should
do for a member of the Canoe Club, for I should
never care to undertake the extensive voyages on
which they pride themselves. Depend upon it, a
canoe was never intended for anything of the kind.
A canoe was meant for dreaming and mooning. It is
just the thing on some fine summer day to take up
into the backwater or under low drooping boughs,
and to read your favourite author and to smoke
the lazy pipe. You can run up into the rushes,
you can listen to the swirl of the stream, the distant roar of the weir, the rustle of the leaves overhead, or the hum of the dragon-fly. You can
moon, you can dream, you can read, you can
smoke, you can sleep. One stroke of your paddle
will put your canoe in a different position, one
languid turn of your hand can alter your prospect
altogether. The lightness of your boat is greatly to

its advantage.   You can take it where other
craft could not by any possibility penetrate, you
may ride over water-lilies and browse among for-
get-me-nots.   And thus I drifted about in the
spring sunshine the other morning.

As I before said, this is just the purpose for
which a canoe is suited.   A man who can go for a
thousand miles by himself in such a craft must
certainly be of a most superior order.   I know that
if I were to attempt such a voyage I should get so
disgusted with myself after the first fifty miles
that I should endeavour to upset my canoe, and
put myself out of my misery as speedily as possible.   A man must be peculiarly constituted to accomplish such an excursion.   I am not peculiarly
constituted, therefore I should never think of attempting it.   There are times, however, when it is
pleasant enough for a man to loaf about by himself
and moon and meditate in the open air, and then
a canoe becomes a most desirable acquisition.   And
so I found it the other day as I paddled about
amongst the backwater, as I sometimes went forward, sometimes backward, taking excursions round
old tree stumps, making trial trips over doubtful
looking shallows, and whirling along rapids, and
getting nearly shipwrecked among boulders.   Floating down with the stream, occasionally putting
my paddle across so that the blades would catch
the breeze, lighting up my ancient black clay,
and drifting down with the stream.   Running my
craft into some tiny harbour and being lulled to
sleep by the current gurgling beneath it.   Then
getting suddenly energetic, and putting my canoe

about, paddling violently up stream, taking short
cuts between ancient willows, and nearly oversetting
my ship in attempting dangerous north-west passages between osier beds. At last emerging into
the broad Thames again and struggling against the
stream, keeping out of the main current, and paddling up to the old weir.

Over the flashing waters, dancing amongst the
white foam, riding over the merry billows glittering
in the spring sunshine to the roar of the old weir.
Right up to where the green and white waters come
savagely sliding from between the weir rymers over
the apron. Close to where they seethe, and boil,
and roar as they come bowling through the tumbling bay. Then putting the head of my craft round
and letting the miniature breakers dash over her
and go drifting swiftly and dancing merrily down
stream. At last, quite hot with my exertion, I think
I will land and have a look at the old weir. I drift
across into comparatively smooth water, an active
gentleman, something between a cab-driver and a
fisherman, sees me approach. I land beside a punt.
I leave my ship in charge of the active gentleman,
and I enter an hostelry hard by. I sit down
and the landlord soon makes his appearance and I
take a glass of excellent ale. The landlord seems
to be cheered by the spring sunshine, he is brisk
and lively : the ale seems to feel the influence of
the spring sunshine, it is brisk and lively, and I
drink it with a wondrous relish. I then bethink
me that I will go out and examine the old weir and
see if it remains pretty much as it did in the old
time. It used to be a glorious lounging-place in

those days of long ago. Alas and alas, I find it to
be vastly altered, and I am afraid if my friend were
to see it in the present day he would find but little
inspiration for his muse. I suppose the place is
very much improved : in a practical, business-like
sense it undoubtedly is. The grand old stream is
as grand as ever, and its roar is quite as musical as
formerly, but beyond that little remains of old
Blankton Weir. It has been modernized, refur-
bished, polished up—in a word, rebuilt. Some
corporation of improvers have taken the ricketty
old structure in hand, and have made it as safe, as
substantial, and as unpicturesque as the most
practical man could desire.

It is very sad to see all this. It is a grievous
thing that the useful and the picturesque can scarcely ever be combined. The battered piles, moss
o'ergrown and weed-covered, are gone, the creaky,
wheezy old gates have disappeared, the shattered
wood-work, so superb in colour, has been removed,
and a painful respectability, a fearsome church-
wardenism, reigns in its stead. The amusing old
lock-keeper, who used to be one of the most expert swimmers on the river Thames, is gone. I
wonder whether that amiable old Waterloo hero,
who used to fish so enthusiastically here every
evening, still exists. What many talks I have
had with the gallant old colonel in the twilight
when lounging about here! I will walk across and
see if I can find him anywhere over the weir. When
I reach the entrance to the lasher I find a most
painfully white, obtrusively churchwardeny gate,
securely locked, bars my progress. Thereon is

written, in most well-conducted, severely correct
characters, a notice to the effect that no one is
allowed on this part without especial permission of
some board or another. Is not this too much ?
Boards are becoming the bane of my life, and perpetual ' notices, ' ' by orders,' and bye-laws are
making existence wearisome. What does this
board mean by closing my favourite lounging-place,
and what right have they to interfere with my
mooning propensities ? This place would have
been the place of all others to study spring sunshine
in all its glory, and to watch the waters sparkling
and making merry beneath its influence.

I am disgusted with the trimness of the machinery, the new tightly fitting lock gates, that
appear as if they were well polished over every
morning by a detachment of the Shoe-black Brigade.
I am out of patience with the method and order
that seems to reign about the place. I loathe the
new white stone pound that looks so painfully like
a fortification, and I sigh for the glorious tumble-
down picturesque place that I used to know. All
the surroundings, however, are pretty much as they
used to be, so I once more take as comfortable a
position on the gates as these emblems of modern
respectability will allow me, and I gaze down stream.
I see the stream foaming and sparkling and running
away from me in a vast hurry. I note the whiten-
ed banks, muddy from the recent floods ; I observe
the grand old elms, with their delicate tracery,
reddening with buds against the pale clear blue
sky ; the eyot just below with the tall old willow
and the tangle of branches and osiers at its foot ;

the dazzling bright green meadows on either side; the thin smoke going straight up from the chimney of my hostelry; the windows of distant houses winking and blinking in the sunshine. I gaze upon all this as I listen to the everlasting melody of the rush and the ripple of the waters. I drift back in thought to the old times, and I almost forget that we live in an age of detestable improvement and of oppressive respectability. I strive to shut my eyes to the alterations that have taken place in this spot as I dreamily bask in the bright spring sunshine.

The village clock, with its quaint chime, rings out twelve distinctly on the bright clear atmosphere. It is terribly unromantic, I know, but it reminds me of luncheon and I begin to feel awfully hungry. I shall just be able to get back in time. So I once more get into my canoe and drift merrily down stream, dancing gaily along over the ripples in the glad spring sunshine.

EARLY TO BED.

'EARLY to bed and early to rise makes a man healthy, wealthy, and wise.' So says an old proverb. Though I have been brought up with the highest respect for old proverbs and an implicit belief in their teachings, I have gradually and gradually become an utter sceptic. I may state boldly that I consider nearly all of them to be pleasantly phrased lies, I consider all their principles to be wrong and their teachings invariably unjust. Possibly they might have been true at the time they were invented, perhaps their principles were right a hundred years ago, perchance they exactly suited our great grandfathers. Be that as it may, they will not do now. I assert boldly that they must be altered. They are old-fashioned, worn out, and entirely behind the age! We alter our laws to suit the requirements of the age with the utmost ease and the greatest freedom, and why should we not alter our proverbs? Among the many excellent societies that I have founded, or rather that I have talked about founding, it comes to pretty much the same thing, in my time—it surely is quite enough for me to invent societies, and look to others to carry them out—I mean to include another. It will be called the ' Society for the Suppression of Ancient Proverbs.' There is no reason why this should not be at once started, and the good work immediately set about. There is nothing irreverent, unreasonable, or impossible in this proposition. This is an iconoclastic age. We want to reform everybody, improve all men, and do away with most things. We have altered the Prayer Book. We are proposing to bring out what is called an amended edition of the Bible, and is it to be imagined that our poor, decrepit, senile, broken down, useless proverbs are to be spared? No, certainly not. Not for a single moment! I have striven my hardest to hold to my original belief in these proverbs, for I have had them dinned into my ears from my youth up. But reason has proved too strong and my faith has been shaken. I have been convinced of the hollowness and mockery of proverbs, and one by one have the traditions of my childhood been demolished. All this, however, has been a gradual business. I have lingered fondly over many of the pretty conceits, but little by little I have been compelled to discover what falseness has been sheltered beneath a showy exterior, and I have put them from me as many of us, my brethren, have relinquished a pretty girl when we discovered that in reality she was nothing but a heartless coquette. It is sad work this disillusionment. But the sooner it is accomplished the better. When my great volume is published, 'The Disestablishment of Ancient Proverbs,' I shall be able to show you how gradually my faith was shaken, and how one by one I analyzed these proverbs, found them wanting, and proclaimed their falseness to the world. It is sufficient to me to say now that it was till only a few nights ago that I held implicit belief in the last of the bunch. The last of the bunch was 'Early to bed and early to rise makes a man healthy, wealthy, and wise.'

Now this proverb certainly sounds reasonable. There is something reasonable about going to bed early, and if you go to bed early you would naturally expect to have a good night's rest, you would imagine you would be able to get up early and go through that unaccountable feat of gymnastics, taking Time by the forelock. For my own part I believe Time to be entirely bald, consequently he has no forelock, if he had one I am quite certain he would resent my taking such a liberty by probably wounding me severely with his scythe. (This you see, is another asinine old proverb, but no matter, it is a terribly long parenthesis, too, a parenthesis within a parenthesis, like the carved Chinese balls, one within the other, and about as useful but also no matter.) Having taken Time by the forelock, you were supposed to become healthy, wealthy, and wise. Now, though I know some of the most sickly, the most impecunious, and the stupidest people habitually get up early in the morning, I believed implicitly in this proverb. I say *believed*, because it is only a few days since I forsook the faith of my youth. I was everlastingly preaching sermons from this text, though I am bound to say I very seldom practised what I preached. Well, I began to think it was time I turned over a new leaf. I resolved to go early to bed. I am thankful to say I am tolerably healthy,

I never expect to be wealthy, and I doubt if I ever shall be wise. But still if these things could be accomplished by going to bed at ten or eleven o'clock, most certainly the experiment was well worth trying. Thus it came to pass that the other night I resolved to test the last flower of my bouquet of proverbs that was left blooming alone—'Early to bed and early to rise makes a man healthy, wealthy, and wise.'

I felt clothed in virtue, my very boot soles felt worthy of Exeter Hall platform, my necktie seemed to be morality personified, and I fancy my great coat might have gone as missionary for the Society for the Suppression of Vice, when I left the club smoking-room at ten o'clock on Wednesday night. People were just beginning to be comfortable; there was a nice little knot of pleasant talkers, and the clock hands were beginning to quicken their pace, though they had not got to the express speed in which they always canter after midnight. I bade one or two men goodnight, and slunk away as if I meant to search for the best great coat in the hall, run away with the newest hat, and appropriate the choicest umbrella. I must say that virtue did not sit well upon me. I never felt more like an abandoned criminal in my life. I felt half inclined to go back and apologize, and say I would never do so any more, and pray that every one would look over it, and beg that no one would think of mentioning it to the committee. I walked briskly home. I felt so good, so intensely moral, so aggressively virtuous. The streets were unpleasantly crowded, I was jostled about and was cannoned off by drunken men. I began to lose my temper, and then settled down into the sour, unsatisfactory, self-satisfaction of a martyr. I wondered how my portrait would look in ' Fox's Book of Martyrs.' Rather well I fancied. I imagined myself facing the cut of Saint Lawrence, being broiled on a gridiron into ' rotheramdakes ' of the period, which I recollect seeing in that ancient book when I was a very small boy. When I arrived at home I felt more rigidly virtuous than ever: the house seemed noisy, and I could not make out why people were up at that hour. How could Jane, the housemaid, expect to be up in proper time when she was singing selections from Madame Angot in the kitchen at that time of night, and how could Margaret, the cook, expect to be down early enough to let the sweeps in if she was rattling saucepans about at half-past ten? You cannot burn the candle at both ends, I say to myself — I should like to know any one, out of a lunatic asylum, who ever wanted to go through this most ridiculous operation—and at once think that I will have printed in large characters, and nailed up over my kitchen dresser, ' Early to bed and early to rise makes a man healthy, wealthy, and wise.'

There is a nice fire in my room, but I will not sit down. Not I. I did not tear myself away from a pleasant club to sit by a fire, did I ? Of course I did not. There is the tobacco jar, there are pipes on the table, there are bottles and ' materials.' But I did not come home to drink or to smoke, did I ? Of course I did not. No! I came home *to go to*

BED ! And to bed I will go. It seems to be an unreasonable proceeding. I have a feeling come over me such as I have not experienced since I was a tiny child, and sent to bed by daylight in disgrace. I find everything wrong. Going to bed is not an easy matter, as it usually is with me. It is an actual ceremony. I potter about. Everything is obstinate. I cannot find my brushes. I knock over the water jug. I break a tumbler. I upset a bottle of hair oil. Upon my word, I believe all my furniture has conspired against me, and that they are holding an indignation meeting to protest against my retiring so early. Anyhow, they all seem to be endued with a kind of life of a most awkward and annoying description. I lose my temper, and I must say I use language which is not at all in harmony with the halo of virtue and the atmosphere of morality with which I fancy I am surrounded. However, I console myself with the thought, how nice it will be to be up so early. It is one thing, however, to determine to go to bed early : it is another to go to sleep. Instead of tumbling into bed as usual I find there are all sorts of things that distract my attention. I begin to discover that my bed-room is badly arranged : that pictures hang in the wrong places, that the wardrobe is the wrong side of the room, that I do not like the patterns of the paper, and that the carpet is simply hideous.

I gaze at myself in the looking-glass, and think how terribly old I am looking, and how the grey hairs are beginning to assert themselves. I turn away in disgust, and nearly fall into my bath. At last I will have no more trifling. I plunge boldly into bed and determine I will go to sleep. But, as I said before, it is one thing to go to bed : it is altogether another matter to go to sleep. The bed feels as though it had been iced, and the pillow as if it were stuffed with parchment shavings. However, I dare say it is all right. I shut my eyes. I not only shut them but screw them up tightly so that there will be no chance of their opening by accident. Hitherto shutting my eyes has been synonymous with going to sleep, but now I find out my mistake. In about five minutes' time I open one eye cautiously and look round and discover I have not been to sleep at all. I roll over and tell myself that this will not do at all ; if I put myself to bed before eleven o'clock I expect myself to go to sleep at once. And then I discover that peculiar phase of existence which, I imagine, is common to all of us in a state of partial sleepiness or semi-wakefulness—namely, that of a dual existence. I am distinctly two persons contained in one body, and two persons of a most antagonistic nature. My better self wants to go to sleep, but my worse self absolutely refuses to do anything of the kind. Good and bad self are continually quarrelling all night long.

I think I could possibly get to sleep if it were not for the noise. People *will* chatter and sing and shout as they walk through the square. Why on earth cannot they go to bed early as I do ? I am beginning to doubt if going to bed early is a good thing, and feel half inclined to register a vow

that I will never do so any more. There is a cab
just stopped at Number Ten. How painfully distinct every sound is! I can hear the grate of the
wheels as they scrape the kerb, the clump of the
cabman as he jumps down on the pavement. I
can hear him clump up the steps, give a tremendous
double rap and clump down again. I can distinctly
hear the ' scroop ' of the cab door when it is opened,
the *frou frou* of dresses, and the patter of feminine
feet. I hear a conversation in an under-tone. I
can distinguish the phrases ' leave it to you, sir,'
' such a norful night,' and the like. I hear a jingle
of silver, a hearty but gruff good night on the part
of the cabman, I hear the cab turn round—I became
tremendously interested, for it turned round so
sharply that I thought it was going to turn over—
however, it righted itself, and I heard it slowly rattle
out of the square. I could hear it clattering over the
stones in Great Rumble Street, and I wondered
whether it was going to turn into Spattleton's
Mews for the night. Then I recollect that Spattleton's is rather an aristocratic mews, and certainly
would turn up his nose—the idea of a mews having
a nose to turn up!—at a cab. I wonder what becomes of cabs when they are not on service. Did
you ever see a gigantic ' cabbery ' ? I once in my
prowls came upon an extraordinary back-yard, in
which there were seventeen hansoms without
horses or drivers; they seemed as if they were
holding a special meeting of the Society for the
Suppression of Cruelty to Cabs. I never saw anything so ghastly or appalling. I was as much
startled and horrified as if I had strolled into an

hospital dissecting-room by mistake, and I ran
away not daring to look behind me in case I might
find myself pursued by a troop of infuriated, noise-
less, driverless hansom-cabs trying to gore me with
their shafts.

I have given up all idea of going to sleep now.
It is of no use whatever. All my senses have become painfully acute. The least noise gives me
an alarm of burglars. I fancy I can detect a smell
of burning, and the lurid reflection of the street
lamp becomes almost as painful as a pattern on the
brain. I never knew my bed-room was so draughty
before. There are about fifteen different draughts
coming from all sides at once. Directly I put my
head outside the clothes I seem to put it into an
air needle-bath. I can *not* go to sleep. Why
have I not something to help me? Why have I
not Indian hemp, chlorodyne, hydrate of chloral
opium, laudanum, hasheesh, syrup of poppies,
brown brandy, or bottled stout? Why have I
not all these things arranged in a goodly row along
my mantel-piece? Why? Simply because I never
required any artificial stimulants to sleep till I was
such as ass—such a *silly* ass—I say—as to go to
bed early. I am not going to be treated this way.
I will endeavour to put in practice all the receipts
I have heard of for provoking somnolence without
recourse to narcotics. I will trace the course of a
river from its source to its mouth. Of course I
think of the river I know best, and I begin at the
source of the Thames. Then I think of people
dwelling on its banks. I think of the Bonnybelle
girls. I then remember that they are coming up

to town next week, and I promised to get them some stalls at the theatre. I have forgotten all about it. Upon my word I must about this the first thing, the very first thing to-morrow morning. This throws me into a state more wakeful than ever, and I begin to wish that the morning were come in order that I might rush off to the box-office at once. The morning, indeed! The morning is so far off that I look upon it as the year after next.

It has just struck half-past twelve. In the usual way I never think of leaving the club till after this time. I am told that the majority of fires always take place between twelve and one, and I have been given to understand that that is the most favourable period for burglars. Now I come to think of it that smell of burning is certainly getting stronger—very much stronger! I hear mysterious thumpings and rattlings about the house that I cannot account for. I just become conscious that I am very hungry. If there is one thing that is more annoying than another it is being hungry in the middle of the night. I really am prodigiously hungry. I could do with a few slices of cold tongue and some bread and butter. Shall I boldly get up and go down-stairs in search of it? No, I think not. My kitchen in the dead of night is not a cheerful place, I can tell you. Besides, I have been considerably frightened with the burglaristic noises I have heard ever since I was in bed. No, I will not go down. But what a lot of nice things I begin to think about. A good thick, lean chop, with

potatoes such as Paddy Green used to give you ;
a Welsh rare bit to follow, and a pint of stout
out of the pewter. Dee-*li*-cious. Num! Num!
Num! Num! *Num!!* Nᴜᴍ!!! And to think
that if I had not been an absolute donkey I could
have been enjoying my supper at the club at this
present moment. What an idiot I have been!
I begin to toss about and feel very feverish. My
tongue begins to get dry and feels as if it had been
sand-papered. I would give anything for a cyder
cup—a cyder cup, craftily compounded, just as they
give you at the Carnation Club. Bah! What is the
use of wishing? I bury my head in my pillow and
resolve that I will either go to sleep or be suffo-
cated. I do neither, but presently find myself
sitting bolt upright in bed and staring about me.
I try hanging my head over the foot of the bed,
and putting my feet on the pillow, but only succeed
in getting icy cold feet and a determination of
blood to the head. I then roll myself up tightly
in the blankets and pretend to be a mummy. I
toss about, I roll, I gnash my teeth, I groan, I
hear one o'clock strike in all its varieties, two,
three, four, five! Just as it begins to be getting
light I feel to be a little drowsy. When suddenly
I am startled with a tremendous rapping and ringing. The burglars at last—or the fire engines, I
say to myself. I do not hurry myself for I am
really feeling somewhat sleepy. The rapping and
ringing continues. At last I hear a shout of ' Sur-
weep!' from below. Let them rap and ring, I
say to myself, I dare say they will get in somehow.
And I suppose they do, for presently I am again

5

awakened by brushes rattling up the chimney and a general smell of soot everywhere. I get comfortably off to sleep about eight and get up about eleven. I miss an important appointment at ten, I feel very unwell and am fit for nothing all the next day.

My brethren, let there be no mistake about the matter. Early to bed and early to rise neither makes a man healthy, wealthy, nor wise !

IN CLOVER.

IT is very late at night. I know I ought to have been in bed hours ago. But it is so hot, so still, and I feel so sleepless, that it is impossible to go to bed. I have my bed-room window wide open, the flame of my candle is motionless, save when some silly moth flies at it and falls maimed for life, like some poor mortal who has put faith in woman's smiles. The moon is shining brilliantly and sends its silver light across the floor of my room and glints upon the bath which looks so cool and so tempting that I am in a great mind to get into it, tie a wet towel round my head and try to go to sleep. I am so hot that I am certain I should make the water boil if I attempted to do this; I give it up then altogether. It is the first time I have felt at all energetic for the last week, so I think I will try and do a little writing. I am sitting before the window in a costume as near approaching that of an ancient statue as is consistent with my severe ideas of decorum. I have placed my writing materials on a marble table, which I find to be delightfully cool to the bare arms. It would be all the better if I could have it iced every five minutes, but in this sublunar sphere I find it is impossible to have everything you can desire. I find my writing does not progress so swiftly as

sometimes, for I am obliged to hang my head out
of window every now and then and gasp. I wonder,
if any one sees me, whether they will take me
for a ghost, or a madman, or a burglar? Supposing they were to take me for a burglar and
arouse the house and bring down a body of the
rural police. This very idea makes me hotter than
ever and causes me to poke my head out of window
once more, and, to quote Mr Boucicault, 'Come
out into the moonbames.' There is something delightfully cool too in having the moonlight full on
your face. My favourite versifier has sung somewhere something to the effect that 'lunatics thrive
in the light of the moon.' According to many of
my friends, I have now an excellent chance of thriving. But I do not care whether I am thriving or
not, I know I am enjoying myself very much indeed, and I think I shall continue to gaze out of
window and endeavour to get a cool breath of air
all night. There is a lovely scent of clover comes
wafted to me, it changes presently to the fragrance
of laurels, and again a sweet perfume of thyme and
hay takes its place. There is a faint air, the tiniest
breeze in the world stirring, but it is so faint, so
tiny, that it will not move anything that offers to
it the slightest resistance. The tall poplars, in
the middle distance, that are ever ready to bend
and to sway, are as rigid and motionless as the
spruce, well-trimmed, decorous little trees on
stands, that we used to plant in our farmyards in
our extreme youth. Not a leaf seems to flutter,
and a few thin clouds in the clear sky are absolutely stationary. There is not a sound to be

heard save the intermittent rustle of the ivy outside my window, the occasional barking of a dog with an ill-regulated mind, the crowing of some energetic cock who thinks the night bright enough to be morning—and he is not far wrong—and once or twice the subdued shriek of a peacock many miles off, and the melodious roar of the weir far away in the distance.

I am delighted to think that nobody knows my address at the present moment. I shall keep it a profound secret for the present. You see I do not want to be bothered. I know that I am ' wanted' by a good many people. It is much too hot to be bothered, it is far too sultry to be wanted. I know there are a lot of people in town who want me to go out to dinner, to dance myself silly, to swelter in hot theatres. And these people would make me do all these things if they knew my address; so I keep my whereabouts a profound secret. I point the finger of scorn at all these well-meaning but misguided individuals, and say unto them ' Yah !' I will let them into the secret, however, so far. I left town with the intention of going somewhere, but I have stopped on my way, and think it very doubtful whether I shall get any further. I am in most delightful quarters, and I do not see why I should bother myself to make myself hot with broiling in the sunshine, or uncomfortable by moving. I may accomplish these things sometime, and I may not. It will be just as the fancy takes me. Why should you always do what you intend? Why, too, by the way, should you always look in newspapers for what

you know will be reported? You never have
pleasant surprises in newspapers in the present
day. They never leave out something that you
expect to see, or put in something that you do not
expect to see. I mean to start a new journal some
of these days. I shall call it *The Surprise;* a
newspaper for lazy people. But I did not sit down
this evening in the costume of an ancient statue, I
did not cool my arms on a marble-topped table, I
did not 'come out into the moonbames' for the
purpose of talking about newspapers. Newspapers?
Yah! The very name makes me hot. Gas-heated
rooms, clattering machinery, bustle, row, hurry,
worry, smell of oil and printer's ink. No. I sat
down and endeavoured to get myself into something approaching coolness in order that I may tell
you how I am enjoying this delightful summer
weather, and to inform you that it is a matter of
the gravest doubt whether I get any further as
long as it lasts.

Where I am at the present moment staying—
please copy the address, "In Clover," and I will give
any one leave to find me if he can—is the very
place to enjoy this superb weather. You can do
exactly as you like: you are not hunted about:
you are not compelled to do anything. You are
not worried to go rides or drives, neither are you
obliged to undertake that most terrible of all penal-
ties 'excursions.' An excursion has been well
defined as an expedition to see something which
never, under any possible circumstances, comes
up to your expectations. This is true enough, and
excursions during this broiling hot weather must

be something terrible. In this pleasant mansion
you never have excursions inflicted upon you, nor
are you compelled to do anything that does not
please you. If the old motto, *Fay ce que voudras*,
were carven over its porch it would be, indeed,
appropriate. What a delicious dreamy day did I
have to-day! It was the very day for doing nothing, and I believe I did it very thoroughly. I
mooned in the smoking-room after breakfast and
smoked. I smoked and I mooned. I gazed out
upon the lawn and noted the pleasant shade under
the mulberry tree and wished I could get there. I
saw the broad expanse of brilliant sunshine which
lay between me and this cool haven and I hesitated.
I knew I should be nearly frizzled if I attempted
to cross it. The man who hesitates during this
hot weather is lost. So I lounged back in my
easy-chair and lost myself in a cloud of smoke. I
see two figures pass across the lawn, pass under
the roses, walk over a carpet of rose leaves and
take their way in the direction of the mulberry tree.
Who are these young people? Softly. Let me
put up my hard sharp-pointed rapier-like Gillott
and take a dove's quill before I write of them.
Verily, their path is figuratively as well as really
one of rose leaves at the present time. These two
young people who are staying in the house at the
present time, are, let me whisper it softly, 'our
lovers.' That is to say, they are engaged and are
very much in love one with the other. I mention
these two facts, because you may be engaged
without being very much in love, and you may
be very much in love with no chance of being

engaged. When these two happy conditions
are combined, as they appear to be in the case
of our young friends, the result is eminently
satisfactory. It affords me the greatest amusement to watch this couple as they are slowly
dreaming about the garden, now in sunshine now
in shadow : now plucking roses and pulling them
to pieces, now whispering in the broad chequered
shade of the mulberry tree. It reminds me of
times agone, ' when girls were girls and hearts were
hearts.' I dare say if I were to ask my excellent
young Cambridge friend he would tell me that
girls are girls and hearts are hearts even in the present day. And I have no doubt, from his point
of view, he would be perfectly right. If I were to
propound any cynical theories to that dainty
damsel, in her charming white *piqué* dress, in her
pretty crushed Dolly Varden hat twined with roses,
she would probably inform me I knew nothing at
all about such matters. And possibly, from her
point of view, I should be perfectly right. But this
by the way. As I watch these two young people
I think what a picture they would make, and I
think how George Leslie would love to paint the
little scene that I see beneath the roses just now.

As the day wears on I do not become more
energetic. Indeed, I fancy I become rather the
reverse. I find it really too much trouble to smoke
a pipe, so I make an artful arrangement of sofa
cushions on the floor of the smoking-room. I
lie at full length. I light a cigarette and watch the
blue rings as they curl up to the ceiling and nearly
go to sleep. The young people have left the shade

under the mulberry tree and have gone up the river, and are probably telling one another the same tale to the ripple of the stream as they did to the music of the leaves. I remain precisely in the same position, only keeping cool by keeping motionless. The sun becomes hotter and hotter outside, and the house gets stiller and stiller. There is no sound to be heard but the chirrup of birds outside and occasionally the hum of insects or the boom of a bee. I can hear the tick of the clock in the hall and the occasional hoarse screech of the old parrot as he scroops in his cage. I think how dry and thirsty the utterance of all these noises must make him, and suddenly I find my tongue is dry and rough even as that of the parrot. I never knew my tongue was like a parrot's before. I now find the resemblance is striking. I am fearfully and wonderfully thirsty. I think I could take a glass of cool bitter beer with great satisfaction, and I am sure it would prevent my tongue cleaving unto the roof of my mouth. It is always a good thing to prevent your tongue cleaving to the roof of your mouth if possible. It is too much trouble to ring for the servant and ask for a glass of bitter beer. That would involve a ceremony that would worry me. I am certain it would make the servant hot to bring me up a tray with a jug and glasses upon it, and the very idea of making any one hot throws me into a profuse perspiration. There is a much better way than this. I know my way to the cellar, and I wot of a certain cupboard where glasses are kept. I slowly and languidly raise myself up, I totter round to the cupboard to get a

glass. I take my way slowly but surely down a
flight of cool red brick steps, and I find myself in
a deliciously cold cellar giving on an underground
dairy lined with quaint tiles depicting Moses and
Aaron in periwigs, the Prodigal Son in knee-
breeches, and other scriptural subjects marvel-
lously illustrated. In the cellar I find six happy-
looking casks — we are told those who give
happiness to others, always themselves look happy
—standing ' magnanimous all of a row.' I turn
the tap of one of these and a pellucid amber liquid
gurgleth with a refreshing sound into my tall glass.
I fill my tall glass and I retire to the dairy, I
refresh my memory in scriptural history and I
moisten my throat at the same time. The bitter
beer is so excellent that I again moisten my
throat and continue my study of scripture history.
I feel as though I should like to stay down in the
cellar all day, and the six happy-looking casks
give me a pressing invitation to do so, but I am
firm. I take just one more glass in order that they
may not think I am rude, and return to the surface of the earth very much refreshed. Upon
my word, this operation of descending to the
cellar and studying the tiles is quite a new sensation. It is so charming that it requires to be
repeated many times in the course of the day.

I am in a delicious state of independence.
When I am at home I feel I am in a state of blind
ignorance if I have not gone through the *Times,*
Morning Post, Daily Telegraph, Standard, Hour,
and *Daily News* by this time. I have seen none of
these valuable dailies yet. I do not care if I should

never see them again, and if one of them were brought to me at the present moment, I do not think I should condescend to read it. I feel a little revived by my trip to the cellar and somewhat stimulated to exertion. I therefore summon up sufficient courage to rush across the broad belt of sunshine and throw myself down beneath the shade of the mulberry tree. I amuse myself by watching the gambols of a large Persian cat, who has caught a mouse, and who is playing with it in the sunshine. She lets it go, and then pretends she does not see it, and when the mouse thinks it has a chance of escape, and limps feebly across the grass-plat, its tormentor leaps upon it and gives it a pat, just to show there is no prospect of its living much longer. Then the cat pretends to go to sleep again, and in a few minutes repeats the performance. It keeps on at this kind of thing for more than an hour. At last I become weary and drop off to sleep. I wake up suddenly. I have not the least idea where I am. I find tobacco ash scattered all over my coat, and I feel as if I had dislocated my neck. I get up with considerable difficulty and I I think I will go for a stroll round the garden. I light a cigarette, I move out in the sunshine perfectly uncertain as to when I shall get back again or whether I shall return again at all.

I propose to meditate and ponder under the limes, I think it would be just the very place of all others to polish up an exquisite sonnet that I have had in my pocket for months past. I am always saying to myself that I will go down in the country and have a rest and intense quiet and polish up my

verses. I frequently go down into the country and
have rest. I seldom have intense quiet. I never
polish up my verses. I should do it now, but that I
am turned aside from my original intentions, as I
commence my perambulation beneath the limes, by
seeing a magnificent mountain ash, with glorious
deep orange-coloured berries. I pause and look at
this. I patronize the mountain ash, and approve
its orange-coloured berries. I see curious insects
—with all my faults I never was entomological, so
I am unable to give the names of these insects—
crawling over the berries, and I think it is time to
interfere, and therefore blow a cloud of smoke over
the berries, and have the satisfaction of seeing
three of these insects rolling on their backs and
flourishing their legs wildly in the air. I think
what an immense deal of good I am doing, and
think that I might persevere and extend my labours to other branches and other berries, but find
the insects take a deal of smoke, and that they
persist in reviving directly my back is turned. I
think I will go in-doors again, and then I come
to the conclusion I will not, but take my way
across the grass-plat till I reach a wire archway
crossing one of the paths. A creeper of some
kind—I cannot bother myself about names—is
climbing up the trellis-work. I find there are
several long shoots that require twining in between the wires. It appears to me to be of the
utmost importance that this should be done at
once. Therefore I devote my whole energies to
accomplishing it. What a deal of good, I think to
myself, am I doing. What a philanthropist am I!

And forthwith I begin to inflate myself after the manner of philanthropists. I very much enjoy standing in the sunshine and twisting the bright green leaves and the long shoots between the wires, as I smoke the while. After I have done all this to my satisfaction I begin to wonder what I will do next.

There is a magnolia about to bloom against an old brick wall, and the gardener has left a ladder hard by. I never in my life climbed up a ladder and looked at a magnolia. I protest it will be a new sensation, that is to say if I do not fall down. If I fall down before I arrive at the magnolia there will be no novelty whatever in it. I have frequently fallen from ladders before. The ladder is decidedly ricketty, and seems to have an inclination to break off short in the middle. I am courageous, and proceed. I reach the magnolia blossom in time; I sniff at it and patronize it, and descend, solemnly thinking I have not gained very much by the proceeding after all. However, I think I have done some good, and think I ought to be rewarded. I do not imagine any one will reward me, however, so I reward myself by lighting a fresh cigarette. I then proceed a little further and reach a dilapidated grey stone sun-dial. It is very ricketty, moss-o'ergrown, and lichen-covered, and all trace of dial has disappeared many years ago, so for time-keeping purposes it is of no use whatever. Hard by a sun-dial is the sort of place to moralize. I know not why, but I feel I could improve the occasion at the present time if I gave my mind to it. But you see the dial has been removed from the pedestal, so I fear a great many of my remarks would lose their point. I very much regret the removal of the dial, as I could have made a great many very pretty and apposite remarks. I drift across under the shade of the mulberry tree, and find there are plenty of ripe, juicy mulberries hanging just within biting distance. Do you know it is infinitely better; you get the fruit fresher and juicier by biting it from the tree instead of gathering it in your warm hand and conveying it to your mouth. This is a thing that is not sufficiently known even amongst your most sybaritic lovers of fruit. You can have no idea, unless you have tried it, how you get the most exquisite flavour of the fruit and distil its most subtle essences. Try it anywhere, at any time you please, whenever you have the opportunity. Nibble grapes off the vine, bite apples off the tree, and browse among peaches on the wall. Having tried the mulberries in this way, and gradually made the circuit of the entire tree, I espy an apple tree not far off, which seems made for the purpose of performing the same operation. It is a small, low, gnarled tree, heavily laden with fruit, and stretches its arms temptingly across the path, just at mouth height from the ground. I cannot do other than make an experiment on this, and find that the apples are even better than the mulberries. Certain savage tribes in Abyssinia aver that no meat is equal to a steak cut from the living animal, and I am quite sure there is no apple equal to that bitten from the living tree.

I cannot, however, be nibbling apples all day

long, so I pass under the apple tree and go and
inspect the bee-hives. I have always rather a dread
of bees. I do not altogether believe in bees. I
have a sort of idea that the bee is the Pecksniff of
insects. I have a firm conviction that he is the
greatest entomological humbug in existence. Some
day I propose write a pamphlet, to be entitled ' The
Bee Exposed, and his True Character made Mani-
fest.' There is a great affectation of business about
the bee, which I take for about what it is worth.
Directly I approach the hive they all pretend to
have a deal of business in hand ; they keep on
crawling in and out in such a monstrous hurry, that
you might almost fancy this hive was the Capel
Court of the insect world. Round and about they
are humming and booming, and seem to have a
desire to cluster round my hat. Perhaps they have
heard of my pamphlet which is to disestablish them
as models of industry in future ages. If they have
it is all up with me. The bee is a most vindictive
animal, and they would all band together and not
rest until they had stung me to death. I think I
had better move to another part of the garden. I
protest I feel quite tired with my exertions. I
will roll down under the shadow of the limes, and
I will meditate. Ah ! now will be the time for me
to polish up my sonnet. I have a pencil. That is
all right. Now for it. Alas and alas, I cannot find
it anywhere. I must have left it in my other coat.
What a pity ! No, now I come to consider it I am
rather glad that I cannot find it. You see I should
be obliged to think, and I hate being obliged to
think. Thinking is all very well when you are not

obliged to do it, but thinking when you are obliged
is as bad as doing anything else you are compelled
to.   I refuse to think unless I like ; so I will roll
down on the grass plat, I will bask in the sunshine,
and I will go to sleep if I please.

Much refreshed by my brief rest I arise and
manage to move slowly on.   I come to a good old
brick wall, with peaches ripening upon it.   What a
study of colour is this brick wall.   Look at the infinite variety of tint.   See the toned red, the specks
of vermilion where the bricks have been chipped,
the grey-green lichen, the yellow lichen, the bright
green moss.   Note how all these tints interlace
and what delicate combinations they bring about.
There is nothing vulgar, nothing garish, nothing
commonplace about this brick wall.   Contrast this
with a wall that Buggins the builder would erect.
There would be as much difference between the two
as there is between a fine old Tory squire and
some third-rate inflated ' working man's ' orator.
Do you note how admirably every part of the wall
is in harmony ?   Will you please observe what
value there is in those dull red staples, those cor-
roded iron braces and rusty nails.   Again, look
how the wall in parts is speckled with snowy spots,
see the weather stains and the faint fungoid
growth here and there.   Please to note the mossy
edges of the top of the wall—there are no hard
lines or sharp corners in any part—the stalks of
long grass nodding in the summer breeze.   This
wall is an extensive province for the tiny traveller.   Then do you see the round peaches ripening in the sun, soft, plump, and rosy, like unto

a maiden's cheek? A few have fallen down over-
ripe. In one of them do I see a rascally bee,
wallowing. According to popular belief, the bee
is one of a large company who go about ' gathering honey all the day from every opening flower'
for the good of the common hive. I never
thought he acted in so disinterested a manner,
and now I have substantial proof that my supposition is correct. Here I find this pattern insect, this model of virtue and of industry, no more
devoting himself to the common weal of bee-kind
than I am. He is, in point of fact, having a quiet
debauch all by himself, and he is be-fuddling himself on the sly. He is absolutely drunk, and he
turns over and over within the fractured peach :
he rolls on his back and shakes his legs defiantly.
I never saw so depraved a bee before. If I were
only to report him to the hive what trouble he
would get into. I wonder whether he will regain
the use of his wings again or whether he will come
to an untimely end within the recesses of the
peach. It is impossible to say. I shake my head
solemnly and ask him why he does not ' bee-hive '
himself and walk on ? . Strange to say he does
not laugh or even give a hum of satisfaction at my
little pleasantry. He wags one leg mildly, he
wallows in luscious laziness, and wriggles himself
further into his peachen grave. I have no doubt
in my own mind that that bee came to a bad end.

I begin to be conscious that it is just luncheon
time, so I moon slowly back again. I find people
having luncheon. They are pretending to eat,
but they are drinking a great deal without any

pretence. I wonder whether they all have parrot tongues like mine. Upon my word, I should like to read a paper at some medical society 'On the Development of the Parrot Tongue in the Human Species.' I wonder whether the parrot tongue is particularly prevalent in hot countries. It would be very iuteresting to have some statistics on this matter. We do not talk much at luncheon. It is too hot. We make signs, and if there is any conversation it is carried on in languid undertones. After luncheon I stroll back to the smoking-room. It is far too hot to think of going out or taking any active exertion. I once more roll on the floor. I roll, and roll, and roll till I roll myself into a comfortable position. I manage to light a cigarette, which goes out in about five minutes. It is quite too much exertion to get the matches, which are about a yard from my hand, so I gaze at the half-burnt cigarette till I go to sleep. I awake and find it to be about two hours off dinner, so I think there will be just time to go and dress quietly. With a vast amount of exertion I am enabled to mount to my bed-room, have a cold bath, make a complete change, get through my toilette in the slowest possible manner, and creep down-stairs again just as dinner is ready.

I find I have been writing away, striving to give an account of my dreamy days in this delightful weather. I suppose I have been writing slower than usual for I fancy the morning is beginning to break, and I hear a few of the earliest of early birds rehearsing their morning carol. I know my candle has burnt very low, and notwithstanding.

my classical costume, my open window, and my cool marble table, the exertion has thrown me into such a profuse perspiration that I can scarcely hold my pen. I will tumble into bed and strive to get an hour or two of sleep before the heat of the day again sets in.

HUNTED BY THE EAST WIND.

NOTWITHSTANDING my profound admiration for the author of 'Westward Ho,' I propose to start a 'Society for the Suppression of Kingsley.' Ever since he uttered his memorable words in praise of the east wind, this abominable blast has persisted in blowing with more untiring constancy and more blighting bitterness than formerly. It is high time that some protest should be made. If the great writer already alluded to likes to be poet laureate to the east wind let him, but let them both go away to some uninhabited island and shiver and howl to the music of chattering teeth. We want none of the music of the east wind, nor songs sung in its praise here. I think I am expressing the feelings of the entire population of London when I say we are absolutely disgusted with the east wind.

The east wind is totally different from other breezes, it has not a blusterous honesty about it. Not by any means. It is a nasty, sneaking, insidious, underhand, unprincipled kind of a wind. It appears to open the pores of your skin till it is like a colander; it riddles your bones with fine pin holes, and then blows through them till you seem to have neuralgia all over your body. It penetrates the thickest of cloths and the most formidable of friezes.

You may fortify yourself with flannel waistcoats, you may don double-breasted sealskin waistcoats, you may wear three or four pairs of trousers, but the east wind will penetrate everything and make you as miserable, as hopelessly wretched, as man can possibly be. And yet a man of such eloquence and erudition as Canon Kingsley can be found to sing in praise of it.

Far more sensible was a certain obscure individual who sang simply but expressively ' The wind in the east is neither good for man nor beast.' How beautiful and how true is this! How true in its simplicity, and how simple in its truth! I am inclined to think that there must be a mistake in the proverb ' It is an ill wind that blows nobody good.' It should run in this wise : ' It is an *east* wind that blows nobody good.' Did you ever know an east wind blow any good to anybody? Did you ever know it to do any good to anything? A bitter, remorseless, scathing, revengeful kind of wind is that of the east.

The worst of it is you cannot escape from it. It follows you everywhere. It hunts you down. Like the famous ' Goosey Gander' of nursery lore celebrity, it goes ' up-stairs, and down-stairs, and in my lady's chamber.' You cannot get rid of it. If it were like that unprincipled elderly individual spoken of in the same poem, who omitted to perform his devotional exercises on every possible occasion, you might treat it in the same summary fashion. You might 'take it by its left leg and throw it down-stairs.' There is, however, no getting hold of the east wind. It is a nasty, dodgy, disreputable, sneaking kind of wind that would not meet you in *duello* in an honest gentlemanly fashion. It will wait for you round corners, and give you a stab in the back when you are not looking; it will come upon you suddenly in the dark and wound you. It holds an everlasting and blasting *vendetta* against every man, woman, and child in the universe.

The east wind loves to wait in the lobby of the theatre. It delights to catch young beauty before she can get her warm cloak over her soft white bosom, and to implant one of its cruel shafts. It glories in sowing the seeds of consumption and inflammation of the lungs; bronchitis, neuralgia, and rheumatism are some of its most particular friends. The east wind, too, is very good at touching up devout congregations on Sunday evenings. My word! Does it not eddy about those large family pews, and give the ancient dames in the free seats a benefit? Does not the popular preacher feel it whistling—in a most irreverent fashion—up the stairs of the pulpit; and does not the asthmatic old clerk experience its torture as he wheezes in the reading desk? And then with what fierce power, with what biting vindictiveness, is it down upon the sparsely clad and the thinly shod as they walk home in the dark. How fiendishly it delights in adding cold to cold, and piling cough upon cough, until it strikes its victim down!

I think it is high time that a protest was made against Canon Kingsley's praise of this most abominable of breezes, otherwise people may begin to believe that there really is some good in the east wind after all. I own that I should love to write a satire, for which I would like Mr Arthur Sullivan to compose the music. I would call it 'The East Wind : a Catarrhic Cantata, in Three Blows.' I have a host of characters I could introduce most effectively. Fancy Baron Bronchitis, Prince Pneumonia, Sergeant Stethescope, the Fair Neuralgia, Rheu Matticks the Robber, and Tic the Dolorous. Imagine a sneezing song, a coughing trio, and a gargling duet. I see a wide field for both musician and librettist in this work, and I fancy we should be doing good work in undoing the harm that the powerful influence of the Kingsleyan pen may already have accomplished. Some years ago I endeavoured to establish a musical society especially with a view to people who were suffering from the evils of the east wind. No one was eligible for election unless he had had at least three severe colds during the preceding two months ; and no member was allowed to sing at the concerts unless he could produce a medical certificate to the effect that he was totally unfit to appear in public and ought to be in bed. The following is one of the programmes :—

FIRST CONCERT OF THE ACRID PULMONIC SOCIETY AND COUGHRAL UNION, AT THE ASTHMATEUM, COLD HARBOUR LANE.

Conductor .... MR HOARSLEY.

PART I.

Overture, ' La Influenza ' .... Tramontana.
Duet, ' Rub in the Croton Oil ' .... Smart.
Tenor solo, ' Come and have a Gargle, Maud ' Bron. Chitis.
(With catarrh accompaniment.)
Glee, ' The Cough and Cold ' .... Tischoff.
Galop, ' The East Wind ' .... Kingsley.
Polka, ' The Sore Throat ' .... Hoarsley.

Song, 'Cough, Cough, said the Stranger.'
Russian Melody, ' Tishooatishoo ' .... Prince Gotsuchacorff.
Selection from ' Il Lumbago ' .... Oftenback.
Galop, 'The Treacle Posset ' .... M. O. Lasses.
   (Possetively the first time of performance.)

Between the parts, Mr Titkins will gargle for ten minutes, in
 eighteen different languages ; and the Committee will sit with
 their feet in hot mustard and water and have their noses
 solemnly tallowed to slow music in a minor key.

PART II.

Overture, ' Garglielmo Tell.'
Glee, ' The Hardy Hoarsemen.'
Comic Song, 'The Sneeze.' .... Leschetitzky.
This song will last five minutes, during which the performer will
   sneeze no less than 568 times.
Madrigal, ' Come, let us all a Coughing
 go ' .... Grufflin, 1582.
Tenor solo, ' Who shall be Gruffest ? '.... Snorter.
Catarrhic solo, ' So eardy id the bordig '.. Hollah.
Valse, ' Black Currant Tea ' .... Frohsdorf.
Song, ' A cup of Cough Mixture come fill,
 fill for me ' .... Tschubert.
Sneezing Trio, from ' Der Tischutz ' ...... Tschumann.
Selection from ' Il Corfnomore ' .... Tryfisher.
Slipper Sonata .... List.

 Stalls (with an endless supply of gargles, mustard-and-water,
and every other catarrhic luxury), 5s. ; area (with cough lozenges),
2s. 6d. ; back seats (with unlimited draughts), 1s.

 Doors open at half-past seven. Performance to commence as
soon as people are a little comfortable, and their coughs easy.

N.B.—A medical gentleman will be in attendance.

The society, though favourably noticed in
some of the musical journals of the day, failed to
command the success it deserved.

I feel strongly, I may say very strongly, on this
subject. I have been hunted by the east wind for
many days past. I have dodged it as well as I
can. It is, however, stalking after me, it is following me, and will run me down sooner or later. It

chivied me to the opening of a new theatre the other night, it crept under the stalls and caught hold of my legs in the most unceremonious manner. It obliged me to rush to an hostelry between the acts and imbibe brandy-and-water, very strong, very hot, and very sweet, It caused many individuals, even more celebrated than the present writer, to do likewise. I saw several of the most distinguished dramatic critics in London thawing themselves by means of libations of a similar nature. I subsequently went by underground railway, and was pursued by the east wind through its cavernous depths. It caught me at the back of the neck, it nipped my ears, it iced my teeth, it gripped me in every conceivable way. In vain I tried to shake it off. It hunted me from pillar to post. It pursued me until I reached the comfortable smoking-room of the club. Here I left it at the door for awhile and forgot all about it when basking in the genial warmth of the fire. O, vile east wind, thought I, I have jockeyed thee at last!

I was mistaken. The east wind is not so easily thrust aside. I felt a sharp twinge at the back of my neck, wafted through a crack in the window frame that showed me my enemy was waiting for me outside, and reminded me there was more torture in store for me on my way home. I endeavoured to put off the evil day. I remained in front of the blazing fire far into the small hours, endeavouring to put off the evil hour. But, alas! I knew it must come! It came! My old enemy was waiting round the corner, and pounced down on me with his vile talons directly I emerged from the warm shelter of the club. I put my coat collar up, I muffled my neck with a woollen comforter, but all to no purpose. Pitiless and savage, he persecuted me all the way home. He was persecuting everybody in the same way. Thick-booted, heavily-coated policemen, on their weary tramp cursed the east wind heartily as they paraded the cheerless streets, and night cabmen anathematized it in their slumbers. I suppose I am, by force of circumstances, out as late at night as most men—I do not think that night policemen or night cabmen could well beat me on the score of lateness. But when this weary vigil has to be kept with the vile east wind gripping their necks or biting their legs the result must be something fearful. O! east wind, O! terrible east wind, mayest thou blow for the future only upon him who has sung thy praises.

I have declared battle against the east wind, and I suspect he will pay me out. He is paying me out. He is taking every mean advantage he can of me. He is circumventing me whenever and wherever he can. He has at last had the impertinence to insinuate himself into my chambers. These chambers are warm and comfortable: they are cosy and quiet. They were a perfect little paradise—as far as we can construct a paradise without angels—but the east wind has converted them into a howling waste; an abode of misery and despair. My old enemy has found out sundry chinks in the doors and window frames, and he has pierced and widened them. He has found one or two cunning apertures in the flooring,

through which he blows most persistently. He
delights to chill me in my paradise, and to make
my comfortable rooms a region of perpetual
draught. At the present moment I am shivering
as I write, and although I have a roaring fire, and
am sitting nearly close to it, my feet are more like
two lumps of ice than anything else. However,
I will have my revenge. I will jeer at the east
wind; I will pillory it and gibbet it, notwithstanding all that the great Kingsley has sung in its praise.

The east wind delights to pretend it is not the
east wind. It likes to make belief to leave off
blowing when the sun is brightly shining in order
that it may tempt delicate people out of doors, and
then strike them down with a remorseless cruelty.
It delights to devour delicate maidens and to anni-
hilate young children. It is cruel, vindictive,
heartless, and inhuman. It loves to blight the
flowers and to hinder vegetation, and its greatest
joy is to make havoc with early spring and trample
under its cloven-foot violets and primroses. The
east wind loveth desolation, despair, and death.

The east wind is terrible. It loves to visit the
habitations of the poor: to blow the last rag of
clothing off their backs and the faintest spark of
fire out of their grates; to torture them till they
are so numb and faint with its cruelty that they
have scarcely any feeling whatever remaining. It
loves to do the work of the destroyer: to blight,
to wither, and to blast. O, terrible and remorseless east wind. It seriously interferes even with
the tiniest of travellers and hinders him from
taking his walks abroad.

I had projected some vastly pleasant travels, but all my time has been taken up by fleeing from the east wind and dodging it in every possible way. I have become a species of iced Wandering Jew: I am driven from one place to another, I have no rest, I am weary and sad, and shall never return to my accustomed joviality, and usual health and spirits, till the east wind ceases its persecution.

LIFE AT BAVENO.

SITTING under the shade of a catalpa tree in the gardens of the Hotel Belle Vue I come to the conclusion that life at Baveno is the pleasantest in the world. And then I discover that the tourist mind does not know how to make the most of its advantages. People come here to see the Isola Bella. I do not know why they come to see the Isola Bella, unless it is that it has a pretty name, and that their grandfathers have been to see it and their great-grandmothers have paid a visit to it, and they have read about it in books, or they have seen pretty steel engravings of it in the old annuals. It is a vastly difficult operation to disestablish a lion, and this little island has been established as a lion for so many years that I am under the impression that it will roar loudly until the end of time. There is no doubt whatever that Isola Bella is a humbug. I thought so when I first saw it—when I was younger and more gushing than I am now—and I was doubly convinced my opinion was right when I viewed it again yesterday. I could name at least half-a-dozen gardens in England that are infinitely better in arrangement and effect, and there are many in Italy and France that have a far greater right to be raised to the dignity of lion than this pretentious little island. There is a tea-gardeny taste of the worst kind pervading the whole place: the palace is tea-gardeny in feeling: the collection of pictures is worthy of a tea-garden: the grottoes recall the tea-garden most forcibly, and the arrangement of the grounds is tea-gardeny in the highest degree.   Were it not for the glorious views one gets on all sides of the Lago Maggiore, with its luxuriant slopes, with its little white villages winking and glittering in the sunshine, with its glorious hills, with the snow-clad Alps in the background, the place would not be worth a visit. The whole thing is one vast sham sustained at an enormous expense.   We may go there and look at the camphor trees; the orange, the citron, and pomegranate trees: we may gaze upon the myrtle, the aloe, the cactus, the gigantic laurel, the cypress, and the lemon, and the vine. On a fine autumn day, in a revel of delicious perfume, we may think what a wonderful place this is: but when we are informed that this island was originally a barren slate rock; when we are told that every spoonful of mould was brought from a long distance and requires to be constantly renewed; that the terraces are all boarded over in winter, and that stoves are heated beneath them, and by so doing the island is converted into one vast hothouse—when we are told all this we do not think quite so highly of the Isola Bella as guide-books wish, or gushing tourists insist upon. It does not matter, however, whether you think highly of it, or whether you despise it, go and see it you must.   You have no will in the case: it is as much a matter of compulsion as going to see the Giant's Causeway when you are at Port Rush, or

visiting the detestable old Lion when you are at
Lucerne. So you may just as well get your Isola
Bella done at once, for you may be certain you will
not be permitted to leave Baveno till you have seen
it. We were so well assured of this that we had a
boat directly we arrived, and were taken over there,
made a rapid run round the place, returned in a
profuse perspiration just in time to change and sit
down to dinner, and talk Isola Bella with any tourist in the place. I did not mean to have said anything about the Isola Bella, but I knew people when
they heard that I was at Baveno would think me
mad if I said nothing about this islet. So I have
just mentioned it to show I have done my duty as
a British tourist—a term that is often synonymous
with British idiot—and now I will settle myself
down to a much pleasanter task, that is, a description of 'Life at Baveno.'

The garden of the Hotel Belle Vue, I should
tell you, is a very charming place, especially if you
can secure a comfortable chair, a patch of cool
shade, and a good view. All these I have been
fortunate enough to obtain, and it is quite necessary you should lose no time about this if you wish
to pass a quiet morning in these gardens. Everybody gets up very early and everybody has a disposition to take advantage of the glorious out-of-
doors life to which this garden lends itself: consequently, if you are not in good time you will find
all the shady nooks occupied and every advantage-
ous situation crowded. At the present time there
is a fresh, plump, bright, fair-haired, English girl
writing letters at the stone table close to the

lake: there is her comical, good-humoured mamma
sitting beside her with her work, and the two are
chattering and chattering as only a couple of
women can, in any climate. There is a deal more
talk than letter-writing going on I fancy. I notice
the gentleman whom we call the disappointed
diplomatist—a man who looks as if he had been
trying to catch the Speaker's eye for the last
twenty years and had not succeeded—sleeping
peacefully beneath the avenue, and utterly obliv-
ous of the ponderous blue book that has dropped
from his hand. There are three middle-aged
ladies sitting at one of the little round tables
doing some elaborate kind of work in most spite-
ful fashion; they look like three sour old crows in
conclave; they appear to be pecking at one another,
stabbing their embroidery and taking away the
reputation of every one in the hotel at one operation. There is an old gentleman sitting under a
mulberry tree with his pocket-handkerchief over
his head, with *Galignani's Messenger* in his hand,
and snoring so loudly that he disturbs the entire
garden. If I can only find a waiter I shall send
him to the old gentleman with my compliments
and I will take *Galignani* when he has quite done
with it. But it is a great deal too much trouble
to do anything but look at people during such
baking hot weather as we have at present. If you
have a reserved seat in the shade you must not be
so silly as to quit it on any trivial pretext; if you
do it will be snapped up at once. I know there
are plenty of watchful eyes peering from behind
the jalousies in the reading-room and the *salle à*

manger watching for a vacant seat. If we leave our chairs only for a moment in these gardens we pile books and umbrellas upon them, or tie a pocket-handkerchief round their backs, and even after taking all these precautions we are forced to leave them in charge of a well-tried friend in order to make sure of finding them when we return. The only individuals who have any energy at all appear to be three over-grown Italian girls, with their hair in long plaited tails, and who are attired in short frocks and frilled trousers, rivalling the famous garments of Miss Morleena Kenwigs. The hot weather seems to make no difference whatever to these noisy young ladies; they chase one another, they shout, they scream, they tumble down, they pick themselves up again, they tear their frocks, they jump, and they romp as if it were a cold day in December. They do not interfere with me, however. If they do I shall at once go and complain to their governess, who is sitting on the terrace, and appears to be rather a nice sort of young person.

One would be hard to please who would not be content with this garden. With its terraces, its alleys, its gay parterres, its arbours, and its grass plots. What a wonderful growth there is of mulberry trees, of chestnut trees, of lemon trees, and of catalpa trees; of vines, of pampas grass, of roses, and of oleanders! There is a magnificent oleander that I can just catch sight of from my present point of observation. The pink hue in the sunshine against the hazy grey-green of the distant hills reminds one of the delicacy and purity of colour which one

7

used to see in some of Mr Bretts' Italian land-
scapes before he turned his attention exclusively
to sea pictures. Then beyond the low stone wall—
on which you can occasionally catch a glimpse of
a lizard basking in the sunshine—you see the water
so still, so unfretted by the slightest breeze, that
it is literally like a looking-glass, and the mountains, and the little white villages at their feet, are
reflected almost intact on the lake. You can see
the town of Pallanza glittering and blinking in the
sunshine on the opposite side of the bay, and if I
mistake not the scattered white specks you see
beyond it on the other arm of the lake represent
the thriving town of Intra. Our old enemy the
Isola Bella looks really quite picturesque from
here. But many of those islands which have not
half its reputation look twice as well. Just beyond
that point of land is Stresa—beyond that is Bel-
girate, one of the healthiest spots on the lake. I
could point out a lot more things to you, only it is
too hot to point things out, and I am sure no one
would attend to me if I attempted to improve their
minds. The water is pleasant to gaze upon. It
is so lovely in colour: it is so still and unruffled.
Nothing disturbs it except the steamer from Arona
or Locarno, which touches here three or four times
a day, or the lazy paddling of one of those picturesque awning-covered boats—boats which look
like an ancient broad-wheeled country waggon,
with a Cook's excursion ticket, or a Margate bathing-machine grown light and frivolous in its old
age.

It is a pleasure to gaze upon the water, but it

is a still greater pleasure to bathe in it, and that
is how we usually begin our day at Baveno. I say
how *we* begin it, because I do not think the other
inhabitants of the hotel are very enthusiastic about
lake-bathing. A few of them patronize a sort of
faint imitation of a bathing-machine which belongs
to the hotel, and in which you can have a species
of wash and paddle behind a canvas screen, but
bathing in the lake seems to be quite the exception.
They certainly have no proper appliances for it.
All the lake boats are so high out of the water that
when once you make your plunge it is impossible
to get into the boat without being hauled in by
the attendant. None of the boats have any steps,
so getting out is a difficult, if not a dangerous
performance. On the Lago di Como they have
boats with steps, and there is no reason they
should not have them here. It would only cost a
few shillings, and it is a thing the proprietors of
the hotel should look to. This morning our boatmen rigged up a dilapidated ladder with chains,
but the whole thing broke down and flung us back
into the water directly we attempted to mount it,
so we had better have had nothing at all. The
getting in, however, is glorious; you take a header
into clear water of a *celadon* colour, you speed into
deep malachite, you find yourself in *celadon* again,
there is a sparkle of bright blue, you emerge with
a rush, you shake the water from your hair, and
find yourself basking in the sunshine while your
body is immersed in the purest water. You can
float on your back and peer up into the cloudless
sky, and you can look far away to the left and see

the snow-capped peak of Monte Rosa, and the
glorious scenery of the finest part of the Lago
Maggiore, or you can gaze back upon the town of
Baveno, with the Monte Motterone rising grandly
behind it.   Since I have been away I have bathed
at a variety of places. I have bathed at Schevening,
on the coast of Holland, in the Rhine, in the Reuss,
in the lake of Lucerne, and in the Lago di
Locarno, but I never enjoyed a bathing like that
I have had here. After our swim in the lake
we dawdle over breakfast in the long *salle à
manger*, which is kept very dark and very cool by
having all the jalousies closed and all the windows
open.   There is a thorough draught, but not even
a stray sunbeam is allowed to find its way into the
room.   Most people breakfast early here, though
breakfasts are going on from seven o'clock in the
morning till one o'clock in the afternoon.

The place is very full, though the season is
drawing to a close. The majority of the visitors
are English and American. Occasionally there are
a few French and Italians, but these are quite the
exception. I am sorry to say we have not much
beauty in the place at present. I do not know
whether travelling makes women ugly or whether
it is only ugly women who travel, but I think I
never saw a much plainer collection of ladies than
those who sit down to our *table d'hôte* every evening. I am sometimes disposed to question whether
beauty is not rarer than it used to be. Beauty always was rare I know, but I maintain you do not see
half the number of fresh, pleasing, passable-look-
ing girls about that you used to. There is a pretty

little American lady whom we call the Doll, she is
so *petite* and quiet : there are one or two fair-look-
ing married ladies, and there is the bright, fair,
plump English girl, of whom I have already
spoken. I am very sorry to say the ' old cat '
element is strongly in the ascendant. I grieve to
state the scandal-loving old ladies who used only
to be found in second-rate boarding-houses at
Boulogne now permeate the pleasantest resorts all
over the Continent. If some of these amiable
ladies only knew my sentiments concerning them
how fearfully hot they would make it for me. But
this by the way. After breakfast we generally
drift into the reading-room, and if sundry energetic
old gentlemen, who read *Galignani*, put their
elbows on the last number of the *Times*, and sit on
the *Swiss Times*, are not before us we manage to
spend an hour or so over the papers. If they
happen to be first, and they generally are, we sit
and glare at the old gentlemen with as much
energy as the weather will allow. If looks had the
power of annihilation these individuals would have
been shrivelled up long ago. I fear I shall have
to pursue a plan that I adopted with signal success
at the Hotel Bauer at Zurich some years ago. I
used to watch for the arrival of the *Times*, pounce
upon it, and, quite contrary to all regulations, I
bore it away to my bed-room and locked myself in
till I had finished it.

One thing, however, it does not much matter
here whether you see any newspaper or not ; you
are totally careless as to what is going on in the
outside world as long as you stop here. It is

only the Englishman's love of having to fight for his *Times* that induces us to do battle every morning with the old gentlemen. During the morning it is difficult to know what becomes of the people. A few who get good places in the shade sit out of doors, some enthusiasts who have no time to spare rush off to the Isola Bella: some paddle about the lake, but I believe a large proportion of the visitors go to bed and read their Tauchnitz editions till luncheon time. I know the house is astonishingly quiet at this period, and every blind is kept closed in front of the hotel, so that the place looks as if it were shut up and deserted altogether. If you happen to see a blind open you may be sure it belongs to the room of some new arrival, who is so enchanted with the view that he has not yet discovered the value of keeping the sun out of the room all day. At luncheon time we get a little more lively, and occasionally parties are made up to visit the islands, or take one of the few excursions there are to be made in the neighbourhood. Or if we do not feel equal to anything of this kind we go and see the Locarno boat in and find out whether there is any one we know on board.

At the *table d'hôte* at six o'clock, we muster in great force. People wake up from their slumbers and their Tauchnitz editions: they return from excursions, and they give up mooning beneath the shade of catalpa trees, and the long *salle à manger* is generally as full as it can hold. After dinner the garden becomes more like a *café* than anything else, for every one turns out to enjoy the

cool evening air. Every seat is full, and more
seats are being continually requisitioned from in-
doors. Coffee is served on the little round tables
and on the broad stone wall, which seems to be
the favourite seat of many, and cigars, which look
in the distance like tethered glowworms or fire-
flies in fetters, appear at all parts of the garden.
The evenings soon get dark now, but the air is so
deliciously soft that no one dreams of going in till
late. The last few nights, too, we have had the
moon, which has been particularly favourable to
our lovers and our newly-wed. I forgot to say we
had some good specimens of both these classes
here at the present time. The newly-wed are
always supremely uninteresting, but I cannot help
being somewhat amused in watching a couple of
lovers. I know of no institution so well calculated to make people utterly disgusted with one
another for the rest of their natural lives as the
honeymoon. The newly-married couples are a
nuisance to themselves and every one else, therefore I will say nothing about them. But I was
vastly interested in watching last night two young
people who were not married, but who appeared
to be very much in earnest as they whispered on
the shadiest part of the terrace, till they were
interrupted by a stout uninteresting mama. The
young lady was very pretty, there was a puzzled
look in her sweet face upturned in the moonlight;
there was a faith and an earnestness in the expression of those large eyes. The broad-shouldered
young gentleman had his back towards me, and
he leisurely puffed a cigar as he talked, whilst his

companion pulled a rose to pieces leaf by leaf. I
hope he is not making that pretty girl too fond of
him, for he looks like a poor younger son with expensive tastes, and no income to speak of, and I
am sure that corpulent mama would not have a
kind word to say in his favour. Evidently last
night she appeared as a kill-joy, she broke up the
tête-à-tête as speedily as possible and hurried her
daughter in-doors. I could not help quoting to
myself some lines by my favourite singer :—

> ' Then, that night at Baveno whilst smoking—
> When Some-one had lit my cigar—
> To be found there 'twas rather provoking
> By little Miss Floy and mamma !
> How she bore you away in a hurry !
> Despite all excuse I could make,
> And said, quoting from odious *Murray*,
> " Night air was so bad at the lake." '

' Mama,' and ' cigar,' Mr Favourite Singer, are
somewhat ' cockney rhymes ;' but let that pass.
Your verse is quite good enough for my purpose.
The broad-shouldered young gentleman did not
seem to care whether the night air by the lake was
bad or good for him, for I could see the incandescent tip of his fourth cigar passing backwards
and forwards along the terrace long after I was in
bed.

A light breeze has sprung up, which rustles
the big leaves of my catalpa and threatens to blow
my writing paper into the lake. It seems to have
freshened everybody up. The disappointed diplomatist has awakened, and is shaking his head
severely at his blue-book and pretending that he
has never been to sleep at all : the plump, fair-

haired English girl has finished her letter and has just passed by us under an umbrella: the 'old cats' are packing up their work and noddling their wicked old heads at one another: the gentleman under the mulberry tree is yawning and mopping his forehead: the pretty girl I watched on the terrace last night has just appeared at the top of the steps in the most charming of morning toilettes, and is shading her eyes with her hand and evidently looking for somebody: and one of the Morleena troupe has just tumbled off the stone wall, has rent her garments grievously, and is sent in-doors in disgrace. The waiter comes to us with the joyful intelligence that luncheon is ready, so I will gossip no longer concerning our pleasant dreamy life in these delightful quarters.

IN THE SMALL HOURS.

IN the dark, black night, or beneath the moonlit sky where the fleecy clouds seem to be hurrying with wondrous swiftness across the fathomless deep blue vault, and a painful hush—a silence that can be felt—seems to be pervading the town.

When the wicked old city is in slumber, and its inhabitants are recruiting their energies for renewed exertions on the morrow; when the painful stillness seems to be a reproach to those who are stirring, and their footfall echoes with acute distinctness from the pavement; when the gas-lights seem to wear an unwonted pallor; when the most familiar streets look like streets you have never seen in your life before, and the houses with which you are most familiar assume an unusually weird and picturesque aspect; when deep black shadows invest the most practical and common-place buildings with a poetical mystery; when the railway whistle is hushed, and the very night cabmen are sleeping soundly inside their cabs, utterly oblivious of a chance fare, and their broken-down, dissipated-looking horses are taking forty winks and dreaming of copious feeds of corn that they will never enjoy; when the spasmodic kick of a cab-horse, the distant rumble of a cab, or the heavy tread of a policeman will make you start, and you

avoid your belated fellow-passenger as he avoids you,
each mistaking the other for a burglar or a roysterer;
when to-day's work is done and to-morrow's work
has not commenced; when people who indulge in
beauty sleep have had their full instalment, and
market-gardeners have scarcely begun to bestir
themselves, and the earliest workmen's train has
not yet thought of running; when the river is
silent and sad, and the lights are extinguished in
its shipping, and its penny steamers are laid up
alongside their quays as if they never would be
able to turn their paddles any more; when no
lights are to be seen in the windows except at the
newspaper offices, and no one is to be seen about
the streets but policemen, journalists, Bohemians,
and vagrants; when the late public-houses are
closed, and the early breakfast-houses are not yet
open; when the coffee-stalls have not lit their fires,
and the country wagons with their frost-covered
tilts have not begun to lumber over the stones—
in short, in that space of time between when late
men drop off to sleep and early birds begin to
have an uncomfortable sensation that their alarum
will go off every minute, then is the period which
may be emphatically termed the small hours.

Have you ever observed what an amount of
work you may do in the small hours? After there
is no possibility of even the latest man of your
acquaintance dropping in and interrupting you,
when there is no noise in the streets to distract
your attention, when the curtains are drawn and
your fire is lighted, and there is no sunshine to
tempt you to fling down your pen and go out for a

meaningless lounge ! How you are able to tackle
your work, how your ideas flow, and how brilliant
are your similes, and how easily everything seems
to arrange itself in the dead silence, only broken
by the chirrup of your pen as it glides swiftly and
merrily over the paper, or the occasional startling
'plump' of some ill-regulated cinder as it drops
on to your hearth ! How you can write on and on
without stopping for a moment, or having to hammer out an idea or elaborate a sentence ! Writing
in the small hours you find to be an operation of
the utmost ease compared with work done in the
broad sunshine ; there is nothing whatever to
attract your notice either in sight or sound, thus
your undivided attention is given to the work you
have before you, and it is surprising the amount of
matter you can reel off under such circumstances.
By necessity, journalists have frequently to write a
great deal during the small hours, and save for
the reasons already enumerated, I can scarcely look
upon it as an advantage, feeling certain that ideas
are not more brilliant or more fertile then than in
the morning, provided a man has had a good night's
rest. It is a mistake to suppose that any amount
of sleep obtained during the day can compensate
for loss of sleep in the night. I am convinced
light—daylight, mind you—is almost as necessary
to our existence as air, and that we droop for want
of sunshine as much as does a flower. Even in
the present high-pressure degenerate days, we
cannot afford to do without beauty sleep, but it is
a luxury that very few of us are able to obtain at
the present time. However, my object is not to

preach a homily on the subject of late hours, but
to discourse discursively, as is my wont, of the
various phases of peculiarity which the small hours
present to my mind.

Though I do not object to be at work late, I
very much dislike wandering about the house after
everybody has gone to bed. I am not supersti-
tious, but I have a sort of feeling that I may
encounter ghosts lurking round unexpected corners. I am not naturally a coward, but I have
always nervous apprehensions of burglars at such
a time. The umbrella stand always looks as if it
contained phantom umbrellas, and their handles
look gnarled and weird. They assume a semi-
human appearance, and, I fancy, gibber at me in a
subdued fiendish manner; the clock ticks with a
thrilling incisive distinctness, and I wonder why it
ticks so much louder at night than it does in the daytime; my watch ticks almost as loud as the clock,
and I make a resolution that I will have it altered
to-morrow. My candle casts gigantic silhouettes
of myself at all sorts of uncomfortable angles on
opposite walls, and my boots creak alarmingly. I
feel very much as if I were trying to commit a
burglary in my own house, and I start if I happen
to hear a cough or a sonorous snore in the adjoining room. I do not like to see boots left outside
a room door; they look like spectre boots, and I
fancy they turn round and point their toes at me
as I pass by. An excursion into the kitchen in
search of supper is not to be thought of unless
under pressure of the most severe hunger. The
scampering of black-beetles, about eight times

the size of life, the scrooping of bolts, and the grating of locks, the ghostly character of the kitchen range without any fire whatever in it, and the weird aspect of your black cat as she turns her sleepy green eyes upon you, is enough to appal the stoutest of hearts.   Then the difficulty of obtaining supper under such circumstances is extraordinary: you cannot find knives, and you are about half an hour before you can meet with the salt; you have mislaid the key of the beer tap, and hit your head violently against the roof of the cellar, possibly break a plate or two, and the noise you make in so doing alarms you prodigiously.

In the small hours you may perchance have some extraordinary adventures in search of refreshment.   I have dropped in at an early market house in Covent Garden, after a *bal masqué*, long before even the market gardeners had arisen, and made a tremendous breakfast off eggs and ham, greatly to the astonishment of the simple countrymen who did not know whether they were standing ou their heads or their heels, when they came down rubbing their eyes and saw a merry party of gentlemen breakfasting in gorgeous costume.   I have, by means of mysterious conversations with a policeman, induced him to put me in the way of obtaining entrance to a public-house even earlier than the earliest, and there slake my thirst with copious libations of pale ale.   I have gone out in the small hours to post letters for the early delivery, and have been—in fact, am now—an object of suspicion to the policeman on the beat, who fancies I have some base plot for blowing up the pillar post. I try to conciliate him, and invariably wish him good night; he is polite, but reserved and stern, and will never enter into conversation even on the weather. I can never draw him out, and could never venture to tip him, though I should like to. He is evidently virtuous and not to be bought. I feel he mistrusts me and has his 'hi' upon me. Talking of policemen reminds one what a weary life theirs must be during the small hours. One continued wearying round all through the chilly night, from ten P.M. to six A.M., tramp, tramp, tramp, with no amusement but trying the fastenings of front doors and the locks of area gates, with nobody to speak to and with nothing to vary the monotony of his walk, but the chance of a scrimmage with a drunken man or a knock on the head from a garrotter : when even an old lady in a fit or a lively burglary would be an agreeable relief. Again, what a life is that of a night cabman : that hopeless slumbering on the box, and dreaming of fares that never come, must be terrible. The present writer often thanks his stars when he sees these hard-working men during the small hours, that he is neither a night policeman nor a night cabman. What is he, pray, that he should be better off than these men ? What has he done that he should not be obliged to perambulate the streets, no matter how stormy the weather is or how rheumatic he may be, in a felt helmet, heavy great coat, and thick clumsy boots ; or, swathed in many capes and haybands, be compelled to sleep half frozen on a cab-box ?

There are many painful phases with regard to

the small hours that space will scarcely allow me
to mention; among them, perhaps, the most painful is, watching in a sick room. When you are
just beginning to feel most awfully sleepy, do all
you can you cannot hold your eyelids up, they drop
down as if they were weighted with lead. Yon cannot think how it is, you started so bravely; you had
a good nap in the afternoon, and were certain you
could keep broad awake all night, but now you find
it is almost impossible to do so. You straighten your
neck suddenly, you tread on your toes, bite your lips,
and crack your fingers, all to no purpose. There is a
soothing in the hard breathing of the invalid whom
you are watching that lulls you off to sleep; there
is a rhythmical measure about the tick of the watch
at the bed head, which adapts itself to a popular
street tune, and serves as a lullaby; and the professional nurse, pretending to be wide awake in
the comfortable chair on the other side of the bed,
acts as the strongest of opiates. You glare at her
and silently assert that you are wide awake, you
then look silly and commence nodding at her in an
imbecile manner, till your head goes down with a
sudden jerk that nearly dislocates your neck. You
look at your watch feeling certain it must be six
o'clock, but are disgusted to discover it is only
two. You then see the nurse is nodding at you:
you nod at her, you exchange nods, you fancy you
are at an evening party and are taking wine with
her. You keep on nodding till your head gets
heavier and heavier every minute, and finally drops
down on your chest and refuses to move. You
wonder whether she is still nodding at you, and

hope she will not think it rude of you not to return it, but you cannot possibly get your head up again. You change your position and look resolutely at the bed curtain : there you see a lot of your friends ensconced, it seems perfectly natural, you are not at all astonished to see them, and you look without the least surprise at the spectacle of a serious, corpulent rural dean of your acquaintance hanging by his heels, with his head downwards, and grinning like a Cheshire cat. Will the morning never come ? Will the unutterable weariness, the painful anxiety never cease ? Will the constant watching be in vain ? Will hope come with the morning's light ? Will the passing away of the small hours bring hope or despair ? Happiness or sorrow ?

As I write in the stillness of night, as my pen is flying over the paper, the small hours are rapidly becoming larger. I am forced to pull up, not on account of my having exhausted the subject, or of my pen refusing to do any more work, but simply because I have gone to the length of my tether. In other words, I have come to the end of the space at my disposal, so am obliged to refrain from saying any more on the subject. Three miserable individuals with a broken down harp, a wheezy piccolo, and an asthmatic cornet, and who call themselves Waits, have just begun to make a hideous row in honour of Christmas, so I know the delicious solitude and solemn silence of the small hours are at an end.

COUNTRY COUSINS.

I HAVE just witnessed the procession of the Lord'
Mayor's Show. It was one of the worst I ever
saw in my life, and yet I think I never saw so many
people present to look at it. Why it is that people
will assemble in such numbers to see so little is a
puzzle to me? I cannot account for it unless it be
that a very large proportion of the crowd is composed of country cousins. It does not follow that
they need be your particular relations, everybody
in the crowd, I suppose, is somebody's relation, but
I here speak of country cousins irrespective of their
relation to anybody. They are that class of people
—mostly of the female persuasion—who are the
most enthusiastic sight-seers in the world. They
will do anything, they will endure anything, for the
satisfaction of witnessing something that comes
under the head of a sight, and they will stand
patiently for hours in the open air, exposed to the
blighting east wind, just for the transient pleasure
of gazing on a passing pageant so shorn of its
splendour and so paltry in its details as the Lord
Mayor's Show of the present day.

It was a bright, brilliant, sparkling day for the
show, and country cousindom was radiant, was rosy-
cheeked, and laughing. All along the Thames
Embankment did it crop up here and there in most

provoking form. The Benchers of the Inner and
Middle Temple—the sly dogs!—had a parterre of
prettiness, such as never edged their green sward
before. Charming young ladies in coquettish hats,
dainty damsels be-furred and be-dimpled. How
lovely a young girl looks in furs! I wish I had a
lot of money. I would I were a Rothschild, or a
Baring, or had the means at command of a Baron-
ess Burdett Coutts, and I would buy my lady-love
a mantle of otter-skin. Do not you like otter-skin?
It is ever so much better than the finest seal to my
way of thinking. It is as soft as a maiden's cheek
and it is appropriate to wind round her pretty white
throat, and it is a suitable nest in which to hide her
dimpled chin. But this by the way. The Tem-
plars have not had such a show in their gardens for
many years.

There were a great number of pretty girls about
the streets. Indeed, you wondered where all of
them could come from. Did they come up by special trains on purpose to see the Show and to show
themselves? It is not at all unlikely. For, evidently, they came from the country, at any rate a
large proportion of them did. They had that brilliancy of complexion, that brightness of eye, and
that air of hearty enjoyment and undisguised pleasure, that belong especially to country maidens. In
some of the large windows in Cannon Street and
other parts of the City might be seen groups which
were really well worth studying. Fancy the
whole of the merchandise proper being cleared out
altogether and its place taken by a number of
charming young ladies in the most bewitching cos-

tumes. A window full of winsome maidens with
the foil of a stout materfamilias or an ancient aunt
or two. This came as near to one's idea of a girl-
show as possible. I noticed a couple of sportive
young gentlemen pausing before one of these windows, looking gravely in, pointing at one girl,
expatiating on the merits of another, as if they were
merely so many dresses in a draper's shop, and as
if the window was an ordinary shop window after
all. I looked for some irate champion to sally forth
and kick these impertinent youths into the middle
of next week, but I was surprised to see a pretty
pearl grey glove tap at the window from the inside; then there was much laughter, mama tried to
look haughty, the girls giggled, and there was a
deal of nodding and beckoning. Finally the young
gentlemen went inside the house, and I presently
caught sight of their heads in the very back row
of all, screened from the observation of mama, and
apparently enjoying themselves very much indeed.
I saw some terrible instances of the most bare-faced
flirtation going on in many of these windows.

Your country cousin is, after all, not only an
agreeable but a most useful institution. There are
many places in London I should never have seen
had it not been through being taken there by a
country cousin. I should never have gone to the
top of the Monument had I not been taken there years
ago by a very pretty cousin—and exquisite ankles
she had, too; but this is quite in the strictest confidence—neither should I have ever visited the
British Museum, St Paul's Cathedral, the Thames
Tunnel, or Madame Tussaud's Waxworks, nor the

Royal Polytechnic Institution: Talking about the Polytechnic Institution, I recollect once a country cousin wanted me to take her down in the diving bell. This I firmly but courteously refused. I drew my line at diving bells. Besides, I began to be nervous as to what the consequences might be. A girl who could flirt in the presence of the Iguanodon in the British Museum, who could squeeze one's hand in the Whispering Gallery of St Paul's Cathedral, who could flash her eyes beneath the centre of the Thames, and sigh under the shadow of the waxen effigy of Cobbett, might make love, you know, in a diving bell. There might be an action-for breach of promise, and all that kind of thing. It would be so very awkward. No, no. I drew my line definitely at diving bells. I took her to have her mind improved at one of Professor Pepper's lectures and she pouted all the time. I subsequently took her to see the dissolving views, and that she seemed to like very much indeed. I am told that the flirtation that goes on during the dissolving views is something astonishing. Mind, I say I am told, for I know nothing of such matters myself. I am told that if you were to suddenly turn on the light the number of people who would be found wearing other people's arms round their waists would be something appalling. I do not believe this myself. Besides, I have not been to the Polytechnic for many years, and possibly there are no dissolving views and no flirtation at the present time.

The charming class of the population which

forms the text of this discourse is to the fore during
the Cattle Show week. I do not care twopence
about the Cattle Show myself, but I am generally
taken there by country cousins. I do not fancy
they care much about it either, but it is a good
excuse for a week or two's holiday in London that
they could not otherwise obtain. It is a good
standpoint around which they group all other kinds
of amusements. And do not these young ladies
work hard, and what a vast amount of severe
labour they make you go through yourself? You
see these country damsels are in such excellent
training, they keep such good hours all the year
round, that they can go through any amount of
exertion for a fortnight. They will go to bed at
two and be down to breakfast at eight as bright
and as lively as larks. You can *not* tire them out
do whatever you will. They are off directly
after breakfast to get through a vast amount
of shopping; they probably will not have time to
get back to luncheon; they will very likely look
in at a morning concert, and not unlikely do some
more shopping as they return. They will dress
in a great hurry for dinner, for they elect to dine
early in order that they may go to the theatre
afterwards. And going to the theatre with them,
mind you, does not mean dropping in at nine
o'clock. They do their theatre as they do all
their pleasure, thoroughly. They like to be in the
house before the green curtain goes up, and they
love to stay there till they stand a very good
chance of being tied up by the attendants in the
holland seat covers. They get in a perfect fever

if even the overture is being played as they go in, and if the first farce has commenced when they take their seats they really feel seriously aggrieved. If you happen to take them to a theatre on a first night, that is to say a special first night, such for instance as occurs at the Prince of Wales's, on the production of a new piece, they will enjoy themselves prodigiously. You will find all your time is taken up by pointing out the various celebrities as they pass into the stalls or make their appearance in the boxes. But supposing you are with them at the theatre some night when his Royal Highness the Prince of Wales, the Princess of Wales, and the rest—or part of the rest—of the royal family happen to be present, their gratitude will know no bounds. Then they are particular about having bills of the play, and if there are any books of the words they will make a point of securing them. If they happen to witness a pantomime or burlesque they will sure to be delighted with the songs and music : they will want to kuow if they are published and where they are to be obtained, and you will probably hear them carolling bright catchy music about the house for many days afterwards. I know how it will be with me after Christmas. I have promised to take a lot of country cousins to countless burlesques, pantomimes, and *opera bouffe*. They will want all the songs to take home with them, and play and sing them till they drive their parents wild. They will send me out to purchase copies of the songs, and if they are not published they will pout and shrug their shoulders, and probably send me off to the musical conductor to ask the reason why. These country cousins are capable of any amount of small tyranny when their sweet wills are thwarted.

You may study the *genus* to great satisfaction at any time you please between eleven and three in Regent Street. I was there the other day, and I was quite surprised to see how the place was thronged with country cousins. I think they believe more in Regent Street than any other street in the world. For my own part I like St James's Street, of which Mr Frederick Locker has so gracefully sung,

> ' The dear old street of clubs and cribs,
>   As north and south it stretches,
> Still smacks of William's pungent squibs,
>   And Gillray's fiercer sketches ;
> The quaint old dress, the grand old style,
>   The *mots*, the racy stories ;
> The wine, the dice, the wit, the bile,
>   The hate of Whigs and Tories.'

Next to St James's Street I love Bond Street. Now, though the country cousin loves the southern portion of Bond Street for its jewellers' shops— this street will in time become a species of *Strada degli Orefici*—she thinks there is nothing like Regent Street. And here she may be found during the fine weather shopping to her heart's content. The bazaars, I recollect, used to be a favourite lounge of country cousins. They were the only people who visited these places, and looked upon them in the light of an amusement. Other people went there to purchase special articles that were not to be bought anywhere else; but your country cousin went there for a series of exhibitions, she made a progress through the place, lounged leisurely at each stall, not unfrequently lunched there, and occasionally passed the whole day in the bazaarine precincts. It must have been a great blow to country cousins when they heard that the Pantheon was disestablished, and that their pet lounging place had been converted into wine cellars. The Soho Bazaar, I am told, still exists, I have not been there for many years, but I understand it is as much thronged with country cousins as in days gone by.

I must not venture to touch upon, in this paper, country cousins at home. I know it is prodigiously dull after they have left town, after you have been in a perpetual whirl of sight-seeing for a fortnight, and at last you take them to the station with piles upon piles of luggage, and you see them off by the train. Then you begin just to feel a little bit sad, you are sorry to lose them, and fancy you will miss their energy, their ceaseless prattle, and their musical girlish laughter not a little. Nothing is more cheering than to have a few bonny laughing girls at your breakfast-table—I have said 'country cousins' need not be your relations, they may be cousins of cousins, or sisters' school friends, or other fellows' sisters, or even actual cousins, after all—with the prospect of seeing the same bright bevy round the dinner-table in the evening. You feel sad, indeed, when you think this pleasant time is at an end; when you take their tickets, when you hand them into comfortable seats, arrange their wraps and shawls, see that they have foot-warmers, buy them enough newspapers and railway literature to read themselves silly in the course of five miles. You try to look jocular as you commend them to the care of the patriarchal guard—a most rubicund and fatherly personage whom, despite the regulations of the company, you tip in most extravagant fashion—you assume a joviality as you bid them good-bye; you utter some pleasantry—but it hath a hollow sound—when the guard waves a flag frantically; you smile in ghastly fashion as the whistle blows, and as the train slowly moves out of the station you seize by the merest chance in the world the very white dimpled hand you desired to, and perhaps, in the excitement of the moment, squeeze it rather harder than you ought. The face of its owner looks somewhat grave you think, but supremely happy : there is a suspicion of much rain, but 'eyes gleam more brightly through eyelashes wet.' The expression of that face haunts you all day long, and the little damsel feels the pressure of your hand as far as Rugby. And then probably the thoughts of both of you become scattered. You do not marry; of course you don't. It is a very bad plan to marry cousins. A man has quite enough relations without wishing to be more nearly related to them.

I should very much like to say something about the country cousin at home, but must leave it for a future opportunity. The pleasant country life, the picnics, the boating parties, the rides, the drives, the billiard matches, the flirtations, the freedom, the confidence, the Christian and pet name calling, and the thousand and one things which are so pleasantly shielded beneath the cloak of country cousindom, might be treated to advantage. *C'est si gentille d'avoir une belle cousine*—I think said Paul de Kock. I used to have a good many pretty cousins, but I fancy they are all gone married.

A WET DAY AT BRIGHTON.

IF the corporation, the town council, the most worshipful the mayor, the fly-drivers, the Bath-chairmen, the shrimpers—all and every of the various officials, potentates, and hangers-on of the town of Brighton—had a spark of gratitude about them they would present me with the freedom of the town in a gold box. Or, if they were not able to do this, they would build a new terrace fronting the sea and call it after me, or they would give me a free ticket for life for both of the piers, a few shares in the Aquarium, a gratuitous everlasting admission to Brill's Baths, or bestow on me a magic pass by means of which I could 'requisition' anything I pleased at Mutton's or Streeter's. It is due to me that they should do something of this kind, for have I not glorified their town upon all occasions ? Have I not visited it in season and out of season ? Have I not mooned there in November, and have had my head pretty well blown off there in April ? Have I not gone for 'A Cruise upon Soles,' and did I not take an 'Uninteresting Walk,' and record my experiences in a certain volume entitled the 'Shuttlecock Papers' ? Have I not done much in, say a thousand and one articles, towards the glorification of Brighton, the exaltation of its inhabitants, and the praise of its climate ? And yet what has Brighton done for me? Has it ever given me so much as a free shrimp as a testimonial? Did Mutton ever present me with a raised pie free of charge, or did Streeter ever accord me a gratuitous bun? Verily they did nothing whatever of the kind. The climate is the only thing that has done anything for me in return for the fulsome praise with which I have bespattered the whole township. The glorious breeze, the briny atmosphere, the brisk, bright, laughing sunshine of its climate, has repaid me a thousand-fold. It has brought back the brown and the red to my cheeks, it has brightened my eye and it has lightened my heart. Is not this the best testimonial I could desire? Go to, then, ye inhabitants of Brighton! I will not have even a paltry shrimp in the way of a testimonial. (N.B. A delicately carved prawn in pale pink Neapolitan coral, set as a pin, I dare say it might be procured at Mr Phillips's, in Cockspur Street, might perhaps be entertained.) And Mutton may bake himself in one of his own pies, Streeter may roll himself into bun-paste, and Brill may drown himself in his own bath. Testimonials indeed! Look at your climate and be thankful. Did not the great Michael Angelo Titmarsh write many years ago: 'It is the fashion to run down George IV., but what myriads of Londoners ought to thank him for inventing Brighton! One of the best physicians our city has ever known, is kind, cheerful, merry Doctor Brighton! Hail, thou purveyor of shrimps and honest prescriber of South Down mutton! There is no mutton so good as the Brighton mutton; no flys so pleasant as the

Brighton flys ; nor any cliff so pleasant to ride on ; no shops so beautiful to look at as the Brighton gimcrack shops, and the fruit shops, and the market.' I cordially endorse the foregoing remarks, but I cannot help wondering whether Thackeray ever endured a wet day at Brighton.

April showers are all very well in their way, but—as Mrs Brown remarks—'I do not 'old with 'em when you're agoin' out a pleasurin' I ses.' April showers, which are provoking enough in the ordinary way, are not particularly hurtful at Brighton. You can run into shelter immediately, and by the time you turn out again the pleasant brick pathways are dry enough even for the most thinly shod. But there are April showers and April showers. There are April showers that are as charming as a pretty girl smiling through her tears, and there are April showers that begin long before you are up in the morning and have not finished until long after you are in bed in the evening. Now this was that state of things that I found when I came down to breakfast at London-super-Mare the other morning. It was blowing spitefully, the windows were bespattered with gigantic rain-drops that were running races down the pane, which they seemed to enjoy very much unless they were blown clean away from one another or coalesced and run the race as one drop, pretending that they were not running a serious race after all, but were only out for a morning sport. The balcony was in puddles and prize rain-drops hung on the ironwork, rain-drops so large that you wondered how it was they could hang for such a

long time without falling. You might watch as
you please, but you never could see them fall.
They seemed to swell and swell but you never saw
them either fall or burst.   My private belief is that
they waited until your back was turned and then
quietly slid down the railings, as active boys
home for the holidays will slide down the paternal
bannister, greatly to the detriment of their own
trouserloons.   It must have been done in this
fashion or else how could the balcony get so full of
puddles.   Gazing beyond the balcony I must say
the prospect looked hopeless. Dull, heavy, uniform
grey; no break in the clouds and no hope of a
break.   A misty blanket seemed to enwrap everything.   There was no sharpness whatever about
any portion of the view; everything was blurred,
hazy, indistinct.   It looked like a water-colour
drawing that had been well sponged by a strong
hand.   Every portion of delicacy, every atom of
fine minute detail was absolutely wiped out of it.
Everything was reduced to a damp monotone. The
roadway was softened into the path, the path into
the railings, the railings into the sea, and the sea
into the sky. As for the horizon, it had disappeared
altogether.   This was altogether a very cheerful
prospect, and calculated to raise one's spirits !

I say to myself it will be better after breakfast.
So I take a longer time over breakfast than usual.
I shall have plenty of time to read the papers this
morning, and get through them quietly without
interruption.   The papers generally arrive before
I am down, this morning they have not come at
all.   A very nice state of things certainly.   On fine

mornings when the papers are rather a bore—of
course they arrive.   On a wet morning they would
be an inestimable boon—of course the boy neglects
to bring them.   What can I do to amuse myself?
I have a sort of idea it would be very good fun to
boldly walk out and get wet through, to sit on the
rails opposite and smoke a pipe, and pretend I did
not care at all about it.   Flyman opposite to my
window is evidently a philosopher.   He looks like
a St Swithin in reduced circumstances.   He appears to have abandoned his bishopric and taken
to fly-driving late in life as a penance.   After all,
he does not look so penitential as I could wish.
On second thoughts, I fancy he must be the adver-
tising medium of some great water-proof house.
What does he mean by standing out in the rain
when he could be so comfortable inside his fly ? If
I were Mr Flyman I would fetch a pot of half-and-
half from the nearest public-house, and would get
inside and pull the blinds down and smoke myself
silly.   Mr Flyman seems to rather enjoy being a
martyr when anybody is looking.   I have a sort of
idea that martyrdom is rather a pleasant thing than
otherwise when there are plenty of spectators, and
fancy that the fewer spectators there are the fewer
martyrs we should find, as a general rule.   The
martyr before me is dripping, he looks like a perambulating sponge : he is just the sort of man to
fling at the head of an unpopular member of parliament.   He would not hurt much but he would
be vastly disagreeable.   He has already swollen to
about twice his natural size, and his fly looks as if
it would begin to sprout directly the sun came out.

I begin to have a feeling of sympathy for this many-caped philosopher, and I think I will employ him in order to give me some amusement on this miserable morning. After all, Brighton is not much better off for amusements on a wet day than other seaside resorts. Indeed, I do not think it has improved in proportion to the increase of its population. Fifty years ago I imagine it was even superior in this respect than at present, for, turning to a charming little child's book, called *A Visit to Brighton*, which has been many years in my family, and which used to be one of my favourite volumes when I was a very small boy, I find the libraries were great resorts in those days. Those must have been primitive days indeed, for in this little book we read the following, which is given as a startling fact, and something really well worth noting :—'The road from Brighton to London is so good, and the travelling so expeditious, that, though above fifty miles distant from each other, several coaches perform the journey in one day, and allow their passengers two or three hours between the time of their coming in and returning.' In those days Brighton had to find its own amusements, and was not merely a maritime suburb of London. I cannot refrain from quoting a few lines of description of the scene which met the eye of Caroline and her papa, when they walked out the first evening of their arrival at Brighton :—'They were not far from the Steyne. But ah ! what a motley group was there ! It was an immense crowd. The military band was stationed before the library. The castle rooms were opened for a

9

promenade concert, from whence piano and harp
resounded whenever the louder instruments ceased.
Music was heard in the library, and from several
bands of itinerant performers the sound of fiddles,
pipes, and tabors, and hand-organs came echoing
through the different streets. In another place
one or two French women were exerting their
voices to attract attention. The mania for music
seemed to have seized the whole community.'
Now, I have made inquiries with regard to these
libraries, and find that the principal one is now
occupied as the electric telegraph station, and the
smaller one forms the office of a very respectable
and energetic firm of house agents. Both these
places, therefore, are still very useful in their way,
but they are scarcely the spots you would choose
to find amusement or distraction in on a rainy day.
It is true you might pass away a few hours pleasantly in getting ' orders to view ' houses you
never meant to look at, or, if you did intend to
look at, your means would never allow you to
take ; or you might kill time by sending off face-
tious or abusive telegrams to your numerous friends.
Both these diversions would, however, become
somewhat wearisome after a time. The one would
prove very expensive, and the other might result
in your being kicked from the Steyne up to Kemp
Town by indignant house agents' clerks. My only
hope of amusement, then, is my St Swithin in reduced circumstances.

I tap sharply on the window-pane and St
Swithin in reduced circumstances looks up. I
seize an umbrella and rush out. He opens the

door briskly. I am somewhat disappointed to
find that he does not bless me in sacerdotal fashion,
that he does not wear a waterproof mitre and does
not carry a crozier reversed for a whip-handle. He
merely says something about it being 'a norful
day.' Some one once said that the depth of misery
was to spend 'a wet Sunday all by yourself in a
hack cab in the middle of Salisbury Plain.' I
imagine this individual had never tried what it was
to spend a wet Tuesday morning in a Brighton fly
and do the regular 'half-a-crown an hour' business
between Hove and Kemp Town. I put both the
windows up and light a short pipe and smoke furiously. I discover that the top of the vehicle is by no
means water-tight, and a corpulent rain-drop—a
very Banting of rain-drops—rolls down between
my neck and my collar, and generally distributes
itself between my shirt and my back. This is not
cheering, but I am Tapleyan and laugh at the oc-
currence. I look out of window and begin, as
people say of babies, to 'take notice.' I see that
all the horses that pass me have changed colour.
The white horses have become grey, the grey
horses black, and the black horses look as if they
had just received a hearty polish of Day and
Martin at the hands of an energetic 'boots.' As
for the bay and brown horses, they are so much
changed that their own proprietors would refuse
to acknowledge them till they were dried. The
sparrows, I see, seem to think it is time to go to
roost—I do not see why they should desire to go
to sleep in a pouring rain—and have taken up
positions in rows all along the railings. The

Brighton sparrows know not trees, leaves would probably frighten them, and I believe their bed-rooms are usually fishing-boats or iron railings. Not a single bath-chair is to be seen anywhere. I cannot help wondering how the Bath-chairmen amuse themselves on such a day as this. I wonder whether they have a club to which they can go and exchange experiences on the matter of invalids. I have heard of a Cabman's Club, and I should think the Bath-chairman's Club would be a most lively institution.

There is scarcely any one about, and the red-brick footway shines and glistens as if it were polished porphyry. I see one or two trim damsels with umbrellas and neat waterproof cloaks. They are faultlessly shod, and for the most part carry rolls of music in their hands. I imagine they are daily governesses. I pity them from my heart, having to trudge about on a day when you would not send your cat out, even if you gave it a mackintosh and two pairs of india-rubber goloshes for its feet. I have a great mind to ask one of these young ladies if I can 'give her a lift' in my fly, but I suddenly recollect it would be scarcely 'proper,' and that my excellent friend, Mrs Grundy, would hardly approve of such a proceeding. Dear, dear, what many acts of politeness, of charity, and of kind-ness we are compelled to neglect because we fear the censure of Mrs Grundy; I wish I could start a society for the suppression of this terribly moral old lady. There is not a boatman to be seen any-where. I should have thought these case-hardened, salted, high-dried, tanned, be-pitched, water-

proofed individuals could have stood any amount
of weather. But it seems such is not the case.
Your Brighton boatman always disappears at the
first omen of foul weather. I am afraid your
Brighton boatman is a bit of a humbug. I
wonder whether he is a ' property boatman ' laid
on by the mayor and corporation for the amusement and mystification of visitors during the fine
weather. The Chain Pier was entirely deserted, so
was the West Pier, except by a shabby dripping dog,
who looked as though he had come in with an order,
and appeared to be enjoying himself amazingly.

Notwithstanding all these depressing circumstances I went through my work bravely. I
thoroughly ' did ' the sea-board of Brighton from
Cliftonville in the west to Kemp Town in the east.
I smoked furiously till I fear I must have scented
the linings of that proper old fly, so that ancient
dowagers and particular old Mrs Grundys will
have a perpetual fit of sneezing if they happen
to ride in it during the next month. I became
ultra-Tapleyan and enjoyed myself tremendously.
I felt I was the Juan Fernandez of Brighton. I
was monarch of all I surveyed, my right there was
none to dispute : in the terrace, the square, and
parade, I was lord of the fly and its brute. I
finally discharged my St Swithin in reduced circumstances with a magnificent gratuity in addition
to his fare—as he said something about being
' werry dry,' alluding, probably, more to his internal condition than to the state of the weather—
and sent him dripping away with a merry smile on
his rubicund countenance.

UP THE THAMES.

I AM up the Thames! I am sorely tempted to shout out Hooray! Indeed, if I were not in the most delicious state of laziness, I would shout hooray at the top of my voice. My spirit is willing, but the flesh is weak, and so I will do nothing whatever of the kind. I believe I started with intention of going to the Henley Regatta. Possibly we may get there in time to see the races run, perhaps we may get there after the races are over. For my own part I do not care twopence which it is. I do not care whether we arrive there the day after to-morrow, or the middle of next week, or next Saturday fortnight. I would sooner of the three name the last of the times indicated, but I really do not care much if we do not get there at all. I really think—if it is not too much trouble to think—that I would rather not get there at all. I am enjoying myself prodigiously in the laziest sort of fashion. Imagine me, if you please, most gentle of readers and most indulgent of British publics—I am in a good humour with you all at this present writing—imagine me, clad in canvas shoes, in white flannel trousers, in a straw hat, and a rowing zephyr, and a pea-jacket. Basking in the sunshine when it comes, and entirely indifferent to the rain when it pours. Figure to yourself my

being in company with two stalwart oarsmen,
capital fellows in every sense of the word. Picture, if you please, a boat admirably adapted for
such an excursion, and know that there is a wonderful square wicker-basket, containing well-select-
ed provisions, hampers with a variety of bottles of
attractive mien, and Brobdignagian stone vessels
of suspicious appearance. Add to this a goodly
store of tobacco, and a number of black clays that
would be worthy of Titian had he devoted his attention to colouring pipes instead of pictures.
Think of all these things, and ask yourself if it is
possible any one can write a connected narrative
under the circumstances. Any one, possibly,
might do it, but your floating philosopher is not
any one, so he cannot do it. And he would not
do it if he could. As I loll in my boat, in the intervals of my taking my turn at the oars, I will pull
out my sketch-book and make little sketches of
anything that happens to take my lazy fancy.

A pretty bend of the river, the prettiest bit
after you pass Egham is, without doubt, at Anker-
wyke. Cooper's Hill to your left and the grand
old trees to the right dipping into the water. I
have seen this bit under all sorts of aspects of day
and night, and I do not know whether it looks best
in the glorious sunshine, as it is at present, or in the
mysterious moonlight of a summer night, when all
is still, save the distant roar of the weir miles below.
What a place it is, under the shadow of that over-
hanging chestnut, to dream and meditate in the
noon-tide heat : you can run your boat beneath it
and be totally hidden from all passers-by. You can

roll on your back and peer up into the glorious canopy of green and count the leaves till you go to sleep, lulled by the swirl of the stream and the hum of the dragon fly. And, O, what a place is this for flirtation! Either in the daytime, when the sun outside is broiling, or in the still moonlight, which can scarcely manage to silver the ripples beneath the overhanging boughs, it is a superb place for such light amusement. I fancy a good many hearts have been led captive at one time or another in this bower known only to the initiated. Sweet voices have sung sirenlike songs in this pleasant haven, and the 'inner light' of girls' eyes has flashed dangerously in this secluded spot. It was only a few evenings ago I was there with a couple of very charming damsels. We did not flirt, of course. O, dear no, we did nothing of the kind. But I own I felt somewhat sad, and sighed 'To be brave, handsome, twenty-two; with nothing else on earth to do, but all day long to bill and coo'—But, no matter.

Supposing you married the girl of your heart—as if any one ever did marry the girl of his heart—but *supposing*, I say, you married the girl of your heart (I take for granted that there are girls and that they have hearts in this degenerate age)—I can point you out a charming little residence which would be just the place to take her to, hard by the spot we have just left. It is Mr Clifford's dainty little cottage on Magna Charta Island. It is the very place of all others to take a pretty young wife. It is far enough distant from town to prevent disagreeable people dropping in. It is surrounded by water : you could cut off all communication with the mainland if you pleased, and be as secluded as Mr Wemmick, when he pulled up his drawbridge in his castle at Camberwell. And, better than all, there would be ample facilities for drowning your mother-in-law if she became in any way obnoxious, as most probably she would, if you gave her the smallest encouragement. But I want you to notice the pretty porch overgrown with rose and honeysuckle, and say if you cannot picture a young lady of your acquaintance looking very charming standing within it. Look you at the quaint mullioned windows, and tell me if you could not imagine snug rooms tastefully furnished with antique chairs and tables within them. Say, do you not admire the smoothly-shaven lawn, sloping to the river, the gay flower-beds, and the ornamental shrubs ? Could not two people be tolerably happy together there, think you ? Or is it possible they might quarrel, or find existence monotonous if nobody stepped in to see them ? I am sure I cannot say how this might be, and in my present lazy frame of mind it is a great deal too much trouble to inquire.

Like the old dissolving views at the Polytechnic, one view soon puts another aside, and whilst I have been speculating with regard to the Magna Charta cottage we have reached the Bells of Ouzely. There is a goodly look about this hostelry. There is nothing slap-bangish about it, and no suspicion of the garish modern public-house. It looks old and well-seasoned ; there is a good, gentlemanly, Conservative look about its very window-sills, with the

gay geraniums decorating them. There is nothing
caddish in its aspect, neither is there a suspicion
of Buggins the Builder about a stick or a stone in
the entire building. I own I should like to stay
here and not go any further. The prospect is
mighty pleasant : the landlord has a superb tap of
ale. Rowing is a nuisance and Henley Regatta is
a weariness to the flesh. Why should we go there
at all ? I would propose that we should stay here,
only I know my friends would not listen to me for
a moment, and it is a great deal too much trouble
to propose things that people will not listen to. I
give a glance of languid regret at the Bells as we
sweep by.

We pass a pretty girl with lustrous brown eyes,
steering a boat which is pulled by a lazy young
gentleman, who is evidently more occupied in
love-making than in rowing, if you may judge by
the way in which he rests on his oar and gazes
straight into the damsel's eyes. Why is not my
boat steered by a fair young girl, and why cannot
I spend my time in gazing into fathomless brown
eyes, instead of worrying my life out in order to
reach Henley by a certain time ?

Three contemplative gentlemen in a punt look
upon us with pitying glances as we pass by. They
have been toiling all the morning, but they have
caught nothing ; they will toil all the afternoon,
and will not catch much more, but they are
perfectly happy. They sit blinking in the sunshine, like ancient owls who have taken their
degrees, and enjoy themselves prodigiously. I
envy these contemplative gentlemen as I bend

over my oar, or as I see my companions bend over
theirs. For, after all, it is nearly as irksome to
see people exerting themselves as to be obliged to
do a little exertion on your own account. I should
like to sit in a punt, even if I did not fish. I should
like to bask in the sunshine, even if I held no rod
in my hand; and I should enjoy to gaze down into
the deep waters, even though I watch no bobbing
float. I should love to look at the sinuous hanks
of long weeds waving with the stream, like unto
the luxuriant tresses of a water nymph, and to
listen to the summer breeze singing through the
rushes : to gaze down into the deep water, and to
see a yellow water-lily far beneath the surface
wabbling about—there always is a yellow water-
lily far beneath the surface wabbling about—and
to wonder how it ever got there.

In Boveney Lock we meet a friend in a light
boat, being towed by a horse in charge of a man.
Another man in the boat to see that everything
goes right, to pay locks, halloo at people, shove
off, and all that sort of thing, you know. Our
friend lolls back on soft cushions on a luxurious
stern seat, and steers in right regal fashion. If he
does not steer it does not much matter : if he is
lulled to sleep by the stream gurgling beneath his
boat, there will be no chance whatever of his being
shipwrecked. For is there not the man in the
head of the boat with a hitcher, to ' chyike' the man
on horseback, to shove off, to hold on, or playfully
prod anybody or anything with his dangerous-
looking implement. It is a pleasure to see any one
who is more practically lazy than I am myself. Of

a truth our friend is of a most luxurious disposition,. and he hath a locker of comfortable dimensions behind his seat, which looks as if it contained many useful and cheering things for a long voyage. A far more luxurious fashion this is of travelling than by the dainty steam-launch which has become so common on the Upper Thames now. There is a want of rest about the best-regulated steamer; there is a fretful fussiness, there is a nineteenth century hurry that is out of harmony with any feeling of laziness you may possess. There is something about its matter-of-fact snort and its sharp shrill whistle that at once removes any idea of repose. But our friend in the boat is something delightful. We christen him the Sybarite of the Stream and let him pass by.

I find no more pictures in my sketch-book for some distance. There is no note of Surley Hall, neither is there any mention of the pleasaunces on the left-hand side of the river between this hostelry, beloved by Eton boys, and Monkey Island. I think I must have been condemned to hard labour all this time, for a halt in Bray Lock is the next picture that meets my eye. Same old lock-keeper, who has been complaining of 'hardenin' of the stummick,' by reason of pressure from opening the lock-gates for years, is there. He is as pleased with the offer of a pipe of tobacco and a drink of beer as ever. I have a sort of notion we paused for a considerable time in this uninteresting, ram-shackle old lock. A few hard-boiled eggs and biscuits were, I fancy, ravenously consumed, and pleasant views of the surrounding country—through an amber medium—were taken through the glass bottom of our silver tankard. This really was a sensible proceeding, and I even ceased to envy the Sybarite of the Stream, who must be almost at Cliefden by this time. You see, if you have a man with a horse you must keep him going, or he will think you a fool. It never does to be thought a fool by your own servants. So, after all, there is some advantage in our mode of travelling.

Under pretty grey Maidenhead Bridge we pull up at Skindle's at last. We are not going to stay there, but we cannot refrain pausing a little while and looking about us. Shall we land ? Of course we will. Just to stretch our legs, you know. We find a number of friends in the coffee-room of the 'Orkney Arms,' and I fancy a certain tankard goes round and is replenished, and goes round again. It seems a pity to think of tearing ourselves away when one might be so happy at Skindle's, and might moon and smoke so pleasantly on his velvety lawn, sloping down to the stream. It is a sin to be obliged to speed away, just because there happens to be a tournament of boats at Henley, just because a number of misguided young muscular Christians choose to overheat themselves and over-exert themselves in the sunshine for the purpose of winning a few trumpery silver cups. Don't you think so ? Why cannot people go up to Henley when there is *not* a regatta ? It is twice as pleasant as when the town is so thronged that you can scarcely move. People who have seen Henley in regatta time do not know what a doubly de-lightful place it is when it is its own quiet, old-fashioned self.　There are three very lazy-looking men in grey jackets smoking very big cigars and reading newspapers on the lawn of the Household Brigade Club: there are two little girls in very short frocks and very long hair romping with a big St Bernard dog on the green sward of the Orkney Arms; and there is a charming young lady about to enter a boat in which a handsome young fellow in flannels is already seated.　We watch this proceeding with a great deal of interest.　There is a deal of parleying going on: the young lady pouts, and smiles, and nods her head, and shakes her shoulders.　The little damsel is quite a coquette: she is pretty, and knows it; she has a neatly-turned ankle, and shows it.　At last, after a deal of hesitation and shrinking, a skilful manipulation of diaphanous skirts and no little display of snow-white frillery, she seats herself in the stern of the boat and beams triumphantly on her slave.

Boulter's Lock!　Prettiest and most picturesque of locks on the river from Henley downwards. The 'bower of roses by Bendemeer's stream' may be all very well in its way, but I doubt if it would equal the marvellous show of roses of every variety, white, blush, deep pink, blood red, and pale yellow, that abound in this little garden.　Could you not be contented to live here for the rest of your life? Would not the office of lock-keeper be entirely in harmony with your notions of mooning and enjoyment?　I protest it would be superb.　If I could only induce Someone to wear print dresses—she looks lovely in print dresses, I can assure you—to be satisfied with a coquettish little brown straw hat,

and to confine her notions of jewellery to one plain
gold ring, I would try for the appointment of lock-
keeper. I would do a little fishing, a deal of mooning, would see a newspaper, perhaps once a fortnight,
would finish my three-volume novel, and complete
my book of poems. My friends would come down
to see me, they might invite me to dinner either at
Skindle's or the Ray Mead Hotel, I should not be
particular which. I should have a boat, and could
row them up to Cookham to lunch, or to dine at
the Complete Angler at Great Marlow. I will
certainly propound this matter to Someone next
time I see her. Would it not be dull? Dull?
Not a bit of it! Just fancy what a lot of callers
we should have during the Henley week! How
all the fellows would look in during the Henley
Regatta, and how thirsty they would be. Our
'bountiful beaker of boraged Badminton' would
want replenishing pretty frequently. Besides,
could one afford to give everybody who called,
Badminton on a lock-keeper's salary? I do not
know, I am sure. I do not fancy I know much
about 'housekeeping.' The matter is worth thinking of. I could not be dull with fathomless brown
eyes, even in a fortnight of Sundays, could I?
Boulter's Lock would be 'rayther' a long way from
the club, would it not? And perhaps Someone
would become just a 'leetle' bored without her
Lady's Mile in May and her Opera-box in June.
Who knows?

I am still feeling very lazy. I am in no hurry.
I do not care whether I get anywhere or not. Of
the two I think I would prefer not, but it does not

much matter. So long as I can go on sketching
and dreaming and mooning and pottering I am
happy. Who was it once wrote thus of me?

> 'A lazy lounger is he, and a youth,
> Who always speaking, ever pleasantly,
> Of pottering and kissing, rattles on.
> He's an authority on bitter beer;
> He writes on ankles like Anacreon,
> Poems on petticoats; "diaphanous"
> Is to my friend the sweetest word on earth;
> Flirting with frills, he wanders week by week,
> And loves to tell us how he once was loved.'

Do not you think the poet painted my portrait
to perfection. I seem to fancy so as we dream
along under the shadow of Cliefden Woods. Now
I find I am on the look-out for another appointment. I should like to be keeper, or gardener, or
something of the kind to the Duke of Westminster, and live in one of those pretty cottages
embowered in foliage. I think that would suit
me admirably. No worry, no responsibility, a fixed
salary a year, and the woods of Cliefden all to
myself. Just as good as if they were my own, you
know. For I could wander here and there. I
could shake my head at the firs, frown at the
beeches, and nod approvingly at the oaks, just as if
they were what the children call my 'very own.'
I could, when we were not very busy at Cliefden,
drop down in my boat—or rather in the Duke's
boat, for of course he would keep one for my delectation—as far as Boulter's Lock, and have a gossip
with the lock-keeper, and when it was my 'Sunday
out,' I would get as far as Amerden Bank and
have dinner with a few of my old friends. I certain-

ly think that nice little situation of the description alluded to should be reserved for highly-cultured impecunious gentlemen with a strong love of the beautiful. I think some one ought to get me an appointment of this kind. I have a strong love for the beautiful, I may not be highly-cultured, but there is no doubt about my being impecunious. To live by the side of the Thames, to be lulled to sleep by the rustle of the leaves of the woods of Cliefden, would be worth more than a handsome annuity.

But I came out to make sketches, not to moralize. I was forgetting all about my sketching. One of my friends has got out of the boat. He has fastened the tow rope to his body, he is evidently pretending to be a horse; he pulls the boat steadily along, the stream gurgleth pleasantly beneath us, and I endeavour to steer, in a sleepy sort of way. The rushes whistle as we brush by them. A magnificent black Labrador dog looks good-humouredly at us through the reeds. We remark to its proprietor that it is a fine dog. Proprietor, who is a pleasant-looking High Church clergyman, says yes, it is. He asks us if we are going far. We say no, and then he makes some jocular remark with reference to the size of our hamper. When we come to look at our boat-load it certainly does appear more as if we were about to emigrate than going for a quiet moou on the river. We invite him to lunch with us, for we are approaching our usual ' pitch,' a spot where we have lunched many times before. He thanks us, but declines, and we wish one another good morning.

When we arrive at our 'pitch,' that is to say the seat beneath the spreading beech, just opposite the most glorious portion of Cliefden Woods, we find it has been taken possession of by a trim little governess in black and her charges, a girlish boy of ten and a boyish girl of twelve. One cannot tolerate a girlish boy, but a boyish girl is certainly very amusing. The boy was a pale dreamy youth with his hair parted down the middle, he moved languidly and carried a book in his hand; his dress was neatness itself. The girl was ruddy, her shock of short hair was all a-tangle, her hands were brown and freckled, she was never two moments still. Her spirits were too great for her strength—of clothes. She was continually, 'coming to pieces;' buttons flew, bobbins came undone, and tapes had to be retied every moment. She was continually tearing her frock or losing her hat. She had a fishing rod, but she had not patience enough for a lover of the gentle art. She plagued her poor governess about lines and hooks, and made her life a burden unto her by reason of groundbait. I think the sight of three gentlemen in white flannel with low necks and bare arms considerably alarmed the governess, for she beat a retreat from the seat almost directly our boat touched the shore and she noted our intention of landing.

Not so the High Church clergyman. He reaches the seat with his Labrador dog just at the same time we do. He has—let me whisper it very softly, or it may reach the ears of his bishop, or what would be worse, the old ladies of his parish

—he has ' put on a pipe.' He is smoking it as if he enjoyed it. With such an example before us, we can but follow. We put on our pipes. Our friend steadily refuses to take luncheon, and we come to the conclusion we are hardly hungry yet. However, we get out our tankard and a couple of foil-necked bottles, we fill up a foaming cup. We pledge our clerical friend, he pledges us, and the cup goes round merrily. The boyish girl sees this proceeding from a distance and evidently would like to join us. She is only prevented from so doing by the governess threatening to ' tund ' her with her own fishing-rod : she takes her revenge by bounding off like an untamed colt, clambering over a gate and falling in most ungraceful fashion into a ditch on the other side. Evidently this bonny damsel is like Robert Brough's ' Neighbour Nelly '—' she regrets the game of leap-frog is prohibited to girls.' We spend some time chatting and smoking here, we find ourselves in a comfortable groove and are reluctant to move out of it. The tobacco is so soothing, the conversation of the clergyman is so amusing, his eyes twinkle so pleasantly through his spectacles, and the green leaves are so brightly reflected in the silver tankard, that we do not feel inclined to move.

Another sketch—As we drift by the pretty grounds of ' Formosa.' A young lady, in a light diaphanous dress, sitting on a rustic seat beneath the trees. The sunshine comes through the leaves, it chequers her dress, it spots it with flecks of light here and there. Her face is entirely in shadow, but becomes wonderfully luminous by means of reflected light. , Has any artist ever ventured to paint a portrait in this fashion? O, ye portrait painters of the present day, I say to myself—I would not for worlds say it aloud— what a set of fools are ye! Everywhere are to be seen admirable suggestions, accidental effects, for making portraits real works of art, and yet these opportunities are neglected, and the fashionable portrait painter really does not display so much taste and art in his posing as your first-class photographer. A portrait painter, if he were only to take his sketch book up the Thames, might find enough hints to make his fortune, if he only had sense enough to profit by them.

Cookham Lock. I like going through these old locks. It makes a break in the journey. You come up with other boats, and you can begin the race again with them if you please. We do not please to race, but if we did we should find that the lock is a mighty leveller. At Cookham Lock we find a few boats in the pound, but there are several spectators on the bank. There are bronzed, weather-beaten labourers, there are chubby children in sun-bonnets, belonging to the lock-keeper. And there are three damsels whose united ages would probably be about forty-five. Three sisters. Thirteen, fifteen, and seventeen, I should say might be their ages, and I am a pretty good judge. Troublesome thirteen, bashful fifteen, and sweet seventeen. There they were. Very bonny they looked. A strong family likeness, but yet the three were as different as different could be. I would that I were a poet, and I would write a poem on Thirteen's dimples, on Bashful's pouting lips, and on Sweet's brown eyes. As I am not a poet, I can merely rave over their coquettish little hats, their dainty *écru* dresses, and I may tell you in confidence, most trustworthy of readers, that the neatest ankles and the snowiest frills you could wish to behold were revealed as these damsels lounged by the lock gates.

Quaint little Cookham! How we miss the dilapidated old bridge that used to give such a charm to this bit of the river. The hideous, practical, utilitarian, iron bridge which takes its place is altogether out of harmony with its surroundings. It looks like a rich shoddycrat, a wealthy puddler, a cotton-spinning vulgarian, amongst an assemblage of poor, courtly gentlemen. What a discord it seems with the grand old trees, the grey church tower, and the quiet village in its immediate neighbourhood. Did ever any one see such a vile combination of girders, of plates, of braces, of pillars, and of rivets? Why is everything connected with the metal work of the present day so uncompromisingly ugly? We would fain land at the Bell and Dragon, and wander about the old-fashioned High Street—of which, if my recollection does not deceive me, Mr Frederick Walker gave us such a charming transcript in the Water Colour Gallery some seasons ago—and strive to forget this vile age of steam and iron. I have no space, however, for all the sketches I would give you hereabouts, so must pass on.

Bathing at Marlow! Bathing at Marlow, if

you care about bathing, and happen to be a fair swimmer, is worth—well it is worth anything you please. I know that I would give a goodly portion of my limited earthly possessions to be able to bathe at Marlow whenever I pleased. Secure the services of good-looking Mr Bob Shaw, politest of boatmen, and most skilful of fishermen, and he will put you in the right way of obtaining this luxury. He will take you in a punt below the weir. You will be able to stand on the apron with the water rushing over your feet, you can hold on tight by the weir paddles and gaze through them up the river; you can see the suspension bridge, the church, the town, and see the whole body of the stream swirling down upon you, whilst you receive a glorious douche that you can scarcely stand against, right over your body. It seems to wash all the dust and drouth of London out of you; it scrapes you as well as washes you, it thoroughly invigorates you, and seems to put, at the very least, ten years on to your life. And then the best of it is to come. You can step into the punt again and walk to the other end, glowing, well-knit, and elastic, and take a glorious header into thirty feet of water. Down, down, down into the dark green waters, with the stream pleasantly singing in your ears. Down, down, down, not wishing to turn, feeling as though you could almost live under water, and wander for ever amongst the waving weeds. You continue to go down till you fancy you see a vicious-looking old pike gazing at you. You think he winks in fiendish fashion, and waggles his wicked old fins at you.

This somewhat frightens you. You elevate your
hands, the water becomes less dark, it changes to
a clear green, a shoal of minnows seem to flash
away from you. It becomes silvery, you can see
bubbles on the surface illumined by sunshine, there
is a sudden rush in your ears, and you are once
more out again in the daylight and swimming as
if water were your natural element. Into the punt
again. A tremendous rub with a rough towel.
You are in a glorious glow, you seem to be washed
young again. You feel you can shout, sing, stand
on your head, turn cart-wheels, dance breakdowns,
in short, do anything wild or ridiculous. And,
as John Leech's rude boy in *Punch* observed,
'Doesn't it make you ready for your grub neither!'

SIDEBOARD-SQUARE.

UNDER the shadow of St Paul's cathedral at sunset, not far beyond the jurisdiction of the Dean and Chapter, within earshot of the clank and clamour of the printing machines of the *Times* newspaper, at no great distance from Stationers' Hall, not above a hundred miles northward of Ludgate-hill, and near enough to Doctors' Commons for people who want a marriage license in a hurry, or require to look at a last will and testament on the spur of the moment, may be discovered Sideboard-square. I say may be discovered advisedly, for Sideboard-square is, and always was, a matter of discovery. Ordinary people—people who know London well—are unaware of its existence. Nobody has any friends there as they have in the old-fashioned squares of Russell, Bedford, Brunswick, Mecklenburgh, or Fitzroy. Nobody has any business there as they might have in the squares of Billiter, Crosby, Jeffery, Devonshire, and Great St Helen's. Nobody has any political argument, with the chance of a free fight there, as they might have in Trafalgar-square, nor pleasure, as they might have in that of Leicester. It is a square that nobody has any occasion to go to unless particular business takes him there, and a square that nobody visits unless he drifts in there by accident. Instances have been known of a wild young gentleman from the country losing himself in this quiet haven, and knocking at every door in succession, and inquiring where he could get a marriage license. Flushed young fathers, with the glory of their first baby fresh upon them, have insisted upon leaving the announcement of the fact, together with six-and-sixpence in money, at Number One, under the impression that they had discovered Printing House-square, and would see the important announcement of their son's birth in the *Times* the following morning. Unfledged authorlings have rapped boldly at Number Five, and have been very indignant because they were not allowed to register the title of a work that nobody would ever think of publishing, and made uncalled for remarks relative to the law of copyright in England, because a respectable citizen refused to receive their five shillings, and requested them to apply to Stationers' Hall. People who are great in making short cuts have occasionally drifted in here, and generally made it a personal grievance that there was no outlet at the end of the square. A lost child has been known to stray into it for a sanctuary ; a postman new to the neighbourhood has delivered letters intended for some other square there by mistake; two or three people have strayed into it during a dense fog, and have wandered round and round without finding any outlet, and have never expected to reach the realms of civilization again. It is not a square much affected as a playground for children. Occasionally a ball or a tip-cat will fly in from the lane outside, and then the ragged boys will parley with one another for a time, and the most courageous of the band will rush in, secure the toy as quickly as possible, and bolt out again as if he had a policeman after him.

The entrance to the square is under a low broad archway. It is broad enough, but there is no thoroughfare for carriages, though the dwellers in the square all have the aspect of the people who, if it had not been for so-and-so, or such a thing, would have been riding in their carriages by this time. The inhabitants are by no means proud, though they are severely respectable. I am inclined to think that the word ' genteel ' would precisely describe their status in society. There is the entrance to an office under the archway, and this office is very grand in the matter of subdued brass plates, dim knockers, and captious-looking bell-pulls. You cannot help wondering what business is carried on at this office. There is a legal aspect about the place, chastened with an ecclesiastical flavour ; there is a suspicion that it may be the haven of a litigious parish official in reduced circumstances, if one may judge from certain beadlesque insignia that may occasionally be found about the portal. On week days, about one o'clock, a pleasant odour of Irish stew pervades the neighbourhood, and on Sundays, at two, an appetizing savour of roast goose and sage and onions has been wafted half-way round the square, and made the children at Number Ten turn up their noses at the excellent roast leg of mutton and Yorkshire pudding provided for their dinner. It may be argued from these circumstances that this parish official has in his old age fallen upon his feet, and that the wind of winter has been providentially tempered for the shorn beadle. This gentleman is not officially connected with the square : he does not perambulate its area in gold lace, and threaten small children with a large cane, nor crack walnuts with the policeman at the corner. No, no. Nothing of the kind. But the very fact of his residing at the entrance to the square, and sallying forth in gorgeous gaberdine every Sunday, strikes terror into the hearts of the lazy 'prentices and dirty little boys of Limpin-lane, and prevents them from entering the sacred precincts. His magnificence awes them ; they look upon him as the Bishop of London and the Chief Commissioner of Police rolled into one—the clearest idea of the church militant these young rascals possess.

Passing under the somewhat sombre archway the traveller emerges into Sideboard-square. You have left the narrow crowded thoroughfare of Limpin-lane but a few yards, but you seem to have entered a different world. You have escaped from the swift current, you have drifted out of the stream into a pleasant backwater ; you can here move and paddle about to your heart's content, as long as you please, without any strain upon mind or muscle. You would think the great City had suddenly retired from business, and gone down into the country, were it not for the fact that the hum of the traffic and the buzz of multitudes is roaring like a weir in the distance. And ever and anon the clock-bell of St Paul's comes booming

over your head, as if the Dean and Chapter were
firing a species of horological gun at distant
steeples to remind them that they were somewhat
behind the time. A delightful flavour of the City
of the past, a delicious savour of behind the time,
lurks about the atmosphere of Sideboard-square.
Progress seems to have turned aside from it,
Enterprise has forgotten it, and ruthless Improvement has left it high and dry—a pleasant, ancient,
mouldy island, amid a sea of modern stucco. It is
paved all over with corn-punishing stones. There
is not much traffic, either wheel or foot, over
them, you can see by the long blades of bright
green grass that are springing up here and there,
which are a source of infinite joy to the plump
City sparrows. There is one lamp in the square,
and one grand old plane-tree. This tree is looked
upon with the utmost veneration. It is regarded
as almost sacred. A dowager hamadryad, whose
name is Gentility, lodges somewhere in its
branches and watches o'er the welfare and shapes
the destinies of her worshippers. It puts forth its
leaves earlier than any other tree, and they remain
upon its branches when the rest of the City trees
are utterly bare; it is true the leaves become
shrivelled and dusty and hard, but still they are
leaves. It has been hinted that there is only one
lamp in the square. This is true of the square as
a public corporation, but private enterprise is not
dead in this behind-the-age little cluster of dwellings. The doctor has a lamp projecting from his
lintel of a very magnificent nature. It has a
blood-red pane on one side of it, which at night

glares like an inflamed eye at the harmless passers-by in Limpin-lane. It also sheds ensanguined reflections upon various parts of the square, which are very terrible to nervous old ladies from the country, when they wake up suddenly in the middle of the night, and find these reflections flickering on their bed curtains. The doctor, however, has not contrived his lamp well. He only has the crimson pane on one side of it. The consequence is, if you are running for a doctor at the top of your speed in the middle of the night, you see the lamp in the distance, and you steer for it; probably overshoot the mark, and then look up and see a white light. The 'danger' signal has suddenly changed to 'all right,' so you hark back, go round the square again, and it is just possible in your haste that the same fatality may once more occur, and you may—if you are not careful—keep on at that game all night.

It is, however, the aspect of the square by daylight that must first be treated of. Your first idea of the place is, that it must contain some valuable treasure, that it must be the depository of papers of very great worth. You notice many of the windows are barred, most of the upper windows are fitted with strong little balconies—which seem more like defences than ornaments—and all the lower windows are provided with massive green shutters, rivetted and plated with most elaborate contrivances in the way of bolts, bars, hasps, latches, staples, and rings, for keeping them fast. Whatever may have been the original condition of the place, it may be easily seen that the present inhabitants have no gold nor silver nor important documents that they wish to guard, for many of the shutters are never closed from one year's end to the other, and the balconies are gay with geraniums in pots, Virginian creepers, mignonette, or any popular and inexpensive plant that happens to be in season. All the houses are somewhat ancient. Most of them are of the Queen Anne period. They were originally of good, honest, healthy red brick, but more than a century and a half of London smoke and dirt has so smirched their faces with grime, that at the present time they have rather a mouldy appearance. You may notice two houses, however, which seem to have attempted to infuse some novelty amongst their neighbours; they have wrenched the shutters from their hinges, they have hearthstoned their steps, and also a little crescent-like oasis on the pavement, to snowy whiteness, and have assumed an air of mild joviality, an aspect of pale conviviality. These are the two—let it be whispered softly—the two inns of the place. The inhabitants do not acknowledge them as inns, nor do their proprietors, but still inns they are to all intents and purposes. They look like inns pretending to be private houses, or private houses playing at innkeeping, you cannot be exactly sure which it is. At any rate the pretence does not take many people in. The first might perhaps deceive any but an expert; the door is closed as in a private house, there are three brass bell-pulls on either side, polished to the last pitch of intensity, and there is a tiny brass plate in which you may see a bilious reflection of

your face, and read the word 'GRIGGS.' It is not
easy to read this, for years of friction and unlimited
oil and rotten-stone have effectually rubbed all the
black out of the name.

The establishment facing the mysterious, rusty
padlocked pump on the opposite side of the way,
which may be known by a quaint carven canopy over
its doorway, attempts to assume an aspect of old-
fashioned hospitality, and leaves its door wide open
as if it expected so many people to be dropping in all
day that it were scarcely worth while to shut it. It
also boldly advertises its calling to the world. On a
plate large enough to serve as a monumental brass
for the proprietor when he retires for ever from
inn-keeping, may be seen, 'PRAWN'S COMMERCIAL
BOARDING HOUSE.' The difference between the two
establishments may be thus described : Griggs's
looks like an inn pretending to be a private house,
and Prawn's appears like a private house playing
at keeping an inn. Prawn is quite a different man
from his neighbour. Prawn gives an air of festiv-
ity to his lobby by putting on either side of it
measly Portugal laurels, in pots. He may be seen
on his door-steps sometimes very early in the
morning in his shirt-sleeves. Prawn is very active
about his own establishment : he gets up betimes
and goes to Covent Garden and buys his vege-
tables ; he knows where the best meat is to be
purchased and at the cheapest price ; he is not
above blacking a pair of boots at a pinch, or carrying a portmanteau to a cab when necessary. Mrs
Prawn does not come much to the front ; she is
very useful behind the scenes, and knows what

cooking ought to be. Her life is made a burden
unto her by three mischievous tomboys of girls,
who are ever and anon running away with the
commercial gents' collars, sliding down the
banisters, breaking crockery, and stealing choice
bits of pastry. The commercial gents are not
unfrequently disturbed by yells from below-stairs,
and on inquiry they will find it is Joey being
lectured, Tilly being carried off struggling to bed,
or Poppy being whipped. Mrs Prawn is a Scotch
lady, and believes implicitly in Solomonian discipline, and if the Miss Prawns are spoiled it is
certainly not by reason of sparing the rod. What
with attending to the cooking, looking after her
servants, and spanking her daughters, Mrs Prawn
is generally pretty well tired by ten o'clock, and
leaves matters to her husband. And when left to
himself, over his pipe and rum-and-water, Prawn
sometimes is really amusing; he gives the commercial gents to understand that he has been a
gay dog in his time, and could divulge a thing or
two, if he were so minded. To this house come
energetic gentlemen who breakfast punctually at
eight o'clock, who sally forth with unaccountably-
shaped cases and parcels, who, directly they come
in, want to write letters — it does not matter
whether they return at eleven or five, they must
begin to write letters at once. If they return at
five it becomes an absolute mania, and the scratch-
ing of pens in Prawn's parlour is so furious as post-
time approaches, that it has been likened to a saw-
pit in full work, softened by the distance.

At Mrs Griggs, or Griggs's, as it is more

familiarly called, you meet with a very different class of people. The landlady is sad and placid, and the arrangements of her house are sad and placid also. It would be difficult to find a house pervaded with such a dull dead level of harmonious sadness. The curtains hang in a drooping fashion, as if they were sick of the vanities of life; the sofa groans dismally when you sit down, as if its having seen better days were an apology for its hardness. The very feather-beds have an injured appearance. The pillow submits to be punched with a querulous murmur, and the severe, rectangular, ascetic gaseliers look as if they might have been made out of worms that had been trodden on for so long that they had given up turning. There is no springy feel about the carpets; they seem as if they had been ground down by the iron heel of oppression for so long that they had not a particle of softness left in their constitution. There is an air of resignation, an aspect of comfortable despair pervading the whole place; there are a couple of mild martyrs in the shape of waiters, three or four mortified chamber-maids, a cynical cook, and a misanthropic ' boots,' contained within this extraordinary establishment. And yet, if you are of a sad and placid disposition, you may enjoy yourself very much at Griggs's in a tearful sort of way. If you appreciate a place which ' combines all the advantages of an hotel with the comforts of home ' —if you can contrive to be happy on a wet Sunday with serious people, and with nothing more lively in literature than the week before last's *Guardian* —you cannot do better than patronize Griggs's.

11

The proprietress has discovered that sadness and placidity are not to be maintained upon pilgrims' rations, so she supplies a generous bill of fare, though there is a suspicion of sackcloth about the table-cloth; one looks for ashes in the salt-cellar; the pigeon-pie seems as if it had rent its clothes; and the smoking joints only consent to be comforting under protest. Hither come country clergymen —most of them very Low Churchmen, with a goodly sprinkling of dissenting divines—during the May Meeting. Hither come country cousins by mistake, because they are under the impression that Griggs's is close to St Paul's, the National Gallery, the Bank of England, all the theatres, and the parks. They make the martyr-waiters think of impaling themselves upon forks, or suspending themselves by their own serviettes; they cause the mortified chamber-maids to have serious thoughts of going into a nunnery, and they nearly drive the misanthropic 'boots' into a lunatic asylum by keeping him up to some ungodly hour, on account of their visiting the theatre and coming home in a most hilarious state of mind and clamouring wildly for supper. They cause the clergymen to sigh during the long preprandial grace, because they begin crunching a piece of toast to assuage their hunger, and when a couple of bouncing, healthy, fresh-coloured lasses come bounding into the room in the middle of family prayers, the officiating divine looks very grim indeed. Charming little faces, fathomless brown eyes peeping from under a fringe of soft hair, such as Gaiusborough might have limned; eloquent grey eyes and delicious dimples, such as Millais would love to paint; round pouting country beauty, such as John Leech might have drawn, have occasionally been seen framed and glazed in the windows of Griggs's.

Law, physic, and divinity are all represented in the square. The beadle is the representative of divinity; then there is the surgeon, and, besides him, we have a proctor. No one in the square has a very clear idea as to what a proctor may be, but it is generally supposed to be an office of an importance little inferior to that of the Lord High Chancellor. This particular proctor, whatever his rank may be, is not at all proud; although he occupies the largest and most comfortable house in the square, he is not above taking notice of his neighbours. He may often be seen chatting affably with the beadle; and it has been said that distinguished functionary has consulted him upon parish politics and investments—the beadle is reported to be a somewhat 'warm' man. It was he who headed the subscription for the ancient Waterloo hero who lodges in the corner house; it was he who went for the doctor when the young lady was so ill at Miss Tank's, the milliner's, and, what is more, found the money for the doctor's bill; it was he who paid for the crimson lamp when Poppy Prawn threw a stone through it; and it was he who took the tiresome romp home crying, interceded with her mama, and prevented her receiving the whipping that the young lady knew was in store for her; and it is he who does many acts of quiet kindliness and unobtrusive charity in the square. He is getting somewhat old, his hair is almost white, and they say there is some story of his life having been hopelessly broken by the faithlessness of woman in his youth. He is very well to do; he seldom goes out; he amuses himself by playing the violoncello of an evening; and his only dissipation is going to the performances of the Sacred Harmonic Society in the winter. He appears to have no relations whatever; he seldom has any visitors. His place is looked after by a Welsh housekeeper, who is the terror of tradesmen and the bane of butchers' boys. Visitors to Griggs's or Prawn's are often puzzled to know what that crooning noise is that they hear of an evening when the windows are open. It is only the good old proctor, with gold spectacles on nose, trying to master some favourite passage on his violoncello.

Miss Tank's millinery establishment has always been a cause of some trouble to the dwellers in this secluded haven. Miss Tank has been a beauty in her youth; she is good-looking now. She is just one of those persons who seem to focus beauty, and her young ladies are like gleams of sunshine as they pass to and fro. It is pleasant to hear their light laughter amid the clatter of knives and forks at the one-o'clock dinner. She looks after her flock in most motherly fashion. Once when she caught an apple-faced boy-curate waving a towel from his bed-room window at Griggs's, at one of her young ladies, she went over and lectured him till the poor young man blushed all over, stammered, apologized, and protested. She talked to him like a mother, and told him he was a silly boy, and if he did so again she would write and tell his father. But when a long, slimy schismatic, the Reverend Boanerges Bageye, wrote a note interlarded with texts to her favourite assistant, Cissy Clare, it was a very different matter. She gave the Reverend Boanerges a bit of her mind, and no mistake. She talked to him as no woman had ever talked to him before ; she made him give her a most abject written apology, and when he attempted to back out of it threatened to go down to Sniggleby-in-the-Dingle and give all his congregation full particulars of the whole affair. There was some talk about one of Miss Tank's young ladies and a dashing young student who resided for a considerable period at the doctor's. This young man was of decidedly too sportive a tendency for the square ; he was given to ring the wrong bells very late at night ; he once brought some of his companions, and they danced a breakdown underneath the lamp at three o'clock in the morning. But worst of all, one summer morning, when he felt more light-hearted than usual, he clomb the sacred tree, tapped at Griggs's firstfloor window, and when an estimable old lady appeared at the window in a marvellous night-cap, he gibbered at her, and made hideous faces. In his sudden descent from the tree he broke several branches ; this was a thing the inhabitants could not possibly stand, and the doctor was obliged to discharge him forthwith, though he was very clever in his profession, and there was much weeping and wailing at Miss Tank's on the day of his departure.

Then on the other side of the way resides a serious stevedore and his stout wife, who gives herself airs because she had an uncle who was a lieutenant in the navy. There are two fat daughters, who also give themselves airs, and decline to 'sit under' the awakening exhortations of the Reverend Hezekiah Hotanstrong in some stuffy little chapel down Shad Thames way, but prefer to go to a fashionable church, and may be seen in gorgeous attire 'flaunting,' as their father would say, out of the square on a Sunday morning. There is also the German gentleman who deals in toys and beads, who has his ground-floor filled with mysterious packages and gigantic brown-paper parcels, who smokes furiously, and has a favourite cat, which is shunned by all the other cats in the square, as its master is by his neighbours. He is currently reported to be a Communist, and affiliated to several secret societies. He has been seen smoking at his window on a Sunday morning and perusing a paper printed in the German character, which, as his neighbours are unable to read, they at once put down as a scurrilous and immoral publication. By the children he is looked upon as an ogre; they cannot conceive any one having a room full of toys and beads and never giving one away. Hard by the German toy-merchant lives a bank clerk with a bonny wife and half a dozen bonny children. The children have all been born in the square, and they are about the only ones who dare to play and romp under the shadow of the plane-tree, and they do this in a subdued fashion. There is something about the whole place that lends itself to the suppression of noise. The butcher-boy shouts less stridently, the baker puts down his basket softly, the milkman ejaculates ' Mee-yaw ! ' in confidence, as if it were a profound secret, and subdues the clank of his pails. No German bands or niggers would dream of invading this quiet retreat. Occasionally an organ may drift into the square, but the grinder always keeps it covered with a green baize cloth, so that it sounds as if the performer were playing in bed with all the clothes over his head. If a policeman ventures to walk round, he shows a strong disposition to go on tiptoe, and the muffin-man muffles his bell and murmurs ' Muffins, O, crumpets,' in a soft unctuous voice, which is really quite suggestive of melted butter. If there is one thing the inhabitants of the square are agreed upon, it is muffins and crumpets. Even the grim toy-merchant's features relax . visibly when he sticks his teeth into what he is pleased to call a ' grompette.'

Perhaps the best time for a stranger to make the tour of the square is about nine o'clock at night. They are not particular about pulling down the blinds, so the chances are you will be able to see a good deal of its internal economy. You will doubtless make an especial pause in front of the largest house in the square. You may hear some charming old melody being lovingly interpreted, and you will fancy to yourself that it is the proctor, the beadle, the doctor, and the stevedore—law, physic, and divinity, with the stevedore thrown in for ballast—executing a stringed quartette for

their own especial amusement. You will wander
up and down and listen to the pleasant harmony,
as it comes floating out of the red-curtained open
window from the cosy old-fashioned room ; you will
fancy that they will have something hot for supper
afterwards, concerning which the Welsh housekeeper is troubling herself mightily—they are
great believers in hot suppers in Sideboard-square
—and then there will be a quiet rubber and a bowl
of punch. You feel certain the proctor is just the
man to brew exquisite punch and to keep the
secret of making it locked up in his heart of
hearts ; you can imagine him filling long-stemmed
glasses from a choice china bowl, with a ladle, in
which a Queen Anne guinea glitters ever and anon
through the generous liquor. You walk up and
down and notice the queer radiation of shadows
cast by the one lamp in the centre, the ensanguined
reflections flung here and there by the doctor's
danger-signal ; you note the point where the yellow
and red rays and the unaccountable shadows seem
to meet in a tangle and have a fight for supremacy,
in which the yellow rays generally somehow or
another seem to have the best of it. Probably
you will meet no one but Mrs Griggs's tom-cat,
who glares at you with its green eyes, but treads
softly and mysteriously as if it were shod with
velvet. It does not scream or spit. Even the
very cats partake of the subdued gentility of the
place. It is said they caterwaul in a whisper, and
use spittoons.

Later on in the evening, if you choose to
stay, you will see queer little shadow pantomimes

behind the down-pulled blinds of the upper windows. After the proctor's music has ceased and
his guests have quitted, and doors have been
softly closed—people seldom bang doors in Sideboard-square—you will notice lights one by one
extinguished in the windows, and in a short time
there is nothing left but the centre lamp, and
the doctor's danger-signal. The doctor's light is
at last somewhat turned down, and the centre lamp
seems to burn paler. There is no sound to be
heard but the rustle of the leaves of the plane-
tree, mingled with the persistent snort of a serious
snorer at Griggs's. Faintly may be heard, when the
snorer pauses or the wind ceases to rustle the
leaves, the hum of the everlasting London traffic
in the distance.

And ever and anon do the Dean and Chapter
continue to fire horological guns over your head
to remind the backward steeples of their slothful-
ness, and ever and anon do the slothful churches
reply and quarrel with each other and keep up a
tintinnabulatory fusillade among themselves. So
quiet is the little square, so strange, so quaint, so
behind the age, that you take your departure
doubting very much that this is the nineteenth
century, and that you have been wandering in the
very heart of the busiest part of the busiest city in
the world.

AT BALLYSHANNON.

NOTHING but the pursuit of the wily salmon and the desire to beard him in his own den and ensnare him in his private fastnesses, would have induced us to come to this part. There is one comfort about this place—you do not meet any tourists. This is certainly a very great luxury. The only people you meet are fishermen, and generally fishermen of a most enthusiastic order. If you happen to meet a stranger, you may safely ask him what sport he has had. For if he is not a fisherman, the chances are he is a lunatic : some people say the two conditions are often combined, but I do not believe them. But no matter. Ballyshannon is not by any means a lively-looking place, but to people who have passed a wet week at Toome it is a scene of rampant hilarity. It looks very picturesque from a distance, and distance, which proverbially lends enchantment to the view, does its duty nobly as far as Ballyshannon is concerned. It has the appearance of a bankrupt town altogether ; it is bleak, desolate, and ruinous. The High Street —I suppose it is the High Street, for there are to be found the principal hotels, the police station, a chemist's shop, and a watchmaker's—is a steep ascent with melancholy, hopeless-looking houses on either side. It reminds one more than anything

else of those melancholy wo-begone villages you see
when you are going over the Saint Gothard Pass ;
villages that even the great *Murray* deigns not to
record ; villages that you do not notice much at
the time, but whose misery and louesomeness is
photographed on your brain, and comes back to you
with vivid distinctness years afterwards ; villages
that you dream about in connection with an atro-
cious murder after you have taken a late supper ;
villages that you feel if you resided there for a
fortnight you would be able to pass with credit an
examination in gibbering idiotcy, and would be able
to grow a prize *goître* against all comers.

This is just the impression that Ballyshannon
gives you. We have been here for some days now.
I feel confident that I have said at least fifteen
silly things, and I have a sort of idea that my throat
is beginning to swell. This, however, by the way.
I said Ballyshannon looks like a bankrupt town,
and so it does. It must have been very prosperous
at one time, but now it seems fast going to decay.
There are a number of commercial travellers come
to this place, but what they sell or who buys it is
difficult to say. There is a general air of desolation about the whole town. ' Many houses are shut
up, a great many in ruins, and a large proportion
are of the very humblest description. There is a
very large factory that has been closed for many
years and is gradually dropping to pieces : the
picturesque old bridge, according to report, is
likely to fall into the river before long, and the
roads would be all the better for a little decent
repairing. There are some gas works of consider-

able size, and the gas is laid on throughout the
town, but for some reason or other the Company
have ceased to make gas and of an evening the
town is in darkness. Nothing could induce anybody to come to Ballyshannon except the salmon
fishing, and that certainly is some of the best to
be had in Ireland. It is not such a great distance
after all. For instance, you may leave Euston
Square by the eight o'clock—or half-past eight is
it?—I have no *Bradshaw* or railway guide with me,
so I cannot be particular to half an hour. Well,
say by the eight o'clock night mail, and if you are
enthusiastic about the matter you may be wading
up to your waistcoat buttons and pulling a salmon
out of the Erne the following afternoon.

The fisherman would be surprised to hear that
there is a good inn in this town. He cannot do
better than go to the 'Imperial'; it is a large,
rambling, old-fashioned building. I do not think
its floors would survive a fortnight of violent Irish
jig dancing. If piscatorial gentlemen persisted in
such terpsichorean exercises there is just a chance
that they might dance a large quantity of lathe-
and-plaster down on to the commercial gentlemen's
dinner. The fact is the Imperial is a very old
house. But it will last my time and yours. You
can get plenty of good plain food and excellent
drink, and, moreover, the waiter thoroughly under-
stands the Englishman's predilection for his tub,
and a capacious bath is brought with unerring
regularity every morning when you are called.
The hotel is comfortable enough, but you must not
stop in it all day. The natives know so well that

the attractions of their town are so few, that a sane man can only come to Ballyshannon for the fishing. If he does not fish they set themselves to work wondering what on earth he comes to the place at all for. I have been indoors all to-day writing and reading. I am certain the landlord and waiters think I am not quite right in the head. The waiter rushes in occasionally and asks me if I rang, and looks at me with a terrified expression, as if he expected to see me hanging by the neck from the bell-rope. The postmaster at the little post-office cannot understand me. I have such a quantity of letters and newspapers arriving every day, and have sent off some dozen telegrams since I have been here. He looks upon me with suspicion. It may be my morbid fancy, but I think I have noticed two very muscular members of the constabulary paying particular attention to my movements whene'er I take my walks about the town. Perhaps I shall be taken up for a Fenian. I wonder whether I look like a Head Centre.

This has been quite an exceptional day with me, I can tell you. I have been hard at work all day, but I generally am hard at work in another way. Instead of plying the steel pen in a pool of ink I am wading in the swift-flowing Erne, and wielding the gigantic salmon rod, and developing my *serratus magnus*, my *trapezius*, and my *latissimus dorsi* to such an extent that when I get into the frock coat of private life again I am afraid my back will look as if it were breaking out into nobs all over. As a general rule I am awakened early by a noise in the next room, which sounds very like prolonged knife-grinding, pretending to be a tune. I know what that is; it is Micky Rogan—smallest of boys but most expert of fishermen—winding the lines off the chairs, where they have been placed to dry, on to the reels. That boy is a most wonderful little fellow. I would back him against any boy of his age in the United Kingdom, either for his skill in throwing a salmon line or his celerity in making up a cast of flies. When I hear that whirring noise of a morning I know there is very little more sleep left for me. I know that presently the waiter will come bustling in with my bath, I shall hear the clink of breakfast things, and Micky will be coming in to ask all sorts of questions. Micky bustles us up: he does not allow us to dawdle over our breakfast. He is continually suggesting that the car shall be brought round long before we are ready: he has our rods stowed away, he takes good care that a substantial luncheon basket shall not be forgotten, and he is never happy till he gets us on board the car and speeding away from the hotel. It was a source of great grief to him when I declined to accompany the expedition this morning.

A little distance above Ballyshannon the Erne becomes very picturesque, and about Mr Connolly's park, towards Belleek, is one of the best bits of river scenery that I have seen in the north of Ireland. It is a very pretty bit, however, about one of the best salmon throws on the river known as the 'Captain's Throw.' Here you have bold grey rocks close to the water's edge, surmounted with trees on the one side, and a broken shore from which you can wade on the other. The bottom is very bad; it is full of holes, and requires a good deal of caution, especially when the water is very high, as it happens to be at present. This throw has a great reputation, and I suppose more fish have been caught at this point by the angler than in any other portion of the river. There are many other throws, however, besides the one already mentioned. There is the famous throw from the ancient bridge itself, also above Red Hugh's Fall and above Kathleen Fall. Besides these there are throws whose names become as familiar to you after you have been here for a short time as the names of Bond Street, of Piccadilly, of Pall Mall, or the Strand do in London. Amongst the best known of these may be mentioned Nova Scotia, Allingham Point, Point of the Mullens, Bank of Ireland, Laputa, Grass Yard, Moss Row, the Angler's Throw, and the Sod Ditch. None of these, however, are more popular than the Captain's Throw, and I am told that in June and July you frequently have to wait your turn some considerable time to fish it. There are only nine rods allowed on the river, consequently it may be imagined the sport is excellent. Below the fall, during the present month, some very good white trout fishing may frequently be had. If the angler wishes for a change, he can take a boat and row down towards the Abbey of Asheroe, and he will stand a very good chance of an afternoon's sport. Or, if he does not like this, he can take a car and drive over to Lough Melvin and amuse himself with

pulling out the gorgeous gillaroo, or the savage
sunahun.   The angler need never stand still for
want of employment of his rod at Ballyshannon.   I
may mention too, that Mr Moore, the proprietor of
the fishery, always treats fishermen with the utmost
hospitality and most courteous consideration.   *The*
professional fisherman of the place is Rogan, the
father of Micky, who is also celebrated as a tyer of
flies and a maker of tackle.   He thoroughly under-
stands his business in every way.   You have the
advantage of having your rods and your tackle
made by a practical man, an enthusiastic fisherman,
and who knows exactly what the angler requires.
Most of the rods in London · are made by men who
never saw a stream, much less threw a trout fly, or
put their back into a salmon rod.   If you can get
Rogan to build you a rod, make a point of doing
so.   With a trout and a salmon rod of his manufacture, you will be a happy man; you may whip
all the streams in creation, and it will be your own
fault if you do not catch anything.

As yet we have stuck to our work pretty well,
but we have not had any great sport.   Still we are
enthusiastic, and persevere.   We wade and we flog,
we flog and we wade, from directly after breakfast
until about two o'clock.   At two o'clock luncheon
is sent out from the hotel by a boy.   It is curious
how he finds us, or how we find him.   I dare say the
matter is arranged in some clever fashion between
Micky and himself.   Be that as it may, whatever
part of the river we may happen to be in, we are
sure to run up against the luncheon-basket, or the
luncheon-basket is sure to run up against us about

two o'clock. We generally find ourselves pretty hungry by that time, and we are as delighted to see our *luncheonbadar* as Micky is. Our rods are laid aside for a time, we emerge dripping from the stream, and try and squeeze the water out of our boots. We select a soft green sward or a convenient flat rock, and spread out our eatables and enjoy half an hour's rest from our labours. Possibly one or two brother fishermen may join us. If any of the professionals or water keepers happen to pass by you may be sure they will not disdain to assist us with our modest banquet. And then you may be certain we shall hear some marvellous accounts of wonderful fish. If anybody has done any particular trick on the river, anywhere between Ballyshannon and Belleek, you are sure to hear of it. You casually ask if Mr So-and-so has done any good to-day, or what was the weight of the captain's fish of yesterday, and whether it was true that the colonel lost a twenty pounder over the fall. Then tobacco pouches are produced and handed round, pipes are filled, and we are allowed a few minutes for reflection before we start again. It is only a few moments, however, for Micky, who does not smoke yet, bustles us up, and says it is high time we began work again. We dare not disobey his orders, so we quickly shoulder our rods and betake ourselves to the 'throws' to which he commends us, and flog away until evening. For my own part I do not believe much in fishing after four o'clock in the afternoon, but as for Nomad he is so 'keen' that I verily believe he would flog a damp turnpike road until twelve o'clock at night if he thought

there was any chance of a ' rise.' So it is generally
half-past five or six o'clock before we strike work
for the day.   If wo happen to be fishing ·up
above the ' Captain's Throw,' and the chances
are we are, we have a good tramp then before
we reach home.   It is from the road as we walk
homewards that we get the best view of Bally-
shanuon.   With its pile of houses on either side
of the river, with its church perched up on the
hill, with the sun setting just behind the old
bridge, and glimmering on the large sandhill at the
bar down Bundoran way, it really looks quite picturesque.   But, as I before remarked, all this is
dissipated when you enter the town and see its
dilapidated buildings and poverty-stricken inhabitants.

The mention of Bundoran reminds me that it is
one of the few excursions that are to be made from
Ballyshannon.   What manner of place would my
readers expect it to be?   An eastern arid place;
a town suggestive of tropical atmosphere, of palm
trees and bungalows, of natives in no costume to
speak of, of a land of perpetual thirst?   As a
matter of fact Bundoran is nothing of the kind.   It
is a bare, rugged coast, it has moist sloppy green
pastures and muddy roads, and it has a glorious
breeze blowing in from the Atlantic.   It is situated
on the finest part of Donegal Bay, but it is bleak,
desolate, and cheerless.   If you ask if there is anywhere to go for a walk at Ballyshannon, they will
be unable to tell you of more than three places—
Bundoran, Belleek, and Lough Melvin.   First and
foremost in their affection is Bundoran—the bleak

village with an eastern name—so I will give it the
place of honour in this paper. They call it four
miles from Ballyshannon. My private opinion is
that it is a great deal more. Sometimes they
measure by English miles, sometimes by Irish, but
I believe very often by the two added together, or
one subtracted from the other or multiplied by itself. It is the most difficult thing to obtain any
accurate information with regard to distance in
Donegal. If you ask a car-driver he will think you
are going to cut him down in his fare, and so tell
you it is double what it really is ; if you ask some
one who is interested in it being a shorter distance
he will at once proceed to shorten it one-half in the
coolest manner possible. No matter, then, what
distance Bundoran may be from Ballyshannon. It
is a weary uninteresting walk, plenty of uphill
work, and plenty of those interminable straight
roads of which the Irish seem to be so fond. It is,
perhaps, as weary a walk as one could take.
Nearly all the time you are walking you are unable
to lose sight of the sandhill just by the bar at the
entrance to the Erne. It never seems to get any
larger, and each time you look at it it appears to
be further off than it was before. At last, when
your view of this is shut off, you begin to make
some progress, and straggling houses gradually
becoming groups, and these groups eventually becoming rows, and at last you fancy you must be in
Bundoran. You are by no means sure of this, for
Bundoran is a curiously shaped straggling town,
and its houses have a predilection for distributing
themselves generally all over the parish.

If Portrush might be considered the Scarborough of Ireland, I should be inclined to rate Bundoran as the Redcar of the Emerald Isle. Indeed, the town itself is not at all unlike Redcar. Most of the houses are small. The majority of the visitors spend their time entirely out of doors, and the place is entirely shut up, as far as visitors are concerned, in the winter. Of a truth, it must be a fearful place in the winter. It is also like Redcar, a great place for bathing; but unlike Redcar, it has not the superb stretch of sand that renders that little maritime resort so attractive. It is true there are one or two sandy coves here and there, but the coast is generally rugged and rocky. You may get fine views of the distant coast on the north side of Donegal Bay. You may see St John's Point, the bays of Inver and Killybegs, and the cliffs of Slieve League and Teelin Head in the distance. The Enniskillen people come crowding down here just as the Stockton-on-Teesians and the Middlesboroughnians come to Redcar. Nearly the whole town—except a few cottages occupied by peasantry—is devoted to the visitors, and the stranger knowing this will be puzzled to account for the fact that he does not find the familiar seaside legend of *Apartments to Let* displayed in windows or dangling from balconies. The Bundoranese do not, however, signify this in the usual way. They stick up an envelope in the window. I do not suppose any of my readers will ever want to take lodgings at Bundoran, but if they do, this is a fact worth knowing. The people from Ballyshannon come here, that is to say, when they can afford it; but I believe the most part of the population of Ballyshannon to be so miserably poor and so low-spirited that I cannot think they can add much to the prosperity of Bundoran.

There is, I think, only one bathing machine in the place, which is kept locked, and no one knows where to apply for the key. This machine is quite useless, and is generally looked upon as a sort of moral monument, a respectable protest against the very free and exceedingly easy style of bathing prevailing on this coast. The bathing here is *al fresco,* not to say all frisky. The ladies and gentlemen bathe in the same cove; their bathing places are only separated by a drain, which cuts the shore in two. There are no bathing boxes or tents. Everyone undresses on the shore, leaves clothes to take care of themselves, and runs down a long distance before he can reach the water. This would be a grand place from which ' Paterfamilias,' ' A True Briton,' or any of those terribly proper people who write letters to the *Times* every year about the bathing at Ramsgate and Margate, to date a letter from. The gentlemen have no costume whatever, and the ladies wear nothing but night-dresses. Occasionally the ladies have as slight a costume as the gentlemen; indeed, I was told by an old visitor to the place, that the night-dress costume was altogether unknown a few years ago. We were sitting on the rocks the other morning, smoking and wondering at the strange manner and customs of the natives, when three shabby, grimy-looking men, who had just bathed and dressed, approached us. They stared at us for a long time, and we

imagined they were about to ask us for a light.
At last the shabbiest and the dirtiest spoke, 'Sor,'
he said, 'could either of you gentlemen be good
enough to lind me the loan of a comb?' And he
evidently thought it rather hard that we were
unable to comply with his request. There is
nothing else to do but bathe at Bundoran, so it
seems odd that some better arrangements should
not be made. People seem to bathe at any hour,
when they please, where they please, and how
they please, and the popular amusement amongst
the natives, after church on Sunday, is to sit on the
edge of the cliffs and watch the bathers. I think
I have described everything of any interest in
Bundoran, so I will now beg you will listen to me
whilst I describe other excursions in the neighbourhood of Ballyshannon.

Lough Melvin is well worth a visit. We have
been there a good many times, and have had some
very fair trout fishing. It is much more picturesque than many of the lakes in the north of
Ireland, more so, for instance, than Lough Erne or
Lough Neagh. It cannot be much more than
seven miles long, and there are many richly-wooded
islands in various parts of the lake. On several of
these there are snug little fishing boxes; on one
close to the south shore are the remains of the
castle of Rossclogher, and on the eastern shore
may be found the ruins of the ancient church of
Rossinver. Till the middle of May there is good
salmon fishing in this lake. It belongs to Mr
Johnston, of Kinlough House, who will readily
give permission to any well-accredited angler to

fish it. We did not get as far as the village of
Garrison, but I am told that there is very good
accommodation for fishermen at the little inn
there. There are one or two sunken islands in
the lake, and a large portion of it is very shallow.
Here it is that the gillaroo trout love to congre-
gate. We caught some very good specimens of
this most golden and richly spotted of all the trout
tribe. In other parts of the lake may be caught
the sunahun, a somewhat ugly and jack-like looking trout, but capital eating. There are no pike
whatever in Lough Melvin. The fisherman told
us that there was something peculiar in the water
of this lake that disagreed with the pike, and that
if any number of fine healthy pike were placed in
it they would be dead in five minutes. The same
individual told us of gigantic trout, as much as fifty
pounds in weight, which he had seen lurking about
in the deep waters : he also told us of a wonderful
monster of the deep that he had seen rising from
the lake and shaking his mane in the twilight.
This monster was something between a pike and a
pony, with a touch of the agility of the kangaroo.
Another fisherman told us, to cap this story, of a
monster of the lake who came out of the water late
in the evening, barked at a man on horseback, and
finally jumped right *through* the horse and killed
him. This tale, I should say, was told when the
twilight was deepening and the whiskey bottle had
been freely circulated, but it was very impressive.
Not wishing to be outdone, I was obliged to relate
the impressive story of the Big Pike at Constance,
with special additional weights and extraordinary

measurements laid on for this particular occasion. There is no doubt, however, that anybody who cared to spend a month on this lake would not only make an excellent bag of trout but would probably pick up an extraordinary bunch of legends. And he might see the pony-pike after all! There is plenty of variety in Lough Melvin. You can fish with a fly as long as you please, and when you feel lazy you may troll. Either system you pursue, you will be likely to have tolerable success. You may reach Patrick Magonaghan's cottage in a car from Ballyshannon in about three-quarters of an hour. Pat is a civil and obliging man, has a very good boat of his own, and knows every inch of the lake; and his cottage is the best spot to make for if you go from Ballyshannon for a day's fishing.

The third and last excursion which I shall introduce to your notice, ladies and gentlemen, is the walk from Ballyshannon to Belleek. Another place with an eastern name, by the way. The walk to this village is certainly one of the best bits of scenery in this part. Turning our backs to the sea we take the left bank of the Erne; we pass Dr Sheil's house 'Laputa,' and soon after that we turn off through Mr Connolly's park. The scenery improves as we go on, the trees are more luxuriant, and we begin to lose sight entirely of the bareness and hopeless blackness that characterizes this part of Ireland. It improves still more after we have past the eel weir. We then go through a thick plantation and presently reach 'Cliff,' Mr Connolly's residence. This gentleman is the owner of the soil around Ballyshannon, and is one of the largest landholders in Ireland. The house itself is not very extensive, but the view from the dainty little garden at the back right up the Erne, which comes tumbling and brawling down a series of falls and rapids, midst bold rocks and a dense plantation of pines on either side, reminds one more of a bit of Switzerland than anything else. If the pedestrian takes the lower path from this point, he will find it somewhat rough walking, but he will be well repaid by the picturesque bits of river scenery that meet his view at every turn. After he gets clear of the park, he will clamber up the ravine and reach the high road, which will take him into Belleek. Just before you reach the railway bridge you should pause once more, not only to notice the grand sweep that the river here takes, but to see that they really have been at some pains to make the railway bridge tolerably picturesque, and that it is not one of those hideous abortions that these structures invariably are in the present day.

An Irishman was once asked if there was any manufactory at Belleek. He replied, ' Sure, I don't know what ye mane by a manyfactree, but I b'lieve they make tay cups there.' He was not altogether wrong, for there is a large factory, built just above the old bridge, where they make a peculiar kind of porcelain, known as Belleek Pottery. This hideous building has perched itself just at the top of the falls, and detracts not a little from the beauty of the view from the grand old stone bridge. There is nothing else to see in Belleek except a disused fort on the top of a hill. The village itself is no-

thing but one street of enormous width, with pigs
and geese marching up and down the middle. The
houses are, for the most part, poor and tumble-
down; there is one inn which, having no sign, is
somewhat difficult to find. It is a tolerably good
one, and serves to accommodate a few fishermen,
who make this their head-quarters for fishing in
Lough Erne. Above Belleek it is permitted to
fish for salmon with a shrimp and a float. Some
gentlemen have been hard at work in this way the
last few days, and I am sorry to say have been
fairly successful. They call this barbarous practice
sport; sportsmen call it poaching.

Nomad has just come in dripping and hungry.
He wants to know why the fire is not lit and why
the dinner is not ready. He has an air of supreme
virtue and intense muscularity about him. He admits reluctantly that he has not had great sport,
but he has the air of a man who has done his duty
and lets me know it. Micky comes in presently
and looks at me reproachfully: he makes more noise
than usual with the reels and the rods, and evidently looks upon me as a deserter from the noble
army of fishermen. I pretend to be very busy,
and not to see him. I dare not meet his glance,
for I feel as though I had lost a day, and com-
mitted a crime of the deepest dye, by not wielding
a salmon-rod when I had the opportunity.

IN THE CITY OF RUBENS.

HERE we are at the Café de la Poste, sitting with our toes in the sunshine aud our noses in the shade, with soothing cigars in our mouths, with vast glasses of excellent Bairisch beer before us, dreaming and resting in the city of glorious old Peter Paul.

We seem to have so changed our existence, to have so utterly cast our London skin with the assumption of flannel shirts and the abjurement of frock coats, that we feel to be somebody else. It is said that people entirely change every seven years. I believe they entirely alter with a change of scene: that people become different as they change from one country and climate to another: that Joues at Madrid and Jones at Venice are two distinct individuals. I know that a certain person whom I saw in London last week is a very different being to a certain person who is now sitting under the awning of a *café* in the Place Verte and looking so extremely happy. There is the Unlimited, too, looking vastly jovial and already seeming somewhat stouter for the change—and there is also an excellent artist friend who knows every nook and corner of the City of Rubens, and who thrusts handsfull of excellent cigars into our pockets and takes us to places where the finest

Bairisch beer is to be obtained. The change has
been so sudden, that is to say we have had no
gradation of changes, for we got aboard the Baron
Osy at St Katharine's Wharf, London, and left her
at the Quai Van Dyck at Antwerp, that we can
scarcely believe it was only yesterday morning we
left London.

There is no doubt, however, about that being
a fact. At the beginning of a lovely autumn day
two distinguished cavaliers might be seen descending—but stay, I am not G. P. R. James that I am
aware of—the cavaliers were in a hansom cab and
they descended St Dunstan's Hill from Great
Tower Street to Lower Thames Street, and I must
say that the cavaliers in their grey tweed suits and
their light hats considerably horrified the good
people who were betaking themselves churchwards
on Sunday morning. The City looked more deserted than usual yesterday morning: more deserted
even than when I went ' In Search of a Church : '
quieter even than when I found myself ' Nothing
in the City.'   Indeed, I felt very much as if I were
going to commit a burglary in Lombard Street or
set fire to the Corn Market in Mark Lane.   I know
that a policeman with evangelical tendencies looked
upon me with a reproachful eye, two maid-servants
with gilt-edged prayer-books enfolded in clean
pocket-handkerchiefs regarded me in the light of
a Sabbath-breaker of the deepest dye, and a lugu-
brious landing-waiter, who was convoying his stout
wife, three stout daughters, and a swollen son in
order that they might ' sit under ' the awakening
exhortations of his favourite preacher, evidently

looked upon me as a sinner of the most hardened description. It did seem odd, I must admit, clattering through those deserted streets, with all the shops shut up so tight that it makes you think they will require a surgical operation in order that they may be opened on Monday morning: with no sound to be heard but the echo of our own cab wheels: the melancholy tang-tang of the bells of the deserted churches and a distant hum of voices and a faint ' yeo-yeoing ' of sailors from the river. Omnibuses and cabs we know are required to go at a slow pace past St Paul's and the Strand churches during service time, and possibly there is a regulation obliging the sailors of St Katharine's Wharf, between the hours of eleven and one on a Sunday, to ' yeo-yeo ' in a whisper. I do not know how this may be, but they certainly seemed to be less demonstrative than usual. The man who opened the cab door: the porter who carried your bag on board: the official who worried you about tickets: in short, all the Baron's retainers did their work in a subdued manner as if the starting from St Katharine's Wharf on a Sunday was a very serious matter. The steward looked very much like a bishop who would deliver a charge before we got to Blackwall, and the stewardess might have sat for the portrait of Mrs Proudie with considerable success : the man at the wheel looked as if he could improve the occasion, and the under-waiter seemed as if he were quite capable of delivering an exhortation to the Buoy at the Nore.

There was an earnestness about the Baron Osy

and its passengers that was very striking. I
must say it reminded me more of an emigrant
ship than anything else. There was very little of
the tourist flavour about the whole affair. There
was an air of business about the passengers : there
was a sense of responsibility : there was no light
nonsense about scampering up mountains and travelling for pleasure about the majority of the
passengers. No, no, we did things in quite a different manner to the majority of Continental travellers I can tell you. There was none of the
flippancy of the Dover to Calais passengers, none
of the frivolity of the trippers from Folkestone to
Boulogne, and even the ponderosity of the voyagers
between Newhaven and Dieppe was light *persiflage*
in comparison with our sober earnestness. As I
before hinted we had an emigrant flavour about
us : we had a touch of the hopeless seriousness
which characterizes the emigrant mind. We had
people to see us off, people who were lachrymose,
people who smiled one moment and cried the next,
people who waved aprons, towels, and pocket-
handkerchiefs long after the vessel was out of
sight. There was one old lady who waved a towel
in such an energetic manner that I should not be
surprised, if she has not been removed by the
police, that she is waving it at the present moment.
The emigrant character of the vessel was still continued after she got under weigh, for then ' stowaways' began to turn up. People who had come on
board to see others off and then pretended they did
not hear the shore bell ring and so had no chance
of being put on shore till they reached Gravesend.

I found my old friend Swellsly turned up, just as the Baron had full speed on, and appeared to be astonished that the ship was moving, and that there was no chance of his landing for an hour. Swellsly endeavoured to argue the point with the captain, and it was only by means of our interference that he was not mast-headed or put in irons for the rest of the voyage. We found as we steamed down the river that many of our friends and acquaintances emerged from cabins, from behind piles of luggage, and from the depths of tankards of ale. People that we knew not were on board, or that we imagined were in quite a different part of England. There was Captain Hawtrey quite oblivious of *Caste* talking affably to some sailors on the fore part of the vessel, and there was Mr Evelyn, to whom *Money* is no object, lighting a magnificent regalia on the quarter-deck. There was a pretty Belgian girl with unexceptionable ankles and with a wealth of light brown hair coiffed in two enormous plaits, and a grim gentleman who kept watch over her, whose company we might well have dispensed with; there was a lady's-maid with wonderful eyes, who made it her business to flirt with everybody on board. She took everybody in turn, she did not mind who it was. Everybody; from the Unlimited down to the Irish footman, who made love in the most demonstrative fashion in the brogue of Kerry. Indeed, I believe she would have enlisted the earl in her string of admirers if he had appeared in public. I forgot to say we had a live earl on board. This you know was very nice. It gave quite an aristocratic flavour to the ship. Something like Dr Blimber's butler, who gave a winey flavour to the table-beer by the superb way in which he poured it out. I am sorry to say our live earl did not show himself, but it was some satisfaction to have the pleasure of seeing his name in the ship's book.

There is not much incident to record in our voyage to Antwerp. The first incident was when the 'stowaways' left us at Gravesend. The captain had been mollified, and the stowaways were allowed to depart unpunished. When we had taken leave of them and their boats had diminished to specks in the distance we began to think that our case was, indeed, hopeless. How should we wile away the many hours we shall have to spend till we reach Antwerp? We have had luncheon: we have already smoked more than is good for us: we have flirted with the lady's-maid: we have explored the vessel in every corner: we have talked to all the people we knew, and we have held lengthy conversations with most of the people we did not know, and we begin to look upon the voyage in the light of a bore. It suddenly struck us that dinner would prove a pleasing diversion. There had been flying luncheons and promiscuous liquorings-up going on all the morning, but we began to think we could do well with a properly-organized meal. On inquiry it was found there was one dinner at two, another at four, and a supper at six. We did not know whether we were expected to partake of all these, but we elected to join the dinner table at four. I believe there were many people on board who took a heavy luncheon at two, a snack at four, and a hearty dinner at six. And if they could stand it I for one do not blame them. The voyage after a time becomes so wearisome that you must do something to break its monotony. After passing Gravesend the Thames is terribly dull: it is true you do not have much of the sea, but the Scheldt is duller than the Thames, and I think even *mal de mer* is preferable to dullness.

There is an undeniable splendour about the Baron: its cabins with white and gold decorations and its rich damask-hung panels, remind one of an ancient assembly room: its attendants have all the courtesy of old retainers, but I do not like the practice of filling the main cabin with sleepers as well as eaters. If you go down to have a bit of supper about nine o'clock it is not a pleasant thing to find mattresses all over the floor, and a row of ladies reposing on one side of your table and a row of gentlemen on the other. If proper sleeping accommodation cannot be found for all, they ought not to be permitted to pay their passage money. Fortunately we had a very smooth passage. I tremble to think what would have been the result in the main cabin had the weather been at all rough.

I stopped on deck late. Indeed, most people seemed reluctant to turn in; it was a tolerably fine night, although it had been drizzling the greater part of the afternoon. The incandescent tips of cigars and pipes like tiny danger signals about different parts of the vessel showed that many preferred the fresh night air to the stifling, stuffy

13

cabin.   However, get as comfortable a position as
you can, make as cunning an arrangement of
camp stools and rugs as you will, in time you get
tired of the ceaseless roll of the vessel, of counting
the stars through the upper rigging, watching the
smoke curl away into the darkness, and listening
to the monotonous beat of the engine.   So in time
I turned in.   I got a mattress on the floor of the
small cabin, and I had as fitful and unsatisfactory
a snooze as you always get on short voyages.   The
wind and the flutter of the engine lulled me to sleep
after a time, but I was ever and anon awakened by
the hoarse shout of 'starboard,' or 'port,' or
'steady!' being given by three different voices,
each one seeming hoarser than the other.   Sometimes the last voice shouted with such energy that
I was afraid it was angry.   I trembled in my sleep
to think that perhaps the captain and the man at
the wheel might quarrel and come to blows, and
that we might be run on a sandbank or broken on
a rock.   Then the heavy tread overhead annoyed
me very much.   It appeared just as if the men were
actually walking on my brain; the clanking chains
above seemed to jingle on my brain, and it appeared
to me as if they were actually coiling ropes round
my head.   Then I would wake up suddenly and see
the dim lamp swinging and casting all sorts of
weird shadows over the weary sleepers; I would
see in my fancy the most comical figures reposing
in the bunks and doing most extraordinary gymnastics in the curtains.   I would listen to a stout
old gentleman snoring in the corner till I could not
be certain whether the engine was snoring or

whether it was the old gentleman pretending to be
the engine. I would watch the steward without
his coat dozing in a chair by the doorway and wonder what he was dreaming about. I wonder whether
steamboat stewards ever fall in love or if they are
ever married. I think there was a steamboat steward in 'Christopher Tadpole,' who said there was
not an instance on record of a steamboat steward
having a wife and family, and I daresay he was about
right. Then I fancy it must be getting very late
and we must be nearly there. With great difficulty
I find my watch and with still greater difficulty I
discover what the hour is. I see to my disgust it
is just about the time that the club smoking-room,
in town, would be getting full, and that we have at
least six hours before we can hope to see Antwerp.
Six weary hours to listen to the snore of sleepers
and the beat and the flutter of the paddles. I am
beginning to get furiously hot. I can stand it no
longer, I get up and find my hoarse-voiced friend
walking up and down the deck. I feel very much
inclined to say to him, like the gentleman who so
improperly spoke to the man at the wheel in the
song of the 'Pilot,' 'I'll come and pace the deck
with thee, I do not care to sleep.' I fear, however,
he may rejoin 'Gud down, this is no place for thee,'
so I pass by him in silence. I am mightily refreshed
by the cool night air, and I light a pipe, sit under the
lee of the paddle-box and listen to my hoarse-voiced
friends still singing a perpetual part-song of 'port,'
'starboard,' and 'steady,' and apparently getting
more and more angry with one another every moment. What a long time the dawn is coming! It

seems as if we should never have morning again.
How often does the grey morning come too quickly,
how frequently would we prolong the night, and
how seldom do we think the 'accusing splendour
of the morn' comes too soon, but now I wait and
wait. It seems as if it would never come. Indeed
it appears to be the longest night I ever recollect.

At last, however, the chill grey of morning
comes, and before the first streak of the eastern
glow has appeared most of the passengers, apparently weary with the tedious night and unsatisfactory slumber, turn out. Before the sun is well up
the cook, the steward, and their merry men are at
work: there is a savoury smell of cooking, and
covered dishes are hurried cabinwards. I never
saw such a ship for perpetual eating and drinking
in my life. Our landing at Antwerp is a matter of
considerable difficulty, and takes not a little time,
as the sailors have to actually build a bridge from
the steamer to the shore before we can accomplish
it. Why a gangway is not made to save all this
trouble is a thing that it is impossible to understand. When we at last get ashore we say good-
bye to Captain Hawtrey and Mr Evelyn and
betake ourselves to the excellent Hotel de l'Europe.
Here we have a halt and a good breakfast: we are
presently joined by our artist friend and sally forth
to take a flying view of the City of Rubens. It is
only a flying visit, however, for we are bound to
start in the afternoon. Thanks, however, to the
gentleman just mentioned and the Unlimited, who
both know every stone in the place, I am enabled
to see a great deal in a little while. I see the

Gothic canopy to the well by Quintin Matsys, and think what a pity it was that he ever gave up iron-work, of which he was so accomplished a master, in order to become a second-rate painter. Of course we have been to the cathedral, and have seen the masterpiece of Rubens. The cathedral authorities must derive a considerable income from this great work; they keep the curtain drawn before it all the morning till one o'clock, after that hour the admission is by ticket, which costs one franc. It is certainly a little too bad that this great work is not allowed to be seen at all times for nothing. We have taken a passing glance at the house of Rubens, still inhabited by his descendants, whose ancestors, we hear, dis-mantled the great man's studio altogether in order to build stables. We have seen the church of St Paul, which our own David Roberts so often painted, and have inspected the curious Calvary outside : we have taken a rapid run through the Museum, and have revelled in the glorious colour of Rubens and the majesty of Vandyke. We have paid a visit to the Hotel de Ville, and seen the frescoes of Baron Leys : we have run round the New Bourse, and walked to the outskirts of the town to call on a very charming lady. We have had just a tasting order of the City of Rubens, and we like it so well that we would gladly stay a few weeks and moon about in the picturesque old town, and become intimately acquainted with its numerous art treasures. Alas and alas, this is not to be done. We are obliged to be at the Hague to-night : we could sit under this awning, with

toes in the sunshine and nose in the shade, and
listen to the musical carillon which rings out from
time to time from the towers of Notre Dame, we
could drink more Bairisch beer, and smoke more
cigars in a dreamy sort of fashion.   But time and
trains are inexorable.   It is quite time we were
thinking about starting at the present moment.
There goes the carillon again.   If we could only
stop here another day, what a lot I would tell you
about this picturesque city.

POTTERING.

IF there is a man above all others who likes to do the wrong thing at the wrong time I believe it is your humble and most obedient servant the present writer.

Having said this much it is no wonder that I purpose to write a dissertation upon 'Pottering' and give my views on its principles and professors. Your potterer must be Tapleyan, he must be lazy, and he must have a mind of a peculiar nature. I do not think the potterer would make a good bank manager, nor a railway director, nor a chairman of a bubble company, nor a fashionable doctor, nor a schoolmaster, nor the editor of a newspaper, nor a theatrical harpy, nor a toll-taker on Waterloo Bridge, nor a dentist, nor an oyster-opener, nor the conductor of an orchestra or an omnibus, nor the general of an army, nor the ruler of the French nation, nor the manager of a theatre, nor a public executioner, nor a sheriff's officer. I feel certain the potterer would be out of his element in all these offices. However, it is not all of us who can be either bank managers, railway directors, chairmen of bubble companies, fashionable doctors, schoolmasters, editors of newspapers, theatrical harpies, toll-takers on Waterloo Bridge, dentists, oyster-openers, conductors of orchestras or omnibuses, generals of armies, rulers of the French nation, managers of theatres, public executioners, or sheriff's officers. It is a good thing there are plenty of people in the world energetic enough to fill these offices a great many times over, so there is plenty of room left for the potterers.

I should tell you I am a potterer of the first order, and, moreover, I glory in it. I may say I have elevated pottering to a fine art. There is nothing so superbly delicious as to have so much to do that you do not know which way to turn, and to endeavour to persuade yourself that you are a man of leisure. This morning, when I woke up, I suddenly remembered that I had more to do than I could get through in the day. I was conscious of having been called a great many times, and yet I turned round and sang sweetly to myself, ' 'Tis the voice of the sluggard, I hear him complain, you have woke me too soon, I must slumber again.' I nestled down, I pulled the blankets over my nose, and snoozed and snoozed till I felt quite awake. I thought what a hard day's work I had before me. I laughed and I chuckled, and said ' Yah!' in a derisive manner at people and things in general; I bethought me that I would potter. So I pottered pretty well all the morning. I hunted for books, not that I wanted to read them, but because I had not seen them for a long time, and I thought it would be good sport to look them up. I commenced a frantic search for a letter, not that I wanted to see it, but because I thought I should like to know where it was. Then I came to the conclusion, being rather busier than usual, that I

would re-arrange some book-shelves. Now, these
book-shelves, I should tell you, had been in their
present condition for months past; they contained
books which I never want to look at, and it would
not matter if they remained in the same state for
a dozen years to come. However, I thought now
was the time do it. I pulled them all down, covered
my hands with dust, and then I thought I would
just glance inside one of them. I discovered
some rubbishing tale that interested me considerably, so I sat down on the floor and began to read
it. I found it left off at the most thrilling part—
it was ' continued in our next '—so I tried to find
the following number. After pitching all the books
about for some time I could only discover the next
number but one, which I diligently read through,
and then amused myself by speculating what had
taken place between the two numbers. I became
disgusted with my books, and left them in a heap
on the floor, and said they might arrange themselves.

I then look out of window. I see the sun is
shining, and I think it will be a nice day for a
walk. I have nowhere that I wish to go, there
is no place that I am compelled to visit; but I
fancy it would be pleasant to potter about the
streets. I should tell you that all this time I have
an immense amount of work to get through; I
ought to be hard at it, and, as for going out for
a walk, this is the very last thing I ought to dream
of doing. If I had nothing to do, of course there
would be no pleasure in pottering. But as I am
overwhelmed with work I take the keenest pleasure

in it—not in doing my work, but in pottering.
So I think I will go out and roam about the streets.
I am seized with an overwhelming desire to stroll
as far as Russell Square and wander about Square-
opolis generally.   I cannot tell you why this desire
seizes upon me.   I believe the real reason is that
I have probably less business in this spot than in
any other part of London; therefore it gives me
the keenest possible pleasure to potter about in
this particular quarter of the town.   I stroll
round Russell Square.   I make it my business to
discover which is the house in which Mr Sedley
used to reside, and where, at one time, our particular friend Miss Becky Sharp paid a visit to her
dear friend Amelia.   I wonder which side of the
square this house could be, and whether it was up
at those old-fashioned windows,—where, at the
present time, I see some bonny fair-haired children
flattening their chubby cheeks against the pane,
—that the Collector of Boggley Wallah held the
skein of silk that very nearly entangled him for
life.   Could it be possible that in the red-curtained
dining-room below, Mr Jos once told those celebrated tiger-hunting stories of his, and discoursed
upon Miss Cutler and Lance, the surgeon?   Is it
likely that I am gazing into the very apartment in
which Rebecca endured such torture by eating
Indian curry with a chili to follow?   I protest I
am delighted to think I have run into such a
pleasant neighbourhood for speculation.   I almost
expect to see Lieutenant Osborne and Captain
William Dobbin ascend those broad steps as I am
waiting about.   The door presently opens, and
instead of black Sambo in livery, with a mouthful

of white ivories extending all over his face, I see
a tall supercilious footman who stands with his
legs outstretched and his hands behind him, evidently wondering what I can possibly want staring
at the house in such an earnest fashion. He
glares at me and I glare at him : he evidently
thinks I have an eye to the spoons, and he looks
to see if the area-gate is securely locked. I wonder what he would say supposing I were to boldly
stride up those steps and ask if Mr Sedley was at
home, to inquire after Miss Amelia, and to ask
when Mr Jos might be expected back from India.
I expect the supercilious footman would look
more supercilious than ever. He would, probably,
on the strength of his powdered hair, call me
' young feller,' and would hint that he knew what
my little game was : he might make offensive
allusions to greatcoats and umbrellas, and be
generally impertinent. I should not like to risk
this, for if he said all, or any of these things, I
might feel inclined to hit him. He is six feet one
at least, and I think in a hand-to-hand combat I
might possibly get the worst of it. It would be
undignified for a person of my standing and years
to be struggling with a footman and wallowing on
the pavement in Russell Square in broad daylight,
so I content myself with glaring at him. I flatter
myself that, if I give my mind to it, I can glare
any one down in five minutes. I give my mind to
it on this occasion, and so scorch the poor man
with my glare that he goes in and shuts the door.
I will be bound he goes down into the kitchen and
discourses at length to Jane, the housemaid, or
Margaret, the cook, about the suspicious character

he has seen lurking about the square. And I have no doubt he gives it as his opinion that the square is 'a-goin down, Mrs Cook, it is not what it was, mum, and our people will most likely be a-movin' before long. It is just a little low, mum. Somewhat *passy*. Yes, mum, somewhat *passy*, is the square.'

I am very fond of having fictitious property. I declare there is a great deal of pleasure to be had in pretending things belong to you. This right over other people's property certainly constitutes one of the greatest charms of pottering. I feel this as I stroll round the square. I look in at one window and glance in at another. It may be very rude, this kind of thing, but I am sure the opulent inhabitants will not grudge me the small pleasure I derive from the proceeding. I find fault with the colour of the curtains at one house, carp at the furniture in another, and quarrel with the arrangement of pictures in a third. I tell myself how I would have such and such a room papered; what alterations I should make in one part of the house, and what improvements I should bring about in another. All this I do with the greatest thought and the utmost deliberation. At this very moment I ought to be hard at work, and the recollection of this gives the keenest relish to my pottering. I see there is a house to let. Now, think I, I must take this house. I do not stay to inquire the rent. It is probably far beyond my means, but that does not matter. It seems to be in tolerable repair, but I should imagine it will want papering and painting from top to bottom. I wonder whether this was old Sedley's house. No, I scarcely think it can be.

It seems to be on the wrong side of the square.
No, I feel quite certain now that the house where
I saw the supercilious footman must have been
Sedley's. But I think I ought, at any rate, to
look over this house. I mount the steps, I ring
the bell. The bell echoes noisily through the
house, as if there was no one there to prevent it
kicking up as much row as ever it pleased. What
a noise it makes, to be sure. Tang, tang, tang,
tang! Each tang getting fainter and fainter till
it dies away altogether. I make another pull with
the same result; a passing boy opines I shall catch
it for breaking the gentleman's bell-wire, and a
policeman looks as if he would like to 'run me in.'
I slowly descend the steps, I shake my head, and
gaze up at the house as if I expected to see somebody's head protruding from an upper window.
As there is no chance whatever of getting in, I am
more determined than ever to take the house. I
copy the agent's name and address, then I bethink me I would like to ascertain what sort of a
look-out my mansion has at the back. Now this
is by no means an easy thing to ascertain. It is
easy enough to find the fronts of houses, but to
discover the backs of them is altogether a different
business. I make a long circuit and lose myself
in a mews. I go down queer streets. I pass beneath unaccountable archways into yards that look
as if they belonged to the bankrupt inn of a country town. I run against men with pitchforks, I
come in dangerous proximity with sibillating
ostlers and horses' heels, and at last I think I must
be somewhere at the back of my house. Now,
however, I am rather puzzled; though I recollect

the number of my house as inscribed on its front door, I have no idea how many houses it is from either one end of the row or the other. I think I can detect my house, though, by the dustiness of its windows. I know it was somewhere in the middle of the row. I then begin to arrange what I will do. The look-out is not bad. It is tolerably open, as London houses go. I shall, however, have to throw out a billiard-room over the garden, and I think I might add a small conservatory. I am waving my stick frantically at my house when I begin to be conscious that I am being observed by one or two corpulent coachmen and irreverent stable boys. They evidently think I am a maniac, or that I am assuming a madness in order that I may steal a horse, or run off with a truss or two of straw. I beat a retreat, I take a wrong turning, I lose myself in a labyrinth of mews, and finally return to civilization in a street far removed from Russell Square.

A curious little street it is. One evidently adapted for pottering. No two houses alike. Shops of every variety. Dear me, I recollect this street. Years, years ago did I come here to be perfected in all the mysteries of the ' light fantastic.' In this very street did a certain person attain the grace, the lightness, the finish that has made his waltzing and *cotillon* dancing famous at all the courts of Europe. At that modest little room over the shop, which you can see from here, did a very charming member of the *corps de ballet* consent to give me lessons in the Terpsichorean art. How we used to spin round the little room as the young lady hummed the air of the last waltz in faultless

time, and with such a *verve* and spirit that made you
dance whether you would or not.   I used to enjoy
pottering even in those days.   We did not always
dance even when I came to have my lesson, and I
was working particularly hard in order to distinguish myself at ensuing balls and evening parties.
No, sometimes I would strike altogether.   I would
bring out a comic paper, or I would volunteer to
give my imitations of actors, I would sing snatches
of the latest of popular songs.   I would gossip
idly and refuse to put on my thin boots.   Ah!
pleasant times were these, my brethren.   This is
the right way of being taught to dance.   I do not
believe in dancing-masters.   I would not care for
the teachings of all the Turveydrops—fathers and
sons—in London.   Give me a pretty girl who is a
good *valseuse,* and she will make the most awkward
of men an accomplished dancer in a month.   I
wonder what has become of my pretty little professor : the remembrance of her trim ankles, her
exquisite little boots, and the faintest hint of white
stockings, as she tripped a *pas seul* to show me
exactly how the steps should be executed, is fresh
in my memory at the present time.

Ah, my brethren, it is a somewhat sad reflection to think that one's dancing days are over, that
we can no longer trip it on the light fantastic.   I
take my way homewards, wondering what can have
become of the pretty little professor at whose feet
I sat, and who taught me so gracefully.   I am
somewhat sad; I have a power of hard labour
looming in the distance, but I have enjoyed my
morning's ' pottering ' immensely.

*

THE PIGEONS OF ST MARK.

THERE is but little doubt that sight-seeing in Venice is very hard work. The Unlimited has just gone off to see some masterpiece of Titian's, but I have ' struck.' I will have no more of it. I will sit down and rest, light up a cigarette and wait till he returns.

I think I should like to come to Venice when every picture gallery was shut up and every church was closed. You recollect Albert Smith's song of the ' Young English Traveller,' who ' got quite bored at Venice, thought the Rialto precious slow, and goes to see the Bridge of Sighs because he thinks must go,' and who finally was supremely delighted when he finds anything ' shut up and can't be seen.' This is true enough, but they will not give you a chance in Venice ; everything is most provokingly open, and the facilities of sight-seeing are something astonishing. They chase you about, they worry you into seeing all kinds of things whether you will or not. They persist in your ' doing' everything and going everywhere. Up to the top of the Campanile and down to the depths of the Pozzi, sweltering in the Sotto Piombi and shuddering on the Bridge of Sighs : visiting first a church and then a palace, then another church, so that you get a sort of recollectionary sandwich,

so to speak, of the three. You muddle them all
up together, you have ideas of the most ecclesiastical things in palaces and matters most palatial in
churches. You get a determination of pictures to
the head. You put down Titian's pictures to Tintoret and Tintoret's to Titian, and those which belong to neither to both : your brain becomes one
ever-whirling chromatrope of pictures and palaces,
of Rogers and Ruskin, of Murray and Shakspere, of
Byron, of Woods, of Gally Knight, and of Rawdon
Brown. You have a dazzling kaleidoscope of *verd
antique* columns and *lapis lazuli* pavements, of
silver altars and golden candlesticks, of bronzes,
sculptures, mosaics, and bassi-relievi, of Doges and
dodges, of Bucentaurs and Brides of the Sea, continually dazzling your mind's eye. It is quite a
relief when you can pause for a moment, and have a
little quiet. I had one of the most delicious naps I
ever had in my life whilst sitting down before Tintoretto's masterpiece in the Scuola di San Rocco,
yesterday afternoon. There are many ponderous
essayists who write in a 'fine scholarly style,' and
heavy poets, that I often find extremely useful to
send me to sleep at home, but I was not aware that
a great master in art would prove such an excellent
soporific. Certainly ' Tintoretto's Soothing Syrup '
proved to be quite as effective as chloral hydrate,
and infinitely more pleasant.

Glad to seize once more the opportunity of a
little rest, I sit down on the cool marble steps of
the Scala dei Giganti and moon and meditate.
I am afraid I am not much impressed with my
situation. It is nothing to me that the Doges used

to be crowned at the top of these stairs.   I do not
tremble though the busts of Zeno, Vittorio, Pisani,
Foscari, Rinieri, and a lot more rascally old Doges
look down upon me.   I know round the colonnade
I may find the busts of Morosini, of Bembo, of
Marco Polo, of Galileo, of Tintoretto, and many
others, but I do not feel inclined to bow down and
worship them.   I am particularly interested in
watching some pigeons as they come fluttering
down and hover about the picturesque bronze well
in the courtyard.   These pigeons are very lively,
they are very tame, and very plump.   They are fed
regularly at the expense of the town : they have
their ordinary every day at two o'clock precisely :
they are the most independent, refined, highly-
educated, blue-blooded pigeons I ever saw in my
life.   I wish my excellent friend, Mr Tegetmeier,
was with me at the present time, I would get him
to cram me on the subject, and I would give such
a learned disquisition on these pigeons, such an
elaborate account of their antecedents, such an interesting history of their manners and customs,
that all my readers would be immensely charmed.
As my friend is not with me, I am left to my own
resources and am obliged to form my own theory
with regard to these birds.   My theory is that
their prosperous condition, their aristocratic bearing, their plumpness, their ' perkyness ' arises from
one fact—*they never have the fear of the pie upon
them.*   This is a very great point.   The most light-
hearted of these pigeons would always feel depressed
if the thought came over him in his gayest moments, that eventually he would be cast into a

prison of the hardest earthenware and half-drowned
in gelatinous gravy : that he would languish beneath a Sotto Piombi of crust or lose all hope in the
Pozzi of steak and hard-boiled eggs, and be finally
thoroughly baked by order of some bloodthirsty
and tyrannical Doge. The ancestors of these
pigeons probably established themselves here more
than eight hundred years ago, so the thoughts of
their descendants would naturally run on the line
of the most ancient form of government in Venice.
They would know nothing of the French occupation,
the Austrian rule, nor the sway of Victor Em-
manuel, they believe implicitly in those who first
fed their ancestors eight hundred years ago, and
who passed a law that the Pigeons of St Mark
should be for ever and ever protected from the pie.
There is a mystery about these pigeons that I
would fain have unravelled. Why are they always
held sacred, and by what superstition did the
bloodthirsty Doges accord them the protection they
refused to everybody else ? I only hope the
present government will continue the protection
that has been afforded these birds for the last eight
hundred years. I am sorry to see indications of a
vile spirit of progress and improvement in Venice
which did not exist when I paid my first visit to
the picturesque city. I grieve to say they have
already one or two steam-launches, and I should
not be at all surprised if some day we should find
a species of Hurlingham established on the Lido,.
and the sacred pigeons of St Mark taken out there
in baskets to be butchered. When this takes place,
mark my words, the glory of Venice, which is so

glorious in its decay, will have entirely departed. If Venice attempts to be a prosperous city it will fail. Venice is mainly supported by visitors who come here because the city is so picturesque, so behind the age, so quaint, so totally unlike any other city all the world over. Once take away these characteristics and the tourists will go elsewhere. As it is they come pretty freely, and are content to pay the charges which are somewhat high on all hands.

Now am I coming to the subject on which I intended to speak especially. Raising my eyes from the pigeons which are gravely pecking beneath the shadow of the bronze well entrance, looking across the courtyard and gazing on the colonnade on the first floor, do I see a very charming little picture. A dainty young English girl is gazing down upon the courtyard, and, probably, surprised at my sitting down on the steps, and wondering what I am doing with a pencil and paper. She has fair hair, large grey eyes, and as some one has somewhere sung, 'sweet little dimples that Millais might paint.' She is leaning over the stonework, her arms are stretched out and her fingers are just touching at the tips, her petticoats are pouting through the balustrade, and I can just catch a glimpse of the patent leather toes of two tiny boots in the shadow; she has one of the most coquettish of hats, a dark travelling dress in perfect taste. The pointed arch, the delicate tracery, the massive stonework, more than three hundred years old, forms a fitting frame for this pretty picture. The perfect taste of the building of 1573 and that of the young girl of 1873 form a pleasant harmony. This damsel is one of the pigeons of St Mark. You would not think it, although her dress is about the tint of the feathers on a pigeon's wing. I know a charming young lady at home whom her friends· call 'Pidgey.' It might be this young lady, only it isn't. Let me explain : the damsel gazing upon the courtyard has only just got rid of a terrible hawk in the form of a valet-de-place, who has been taking her and her party round the palace, telling them things they do not want to know in a hideous polyglot jargon they cannot possibly understand, and charging them an exorbitant sum for so doing. More hawks will await this pretty pigeon wherever she goes. More numerous than the pigeons that come flocking to the Piazza San Marco at two o'clock are the troop of human pigeons that flock to Venezia la Bella during the season. The hawks rejoice and are exceeding glad, and St Mark gathereth a goodly sum into his treasury. Possibly this is the reason that sight-seeing is so insisted upon in Venice : you cannot see anything in this town without two or three people assisting you, and each of these persons expects to be royally ' undamaged ' for his assistance. Who was it sang something like the following relative to the hurry and worry of sight-seeing in Venice ? If I mistake not, it went to the air of the ' Tarentella ' in *Masaniello* :—

> Floating in gondolas, laughing and jollity,
> Cyprian wine of the very best quality,
> At Florian's *café*, midst fun and frivolity,
> Venice the place for a capital lark !

All that the tourist can dream of or hear about
Crowds on your sight as you carelessly peer about,
Quaint water streets you so carefully steer about,
    See the Rialto and Square of St Mark ;
        Musicians in plenty
        Play *Ecco ridente*
Or *Com' e gentil* in the still summer night ;
        If you're in a hurry
        Pray read it in *Murray,*
You'll find his description is perfectly right.

Thousands of thirsty mosquitoes are biting one,
Bright summer sunshine is ever delighting one,
Music and mirth every moment inviting one—
    Dreary old London we quickly forget !
Shylock and Portia, in short the whole kit of 'em,
Readers of Shakspere recall ev'ry bit of 'em ;
Troublesome guides, you can never get quit of 'em,
    Pictures by Titian and old Tintoret !
        The sock and the buskin,
        With Rogers and Ruskin,
Are mixed in a muddle with palace and sight.
        It may be a worry,
        But don't forget *Murray,*
He'll throw on your darkness some excellent light !

Not a bad description by the way of the manner
in which English and American pigeons are hunted
about Venice. Now a word or two concerning the
hawks. After all this paper will be more about
hawks than pigeons and I think the ' Hawks of St
Mark ' would be a better title than the ' Pigeons
of St Mark.' But no matter. Everywhere hawks
abound, the humbler hawks endeavour to extract
coppers and half-francs from your pocket, and the
more magnificent hawks swindle you at hotels and
persist in your buying all kinds of sham antiques
and spurious old masters. As for the first class, their
name is legion. If you look at a boy in the street

or gaze at him from your gondola, he will immediately put out his hand for a gratuity.   Not only
this, if he sees any chance of obtaining even a *cen-
tesimo* he will follow you half round Venice.   He
will take short cuts and turn up at unaccountable
places, and long after you have forgotten all about
him, you will see him suddenly appear upon a
bridge waving his cap, and panting and grinning,
and looking for his reward.   It was only yesterday
that a young rascal offered to swim after our gondola just as we were leaving San Salvatore, and
positively commenced to undress: he became entangled in his garments, and we left him struggling with them and being assisted by a select
committee of his friends to get out of them.   We
went on our way, and had quite forgotten all about
him, when suddenly turning a corner we heard a
terrific shout, a sort of view halloo, and this rascally
little naked boy, looking as if he were curried'
came tearing along by the side of the canal, and
took the neatest header in the world into the water
and swam after our gondola.   Of course he got a
lot of coppers, which he put in his mouth, being
the only thing of the nature of a pocket that he
happened to have on.   The majority of boys, however, do not do nearly so much for their money.
They generally expect from half a franc to a franc
for looking at you when you land.

There is another class of useless individuals who
have grown grey in their hawkery and imbecile in
their mendicancy, and that is the men whom for
want of a better name I call the ' hangers-on of the

gondolas.' Wherever you stop—at church, palace,. or hotel, it does not matter where—you will find these men. They are all furnished with a terrible instrument which seems to be an old mop-stick with a bent rusty nail at one end, with which they hang on to the gondola directly it gets within hanging on distance. They then in a most ostentatious manner try to assist you out of the boat; they do this in such an awkward manner that they often roll you back into the gondola, or hand you into the water. Of course they have to be ' undamaged.' You are afraid not to do this, because they are apt to look fierce and brandish their mopstick. If you did not give them anything I verily believe they would job that rusty nail into your eye as soon as look at you. They are about as useful as those boys in London, who when you have hailed a hansom, got into it, and told the driver where to go, come up, open the doors once more, and shut them with a bang, touch their caps *con espressione* and say ' Where to, sir ? '

A far more dangerous specimen of the hawk tribe is the dealer in antiquities, the vendor of pictures, and the wholesale carver of statues. He is dangerous because most of the gondoliers are in his pay. I believe that they get a certain sum on every customer they bring, and so much per cent on the sales made through their instrumentality. Your gondolier will endeavour to take you to one of these places as if it were one of the shows of the city, and if you are not very careful you will find yourself in a bazaar of bad pictures and a museum of spurious antiques before you know where you are. It is by no means difficult for you to be deceived, as many of these emporiums are in magnificent palaces bearing the name of some ancient Venetian family. If your goudolier mentions manufactures, or statuary, or pictures, or antiques, and he casually states that some of them are for sale, tell him you will think about it to-morrow : then there may be some chance of your escaping from the worst form of Venetian hawk. I do not know whether an ecclesiastical atmosphere is favourable to the development of the hawk tribe, but at all the churches the tribe flourishes and flutters exceedingly. There are generally three boys who conduct you from your gondola to the church door, and then fight savagely and vindictively over a copper you have given one of them till an official comes out and well nigh kicks them into the canal. This official takes you in charge and trots you round the church, and gives a running commentary on the pictures, then he has his tip and hands you over to some one else, who has the care of some especial chapel. After you have remunerated this man liberally a holy friar turns up from some mysterious quarter—he either comes up through a trap-door or out of the confessional—and opines that you would like to see the shrine of San Qualcheduno. Of course, he has his reward. Indeed, at all the churches there seems to be a sort of limited liability company for preying on the pockets of the unwary traveller. At the palaces you may tip people till you are black in the face if you are so

minded.   Everybody, from the most humble scul-
lion to the most pompous *major domo,* is willing
to receive a franc or two.   I never saw it refused
save in one instance, and that was the day before
yesterday, when we attempted to tip an exceedingly
respectable gentleman, who looked like a superior
butler who had recently gone into the church, but
who turned out to be a member of one of the oldest families in Venice, which numbers three Doges
and several distinguished warriors amongst its
ancestors.   The hotels at Venice are for the most
part dear.   Every one goes to Danieli's because
every one talks about Danieli's, but there are quite
as good hotels in Venice as this and a great many
cheaper.   Danieli's has, however, a European
reputation, and I am not going to quarrel with it.
It is good enough for me, and it is too hot to
quarrel with anything.   Were I Murray or Bradshaw I would give you a lecture on the various
hotels in the place.   As I happen to be neither
the one nor the other of these potentates I will
do—.   I begin to be conscious that a rascally
brigand of a *valet-de-place* is gazing at me from
the other side of the courtyard, and will probably
come across and make a fixed charge for so doing
if I do not move out of the way.

The Unlimited has just returned, and is raving
violently about Tintoret and Paolo Veronese.   I
find that I have ' pins and needles ' in my feet, and
a proof impression of the metal *intarsiatura* of the
front of the step all down my back.   It has just
struck two o'clock; the birds have flown; the

young English girl has retired from the colonnade. My amiable pigeons in feathers have gone to dinner, and my pretty pigeon in petticoats has gone to luncheon. I think it is high time we followed the latter, and helped to swell, in the *salle à manger* of the Hotel Danieli, the noble army of the ' Pigeons of St Mark.'

BENEATH THE BLANKETS.

THE 'early village cock' is a species of bird which I have always held in the greatest abhorrence, and I look upon him as a vainglorious nuisance that ought to be put down by act of parliament. I know him with his self-sufficient strut, with his perky carriage, and his obtrusive morality: he proclaimeth his virtue upon the housetop, and 'doth with his lofty and shrill-sounding throat' tell unto all men what an exemplary cock he is. He is the cock who always has his breakfast punctually at eight o'clock, he always keeps his appointments, he is never late for dinner, he goes to church regularly on Sundays, he pays his bills punctually, he never omits to answer a letter, he subscribes to charitable institutions, he brings up his family properly, he returns the umbrella he borrowed, he never missed a train in his life, and he always makes a point of practising that absurd operation humorously described as 'taking time by the forelock.' He is an irrepressible, a preternaturally active bird. You could fancy him going round and knocking at every one's door in his house at six o'clock, and not only knocking, but seeing that they got up, too, confound him. He would not be satisfied with a faint knuckling on your panel, and informing you in a subdued voice that it was six o'clock and your hot water was there. Bless you, he would hammer and kick at your door at six; at a quarter-past he would come and tell you the hot water was there; at twenty minutes past he would come and inform you that the hot water was getting cold; at half-past he would shout out that the hot water was quite cold; at five-and-twenty minutes to seven he would bring your boots and rattle them violently against the door; at twenty minutes to seven he would wish to know whether you were going to stay in bed all day; at a quarter to he would suggest how pleasant it would be to ' take a turn ' before breakfast; at ten minutes to he would tell you he should not wait breakfast for you, and possibly would eventually succeed in hunting you out of your cozy warm bed-room down into a chilly breakfast parlour, with the windows all open, the fire only just lighted, the furniture in a general state of *bouleversement,* and a cold maid-servant, apparently in gardening gloves, and her face black-leaded, dusting the furniture in a per-functory manner. Then, in sheer desperation, you are obliged to go out for what he is pleased to call ' a good brisk walk, which will give you such an appetite,' but which only succeeds in taking away the little appetite you ever had, and making you singularly silent and morose the whole of break-fast time. The ' early village cock,' which has disturbed my rest several times during the last half-hour, has unconsciously led me into a ram-bling discourse on its human prototypes, and I have lost sight of the bird in the man. I number

a few—I am glad to say a very few—of such
active gentlemen amongst my acquaintance; and,
if there is any truth in the doctrine of the metem-
psychosis, I doubt not but what these gentlemen
will eventually become converted into 'early
village cocks,' and disturb the public instead of
their own family, and upset parishes where they
formerly inconvenienced households.

The question is, have I been called or have I
not? This subject admits of such a variety of
argument, and there is so much to say on both
sides of the question, that I could not think of
getting up before it was decided. Supposing it
were to be six o'clock instead of nine. If it were
six it would be dark. Yes; but then the mornings are so foggy now, and that makes a difference
one way or the other; you cannot exactly see how,
but there is evidently something in it. I wonder
whether it is Thursday or Friday. If it is Friday
I must get up at once, as I have a particular
appointment at a quarter-past twelve—I come to
the conclusion it must be nine o'clock by this
time—I decide that it is not Friday: if it had
been Friday, of course I should have been
called, and if I had been called, of course it
would have been Friday; as I have not been
called, of course it is not Friday, that is plain
and logical enough on the face of it. I turn
round, and pull the blankets over my shoulders,
and think what a capital thing early rising is.
Yes, a capital thing, for the country never could
get on without it, British industry never could
have thriven, British arms could never have been

victorious, British literature, art, and science could
never have flourished without early rising. Yes,
yes, no doubt; but there are some constitutions
cannot stand it; it requires an iron constitution to
get up early in the morning. I do not think I
could stand it. It would never do for me to trifle
with my constitution. Oh, yes, of course I could
do it if I was called at the proper time. But when
a man is not called, it would not be proper for him
to get up of his own accord. He might get up in
the middle of the night, and disturb the entire
household. I would not disturb an entire household for worlds. Perhaps it is the middle of the
night now. I will not get up in case I might disturb an entire household. I am glad of this
excuse, and I roll and congratulate myself. I congratulate myself and I roll till I nearly roll out of
bed. I listen to the bells chiming forth the hour
from the various churches. I try to count the
vibrations in each boom of Big Ben. I cannot
make the number of vibrations in each boom agree.
Wonder whether there is a difference in the density of the atmosphere between the period it struck
one and the period it struck nine, and if there is a
difference in the density of the atmosphere, whether
it would account for the discrepancy. Perhaps
after all I am wrong, and Big Ben is right. Possibly we are both wrong or both right. Either
way it does not much matter. Now, I know exactly
what chimes will follow Big Ben, and I wait for
these to ring out in their usual order. One or two
of these I miss. I wonder whether the vergers of
Saint Ticklish Tonsure forgot to wind up the

clock, or whether the churchwardens have refused
to find money to oil the works of Saint Grewsome Gargoyle.   Now, the question is whether
I have been asleep during part of the series of
striking.   There is just a possibility of my having
dropped off when Saint Ticklish Tonsure or Saint
Grewsome Gargoyle ' obliged again.' I must think
this matter over.   I cannot get up till I arrive
at some satisfactory conclusion.   I roll, and roll,
and roll.   I wish it were last night instead of
this morning.   Suppose I pretend it is last night,
and cheat myself into the belief that this morning
is to-morrow morning, that the day before yesterday is the day after to-morrow, or that last Tuesday week is next Saturday fortnight.   I continue
to roll.   ' Clocks may chime and bards may rhyme,
but I roll on for ever.'   This is nonsense, is it ?
I don't care ; it amuses me.   I think it very
clever.   I am not on a platform before the British
public.   I am giving an entertainment to myself
by myself.   I applaud myself, and I encore myself,
and think if I were a dramatic critic what laudatory
notices I would write of myself in the morning
papers.

My ancient clock in the next room, which
always makes a noise, something between a damp
squib and an asthmatic dinner-gong, when it
strikes, has just chimed fourteen in a humorous
manner.   I try to calculate by this what the time
really is.   Let me see : I recollect it striking five
yesterday afternoon when it was two.   So as two
is to five, so is fourteen to the answer.   True, but
then I recollect that the day before yesterday it

struck eight at two o'clock. I remember Albert
Smith's famous Edwards, the engineer, had a
clock which stood at twenty minutes to five and
had just struck three, on which he remarked 'he
knew it meant half-past one, but it wasn't to be
expected that a stranger would find that out.' I
wish I understood the Edwardsian theory, and
could apply it to my erratic time-piece. I wonder
whether I could work the problem out by trigonometry. Could it be worked out by trigonometry,
or should it be worked out by horology, or a combination of the two? By horological trigonometry
or trigonometrical horology? That is a thing that
must be thought over, and solved when I get up.
I hear a rattling of breakfast cups, and a jingling
of spoons in the adjoining apartment, and really
think it must be time to get up. What the Duke
of Wellington said about 'turning in and turning
out' is all nonsense. It may be all very well for
hardy warriors who like to accustom themselves to
sleep on hard knife-boards, but it will not do for
me. I recollect seeing the Duke's bed at Walmer
Castle many years ago, and it gave one the impression that one could only do one thing after
turning in, and that was to turn out again as
quickly as possible. They might well call him an
Iron Duke when he slept upon such an adamantine
couch. I wish the room were not so dark, and I
would get up at once. There is nothing I dislike
so much as getting up in the dark. Must have
some arrangement made in order that I can hoist
the blinds without getting out of bed. Besides, I
really do not know whether the day is sufficiently

15

fine to justify my getting up. I should not mind
getting up if it were not a damp morning. Is it a
damp morning or not? Yes, I am sure it is, or the
cabs would not have that peculiar sound as they
pass along the street. By the way, it must be
very late or there would not be so many cabs
about. I hope nobody will call before I am up.
Hate people to call before I am up. They think it
funny to say 'Good afternoon' if they see a man
breakfasting at twelve o'clock; they say signifi-
cantly they 'suppose you were out very late last
night,' they cannot think how you can manage to
stand it, and talk idiotically about lighting the
candle at both ends, and have such a general air
of activity and spruceness about them that I cordially detest them.

I wonder what time it is. Oh, here is my
watch, not wound up, of course. Why cannot
watches wind up themselves? 'As regular as
clock-work,' indeed. Where's the regularity of
watches, or clocks either, for the matter of that, if
they do not have a couple of men to look after
them? I should be regular and punctual if I was
only half as well looked after as my watch usually
is. The science of horology is evidently in its
infancy. Wish I knew when the Horological
Society held its meetings, and I would call and
tell them so. It must be getting late. I really
would rise at once, but the thought strikes me that
my hot water by this time must be cold enough to
skate upon, and I recollect I did not strop my
razors last time I put them away. If there is one

thing that I hate more than another it is shaving with a blunt razor. I remember once staying down in the country with some serious ultra-punctual people who actually had breakfast at eight o'clock to the minute on Sunday morning. It was a cold winter's morning, there was no hot water, and my razors were blunt. I shall never forget my appearance at that well-ordered break-fast table, after repeated shoutings and knockings at my door, after a fiendish tintinnabulation of 'up-stairs bells,' with my face tattooed like a New Zealand chief's, and a sanguineous white handker-chief bound round my throat as if I had attempted suicide. This was a warning to me that I shall never forget. I know my razors are blunt, so I will not get up. Next to the luxury of stopping in bed and wondering whether you have been called or not is jumping up directly you hear a knock at your door, and then when you are thoroughly chilled and the servant has departed sneaking into bed again. You have all the sensa-tion of Spartan virtue one moment, and the feelings of Sybaritic luxury the next. When snuggling down again under the blankets, you think what a grand thing self-denial must be, but what a set of fools the Spartans were. Once, when living in the country, I tried an exquisite refinement of this luxury. I rose at six on a chill, misty, autumn morning, I hurried on a few clothes, rushed to the Thames, and took a header in the icy stream, ran back again, jumped into bed, lit a long pipe, and smoked and dreamed in delicious lazy languor until I went off to sleep again. The sensation was positively delicious. It is a sort of feeling you experience probably but once in a lifetime.

I wish I knew what day of the week it was. Of course it would be absurd for a man to get up unless he knew this, for he might get up on the wrong day. That would never do. At this present moment I am in a state of hazy uncertainty as to whether it is the day before yesterday, or the day after to-morrow, or the week after the next, or last Saturday fortnight. It would never do to take such an important step with such misty *data*. Besides I have a dream of great consequence to finish. I always like to finish anything I commence; I never like to do anything by halves. If a thing is worth doing at all it is worth doing well. If a dream is worth dreaming at all it is worth dreaming thoroughly. I try to continue my dream, I cover my face with the blankets, but it is of no use, and I begin to feel uncomfortably wakeful. The clothes slip off at one corner of the bed and make my feet feel very chilly. I have a horrible conviction that it is Friday morning, and getting very late, and that I shall miss my appointment after all. However, I console myself with the reflection that I have not been called, and burrow once more amongst the pillows. At last, however, comes a sharp rapping at my door, as if it had made application many times before and had been treated with contempt, but was not going to be put off this time. Knock! *Knock!!* KNOCK!!!

'Yes!' I shout with assumed vehemence.

'More hot water, sir?'

'More? Eh! Yes! What? What's the time?'

'Twelve o'clock, sir, and you've been called four times.'

And so it is. I have to take my bath, dress, shave, and breakfast, and be with old Colonel Precise at Knightsbridge by a quarter past.

THE GIANT'S CAUSEWAY.

'AH! shure yer honour, this is the Wishin' Chair,
and ye must sit down and wish three wishes,'
said the guide, taking me by the shoulders and
thrusting me down upon a particularly hard basaltic
seat, causing me to lean on a most uncomfortable
basaltic back and to rest my arms upon peculiarly
unyielding basaltic arms. Upon my word I do
not think much of the Giant's upholsterer. It
may be vastly unromantic and matter of fact,
but I own that I would much prefer Gillow to
His Most Towering Giantship's cushionless manu-
facturer of chairs. 'Ye must wish three wishes,
yer honour,' repeated the guide, seeing I did not
take any notice of his first remark, 'and bedad,
they're shure to come thrue before a year has past.'
I find there is no getting out of it. Perhaps, after
all, I have a touch of superstition and a grain of
romance about me. So I wish three wishes. I wish
that I may not lose my hat before I get home.
That is wish number one. I wish that they will
not give us salmon for dinner at the 'Antrim' to-
night. That is wish number two. Wish number
three, which is the most important of the lot, I entirely decline to divulge. It has nothing to do
with hats and it has nothing to do with dining. I
know every one will be curious to know all about

it, but I am not going to satisfy their curiosity. I think this would be a good opportunity to write, so, much to the disgust of our guide, who fancies we are only going to remain about half a minute, I pull out a pencil and paper and begin. Well, well, the Giant's Causeway is not at all a bad study to write in ; it is nice and airy and there is plenty of light, and you might after all have a worse writing table than a convex basaltic pentagon, and might sit on a worse seat than a concave basaltic octagon. There is just a little too much wind for writing comfortably, and I am not at all sure but that long before I have finished my chronicle, one part of it will be carried round Bengore Head, another will be blown right out to sea, and the rest will be wafted as far as the other side of Portrush. But no matter. Here goes to begin.

From my earliest youth I have conceived a rooted antipathy to doing anything that people say you *must* do, and have always shunned places that people tell you you *must* go and see. If I am told when I visit a particular town I must go and see some especial object within its walls I invariably refuse to go near it. Years ago when staying at Lucerne I recollect that no power on earth would induce me to go and see the 'Lion' which all visitors to that picturesque and attractive Swiss town feel compelled to visit. Every tourist I met, every young lady I happened to sit next to at *table d'hôte*, asked me if I had not been to see the 'Lion,' and what I had thought of it. I gloried in telling them that I had not been to see the 'Lion,' that I had no intention of going to see it, and that I

questioned very much whether it was worth a visit.
They appeared to look upon me as a hopeless bar-
barian or harmless imbecile: they were not quite
sure whether I was not a terrible combination of the
two: they avoided my society for the future as that
of a dangerous character.   Holding these opinions
it cannot be imagined that I looked with much
favour upon the Giant's Causeway, especially as I
have a wholesome horror of excursions of every kind.
But I should tell you you are not allowed to hold
such heterodox opinions with regard to the lion of
the neighbourhood if you are staying at Portrush.
It is the first thing everybody does when he comes
to the village, and it is generally the last thing he
does before he quits it.   The waiters, the boots,
the car-drivers, will not give him a moment's peace
till he has done this, so he had better accomplish
it as soon after his arrival as possible.   If a man
remained for a long time at the 'Antrim' without
making this popular excursion, or if ho were rash
enough to hint that he had no intention of under-
taking it at all, I am inclined to think that the
chief of the constabulary would keep his eye upon
him as a suspicious character, and the landlord
would keep a sharp look-out after his spoons and
the payment of his bill.   It is, after all, a charming
trip, and many people go there a great number of
times during their stay.   It is always a resource,
and often when you are lounging on the hotel
steps of a morning you make up parties to go
to the Causeway, simply because you have nothing to do and this is a very charming way of
doing it.   You may go to Dunluce Castle, or the

White Rocks, if you like : you may sail over to the Skerries, go to Bushmills, and drink whiskey ; or pass the morning lounging on the rocks, or fishing, if you please. All these things are optional : you may do them or leave them alone. But go to the Causeway you *must*, if you have any desire to keep up a good character among the Portrushians. It is useless to attempt to stem the flood of this fanaticism, so bowing to the popular will, or rather being swept away by the current of popular opinion, we came out here this morning.

A very pleasant ride it is of not more than eight miles. The first part is along the coast, by the White Rocks, and you look down upon the picturesque caverns and rugged coast and gaze upon the superb colour of the water : you pass a curious chasm in the rock called the Devil's Punchbowl, and the grand ruin, Dunluce Castle. Some distance after passing the latter you strike inland ; you see Sir Edward Macnaghten's residence in the distance, and you presently reach the quaint little village of Bushmills. Here you cross the Bush, a small river, but one of the best salmon streams in this part of Ireland. About a couple of miles beyond this we reach the foot of the hill leading to the Causeway Hotel. There is no doubt about it that the Giant's Causeway is as much a show place as any of the common mountains or popular easy excursions in Switzerland. If one had any doubt on this head it would be instantly set at rest by the eagerness with which we were 'spotted' by the guides who were awaiting us at the top of the hill. They started off in a race to meet us; the best man won; he seized hold of our car and he took us in charge. This guide was a very learned person: the peripatetic knowledge which he possessed was something tremendous, and the way in which he talked in a familiar manner of basalt, felspar, hornblende, and columnar formation, and delivered a sort of diluted Polytechnic lecture on the smallest provocation, made us tremble and feel very small indeed. We learn, to our sorrow, that though it is a tolerably fine day, there is too much wind to dream for a moment of going out in a boat. The finest view of the Causeway and the cliffs is undoubtedly from the water. This we must give up, also a visit to the caves of Portcoon and Dunkerry, which can only be approached in calm weather from the sea.

Under these circumstances we make the best of it, and take our way up the cliff, to get a view of the Causeway from above first. It blows furiously, so that we have quite enough to do to keep our hats on, and if they had not been well secured by the judicious hailyard, they would probably have tumbled into the entrance hall of the 'Antrim' long before we had had a glimpse of a single basaltic column. The guide keeps on improving our minds; he babbleth continually of basalt, he jabbereth of fluted crags and mysterious legends, he gives his Polytechnic lecture over and over again, but it does not matter. The wind is blowing so hard that we cannot hear what he says, and if we say 'Yes,' or 'Oh, indeed!' occasionally, we find he is perfectly satisfied. We meet a good many visitors coming down the hill. There are a

number of young ladies, who are nearly blown to
pieces, attended by a number of gentlemen whose
time seems to be filled up by exciting chases after
their own hats. Our guide informs us that these
people are part of a large pic-nic. What a place
to come for a pic-nic to be sure! Why they will
have all their food blown to Ballynastraid long before they have time to carve it. I hear that fre-
quent picnics take place in this part, and I should
not be at all surprised to be told that the surrounding country was strewn with broken victuals: eatables actually fractured by the force of the wind,
mind you. I dare say simple peasants sitting down
to their mid-day meal are often agreeably surprised
by a pigeon pie being hurled through the window,
a few hams deposited in the front garden, or a
lobster salad or two shot down on the doorstep,
and if I had been informed that it occasionally
rained ham sandwiches I confess I should not be
greatly astonished.

Our first glimpse of any part of the Causeway,
is looking over the cliff down upon Portnabaw Bay.
We are somewhat disappointed in this, for looking
down we only see the smaller range of columns,
and from the height they look like the stump
paving of a rustic summer-house. It is only when
we see tiny figures looking like the smallest doll
you ever saw, tripping about from column to
column, that you can form the least idea of the
vast proportion of everything around. We see at
a promontory on our left two curiously-shapen hills
known as the Steucans, and as we skirt along—
keeping at a respectful distance from the edge of

the cliff if you please—Port Ganniay, the view improves very much indeed. The coast is bolder and more rugged, and when we come in sight of the Grand Causeway we find it very nearly comes up to our expectation. The finest view, however, is to come. Our guide takes us by the arm and leads us out on to a narrow promontory, which looks as if one might easily slip down on either side. It is blowing so hard that it is difficult to keep one's feet. When we get about half-way out, the guide suddenly throws himself down on his stomach, as if he were skirmishing, and we are blown down on our backs as if we were shot. The wind is blowing so hard that we cannot get up again, so we take our hats in our mouths and pretend we are slugs, and wriggle along to the edge of the cliff and gaze over. We see on one side the Giant's Amphitheatre, with its rows of towering columns, eighty and sixty feet high, as regular and exact as if designed by an accomplished architect and hewn by a skilful stonemason. In the distance we observe three isolated pillars, which are known as the Giant's Chimney-tops. There is no doubt whatever that the Amphitheatre is even better worth seeing than the Causeway itself.

We have plenty of opportunity of looking at this superb view, for we still keep to our slug-like attitude. Notwithstanding our waistcoats are covered with mud we still wallow in this undignified position. At last, when we have heard all the guide has to tell us—taking advantage of our helpless state, he fires off a lot of the most terrible and elaborate statistics—we wriggle back to a

tolerably safe position. Here, just when I am trying to make out which was the portion of this scene
that was introduced into a pantomime of Mr E. L.
Blanchard's at Drury Lane some few years ago, the
guide seizes me by the arm, nearly shoves me over
the cliff, holds me close to the edge and tells me a
frightful tale of some young captain in the constabulary who fell over just in this very spot—'Just
standin' as yer honour might be now.' I am very
much afraid the guide will go suddenly mad and
hurl me over, and am greatly relieved when he
looses his grip and allows me to drift inland.
After this we descend a steep and winding path on
the face of the cliff, a path infinitely more difficult
than the famous Mauvais Pas at Chamouni, and
when we gain the beach we are set upon by a
number of wretched boys who want us to buy bits
of stone and lumps of rock. If there is anything
more uninteresting than another it is geological
specimens. Of all the absurd things to take away
from a place as a reminiscence I think bad building
materials are about the worst. As my friend
Nomad, who has travelled pretty nearly all over the
world, remarked, if he had brought away a ' specimen ' from all the places he had visited he would
be able by this time to build a moderate-sized village. Some people, especially Americans, have
actually been mad enough to order basaltic penta-
gons to make into baptismal fonts, washing basins,
and spittoons. If I were sufficiently enthusiastic
about the columnar formation to buy a column of
five, six, or seven sides, I would certainly super-
intend its removal myself, for I have heard it

rumoured there is a manufactory of these things, and that there is somewhere a large stock of them kept, like the drags of the Royal Humane Society, ' in constant readiness.'

Our guide became wonderfully active when we were pottering about the Causeway. He was continually shouting out ' Bedad, sor, here's the finest pintagon in the place.' 'Shure, yer honour, this is the most perfect di'mond of the whole lot.' ' Look, sor, at this illigant hiptagon !' He showed us the only triangular pillar, and the only three pillars of nine sides that exist in the collection of over forty thousand columns. He pointed out the column ou which Prince Arthur sat to have his photograph taken when he paid this place a visit not long ago, and he gave us, as a relish, a sea-weed which he called *dulse*, which was about the nastiest thing we ever tasted. Those of my readers who care anything about figures may be interested in knowing that there are very few columns of four and eight sides. Ninety-nine out of a hundred are either five, six, or seven. Our guide was too much used to ' doing ' the place to let us have much peace, he seemed to be surprised that we cared to sit down and ' take the whole thing in ' and enjoy it quietly. No sooner did he get us into the Wishing Chair than he hunted us off to the Wishing Well, where we found an old lady who gave us a draught of excellent spring water which we took, and, mindful of the precept of our dear friend Mrs Brown, tempered it freely with Coleraine whiskey, ' to prevent the water a ranklin' in our constitutions.' We made the ancient Hebe mix a tolerably stiff glass for the guide and we bade him fill his pipe. His heart is softened and he has allowed us to return to the Wishing Chair. We also light pipes; the guide has retired, possibly to graze upon *dulse*, and probably will be very ill, and we sit down and meditate and muse in the sunshine. The pic-nic party, we can see, has assembled at last; they have discovered a soft greensward and a sheltered spot under the lee of the Steucans, and most picturesque do the bright dresses of the ladies look dotted about the grassy slope. I should like to spend a morning or two here pottering about the Causeway, gazing upon the grand old Amphitheatre, and imagining new legends and weaving fresh traditions of Fin McCoul and the race of giants, and watching the superb sea come breaking over and eddying amidst the dark wave-worn columns, in its majesty of strength, in its glory of colour, and in its mournfulness of music.

But stay! I see a couple—the girl is pretty enough and the boy old enough to know better—whom we caught just now 'spooning' at the top of the cliff, and who followed us down the steep path; they have just come in sight. The young lady trips from pentagon to hexagon and from hexagon to heptagon and from heptagon to pentagon again so lightly and laughs so merrily that those stern old basaltic columns must feel quite happy. She comes in our direction: when she sees the Wishing Chair is occupied she gives the prettiest little pout in the world and the most bewitching shrug of her shoulders. She looks towards where we are sitting and holds a whispered conversation with her companion. Ah! Nomad, friend of my youth, let us retire. This boy and girl have possibly important wishes to wish. Let us vacate the Wishing Chair and let the boy and the girl revel in a brief belief in sunshine, beauty, and love!

BUBBLES.

'

IT is a matter of the greatest surprise to me that
the blowing of bubbles has never become a
fashionable amusement. I mean the actual blowing of bubbles; the taking of a long churchwarden
pipe, the mixing of a quantity of soap-suds, and
the floating away in the soft summer air of countless
fragile, iridescent globes, and watching them drift
away till they burst. I see endless amusement for
lazy people of fashion. It would be an elegant
pastime, it would require little skill, and it would
be equally attractive and useful for ladies as gentlemen. When a light breeze was blowing, a bubble
race could be organized and bets could be made,
and the excitement would be tremendous. Fancy
what an excellent game bubble-loo would be!
Each player to back his own bubble to last the
longest for whatever sum he pleased. There should
be no restriction as to the kind of soap used or as
to the sort of pipe employed; the individual who
was most cunning in the manufacture of soap-suds
or the most crafty in the construction of pipes
would probably be the winner. Fancy having
'bubbling parties,' imagine being bidden to a five
o'clock bubble! Figure to yourself receiving a card
thus inscribed :—' Lady Ecume de Mer. At Home.
Bubbles at Ten.' Upon my word I think it would

be an excellent idea. The blowing of bubbles would not be more difficult than the majority of fashionable amusements and infinitely more harmless. What a deal of employment it would give to those tradesmen who live upon the novelties that the whirligig of fashion brings round from time to time. Now that croquet has become a science no one cares about it. Indeed, it is no longer a pretty medium for flirtation, an excuse for the exhibition of shapely legs and ankles, and a competitive display of marvellous *bottines*, elaborate embroidery, and snowy frills. It has become lost in the limbo of learned societies, and the 'Croquet Society' will soon take its place with the Numismatic Society, the Statistical Society, and the like hideously uninteresting corporations, and we shall have ancient, learned, solemn gentlemen read wonderfully erudite papers 'On the Antique Form of Tight Croquet,' or 'On the Gradual Decrease of the Size of the Hoop.' Having come to this melancholy pass, of course croquet, as an amusement, cannot be thought of any longer. We want another amusement.

Nothing then can be better than the blowing of bubbles. Do not you see what a field for invention and contrivance it would give. Each giver of bubble parties would introduce some crafty colouring matter into the soap-suds : hence there would be a new surprise in the way of variously-tinted bubbles at every fresh party. People would be wondering how the *celadon* bubbles were produced at the Marquise de Savonnière's last party, and talking of the gigantic bubble blown by Lady

Brown de Windsor at Mrs Sopesnddes' grand
bubble *matinée*. Then cannet you imagine the
charming things in the way of pipes that would be
designed for ladies for this latest form of fashionable frivolity. There would be elegant little instruments, in silver and in gold, in ivory and in china :
they would be elaborately jewelled, they would be
curiously chased and carved, and most artistically
painted. Then I can see that each instrument
would have a quaintly designed *etui* in order that
it might be suspended from the possessor's girdle.
What a pretty sight would be a bevy of fair damsels blowing bubbles. What anxiety they would
evince over their work ! How they would pout
their ripe little lips ! How they would exercise
their bonny *buccinator* muscles, and swell the faint
violet arteries over their temples, and what laughter and merriment there would be over the whole
business. Cannot I fancy the countless charming
pictures that Mr George Du Maurier would give
us in the pages of *Punch* concerning this new
fashionable amusement. I do not know whether
any of my readers have ever tried blowing bubbles.
If not they will find it is a most charming amusement. I really do not see why the children should
monepolize all the games. The Chinese hold this
view, and only old men are allowed to fly kites.
Unfortunately with us, young, middle-aged, and old
men are permitted to ' fly kites.' But that is not
what I mean,—I mean that the use of the actual
toy-kite of our boyhood is especially confined to
old men. I have frequently said before that I
believe there is a good deal of the Chinese element.

in my nature. People say that I look very like
one of the Celestial race. I worship the extremely
little, I hate improvement, I am somewhat in
favour of retrogression. All these characteristics
are eminently Chinese, and now I have found out
another point of similarity. It is this. That I
would not allow all the good games and all the
most emphatically amusing games to be entirely
monopolized by children. Great minds require at
times a great deal of unbending. My mind may
not be particularly great, but I know it requires
an immense deal of unbending. At one time I
used to amuse myself with the noble game of
' puff-and-dart,' at another I revelled in ' battledore
and shuttlecock,' now my greatest joy is ' blowing
bubbles.'

When I have rather more to do than usual, I
call for my pipe, and I call for my bowl, and
straightway begin to blow saponaceous sonnets,
and let them float out of my window and disappear.
You have no idea what a pleasant employment
this is; you cannot conceive what an excellent
thing it is for the mind, and what marvellous
notions occur to my fancy as I see the prismatic
bubbles vanishing one after the other in the sunshine. It is soothing, in the first place, to put
your pipe into the bowl, and hear the delightful
gurgle it makes as you convert the whole surface
of the soap-suds into a mass of bubbles. You
begin to fancy you are a serious tea-kettle on a
wet Sunday afternoon, or a lazy locomotive waiting
at some out-of-the-way country junction. Then
you can continue to blow, and at last you cover the

whole of the basin over with a crystal roof such as
Sir Joseph Paxton never dreamed of. In fact,
there are innumerable suggestions in the operation
I have spoken of. I think it will lead to my bring-
ing out a pamphlet with regard to the construction
of greenhouses and conservatories on an entirely
novel principle. Well, you can keep on bubbling
away like this all day, if you please, for, as I said
before, it is the most soothing thing in the world.
After you have built one or two Crystal Palaces
and half-a-dozen Kew palm-houses, and a few
Chatsworth conservatories, and become very red
in the face, this amusement will, perhaps, pall upon
you a little. Then you may give your mind to the
operation of blowing bubbles properly and wafting
them gently out of your window.

This gentle and poetical occupation, however,
cannot be carried on without some danger. The
prismatic globes floating out in the sunshine will
be sure to attract the attention of passers-by. The
street boys will ' hooray,' and the old gentleman
with an inquiring mind—who appears to be as
ubiquitous as the street boy, and always comes up
and wants to know ' all about it ' at a street accident or free fight—will look on with wonder.
This old gentleman will gaze admiringly at a
gigantic bubble: he will shake his stick at it and
presently the bubble will disappear; the old
gentleman will make just such a wry face as
children make when they are being washed by a
hard-handed nursemaid, and she gives them an
eye full of soap and rubs it well in. If you are
not very careful he will find you out, knock at

your door, and make a complaint to the police. Some old gentlemen are always so ready to interfere with the enjoyment of their fellow-creatures. It would be as well for you to have all your windows open, and not show your pipe, so that people cannot tell where the bubbles come from. For some men are so unreasonable that they object to have 'blobs' of soap on the top of their new white hats, and I have known a lady become quite indignant at a broken bubble descending on her latest Parisian bonnet. When, however, you get a little experienced in bubble blowing you will be able to avoid all these mishaps. You will be able to land soap-and-water in old gentlemen's eyes with the utmost precision, and they will not have the faintest idea where it comes from. One thing I should say to the tyro in bubble blowing. Never be lulled by the bubbling noise into the idea that you are smoking, and be tempted to take an inspiration by mistake. A mouthful of soap-and-water taken unawares is not by any means exhilarating, I can tell you.

Sitting at your window and watching the bubbles float out, being utterly oblivious of the white hats, the new bonnets, the old gentlemen's eyes in the street below, you may fancy you see the failures of life reflected in their prismatic but evanescent colours. In that vast, strong-looking bubble, that seems so proof against wind and sunshine, which sails slowly and steadily along, do you see the Gum Tickler Silver Mine which was to have made your fortune. See how promising it seems; it looks as strong as a gold-fish globe and as flexible as a foot-ball. You watch it anxiously : it sways to and fro. It even touches a window ledge, but it bounds lightly off again, unharmed in any way. You are willing to make a bet that it will go the whole length of the street without coming to grief. You think what a grand bubble it is; you are just about to send off another to catch it: your attention is called away: you look after it, it has vanished entirely, and there is nought but a greasy splodge on the pavement to mark where it fell. Is not that just like your shares in the Gum Tickler Silver Mine? Did not that marvellous project go on so satisfactorily that if you had only sold out at the right time you would have been very comfortably off, but you were so anxious to make a vast fortune at a blow that you listened to the advice of the directors, and let your money remain in till your shares were not worth more than the paper that represented them.

As you send out bubble after bubble, and watch their colours till they burst, you see all these things reflected. There is your ship that never came home, there is your rich uncle who altered his will just before he died, there is the girl of your heart who married some one else—after the usual fashion of girls of your heart : there is your house in Grosvenor Square, there is your villa by the Thames, there is your balance at your bankers, there is your well-appointed carriage and your magnificent horses, there is your schooner yacht, and there is your Venetian *palazzo*. There is your three-volume novel, your comedy, your volume of poems, and your magnificent picture ; there is your eloquent oration, your lucrative government appointment, your seat in the House of Commons, and fifty thousand other things you meant to have accomplished, typified by these bubbles. All, all of them have faded and collapsed sooner or later, after the fashion of the bubbles you are wafting into the sunshine and watching as they disappear.

You will see that after all there is something more than amusement in the blowing of bubbles.

OFF THE RAIL.

I THINK it must be evident to most of those who do me the honour to accompany me in my tiny travels, that I am not very enthusiastic with regard to matters appertaining unto the turf. I am not what would be called a ' horsey man '—or, to use a colloquialism, more expressive than elegant, ' a nossy gent '—and in racing matters I am altogether in a state of the blackest ignorance. I generally fight shy of horse races as much as possible, but I find it impossible to escape from them altogether. Wherever I go I find races are going on. If I visit the uupretentious hamlet of Bumbleton-cum-Slush, I am received by the landlord of the Golden Beadle with a benevolent smirk, and he informs me that I am just in time ' as the races is a comin' off to-morrow.' Up to the minute of his mentioning the circumstance I was not aware that there was such a thing as a race-course within a hundred miles of Bumbleton. If I pass on from this cheerful place to Sniggleby-in-the-Dingle the following week I am sure to find more races going on. When I express my surprise at the circumstance, I am looked upon with the utmost contempt, and I am told ' O, of course, always is so, you know, Sniggleby races always a week after the Bumbleton Cup Day.' I verily believe that if I

were to make an excursion to the island of Cagay
an-Sooloo, pay a visit to the city of Galena, go for
a tour through the province of Okhotz, sojourn for
a time at Palembang, call at the island of Juan Fernandez, rusticate for awhile in the cheerful region
of Senegambia—in short, if I were to go to the
most unlikely places at the most inopportune times
—I should be sure to be just in time for the first
or second day of the races. Seeing all these things,
it was not at all surprising when I happened to be
in Stockton-on-Tees that I should hear that I was
just in time for the races. What people at Stockton want with horse races I cannot imagine. I
never yet saw the race-course in Stockton. There
is another curious fact about these country races,
you always have a difficulty in finding the course.
It is generally a long way from the town, it winds
about and hides itself in a serpentine, sneaking
sort of way for the best part of the year, as if it
were ashamed of itself, and it is only when lined
by a crowd of howling maniacs who shout themselves hoarse for nothing at all, or by following in
the wake of a company of gentlemen with very
tight trousers, very red noses, and very loud scarves
and breast pins that you can discover where the
course may be. Of the thousands of visitors who
go to Brighton in the race-week I suppose there
are very few who could tell you the way to go to
the course. Indeed, I believe some of the inhabitants of the town scarcely wot of its existence. But
I did not intend to 'improve the occasion' with
regard to horse racing, I merely wished to draw
attention to the fact of the way in which the

Houyhnhnms are perpetually persecuting me. I once behaved in a somewhat mean way, and accepted an invitation to a county far removed from Surrey, the day before the Derby; well, I resolved to repeat my meanness on this occasion, to run away and not return till after the saturnalia were over.

My good friend the Friar, noticing my countenance fall when ho mentioned the races were shortly coming off, and that we might attend them, added, by way of a rider, that after all we need not go unless we liked, what did I say to a bit of a tramp for a few days, get beyond railways altogether, out of the reach of telegrams and newspapers? I, of course, was delighted, but said I, ' My good Friar, where can you find all these good things near to your high-pressure, money-making, smoky, manu- facturing, blasting, busy town?' Replied he, ' In Wensleydale; let's go there.' I shouted enthusiastic- ally ' Let's.' He said he thought he knew a Justice of the Peace who would accompany us. My countenance fell a little, though I had often been up before a—but no matter—there was a great novelty in going out on the tramp with a real, live, flesh-and-blood Justice of the Peace. Imagine being able to laugh with a J. P., to jeer at a J. P., to slap a J. P. on the back. Fancy smoking short pipes with a J. P., and sitting in wayside public- houses with a J. P. I protest the very idea put me in tremendous spirits. Moreover our J. P. was a capital fellow, he stood six feet two in his stock- ings, and I verily believe he knew everybody in Wensleydale, from Lord Bolton down to the parish clerk at Redmire : he was well acquainted with

every short cut and was a superb hand at scaling
stone walls. So everything was satisfactorily arranged, and, at about the period when the bell was
ringing to clear the course for the first race, we
found ourselves seated in the train on our way to
Northallerton. When you go on the Continent
you always have a great difficulty in avoiding
Malines, and thus it is when you leave Stockton,
wherever you want to go, it seems to be a matter
of the utmost importance that you should first go
to Northallerton. My first experience of this
station was being turned out to wait there for
the York express on one of the coldest nights
in January I ever recollect. I believe on that
occasion I expressed my opinion of the place and
its arrangements pretty freely and forcibly. Well,
well, let bygones be bygones, I would only remark that Northallerton Station in summer by
daylight, is only two degrees better than Northallerton Station in winter by night. After the usual
abominable amount of waiting and dawdling, we
found ourselves slowly creeping along a single
line which improved as we went on : the very
names of the stations wore a novelty about them.
Fancy Lee ming Lane, Bedale, and Newton-le-Wil-
lows; and what do you say to Finghall Lane, Con-
stable Burton, Spennithorne, and Leyburn ?

A quaint little terminus is this and a quiet little
town is Leyburn. There are very few passengers
get out of the train and the porter collects the
tickets where and how he can, in fact he does not
seem to care much about collecting them at all. A
wagonette, containing Lord Bolton and some ladies,

drives off just as we turn out of the station. We lounge leisurely through the town. I begin to think what a quiet unsophisticated place it is, when to my horror I see ' County Court ' inscribed over a door. I shudder. We go a little farther on and I observe ' County Court ' emblazoned over another lintel. I feel faint. Imagine a small town like this with two county courts. It is horrible. We are all so overpowered by our feelings that we are compelled to rush into the ' Bolton Arms ' and beg of the excellent landlord to give us a draught of his superb ale. I would fain have stopped some time and chatted with this amiable gentleman, who has exactly the figure and bearing a landlord should have, and one rarely to be met with in these degenerate days of thin red wine, but my companions know it would be as fatal to progress as sleep frequently is to Alpine travellers, if I were allowed to have my own way. We are soon out of the town, and ascending a steepish hill we come to a gate inscribed ' To the Shawl.' I have frequently seen in large linendrapers an inscription ' To the Shawl and Mantle Department,' but I was scarcely prepared for anything extraordinary in the way of ladies' dress in a quiet Yorkshire valley. I inquire. J. P. explains that it is not a portion of feminine habiliment, but a steep hill commanding one of the finest views in the valley. The Friar says ' Shawly!' I frown at him. He immediately begins to dance wildly, and sing something about ' Out on the Shawl, boys, out on the Shawl!' That is the worst of the Friar, he will make fun of serious subjects. Serious, yes, I should think it was. Why, bless your heart there are all sorts of historical associations connected with this place. Presently we come to a Roshervillian summer-house at a place called 'Queen's Gap.' We see on a board, which we at first imagined to be a warning with regard to the prosecution of trespassers, a notice to this effect, '*The place where Mary Queen of Scots, according to local tradition, was retaken in her attempt to escape from Bolton Castle where she was a prisoner under the care of Lord Scroope, A.D., 1569.*' The irrepressible Friar is by no means awed by this announcement, but says something about her being under ' *scroopulous care.*' Upon my word I believe he is writing a burlesque. But let us be serious. The view from the Shawl is superb, over wooded terraces and rocky fields, right down to the river Yore, the vast towering eminence of Penn Hill, Bolton Hall embowered amid its grand old trees, the town of Wensley, the little village of Redmire, and—those wretched Houyhnhnms will not let me alone, even up here, for the J. P. will insist upon telling me that ' Over there, you know, is Middleham Moor.' ' Oh, indeed,' I say. ' Yes, Middleham Moor, you know. All the great training stables there, Fobert's, Osborne's, Dawson's, and all the rest of them. If you'd like to go and see them any time——' I put on an injured look, but J. P. rejoiceth fiendishly, and is exceeding glad.

We gradually creep down from the Shawl, through meadows and stone walls, by means of various short cuts well known to J. P. We pass through pleasant pastures, and see sleepy-eyed

cows being milked by men under the grateful shade
of spreading trees. The milking is nearly all done
by men in these parts, and the conventional milk-
maid is almost unknown. We cross the beds of
roaring torrents—I say beds advisedly, for the
weather has been so dry that there are no torrents
—consequently they do not roar, but by the disposition of the huge stones and the worn aspect of
gigantic boulders we can see at a glance what a
noise of rushing water there must be in the winter-
time. There is everything arranged for a mountain
torrent except the stream. It looks as if the inhabitants of Wensleydale had not paid their water
rate, so the supply had been cut off at the main.
We pass the charming residence of Captain Other,
whose volunteer rifle corps, it should be remembered, forms a worthy successor to the Dale's vo-
lunteers of years ago. At last we arrive at Redmire,
a pleasant little village, which, being neither rubicund nor muddy, altogether belies its name. Here
we meet with a youth on a pony, and being somewhat overburdened with our luggage—which, I
believe, consisted of a tooth-brush and a pair of
socks a-piece—we make a bargain with him to
transport our *impedimenta* as far as Askrigg. A
crowd of healthy children collect and look wonder-
ingly on us, and half fancy we are a party of
Prussian Uhlans about to take possession of their
quiet village. They advance upon us, we make a
feint and execute a masterly strategic movement,
and retreat in the direction of the Bolton Arms.
Another Bolton Arms! These admirable institutions seem to abound in this happy valley. This

child is delighted. It is just the kind of place to suit him. Quiet old room, large fire-place, oak settles, gigantic beams and joists, thick walls and window-seats, and last, but by no means least, an amiable landlady and chubby daughters. J. P. seemed perfectly at home here, he addressed his landlady by name, and he inquired after the daughter's cousin, and wanted to know how the cheeses were getting on. Would we like to see the cheeses? said the landlady. Of course we would, we reply. We are taken into a low cool room and see rows upon rows of prime Wensley-dale cheeses. Now a good Wensleydale cheese, I would inform the uninitiated, is by no means to be despised. If you get it in prime condition it is far before either Stilton or Cotherstone. After a deal of consultation and critical examination we select one which it is said will be in prime condition at Christmas. J. P. says I must come down then and see how it turns out. Won't I come then, that's all! Cheered by a draught of excellent shandygaff and saluted by the 'shrill clarion' of the largest tortoiseshell-coloured Cochin China cock I ever saw—he seemed to be about eight times the size of life—we once more started on the tramp. Again across the fields and through the peculiar stiles that abound in those parts, where stone walls do duty for hedges. These stiles con-sist of a flight of rough, loose, irregular steps, and then a Y shaped opening in the wall. The shank of the Y is generally from three to four feet high and frequently so narrow that if a man's *gastrocne-mius* muscle is tolerably developed he has con-

·siderable difficulty in getting through. Arguing from the general construction of these stiles I should say that the dalesmen were by no means strong in the calf department. I am quite certain if 'Mr Jeames, of Buckley square' had attempted the passage of one of these walls he would have had to leave his calves in the embrasure. I tremble to think how terrible must have been the passing through these stiles in the early days of crinoline for the damsels of Wensleydale. I am glad that I knew not the dales in those barbarous times, though I am informed that the girls of Wensleydale have some of the neatest ankles in the north of England. This, however, is a delicate subject. Let us dissemble.

A curious old gentleman, who followed the occupation of tailor, parish clerk, and whitewasher, accompanied us across the fields. He had plenty to say for himself: he had peculiar views with regard to sacred music : he did not think much of the singing at Aysgarth—the choir at Aysgarth, I should tell you, is one of the best for many miles round—but what he did like in the church was the French horn. 'The French horn!' I said in surprise, 'I never heard of such a thing in an English church. I recollect I once looked in at a church at Rouen and found a priest marching up and down between a double row of choristers and blasting away on a bright brass opheclcide till he turned purple, and I thought he would have blown the top of his head off, but the French horn in the Established Church I never——' 'Well, sir,' he replied, with enthusiasm, 'I used to play it in

17

church, there's nothin' like it, it do sound so 'eavenly and so meller!' We say good-bye to this enthusiast and take our way to the left and presently arrive at the foot of Aysgarth Force. Here we are somewhat disappointed by the lack of water. A waterfall without water, is something like *Hamlet* with the part of Hamlet left out. However, we are enabled to walk up the edge of the stream and creep along from rock to rock till we come to what should be the principal fall ; this we find is shrunken almost to a rivulet, and just as we turn the corner we see a couple of hamadryades trip lightly across it, or in prosaic language, a couple of laughing girls, one in pink muslin and the other in white—both with unexceptionable ankles—jump over it. I am glad to find that the rumour with regard to Wensleydale ankles was not without foundation. We cross over the bridge and pause for a moment to look at the magnificent view, both up and down stream. We pay a visit to Aysgarth Church, a church which appears to have been well restored in parts. It is a pity the restoration has not been altogether carried out so well as it might have been ; there are some fine wood carvings inside, many of these were brought from Jervaux Abbey. I believe I am not wrong in stating that the parish of Aysgarth is the largest in England. After leaving the church we come to Palmer's Flat. I do not know why it is called Palmer's Flat, for it seemed to be about the steepest bit of hill of the entire journey. J. P. here said he felt as if he could take a cup of tea. Some of us talked of pushing on further before

we refreshed, but, as the Bench felt hungry and
thirsty, all opposition was waived, and the Bench
and his friends went in to tea. And, ye gods,
what a tea it was! Give ear, ye purveyors of
Pegwell Bay, and perpend, ye harpies of Tea-pot
Street! We had potted trout of the most delicious
description, rosy crayfish of the most delicate
flavour, broiled ham, eggs, cold shoulder of lamb,
pigeon pie, Bath chaps, muffins, tea-cakes, toast,
and tea. The whole in the most unlimited profusion. And what do you think we had to pay
for this glorious banquet? You will never guess,
O cunning reader. Well, then, I will tell you.
One and ninepence each. Here we met the brother
of the gentleman who shot sixty-two and a half
brace of birds on the twelfth, so we argued from
that fact that we should not be badly off for grouse
when we reached Askrigg.

If we mean to reach Askrigg to-night we think
it is time to start. It is already nearly dark, and
there is no moon. The J. P. is joyous, the Friar is
joyous, the present writer is joyous. We all light
pipes and we have a disposition to walk arm in arm
and shout a chorus. The J. P. does not appear to
be so clear in his geography as he was. He says,
after we get about a mile and a half along the road
we shall find a hole in the wall, we have to go
through it, across a meadow, over some stepping-
stones in the Yore, and there you are. The road
gets worse and worse, it is covered with loose,
sharp stones, we feel as if we were walking along
a pathway paved with cricketing shoes with the
spikes uppermost. It is getting darker and

darker. J. P., after feeling a wall all over for some
distance, says it is all right. He suddenly disappears as if he had been a ghost, the Friar shouts,
' Here it is ! ' and he vanishes into thin air. I begin to think my case is a desperate one, but I hear
J. P and the Friar talking to one another. It
appears to be many miles off. I walk straight on,
find I go right through a stone wall—there is a
crash and a stumble, and I find myself sitting
upon sharp stones in the middle of a field. Like
Mr Micawber, I think I will wait for something to
turn up, and presently I am run over by the Friar
and J. P., who look as if they were playing at
blind man's buff, or practising swimming on dry
land. They announce that they cannot discover the
stepping-stones. It takes us about a quarter of an
hour to find our way out of the field. We are
once more on the road again, we pass through the
little town of Worton, and nearly capsize a most
ricketty, ramshackle bridge across the Yore. We
then indulge in a nocturnal steeple-chase of the
most lively description ; we go over stone walls,
we have showers of boulders down on our heads,
dilapidated gates fall on our shoulders; we go
through farmyards, and invade private property
freely. It seems to be a general axiom in these
parts, you may go wherever your legs can carry
you : if there is no stile you may jump over the
wall. If you cannot jump over the wall you may
kick it down and go through it. After steeple-
chasing in this way for about half an hour, during
which time I must, at a moderate computation,
have gone over, or through, at least sixteen stone

walls, we go up some steps, we go through a cow-
yard, we tumble down some steps, we run up
against a tub, we pass along a dark alley, we
nearly fall down all in a heap on the road, and we
find ourselves in Askrigg.

Not a little weary we are glad enough to find
ourselves at the comfortable and well-appointed
' King's Arms.' It is a quaint, rambling, old-fashioned place, but I find my Nemesis is down upon
me again. The Houyhnhnms are determined ' to
take it out of me ' for running away from Stockton
races. I find that this inn was formerly the mansion of John Pratt, the father of the English turf,
who died in 1785, and who was the first man who
reduced book-making to a system, and who,
strange to say, made a lot of money out of his turf
speculations. Quaint rooms with very wide doors
with their numbers inscribed in chalk, thick heavy
window-sashes, chambers opening one into the
other, about half-a-dozen ways to everywhere in
the house, vast stables and wonderfully-arranged
kennels, a large garden sloping up from the back
of the house, with a terrace-walk, whence there is
a marvellous view of Addlebrough and the surrounding country. Evidently Mr John Pratt had
no mean idea of what an English mansion should be.

Three days we spent pleasantly enough making
excursions in the neighbourhood and returning to
this excellent hostelry at eventide. We went to
Bainbrigg, we bathed in Seemer Water, we visited
Colby Hall, we explored Mill Gill and many other
places in this out-of-the-way neighbourhood, at
present untainted by railway, and unprofaned with

the shriek of the locomotive. The fourth day we proposed to wend our way homewards.

Of course the present writer was late down to breakfast. He came down rubbing his eyes and found the Friar making havoc with the cold grouse and the J. P. nearly up to his eyes in scarlet cray-fish shells. The Friar had been for a walk round the village and the J. P. had been making calls, and they reproached their friend with his laziness. However, he took not much notice of their jibes and their sneers, for he did not expect to be thoroughly awake for the next hour.

'Ah, he isn't up to the mark somehow,' said J. P.

'Went to bed too early,' was the reply almost inaudibly grunted.

'Ah, if you had only gone in with me to see Mr Publius,' continued J. P. I should tell you this gentleman's name was not Publius, but as I remember a certain individual, ' who was the chief man of the island,' was so named, and as this gentleman is the chief inhabitant of the village I elect to call him Publius. ' If you had only gone and spent the evening with Mr Publius,' repeated the J. P., ' you would have been all right. First-rate evening, I can assure you. Young Publius, you know, is a capital fellow. Miss Publius and her sister charming girls. They play admirably. We had plenty of music. They wanted to hear your songs. Jolly evening : capital supper : su-perb grouse pie : magnificent whiskey and long pipes in Mr Publius's sanctum afterwards. Plenty of fun, talk, and gossip : didn't get back here till I don't know what time.'

'My dear J. P., do not babble to me of these pleasures. You see I could not possibly have gone last night. In the first place, I left my razor behind me, and consequently have not shaved for three days; in the second place, I am so lame that I can scarcely toddle; in the third place, the gay and festive throng, the charming girls, the music, the grouse pie, the splendid whiskey, are not for the likes of me. Time was when I could—but no matter. Allow me to drop a manly tear. But no, on second thoughts, I'll have another cup of tea! And so we're going back to smoke and bustle and business and general turmoil to-day, are we?'

'Why, I thought you were tired of this ever-lasting tramp and quiet?' said the Friar.

'Not at all; I am but just getting acclimatized as it were. Just as I begin to like anything, it is taken away from me. "'Twas ever thus from childhood's hour. I never loved a wild gazelle." By the way a wild gazelle is about the last thing I should think of loving. But I never loved a wild young girl but that she was sure to go and marry the wrong man. And now I am just getting to like these Yorkshire dales and I have to leave them——'

'There is no doubt about it,' said the J. P. impressively, 'he is *not* up to the mark. There's something wrong somewhere. But anyhow it is time for us to be off.'

Our bill was soon settled; it came to one pound fifteen the three of us for three days. Our luggage was quickly packed up, and left for the mail cart to call for. J. P.'s baggage was not so easily arranged, for nearly everyone he knew in the dale had presented him with a brace of grouse, and if he had been obliged to carry all these good gifts home, he would have looked more like a perambulating poulterer than anything else. We made arrangements for the birds to be delivered to the official who took charge of Her Majesty's Mails, and said good-bye to Mrs Lee, patted the kind-eyed old hound Sampson on the head, and left the 'King's Arms,' Askrigg, with no little regret. More stony roads ; past pleasant little cottages and farms, we then strike into pastures, and indulge in our favourite occupation of steeple-chasing. We take in our homeward walk the opposite bank of the Yore ; we pass under the shade of gigantic elms, we scatter lazy sheep and ford purling brooks. At last we reach the outskirts of a grand old mansion ; there is a vast avenue of trees, beneath which the cows are milked, and there are grave old rooks sleepily swinging, and clerically cawing, in their topmost branches. We then walk across a soft bit of emerald-green sward, littered with rooks' feathers, and we find ourselves opposite to an arch-way with massive gates, rivetted and beclamped in the most substantial manner, and, moreover, decorated with hinges, and a knocker of most quaint design and ancient workmanship. These doors are partially open, and a handsome little colley pup pokes his head out and yelps a welcome and wags his tail. We enter and find ourselves in a spacious courtyard, and think we ought to hear the tramp of horses and the clank of steel. Sure enough such noises did resound in this court-

yard in past days, for we are now facing the somewhat famous Nappa Hall. This was formerly the
head-quarters of the Metcalfe clan, which is still
so numerous in this happy valley. From this
hall three hundred Metcalfes, all mounted on white
horses and clad in uniform, rode forth in attendance
on the high sheriff, Sir Christopher Metcalfe, when
he met the judges of assizes in York in 1556.
As the Friar inconsiderately remarks, he was not
christened 'Met-calfe,' because he met the judge
of assize. This is frivolous, and at the same time
somewhat insulting to the Bench.

What a grand old place is this Nappa Hall. I
wish some one would leave it to me along with a
couple of thousand pounds to put it in good repair.
I should like to ' make believe' to be a baron. I
should like to pretend, as children say, to be a
feudal chieftain. I really think I would at once
exchange my distinguished patronymic in favour
of Metcalfe, if I had such a chance offered me.
Nappa Hall is at present a farm, and the J. P. being
acquainted with the lady who has it—as I said
before, J. P. knew everybody—we knock at the door
under the massive porch, and she courteously allows us to wander as we please over the grand old
building. The large hall, which it is said was
formerly the kitchen, is a grand old room with a
vast fireplace—just the spot to burn gigantic yule
logs—carven presses and sideboards. What a hall
it would be for Sir Roger de Coverly! Cannot you
imagine perching the village fiddler on the oak
dresser and putting a black jack continually replenished with strong old ale by his side, and then

—going it. 'Fol-de-rol, de riddledy; fol-de-rol, de riddledy! Fol-de riddledy, *riddledy*, RIDDLEDY. —Fol-de-rol, de riddledy!' Through all the intricacies of that interminable dance till the fiddler became blind drunk and the guests dropped exhausted on the floor. The kitchen proper, too, is a grand apartment—its rows of saucepans and stewpans, its bright copper kettles and cauldrons winking and blinking as if they were all sitting for their portraits to Teniers, and were afraid they did not look bright enough. From the kitchen we wind up the tower staircase, and from this ivy-clad battlemented eminence we have a superb view of the valley. The Friar was inconsiderate enough to remark that *Napper* Hall ought to have been situated in Sleepy Hollow. I am glad to say that this remark was received by his friends with that silent contempt it deserved. Half way down from the tower we open a door and enter the cheese-room, and see a wonderful collection of Wensleydale cheeses. The J. P. is anxious to secure one of these: we, however, dissuade him, there are no mail carts handy, and to lug a good-sized unctuous Wensley-dale cheese for fifteen miles in the broiling sunshine is no joke at all, I can tell you. Passing from the cheese-room through a low doorway we see a massive oak bedstead, which Mary Queen of Scots is said to have slept in. It is a very fine piece of workmanship, but is in a most dilapidated condition. I wish Mr Sly, of the 'King's Arms,' Lancaster, who has such a superb collection of ancient bedsteads, or some such enthusiast would take it in

hand.   It is a pity it should perish for want of a
little care and carpentry.

With considerable difficulty do we tear ourselves
away from Nappa Hall.   The present writer would
have liked to stay all day here and indulge in his
favourite amusement of pottering about.   The
Friar, however, cunningly holds out a bait to him
and tells him about a mile further is a certain hostelry at Woodhall, where there is some superb
Burton ale to be had.   Whereat his fellow traveller's gruesome countenance relaxeth and he begin-
neth to chant a merry ditty running somewhat in
this wise :—

> ' O, Wensleydale of pleasure,
>   O, Woodhall doubly blest !
> O, Burton ale and leisure,
>   And—I forget the rest ! '

We presently reach the hostelry known as the
' Fox and Hounds ' and find the landlady busily
engaged in making bread, and her husband, a
weather-beaten, mahogany-coloured individual, of
merry countenance, paring apples and cutting them
into slices for the Sunday pie.   His velveteens, his
thick boots, and his gaiters betoken him to be of
the game-keeping persuasion, and we find out that
he is the hind, or steward, to the crackest of crack
shots and most enthusiastic of fishermen in these
parts.   He tells us of innumerable successes that
the captain has had with his gun, how the captain
walked four men off their legs on the second, how
the captain caught the biggest trout ever pulled out
of the Yore.   The good man's eyes brighten, he stops

paring his apples, and he gets quite enthusiastic as he tells of these great deeds done in field and flood. The captain, one can see at a glance, is his hero and must be a vastly good master as well as the most skilful of sportsmen. Not at all a bad sort of life to lead, after all, would this game-keeper's be. I would just as soon pare apples and think about nothing as weave essays and drive quills for the British public. It would be infinitely more agreeable to walk round the fields with one's gun than to be hunted by printer's devils; and I fancy the roar of the mountain torrent would be pleasanter to the ear than the clank and buzz of the throbbing printing press. We have no time for moralizing however, and if we had, probably our friend in the velveteens would not care to listen to us. We say good-bye to him and leave him paring his apples. I dare say he is paring apples at this present moment, as fit an emblem of eternity as Fuseli's celebrated one of the two serious men cutting fat bacon in St Martin's Lane. We take our way over rocky fields—so rocky, indeed, that we wonder how it is possible for the big trees and hardy thorn-bushes to find any hold for their roots or nourishment for their branches: we come to a high wall over which we climb by means of a craftily-contrived ladder, a ladder that would baffle a dog, puzzle a weasel, and mystify a stoat. We descend into the enclosure and find ourselves in the most celebrated rabbit warren in England. This fact did not, however, overawe the irrepressible Friar, for he immediately remarked that he considered our visit was a most *unwarren-table* intrusion. The

very rabbits shuddered when they heard this frivolous remark, and the J. P. was observed to shed
tears.

I believe there is only one other warren in England where this peculiar breed of rabbits is to be
found, and that I think is in Lincolnshire. These
are the celebrated silver-grey rabbits : the skins of
these little animals are very valuable, they are all
sold to one agent, and the majority of them are sent
to Russia. I wish I could find out where this agent
resided, for I should much like to obtain a set of
rabbit-skins to present unto my lady love. I am
certain my Baby Bunting would look charming in
silver-grey rabbit-skin. A set of sables you know
is getting so common, but really I think a set of
rabbit-skins would be a very great novelty. Despite the Friar's idiotic remark, the rabbits did not
resent our intrusion on their domain at all. They
sat up on their hind legs and winked at us, they
leered out of their burrows at us—they knew, as
that irrepressible Friar remarked, no Reform
Bill could disfranchize them—they gave us a military salute with their ears, and frisked and gam-
boled around us as if they were rather glad to
see us than otherwise, and looked upon the call as
a delicate piece of attention on our part. The
ground seemed literally alive with them : thousands
and thousands were scampering about on every
side, and a select guard of honour consisting of five
hundred picked silver-greys attended us as far as
the gate, presented ears, and winked a courteous
good-bye to us, as we departed. This made things
very pleasant for all parties. Outside this encamp-

ment we come to a formidable moat in the way of
a stream, too deep to wade, and too wide to jump.
We have to retrace our steps until we reach some
stepping stones : this throws us out of our proper
track. We skirt a nut copse, and begin gathering
nuts. The J. P. says he is very fond of nuts, and
tempting clusters lead him on from one tree to another, and at last we lose sight of him altogether.
Presently he is heard shouting that there is a short
cut through the copse. For once we do not believe
him, but fancy his reason is blinded by his love of
nuts. As that incorrigible Friar says, ' He is so nuts
upon nuts that he is off his nut.' We quietly skirt
the edge of the plantation, expecting to see our
friend presently waving his hat from a distant hill.
Nothing is heard of him. We find a soft bit of turf
and sit down. We shout. No answer. O! J. P.,
J. P. ! why didst thou turn aside from the paths of
virtue, and go ahankering after nuts ? At last the
Friar points to the upper part of the nut-copse.
We see the foliage trembling. Period of intense
suspense ! Several of the largest trees are violently
agitated. Moment of acute agony ! ! The J. P.'s
hatless head protrudes from the leafy shade; a
bunch of nuts is gripped firmly in his mouth. He
mounts the wall, he loses his balance, we see one
of his boot soles high in the air. We are prepared
for the worst ! He makes a superhuman effort and
by several Titanesque contortions recovers himself.
Then comes a roar as of thunder, and a falling
shower of stones, as from an avalanche. About a
quarter of a mile or so—at a moderate computation
—of stone wall is knocked down, and the J. P. is

landed safely, but somewhat ignominiously on his
back in the middle of a soft-ploughed field. His
trusty friends receive him with open arms and
shrieks of inconsiderate laughter, and the trio take
their way to Carperby singing a merry song.

Quaint little Carperby, with its ancient village
cross, its grey cottages, its pleasant old houses and
their gay gardens. At one of the gayest of these
the J. P. pauses. A charming old lady he tells us
lives there, and he must make a call. We walk on
and tell him if he is not very quick we shall look
in at the 'Barley Sheaf,' and test the quality of its
liquor. We lounge on a gate : the lady sends out
word that we must stay and dine with her—she
will hear no refusal. Unfortunately, we have to
catch a certain train at Leyburn, and we begin to
be conscious of the misery of once more being
under the thraldom of railways and telegrams.
We are thus reluctantly compelled to refuse her
kind invitation. As a sort of compromise, however, the J. P. presently appears with an armful of
cakes and apricots, and we bless the good old lady
as we munch them going across the fields to Bolton
Castle. The grand old pile looks superb, with the
sunshine full on it, and lowering purple-grey clouds
behind it ; bright bits of colour in the foreground
are formed by the lazy cattle, and flocks of pee-wits
are eddying close to the ground. We enter the
castle and are courteously received by a kind old
lady who looks like a dowager duchess in reduced
circumstances, and who gives us a lengthy history
of the castle to peruse. It is of a kind of literature
that may be denominated Murrayesque, therefore

we do not care much about it.   What, however,
we do care about is the superb view from the tower.
We visit the bed-chamber of Mary Queen of Scots,
and we descend to the deepest dungeon, candle in
hand.   The present writer was delighted with the
vast solid masonry and began to contrast it with
the stucco abominations of the present day ; he
launched forth upon the inferiority of everything of
the nineteenth century, and he wound up with his
customary diatribe with regard to railways, electric
telegraphs, newspapers and ' improvement.'

This lasted all across the fields.   He was luckily
stopped by our arrival at Redmire and the sight
once more of the ' Bolton Arms.'   Here we have
luncheon.   We are treated with the greatest courtesy ; we are shown into an inner room and set-to
manfully at the good things provided.   The J. P.
espies a piano, and when we have satisfied our
hunger he insists upon the Tiny Traveller giving
one of his ditties ; he, of course, bows to the
decision of the Bench, and creates a considerable
sensation.   The landlady is lost in admiration in
the back-room, and her daughters pause in their
occupation in the kitchen ; a travelling packman
who is taking a mug of ale is considerably
astonished, and a farmer on horseback just outside the open window looks not a little horrified.
Leaving Redmire we vary our homeward route
by going through Bolton Park.   The shade of
the grand old trees we find to be vastly pleasant,
and the views at every turn amply repay us for
this slight *détour*.   We notice the deer browsing
beneath the trees, and innumerable pheasants,

arguing well for the 1st of October. Bolton Hall itself is by no means worthy of the park, it is a plain, uninteresting-looking building. For my own part I would rather live in the steward's house, a charming residence with a lovely garden close to the park gates. As we pass this we catch a glimpse of the steward in his library, we hear the sound of a piano, and see two of the steward's lovely daughters idly knocking the croquet balls about on the lawn. I protest I should like to know the steward, and much as I abominate the game, play croquet with his daughters.

Outside the park gates we come to the village of Wensley, from which the dale takes its name. The principal object of note here is a superb elm with a rustic seat beneath it just at the entrance to the village. After this we have to travel one of the dustiest bits of road we ever experienced, a road trying both to feet and temper. We begin to get serious, for our liberty is coming to a close. The J. P. begins to think about his Bench, and, returning to the realms of respectability, feels in his pocket for his gloves : the Friar begins to think about his monastery, and arranges his cowl accordingly : and the chronicler of these adventures begins to think about the miseries that the return to railways, telegrams, and civilization will entail. The three worthies are all sad. They have a final libation at the Bolton Arms, Leyburn, they walk down to the quaint little railway station, they collect their luggage, and take their seats in the train. The bell rings, the whistle blows, the train slowly moves out of the station. Once more they are on the rail, and their brief holiday is at an end.*

* [Note. While this book is going through the press I read the following bit of information in the *Northern Echo*: —'The new line which the North-Eastern is constructing from Leyburn to Hawes will not be finished before 1876. It is only seventeen miles long, and it was commenced last December, so it is evident that the line is not likely to be spoiled by being pushed on too fast. When completed the Hawes branch will have four stations—Keld Head, Redmire, Aysgarth, and Askrigg—and 100 bridges, all built of grit-stone save one, which will cross the Ure before reaching Hawes, which will be of iron girders, 114 feet span. There will be some cuttings through limestone, clay, and gravel, averaging 25 feet in depth—one however, through gravel, is 40 feet deep—and extending altogether two miles and a quarter in length. There will be no tunnels, but a retaining wall on the side of the Ure beyond Aysgarth, for 1,000 yards. The line passes to the north of Bolton Hall, runs close by Aysgarth Force and Bearpark, and runs for a mile and a half past the famous Wappa Warren of Lady Mary Vyner, where are kept the silver-grey rabbits for which the place is famous. Wensleydale is perturbed by the invasion of the navvy, and her natives are unable to accommodate the horny-handed throng; they are, therefore, on several parts of the line, lodged in temporary huts erected by the contractors. The opening of the line may not bring much traffic to the North-Eastern, but it will open up to the public a beautiful and secluded dale, and connect the system of the North-Eastern with that of the Midland.' The glory of Wensleydale is departing, and in a few years' time it will probably be impossible to get 'Off the Rail' in any part of England.]

OVER THE WAY.

'I BELIEVE, sir,' said our old friend, Mr Richard Swiveller, on the occasion of his letting the apartments of Mr Sampson Brass, in Bevis Marks, 'that you desire to look at these apartments. They are very charming apartments, sir. They command an uninterrupted view of—of over the way, and they are within one minute's walk of—of the corner of the street. There is exceedingly mild porter in the immediate vicinity, and the contingent advantages are extraordinary.' It may be remembered that the single gentleman to whom all this was said immediately took the apartments. Whether it was Mr Swiveller's eloquence that charmed him, or whether he was struck with the advantage of being within one minute's walk of the corner of the street, or whether he was a lover of exceedingly mild porter, or whether he prized especially the 'contingent advantages'—it is impossible to say. My own private impression is that he took them on account of the uninterrupted view they afforded of 'over the way.'

You may get more amusement from an uninterrupted view of over the way than you can from an extensive prospect from the top of a mountain. For my own part, I hate your extensive views, where you gaze into miles of illimitable mist, and people declare that you are looking into thirty-two different counties. I never believe this myself. I am quite certain I never in my life looked into thirty-two different counties at the same time. However, I try to look impressed, and as if I thought it were a great advantage to be able to do so. If I thought by raising my little finger I could look into thirty-two different counties at once, I would not do it. It is quite enough—indeed, it is too much for me to gaze into one, and very much better should I enjoy simply to confine my studies and my gazings to over the way. In this paper I shall confine myself to a Lilliputian lounge, a microscopic ramble, the very tiniest of travels. There is nothing I like better than the frivolous, the insignificant, the unimportant, the extremely little. No panoramas of unknown length, no scampering over the boundless prairie for me, I thank you, but a few little miniatures and an excursion or two over the way, if you please.

I am rather fortunate in my situation for prosecuting my studies, for I have a good many ' over the ways' to gaze upon from the window at which I am writing. A variety presents itself to me if I only turn my head to the right hand or to the left. There is a big hall, of vile design, a debased Gothic hybrid monstrosity, approached by a bridge, the whole having the appearance of a theatrical scene. You could imagine a rush across the bridge, and a terrific combat in the moat below. This idea is strengthened by the fact that the bridge is out of proportion to the hall and the moat, and the figures moving across it from time to time look

about three sizes too large for it. I will dismiss
this vile bit of architecture from my consideration
altogether, and I will gaze on a well-seasoned,
dark, brown-red brick building, with grey stone
facings. Such brown-red bricks and grey stone
facings that you always associate, I do not know
why, with Hogarth. Heavy, thick window-sashes,
broad white window-frames, and a tiled roof.
Many of the windows in this stack are very dirty,
and it is very difficult to see through them. A
great many have white blinds. Some pulled right
down, others half down, others a quarter, others
three-quarters, and some not down at all. You
never in the whole course of your life saw such a
number of blinds of every tint of musty yellow
and every variety of dirty white. At one of these
windows which is cleaner than the rest I have
noticed a gentleman who appears to be hard at
work long before I am up in the morning, and I
often see his light burning when I go to bed at
night. He seems to be everlastingly wallowing in
parchment and playing the part of Laocoon to endless skeins of red tape that seem to be eternally
frisking around him. This is the Long Vacation, too! I wonder whether this hard-working
man ever has a vacation, or whether he ever enjoys
himself. Perhaps perpetual hard work, everlasting
wallowing in parchment, and entanglement in red
tape is his idea of a holiday. Perhaps some day
the skins of parchment will close around him and
smother him, or the skeins of red tape will tighten
about his throat and choke him. I wonder whether
this man has any friends or relations. Has he a

wife or a family? Does he ever go home? Or
are those dusty musty chambers his home? A
weary sort of place to live in one would think : a
dreary sort of a place to die in.   It makes me
melancholy to gaze at this exemplary man's window
and see him always hard at work in such a me-
thodical fashion.   He is a standing reproach to me
whenever I look out of window, which is generally
all day long.   I would not mind if he would occasionally relax.   But his persistent virtue is
somewhat monotonous.   If he would come home
drunk, now and then, and begin to pelt passers-by
with inkstands, or wave parchment skins out of
window like a flag, or 'bob' for eminent, Queen's
Counsel with lengths of red tape.   If he would only
do any of these things I should be charmed.   I protest I should be hugely delighted if he would throw
up his window and shout 'Ahoy!' to me across
the gardens, or if he were to make derisive gestures
at me, or flourish a pewter pot in token of there
being 'no animosity' between us.   If any of these
things were to take place I should have some hope
for him.   But I see no prospect whatever of such a
consummation devoutly to be wished coming
about.   His shameless industry, his indecent pro-
priety, and his violent virtue are too much for any
man, and I fear he will come to a bad end.

I turn from this terrible picture to one that is
infinitely more pleasant. Between my sham Gothic
hall and my Hogarthian stack of buildings I get a
glimpse of another old brick house, not so old as
the first stack to which I alluded, but still old
enough to be comfortable, old enough to be quaint,

and with none of the taint of modern carpentry and
little of the curse of stucco about it. There is a
pretty balcony to one of these windows, it is filled
with gay flowers; there is a bird-cage, there are
muslin window curtains, and a brightness, a smart-
ness, and an elegance about the whole place that
show a woman's influence throughout. Now, if I
were put upon my oath I could not swear that there
was a lady resident in these rooms, simply because
I have never seen her, but I know she must be there.
These rooms are not easy to see into, and so my
statement must be taken as somewhat theoretical.
The roller blinds are never pulled quite up, and the
muslin blinds veil the lower part of the window.
But once or twice I have seen the prettiest little
plump, dimpled, white hand shown at the window
on the blind-tassel. Such a charming little hand!
and as Professor Owen is enabled to build up an
entire animal from some fragments of its vertebræ,
so I have pictured the damsel from catching but a
casual glimpse of her hand. I am certain she is a
young lady, a pretty one, and a very charming one.
Moreover, I have further evidence on this matter.
The centre window, with the balcony, is a French
window, opening to the ground, and one morning
I was surprised to see the folds of a fresh lilac print
dress, a suspicion of snowy tucks, and a hint of
pleated frills; beneath all this peeped out from
time to time a pair of neat little feet exquisitely
slippered and faultlessly stockinged. I have established some important points in my theory. A girl
with good hands and feet, with a fresh, crisp, morning dress and spotless *lingerie* must have a great deal

of the lady about her. I had noticed a young fellow
depart every morning at a regular hour, and I had
occasionally seen the white dimpled little hand
wave to him when he reached the street below.
So I concluded that this must be the happy man,
but that his happiness was always interrupted by
his being obliged to rush off to some terrible office
every morning at ten o'clock. One evening, I do
not know whether my young friends were having
a party or not, but the light was unusually bright
in their rooms. The young lady was sitting in one
position for a long period, and I had her profile
reflected on the blind with all the force and distinctness of a *silhouette*. I then could see that her
profile was very pretty indeed. I saw another
profile, which I at once knew to be that of the
young fellow whom I see leave for his office every
morning, approach it. The two profiles seemed to
meet. Ah! well, well, they are happy enough I
daresay. I wonder whether the little lady ever
gazes from behind her ambushment of bird-cages,
flowers, and muslin curtains, and takes pity on the
solitary wretch who glares out of his window over
the way. I wish the little lady would ask me over
to have a cup of tea some evening with them. I
should like to know a great deal more of these
people. I am vastly interested in them. I wonder
whether I shall ever meet the little lady of ' over
the way' and be introduced to her, and whether
she will realize the high estimation—arguing from
her hands, her ankles, and her profile—I have
already formed of her. Let us hope I shall not be
disappointed.

Years ago in Venice cannot I recal some of my 'over the way' experiences? My bed-room was situate at the back of the Hotel Vittoria, looking across one of the smaller canals. It was, tolerably shady, and I used to throw open the large wooden shutters and smoke a dreamy cigarette there of an afternoon. I used to be almost lulled to sleep by the swish-swash of the gondolas passing below, and the monotonous shout of the gondoliers as they swung sharply round corners. I used to gaze at the damp, weed-covered, scaly walls, the odd barred windows, the queer doors, the wonderful colour of the brick-work and tiling, the curious chimney-pots, and the elaborate tangle of rusty ironwork. Up at a quaint window, so quaintly carven were its mouldings that it almost looked like a frame to my picture, was a dark-eyed damsel. She was generally singing to her own accompaniment somewhere in the inner part of the room, and I used to announce my presence by swinging back my wooden shutters with a terrific bang against the masonry. I used to time this so as to come just at the end of her song, and then she used to come to her window, and I used to shout *Brava, brava!* across the canal. She then used to bow and smile sweetly, like a pretty *prima donna*, bowing from the quaintest private box in the world. Then she used to take up some work and pretend she did not see me, but she would occasionally look up slily, and send such glances 'over the way' that well-nigh drove me distracted. We were obliged to confine our love-making principally to glances, for you cannot make love as if you were hailing a ship. Probably, such form of love-making would suit such men as Captain Cuttle or Jack Bunsby; there would be an out-spoken honesty, an ' above-boardedness ' that would be quite in harmony with these rough sea-worthies. But it would not do for us in these days. So we nodded and smiled and blew kisses, and did all the idiotic things that young people usually do under such circumstances. It was not at all a bad way of spending a lazy afternoon, and the picture comes back to me just now with vivid distinctness in connection with studies made ' over the way.'

I once made a somewhat extensive trip in the prosecution of this study. Indeed, it was a sort of panorama, or a gigantic gallery of over-the-way studies. One Christmas-day I took my seat on an omnibus knife-board, and rode from Hyde Park Corner to the Bank, and back again from the Bank to Hyde Park Corner. From my post of observation I was enabled to see all that was going on over the way along the entire route, and then turn round and see what was going on on the other side of the way. Hence I was enabled to study both sides of the way with very little trouble. The variety of views people had about Christmas was something astonishing, and the variety of things that did duty as Christmas decorations was somewhat astounding. Many people seemed to be enjoying themselves prodigiously, and many people looked utterly miserable. I saw the mock joviality, the forced geniality, and the fictitious spirit of forgiveness and love degenerating into blank despair in many instances. From my vantage ground I

could see the assemblage of these most detestable
of all entertainments—'family parties.' I noted
the arrival of the pompous uncles with waistcoats
like unto that worn by Responsible Bonsor, immor-
talized by Mr George Augustus Sala, the mischief-
making aunts with impossible caps and armour-
plated skirts. I perceived the arrival of gibbering
grandfathers and garrulous grandmothers, and the
whole collection of those detestable relations that
always sets everybody by the ears on such occasions.
I saw all this, and I grinned as I was rapidly borne
along. It was not a satisfactory manner of studying over the way, however. You saw too much,
and had not time to appreciate each portion sufficiently.

A very pretty 'over the way' picture is a
balcony full of girls at the sea-side. Indeed, I do
not know anything much prettier. Just imagine
you are passing along the parade of some fashionable maritime resort, and you hear your own name
called out from a first floor, and you look up and
you see a 'balcony of beauties.' Why, bless you,
Tennyson's 'rosebud garden of girls' is nothing
to it! There they are in all their glory, in their
piquante costumes and pretty hats looking as bonny
as girls can only look at the sea-side. You get
every variety of pose in a balcony. See that
slender girl with just the tips of her boots showing
beyond the balcony, and her pretty soft white
drapery pouting through the ironwork, as she
leans forward to speak to you, stretching her arms
over the handrail, and touching the tips of her
fingers together. Note how exquisitely her face is

thrown into shadow by her broad hat, but what pure luminous shadow it is. Observe, if you please, how quaint does Supple Sixteen look as she clasps the verandah's support and coquettishly glances at you through its intricate pattern; observe how Sweet Seventeen has seated herself on a low stool and, half-hidden by her sister's skirts, is dreaming over a novel. Observe how Fretful Five with her spade, her huge sun-bonnet, her sea-stained boots, her loose socks, and her brown legs is pressed up against the railings till one fears she may be trellised for life. Observe how Troublesome Twelve, in the shortest of short frocks and the frilliest of frilled trouserettes, is romping about and threatening to dance the balcony right down at no very remote period. Observe all these things and imagine everybody is asking you different questions at once and all wanting an immediate answer at the same time. Figure to yourself, glorious sunshine and the salt breeze sighing, and say if it is not a perplexing though most agreeable fashion of studying ' Over the Way.'

WHITSUNTIDE WANDERINGS.

'WHENEVER I see a beadle in full fig coming down a street on a Sunday at the head of a charity school,' said Mr Meagles, 'I am obliged to turn and run away or I should hit him.' Now, I happen to have a friend who has just this feeling towards excursionists. He never sees an excursionist but he wishes to hit him, and he never encounters a tourist but he desires to kick him. I expect some day my friend will be locked up in a foreign dungeon for braining some inoffensive be-Murrayed individual with his umbrella in the Colosseum at Rome, or kicking some harmless gentleman, clad in a light suit, from the top to the bottom of the Scala dei Giganti at Venice. The very sight of an excursionist is to him what a red rag is to a bull. This individual, this friend of mine, was a particularly nice person to be with at Brighton on Whit-Monday, was he not? Brighton, which positively reeks with excursionists at such a time, which flaunts its nine hours of sea breezes for three shillings—or four minutes of fresh air for a farthing—in the face of Whitsuntide holiday-folk. Brighton, which offers every inducement in the way of shrimps and cheap dinners, of economical sailing boats and inexpensive conveyances. Brighton, which is within reach of minor lions, such as Arundel, Chichester, Shoreham Gardens, Lewes, the Dyke, and fifty other places beloved by the excursionist. Brighton was certainly a nice place to be at with a man of my friend's peculiar temperament. I could not lock him up in-doors, for he was bent upon going an excursion himself. I was afraid to walk with him along the streets, for the manner in which he exploded, snorted, jeered, glared, and threatened the excursionist was something very terrible to behold. Indeed, I was compelled to resort to any stratagem to get my friend away from Brighton, for I believe if he had remained there for half an hour longer he would have been given in charge of the police. I managed craftily to insinuate that if we were to depart from Brighton we should get quite clear of holiday-folk. I ventured to propose an excursion to Littlehampton. Now in my heart of hearts I imagined there would be quite as much turmoil and Whit-Mondayism at Littlehampton as anywhere else, but you see I am not so well known at Littlehampton as I am in Brighton. If my friend kicked an excursionist or two into the Arun, or choked half-a-dozen ' trippers '—as they are called in the north—with their own sandwiches, it would not so much matter. Possibly the reporter of the *Littlehampton Looker-on* might be squared for half-a-sovereign—at any rate my friend's playful eccentricities would be unknown to the world at large.

With the greatest difficulty I managed to persuade him to start to Littlehampton, and the manner in which he behaved himself when jammed tightly in a seething mass of excursionists, some-

just arriving at and some just departing from the
railway station, were alike creditable to his hand
and heart.   One thing, he was unable to move either
hand or foot, or I think he would have popped in
his left or made some clever play with his boot
heel.   His manly bosom, I am told, has at this
moment the impression of a corrugated straw
basket indelibly impressed upon it, and he has the
mark of a sandwich-box on his back, which, it is to
be feared, he will carry to his grave.   Once in the
train, once clear of the noisy, happy mass, my
friend began to be cheerful: he showed a disposition
to make merry, he chuckled and was exceeding
glad when two excursionists in our carriage who
thought they were on their way to Tunbridge
Wells, found themselves being whirled rapidly towards Worthing.   He lit up a big cigar, he smiled
benignantly, and he hummed softly to himself.   A
very pretty ride it is from Brighton to Ford Junction.   For a long distance we skirt the sea.   We
pass the little stations of Hove and Cliftonville, and
we notice how Brighton is spreading in a westerly
direction. Brighton has long ago ceased to increase
on its eastern side ; it stopped at the extreme limits
of Kemp Town many years ago, and has never
shown any inclination to advance on Rottingdean.
Why does fashion always move in a westerly direction ?   It does so in London, and it most assuredly does so in Brighton.   Brighton has become
almost incorporated with Hove and Cliftonville.
We see, as we are whirled along, the cricket ground
which a few months ago marked the termination of
Brighton proper is now being covered with gigantic

houses; one would not be surprised in a few years to find that rows of houses and shops extended all the way from Kemp Town to Shoreham. At Portslade, hard by a clump of trees, do we see the ruins of Aldrington Church, a church where I believe service is performed once a year, even at the present day. The parish of Aldrington once increased seven-fold between census and census. On the occasion of the first census the only inhabitant of the parish was the turnpike man at Aldrington Gate, and when the next census arrived he had taken unto himself a wife by whom he had had six children. There is but one tomb in this little churchyard of comparatively recent date, and that is one of a boy who fell overboard late at night and was drowned in the estuary of the Adur hard by. Glancing on the other side of the line I can see the quaint little village of Portslade and its ivy-covered church nestling in the trees in the distance. How long ago is it since I took a certain 'Uninteresting Walk' to this place? Do not you remember I gazed somewhat rudely over the wall of the vicar's garden, and saw the vicar's pretty daughters strolling beneath the trees? I daresay those young ladies are married now and have daughters of their own. I wish I could get out and moon about the quaint little village once more. That is the worst of railways, you cannot get out when you please, nor stop where you like. I consider railway travelling to be the devil's own invention. If my ship ever comes home and if I ever inherit my vast fortune, I would never travel by railway anywhere, nor on any occasion. I would either walk or go in my own four-horse coach. But this by the way.

A little further on we come to Southwick. We can see even from the railway Southwick Green, which is as good a specimen of an old-fashioned village green as you could wish to see. There is a quaint little shop, there are curious ancient houses, grand as to old red bricks, and superb as to lichen-covered tiles. You may see, also, the grey little church of Southwick, and not a great distance further, buried amongst trees and hidden behind farm buildings, is the barn-like, tumble-down church belonging to Kingston-by-Sea. There is a comfortable old manor-house looking upon the railway : a manor-house of the rare old sort, where you would like to go and stay a fortnight. Looking towards the sea on the other side you see Kingston Harbour and the lighthouse, which always looks as if it were too big for a street lamp and not large enough for its legitimate call-ing. We rattle into Shoreham, we get rid of a great many excursionists who are going to 'spend a happy day' at Shoreham gardens ; we see the Duke of Norfolk's suspension bridge, and I point out the Adur, flowing rapidly towards the sea, to my friend. Whereat a pleasant smile illumines his face, and he begins to sing ' O, pretty little Adur, charming little Adur, darling little Adur. O, pretty little Adur, flowing to the salt sea air ! ' This is, of course, nonsense, but I take it to be a good sign that my friend is getting better, that he is gradually becoming mollified, and that there is no chance of his being taken up on charge of

assault and battery at present. By the time we
arrive at Lancing the weather becomes brilliant,
the sun is scorching, and I believe my friend
would almost answer an excursionist civilly. You
see he notices they are gradually leaving our train,
and begins to fancy we shall get away from them
altogether. At Lancing I lament that it is not fig-
time, for the figs of Lancing I should tell you are
very delicious. My friend becomes voluble with
regard to the educational advantages of St Nicholas College, which may be seen perched on the
side of a hill. He knows some one who went
there, or he knows some one who is going to
send his son there; at any rate, he knows enough
about it to fling down his glove as champion of
the institution. He very nearly comes to words
with an excursionist who speaks of the place as
a 'sort of charity school.' Fortunately at Worthing the excursionists depart, and leave us the
carriage to ourselves. Worthing does not seem
to be much of a place viewed from the railway.
It is many years since I was in the town itself.
It was dull enough then. Possibly it has improved of late years. We pass by Goring, we stop
at Augmering, and we alight at Ford Junction.
By the time the train has started for Chichester,
or wherever it may be going, we have quite got
rid of all the excursionist element.

Ford Junction is not exactly what one would
call a lively place to spend half an hour, but it is
peculiarly grateful to any one suffering from 'excursionist on the brain' as my friend is at the
present time. There is a fine air, a fresh scent of

lilac, and the little place seems to spend its time
in blistering in the sunshine.   Nobody seems to be
in a hurry.   There is a train for Littlehampton
waiting alongside the platform.   It is in no hurry
to start.   It may go in ten minutes or so, or a
quarter of an hour or so, but, bless your heart,
there is no occasion to flurry yourselves about it.
The engine, with its brasswork glittering in the
sunshine, has none of that officious fussiness that
usually characterizes locomotives.   It does not
shriek and snort and howl and hiss, nor send
forth volumes of white steam and pretend it is
going to blow up every moment.   It simmers
playfully, like the tame tea-kettle of private life;
it diffuses a grateful warmth over the platform, it
perspires, it smiles, and it sings a plaintive ditty,
keeping time with a rat-tat accompaniment executed in an undertone somewhere inside the boiler,
with a muffled knocker.   The engine-driver, who
looks as if he were as good-natured and as well oiled
as his engine, is reading a novel.   The stoker is
sitting on a bench and gazing up at the sky and
whistling.   The porters have an easy and polite
air, and the superintendent examines your ticket as
if he were the steward of a charity dinner and
you were one of its principal patrons.   Our passengers were by no means numerous.   There were
certainly no excursionists amongst them.   There
was no shouting nor singing, no bundles nor
babies, and no 'nose-bags,' as my friend somewhat contemptuously calls the very comfortable
and substantial basket of provisions with which
your true excursionist is invariably provided.   For

myself, I believe implicitly in the 'nose-bag.'
There was no excursion element whatever about
our train. It was by no means crowded. I believe
everyone could have had a compartment to himself had he been so minded. There was a gentleman, who looked as if he might be agent to the
Honfleur packet, established himself in the smoking compartment. There was a young lady hugging a three-volume novel, a quantity of shawls and
wraps, and looking very joyous about something.
She was accompanied by a bonny big girl in short
frocks, who had a shock of straw-coloured hair rippling over her shoulders, and whose attention was
divided between a large doll and a shaggy Scotch
terrier. There was a clergyman and his wife, and
there was a sedate-looking gentleman, who was
either a rural dean or butler to the Duke of Norfolk.
We roam about the platform : at last the guard
thinks we may as well start, the engine-driver
thinks so too, the passengers look at one another.
and say it wouldn't be a bad idea, don't you know.
A train comes up from somewhere and adds one or
two people to our little company. The engine-
driver, having got to the end of a chapter, puts his
book down, nods to the superintendent, gives a
suppressed chirrup with his whistle, and we run
smoothly along about two miles and a half single
line of rail to Littlehampton.

As we get into Littlehampton my friend sees
the Honfleur boat. He talks of doing all sorts of
rash things—he has wild ideas of rushing over at
once and wandering about Normandy. I am only
able to control him by showing him that there are

'excursions' to Honfleur. That settles him, and
he rests content with his Littlehampton. We
find the place literally sleeping in the sunshine—
it seems to be even more asleep than usual.
Certainly no excursionists have come into it. I
have a strong suspicion that all the inhabitants
have taken an excursion out of it. We wander
through the town; all the shops are open, and
business seems to be going on in its usual fashion.
The inhabitants evidently do not care anything
about the bank holiday; indeed, I do not suppose
they ever heard of it. We wander across the
common and endeavour to understand the meaningless notices about roads which do not exist.
We walk along in front of the houses facing the
sea; we wonder where the visitors are; we wonder
if they have a season, and, if so, when it begins.
Most of the houses have the front doors open, but
all the inhabitants seem to be out for a walk or
gone to sleep. There is a ladies' school with all
the blinds down, which looks as if all the pupils
had been sent to bed for being naughty, and the
governess had taken the opportunity of having
forty winks herself.

There is evidently some preparation for a
season going on: houses are being repaired, balconies are being painted, and rooms being cleaned.
There are a number of high-dried, kippered, rugose-
looking individuals who are very busy getting
the bathing-machines out. I wonder where the
bathing-machines live in the winter. I am sure
I cannot hope to investigate this matter. I can
see them from my present post of observation come

in mysterious manner down a lane. I see them put at the top of the bank and trundle merrily over the hillock towards the sea. I am wicked enough to wish one of these machines would fall over on its side. But of course it does nothing of the kind. It never could. There never was anything light-hearted, nor frivolous, nor sportive about a bathing-machine. We seat ourselves under the lee of a stone wall on a very comfortable wooden seat, and we begin to smoke, to moon, and to meditate. My friend is supremely happy, for, to use his own graphic language, he has 'jockeyed the excursionist.' Half-a-dozen damsels come out presently and begin to play croquet close by us. I wonder whether they are the naughty girls who were sent to bed, and whether they have promised to be good and never do so again any more. They look very good, upon my word, and one or two of them are remarkably pretty. Their merry laughter is mighty pleasant to hear. It is a weary game, croquet. I do not mind, however, watching it from a distance. I can see those young ladies are already getting sadly tired of it, and I know presently they will pout and lose their temper and begin to hammer one another with mallets.

Talking about mallets reminds me of mullet, and I ask my friend if he ever tasted any of the famous mullet of the Arun? I have no doubt we could get some at the snug little Beach Hotel. We both come to the conclusion that we are very hungry, that sitting and mooning in the salt sea air has given us a tremendous appetite. We betake ourselves to the Beach Hotel. Alas, we are unable to get any mullet for luncheon, but we find a tremendous bit of cold roast beef, an excellent cheese, and some tankards of ale. This does famously for us. There is no noise, no clatter, no confusion, and there are even no excursionists about the Beach Hotel. A lady and gentleman and their little child were having an early dinner at an adjoining table, but those were all the people we there encountered. After luncheon we again turned out —the weather was too glorious to be in-doors a minute—and strolled to the end of the pier. There we sat down and basked in the sunshine and listened to the water washing against the piles. We watched the brown, mahogany-coloured fisher-children climbing about, whose only notion of true enjoyment seems to be how near they can get to suicide without actually accomplishing it. I think we went to sleep once or twice. We then strolled back across the common. We met the young lady of the train and the bonny big girl with her. The latter was amusing herself by chasing the Skye-terrier, jumping over railings, and exhibiting a pair of shapely legs and a profusion of snowy frillery in the most reckless fashion. We returned to our wooden bench beneath the wall, and we found everything going on as it had been all day. The sun was broiling hot, the men were lazily painting the balconies, the young ladies were getting quarrelsome over their game of croquet, the high-dried, kippered, rugose men, looking more high-dried, more kippered, more rugose than ever, had just trundled their thirteenth bathing-machine down the slope. Everything was repeating itself.

We have just time to wander slowly up to the station to catch the train which will bring us back to Brighton in time for dinner. My friend's countenance is placid, and he wears a smile of satisfaction. This continues till he reaches Ford Junction, where we join the main-line train; and excursionists crowd upon us thick and fast. Happily, however, for my peace of mind, my friend goes fast asleep, and slumbers sweetly till we reach Brighton.

BELOW THE LEVEL OF THE SEA.

GUIDE books of the instructive kind, people who give dull lectures and try to improve the minds of their audience, delight in giving you the population of towns, and they think there is an especial luxury in a mountain being so many thousand feet above the level of the sea. Of course these things are of no possible interest to anybody, you probably forget all about them the next moment, and they are but ordinary facts after all. Every village must have a population of some kind, and the smallest mountain must be at any rate a foot or two above the level of the sea. If I were to head this article ' two thousand feet above the level of the sea,' there would be nothing novel or astonishing in it, but ' below the level of the sea ' is, I venture to think, something out of the common way, especially when I inform my readers that I am not at the bottom of a coal-mine, nor am I at this present moment in a diving-bell beneath the briny ocean. I am sitting in the Oude Doelen Hotel, Amsterdam, and am looking forward to dinner with no small satisfaction. The waiters are like unto ordinary hotel waiters; the chambermaids are not, as far as I know, mermaids; and if the *concierge* has fins, all I can say is they are well concealed beneath his tightly-buttoned uniform. You

do not have to dive to your *table-d'hôte,* nor are
you expected to take your breakfast floating on
your back.   Everything is like an ordinary well-
appointed Continental hotel, and yet when I look
up at that elaborate cornice in the room in which I
am sitting, and think that the level of the sea is
somewhere about at that line, and that any mistake
in watching the tides or managing the vast system
of dykes and locks would probably cause the whole
country to be flooded, and the present writer to be
swept out of the hotel through the first-floor windows and carried on an involuntary excursion about
the Ij and round the Zuyder Zee, I confess it gives
one rather a novel sensation.

The novelty, however, soon wears off, and the
same familiarity which leads a miner to light his
pipe at his Davy-lamp, or would cause one to live
happily with a fire-work manufactory on one side
of your house and a blacksmith's forge on the
other, or would permit you to crack jokes in a
powder-mill, or dance a breakdown on the edge of
the crater of Vesuvius, causes you to think less
and less of the sea being growling above your head,
and only waiting its opportunity to be down upon
you.   Amsterdam is so picturesque; there is so
much to see even in a rapid scamper, that you
soon forget you are below the level of the sea.
'Life would be tolerable,' said somebody, 'were
it not for its pleasures.'   'Amsterdam,' say I,
'would be superb were it not for its stinks.'   *Murray* says, 'There is a good deal of mud deposited
at the bottom of the canals, which, when disturbed
by the barges, produces a most noisome effluvium

when the water is said to " grow." Machines are constantly at work to clear out the mud, which is sent to distant parts as manure.' I suppose we must have been especially unfortunate on the occasion of our visit. Possibly the water was ' growing' more than usual : the machines, probably, had not been at work to clear the mud out, consequently it had not been sent to distant parts as manure, but was allowed to reman and putrify and nearly poison two of the most distinguished visitors the town has had this year. There is scarcely any current in these canals : the water is a slimy kind of pea-soup : so thick and viscid is it that I fancy if you were to pitch a penny-piece into it, the coin would take many days before it found its way to the bottom. The real fact of the case is, I believe, that the whole town lives round a series of open sewers, from which the sewage never passes away, but slowly oozes from one part of the town to another, and then comes back again. Coleridge's seventy-two distinct evil smells of Cologne are perfect fools to the thirteen powerful odours I encountered this morning in a quiet stroll through the town. They came suddenly round corners and nearly knocked you down, they crept across bridges and overpowered you, they gave you a violent slap on the nose, they interrupted conversation, and they made you feel very sick. The proper costume in which to take a walk round Amsterdam would be a diver's helmet, and you should inhale the air through a sponge soaked in Eau de Cologne : you should have your clothes wadded with chloralum, and a footman should walk before you watering your pathway with carbolic acid. If all these things were done I think you might make a very satisfactory progress through Amsterdam. People who live near bone-boilers, hard by tanneries, close to candle manufactories, and in the midst of trades that produce the most noisome odours, always persist that these noisome odours are healthy. Perhaps it may be so, and persons born, raised, and educated in the midst of evil smells may find it difficult to live without them. They have been used to a strong-flavoured atmosphere from their youth up, and they would probably think a pure fresh English breeze insipid. I believe the nose is quite as capable of being debased as is the mind or the palate. I cannot tell whether my theory is correct or not; but this I know, that all the people we met about Amsterdam were of the sturdiest, brightest, and healthiest description. There was none of the sickly paleness of the sewer-cleaners and mudlarks of London, neither did we see any poor, sickly, puny, badly-grown children, such as one may find in the alleys and courts off Drury Lane. They all looked round, rosy, comfortable, and well-to-do, as all Dutch people are. Even in the narrowest streets and in the very midst of the most putrescent odour did we meet with the healthiest and brightest children.

It is very evident that the inhabitants are not troubled much by the stagnation of the waters nor the poisonous character of the atmosphere, for they actually have a swimming-bath in one of the most pea-soupy and stagnant of the canals. You might just as well open a grating in Fleet Street and have a dip in the Fleet Sewer, or take headers in the tanks at Crossness Point as bathe in one of these places. Amsterdam is not a place, I should tell you, for a nervous person to live in. When one gets over the terror of living always ' below the level of the sea,' and the fear that Mr Neptune might drop in uninvited some fine morning, then comes the thought that the piles on which your house was built might give way, and you would find your best drawing-room up to its ceiling in mud some fine day. There is a chance of this you must know. It is scarcely fifty years since the piles supporting the large corn warehouses of the Dutch East India Company gave way; the buildings sunk in the mud, and about 70,000 cwt. of corn was spoiled. You can note the instability of the foundations by seeing how many of the houses are out of the upright ; though they are substantially and honestly built—Mr Buggins the builder, I can tell you, would have not the ghost of a chance at Amsterdam—there is scarcely one of them upright. They exhibit more symptoms of what Mr Buggins would call ' settling ' than do the houses of Venice. I think some one has called Amsterdam ' a vulgar Venice.' But it is essentially different to Venice in many respects. In Venice the canals run close up to the houses, the canals are, in point of fact, the streets. In Amsterdam there are wide quays on each side of the canals ; these canals are planted with thick rows of trees, which make the character of one city entirely different to that of the other. You have more beautiful wall-colour in the back streets of Venice than you have in Amsterdam, but then, on the other hand, a tree is a very rare thing in the first-named city. The one city is that of an accomplished and highly-cultivated aristocracy : the other is that of wealthy, comfortable, well-to-do merchants.

There is no hollow splendour about Amsterdam. Everything is built for use and comfort. Time does not seem to be an object to the Dutch people : they like to do things thoroughly and take plenty of time over them. A Dutchman never killed himself yet with worry. I think I should have made the very best Dutchman under the sun. I am a good hand at pipe-smoking, I am not averse to beer drinking, and I hate to be hurried. All the houses along the quays have an intense—an almost English—aspect of comfort about them. Will you allow me to draw your attention to one or two points ? At the top of every gable is a projecting beam with a pulley and rope attached. I suppose Mynheer does this to save himself any trouble. He sees some one passing along the street with something he wishes to have—let us say a ham—so, between the puffs of his pipe, he hails the man, signs to him to attach the ham to the string : the ham is hauled up, the money is pitched out of window, and nobody has any trouble. You will see, too, little seats at the top of the steps by each front door. So that when you ring the bell and they happen to be a long time in, what is called in servantgalese, ' answering the door ' (as of course they would be in Holland), you can sit down and have a comfortable nap. These seats would be just the very thing to suit Joe, the Fat-Boy, in *Pickwick*. There

is a cleanliness and a 'well-groomed' appearance
about the houses by reason of their being built,
for the most part, of dark brown brick, and all the
window sashes and frames, which are massive and
heavy, being painted a dazzling white. Very
pretty little groups do you see in some of these
windows: plump, healthy Dutch damsels busy at
work behind screens of bright flowers. There is
a dash of Great Yarmouth, a goodly flavouring of
Cheyne Walk Chelsea, a smack of Liverpool, a
suspicion of the West India Docks about the whole
place. But above all these it has a distinct character of its own. What an excellent idea is that
cunning arrangement of looking-glasses, by means
of which you can see up and down the street without going to your window! I wish we could introduce them in England. How glorious it would
be when you saw some especial bore knocking at
your door with a self-satisfied smirk to go out at
the back way long before the servant opened the
door. This is another instance of the genius the
Dutch have for saving themselves trouble. I may
cite still one more instance, and that is in the
balance bridges which cross the canal. They are
provided with a heavy counterpoise and are so
easily raised that a man can work them with one
hand. How much better are they than the heavy
and expensive swing bridges which we have at
most of our docks, and which take three or four
men so long to open. They are not only simpler,
more expeditious and cheaper, but they are infinitely more picturesque, and I cannot possibly
understand why they are not in use in England.

Amsterdam abounds in pictures. If you take one canal, it does not much matter which, the Heeren Gracht, the Keisers Gracht, or the Primsen Gracht, and go up one side of it and down the other you will find quite enough to amuse you for an entire morning. Most of the streets in Amsterdam may be said to have four sides, that is, two quay sides and two sides lined with houses, and you will find quite as much that is worth looking at in the water as you will see on land. The craft of every kind is strikingly picturesque; for the most part of the sturdy solid comfortable kind, which is eminently the characteristic of the Dutch nation. There are ponderous hulls which look as if they had been painted black and then glazed over with asphaltum : they have masts and spars that look almost orange-coloured in the sunshine : they have quaint little cabins painted a bright green, and every bit of brasswork about them winks and glitters as if it had only just been newly polished with rottenstone and oil. If you look inside these cabins you will find they are models of neatness and perfectly Dutch in their cleanliness. You will note in many of them little *parterres* of choice flowers on the windows or on the roofs of the cabins, for these boats are not merely boats of merchandise voyaging from one place to another.   They are the homes of the proprietors and their families.

When a man marries in Holland—so amphibious is the nature of its inhabitants—he does not always look out for a house as we do, but he brings his wife home to a boat, and they commence the voyage of life and the voyage of the canals together. They live entirely on board these boats, travelling with merchandise from one place to another, and a most enjoyable nomadic existence it must be. I wonder if a Dutchman ever grows tired of his wife and she gets knocked off the boat by accident in passing under some of the low bridges. I should scarcely think this would be the case, for a Dutchman is so phlegmatic and so pachydermatous that he is just the sort of man to marry and live happily for ever afterwards. You often in these boats see the husband pushing the boat along with a pole, or hauling it with a rope, whilst the wife steers and a troop of little children are peering out of the cabin window or playing about the deck. Many children are born on board these vessels, and would feel altogether strange if they lived in a house that was stationary, and would not feel at home anywhere but on the water. It is only when the proprietor gets on in the world —and Dutchmen generally manage to do that—and he finds his family getting too large for the boat— which it frequently does—that he thinks about buying a larger one. He very rarely thinks about abandoning it for a house: he is so used to the water, and continually moving about from one place to another, that he would never be happy even if he had the most superb mansion on dry land. Instances have been known of three generations residing for a long period in some of the large boats. It would be a terrible thing, I am thinking, if you did not like your wife, to be obliged to live with her for the rest of your natural life in a boat, especially if she induced your mother-in-law to come and live with her, as most probably she would.

20

Imagine living from one year's end to another with
Mrs Mackenzie in one of these boats. But no, the
thought is too dreadful.   I know, if such a thing
happened to me, I should frequently get the Cam-
paigner to steer, and I should thank heaven there
were plenty of low bridges across the canals.

There, I know what people will say.   They
will remark he has told us nothing about the
public buildings of Amsterdam : he has said .no-
thing about the picture galleries : he has told us
nothing about the ' Banquet of the Archers,' by
Van der Helst, or the 'Night Watch,' by Rem-
brandt, and some wonderful works by Gerard
Douw, Carl du Jardin, Hondekoeter, Schalken,
Teniers, Ostade, and others.   My dear sir or
madam, as the case may be, ' most potent, grave,
and reverend '—objectors, all I can say is that
every picture all over the Continent has been so
much talked about and written about by those who
are well qualified to give an opinion, and also by
those who know nothing at all about the matter,
that I feel there is nothing left for me to say, and if
I said it, it would be supremely uninteresting. There
is one little matter, however, that I must make a note
of, as I think it might be useful to those who pass
our extraordinary and various Licensing Bills.
I am told that the orphan children of the different
asylums wear a particular kind of costume : those
of the Protestant Burgher House wear black and
red jackets.   At the Roman Catholic Orphan
House the girls are attired in black with a white
band round the head : those of the Almosoniers'
Orphan Home are dressed in black and wear a·

black, red, and white band with a number round
the left arm.   This costume is adopted to prevent
their being admitted into the wine *cabarets* and
other places where it is thought the juvenile mind
might be corrupted.   I believe there is a heavy
fine inflicted on persons who admit children so
attired to such places.   I wonder the wise men
who framed and passed the Licensing Bill did not
insist that all, children under twelve should be
dressed in a peculiar costume, and that any public-
an serving liquor to children so costumed should
be heavily fined.   I dare say, however, we shall
come to this in time.

Amsterdam is a place that one might spend
many weeks in, if one could only get accustomed
to the pestilential atmosphere and could brave the
fearful smells.   When we first came here we were
so delighted with the place, so charmed with its
novelty and picturesqueness, that we declared we
must stay here for a week at the very least.   But
we have been fairly driven out of the town by the
evil smells.   Instead of staying seven days, we
only remained seven hours.   Possibly in the winter
time the effluvium is not so terrible as the water
does not ' grow ' so much.   I should dearly like
to visit the picturesque place again.   Till then I
would say in the words of Voltaire, ' *Adieu !*
canaux, canards, canaille,' and I would add evil
smells, which appear to be worse than anywhere
else ' Below the Level of the Sea.'

MOONING.

'WHY should I work?' say I to myself, as I sit down before the window with a pile of repulsively clean-looking slips of paper before me.

It is a lovely day, not a cloud in the sky, a sleepy sea with just enough breeze to give it a sparkle. Everything is bright, joyous, and lazy, and I repeat again to myself, 'Why should I work?' Whereat Conscience—who is always so rude and inconsiderate, and who, by the way, was not spoken to—cuts in. 'Why should you work, indeed? Because you have engaged to supply certain publishers with a certain quantity of copy; because you are under an engagement to cause a certain amount of acute suffering to the British public. Why should you work? Because you are always behind-hand, because you always desire to put off till to-morrow what can be done to-day, because you never take time by the forelock. Why should you——' But there now, I am sick of having hand-to-hand combats with Conscience, in which you always get the worst of it. I am weary of the knock-down blows she always give you before you can put yourself into a fighting position. I am disgusted with the way in which she pinks you and disables your sword-arm before you have time to unsheath your rapier. I have

had so many bouts with Conscience, and she has
pricked me so frequently all over, that I have
arrived at a state of existence which may be described as something between a walking nutmeg-
grater and a human prickly pear; therefore I will
have no communication with this unpleasant individual, and I will turn a deaf ear to what clerical
gentlemen are pleased to call her 'promptings.' I
repeat emphatically I will be persistently idle; I
will be luxuriously lazy; I will be a good-for-no-
thing, a ne'er-do-well, a *vaurien*, if it seemeth
good unto me; I will lounge with both elbows on
the window-sill and get my eyelids thoroughly
warm in the bright sunshine; I will gaze out of
my window; I will loaf; I will moon and meditate.

Where was it I read many years ago of an idle
little boy, who went about asking different animals
and inanimate objects to play with him? If I remember rightly all of them were, or pretended to be,
too busy to indulge in gambols with the lazy youth.
The bee, an insect which I have satisfactorily de-
monstrated to be the greatest entomological humbug that ever existed, and whose affectation of
business, celebrated in halting verse by Dr Watts,
is generally tiresome and oppressive, scorned to
have anything to do with him, but made all sorts of
excuses and found all sorts of reasons why it could
not join in a little innocent amusement. The purling
stream, too, said it had mills to turn, and fish to float,
and clothes to wash, and sundry other matters that
prevented its joining in recreation. Everything
else treated the little boy with similar contempt,
and endeavoured to impress a moral lesson upon

him. If I had been that little boy I would have
told the stream that it might go boil, and would
have seen the bee fried before I would have held
any communication with them. I would have
treated their moral teachings with contempt, and
would have thrown myself down on my back in
the midst of the sweet-scented clover, and would
have gazed up into the blue sky, and dreamed and
slept, and slept and dreamed, with the persistence
a modern Rip Van Winkle. The very notion of
the boy taking the trouble to go round to ask the
various objects to play with him, shows that he
could not have been a genuinely idle boy. He
evidently had a large amount of superfluous energy
which he was obliged to work off; he was one of
those who took no pleasure in business, but made a
business of pleasure. A great mistake, by the way.
Your truly lazy man must absolutely do nothing,
must not even go through the exertion of thinking.

Just fancy, supposing the present writer were
to go to the driver of the fly, which is at this
present moment standing opposite to his window,
and say, 'Come, play with me, O flyman,' the
man would probably look surprised, but would
remark that his charge was two shillings per hour,
and then would cheerfully take off his coat and
'give me a back,' or play at 'jump my little nag-
tail,' or any other insanity in which I might desire
him to assist at. I know, too, that if I were desirous of playing a game of rounders with that
brown-faced expectorating boatman, who is now
occupied in lounging on the rails opposite, he
would be the man for my money, and would bowl

for me at single wicket, or would have a go in at battledore and shuttlecock all day long, provided I paid him three shillings an hour. Indeed, the whole of the inhabitants of Brighton seem to be one vast instrument laying itself out to be played upon for the amusement of the visitors at so much per head. However, the present writer chooses to take his amusement in a quieter and more thoroughly lazy sort of manner. I do not, like the majority of Englishmen, take my pleasure sadly, but I delight in taking it in the laziest fashion possible. I believe I can look out of window longer, and derive more enjoyment from so doing, than any one of my acquaintance.

Looking across the newly-watered road, which seems half inclined to steam in the bright sunshine, do my eyes rest upon a pleasant sward of turf intervening between the railing and the sea. Beyond this do I see the upper halves of bathing machines and the tops of masts of pleasure boats leading me to imagine that there must be a beach beyond. From tho 'dragging' rush of the waves I conclude it is a shingly beach. I am satisfied to conclude that it is. It is too much trouble to speculate on the subject; besides, what does it matter after all? On the green sward alluded too, I observe men busily engaged in picking up something from time to time. I wonder what they pick up on this Tom Tiddler's ground. Is it gold or silver? Brighton diamonds or mushrooms? By the way, why did not I have mushrooms for breakfast? Passes across this verdant field a young ladies' school, somewhat limited in number, and they seem as if they were pretending not to be a school, but trying to make people believe they are a large family. They are walking three and three, too. I object to this as being contrary to all received traditions on the subject. Ever since the world began young ladies' schools have decorously walked two and two. ' Two company, but three none ' is an old adage, consequently the three and three system may have been devised by some cunning governess anxious to guard against any plot for the overthrow of the establishment. By the way, I wonder who kept the first ladies' school. I wonder if I were to ask the question of that prim-looking governess whether she would think it an impertinence. Perhaps she would give me in charge of the police. I am not much afraid of the Brighton police : they appear to be an innocuous race of individuals, something between flymen and greengrocers, who if they ever ventured to ' run you in,' would probably call a fly and perform their painful duty in the most gentlemanly fashion, and are not above a passing joke or a friendly half-pint with the Brighton public generally.

The butcher now drives smartly up to my door. The Brighton butcher is decidedly smart, active, and energetic, and drives a smart little horse, who draws a smart little cart, smartly painted and gorgeous in gilt lettering, something between a newspaper cart and a miniature piano van. He jumps off his cart, deposits his tray on the railings —I should like to know where butchers' trays are made and why they are all made the same shape— and trots down the area steps. As he goes down

I get a bird's-eye view of the top of his head—
Brighton butchers do not go about bareheaded—
and I notice the peculiarity of his cap. It looks as
if it had been originally made of leather, but many
applications of suet to the head had gradually
made it waterproof and shiny. It looks so unctuous in the bright sunshine, that I am almost afraid
spontaneous combustion will take place, and I
tremble for the luxuriant locks of my butcher.
By the way, did anybody ever see a bald butcher?
Butcher is smart and active, and he drives at a
furious pace. I know it is no use to ask *him* to
play with me. His answer would be that he had
chops to deliver at Number Eighteen, a leg to
leave at Number Eleven, and a saddle to deposit
at Number Thirty-six, besides fifty other varieties
of joints and descriptions of meats to supply
two hundred other houses with, therefore he had
no time to waste on such puerile insanities.

Presently up drives, in an elegant basket pony-
chaise, Mr the Riding-master, to know if I require
any horses, any carriages, or any pony-chaises to-day.
Mr the Ridingmaster is a very splendid personage ;
he is bearded, and wears a magnificent signet ring ;
there is a little of the *militaire* and a great deal of
the groom about his bearing ; he is, however, very
polite ; he is an institution, and I do not know
what the young ladies of Brighton would do without him. A pleasant existence has Mr the Riding-
master. He spends his mornings in driving about
the town and soliciting orders, and his afternoons in
galloping up and down the King's Road, or in
trotting across the Downs with some of the pretti-

est girls in the place.　Happy man !　Is it too late
in life for me to renounce literature as my *métier,*
and come and live at Brighton and start as a professor of equitation ?

Here's the boy with papers, confound him !　I
buy the *Standard,* the *Daily Telegraph,* and the
various Brighton papers, and he hands them in at
the window.　I vacantly hand him a handful of
coppers, deposit the papers on the window-sill,
and continue to stare out of window.　He looks
as if he thought I was mad.　I dare say he is not
far wrong in his supposition.

What am I looking at ?　I am looking at the
dumpy Hove and Castle Square omnibus : it is
just like a cab turned the wrong way, and one
of the esplanade benches glued on to its front.
I do not object to the vehicle, but I do object
seriously to a swollen passenger with a very red
nose, who is apparently on the verge of an
apoplectic fit.　What is this man, and why is he
perpetually stationed on the front seat hugging
a large basket and a few brown paper parcels ?
Is he a decoy duck put there to attract other
passengers, the benevolent smirk on his face ad-
vertising the comfort of this method of transit ?
Is he a 'bogus' passenger, placed there to add to
the popularity of the vehicle ?　Is he an omnibus
driver down here for the benefit of his health, and
who, in consequence of that ' fellow-feeling ' which
is said to ' make us wondrous kind,' is allowed by
the proprietor of the Hove and Castle Square
' buslet ' to take a gratuitous ride as often as he
pleases ?　I am sure I do not know how this may

be. It is too much trouble to think the matter
out. But this I know, that I always look out
for my friend every morning, and should be sadly
disappointed if he were not in his accustomed
place. I wonder whether he would be disappointed
if he did not see me at my window. I have an
idea that there is already an electrical chain of
sympathy between us. *Arcades ambo,* that is to
say, we are both mooners, only one takes his mooning sitting still, the other whilst being roughly
jolted over the macadam.

Riding-master passes on lady's horse which he
is training; he has a horsecloth hung down on
one side to counterfeit a habit. He looks like a
fool. I am glad of it, for I was beginning to be
jealous of the riding-master. Flyman opposite
begins to wake up; takes the front cushions of
his carriage and bangs them violently together.
He *is* a fool, no doubt, or he would not take all
that exertion in the sunshine, besides smothering
himself with dust, when he might be quietly
slumbering on his box.

Contiguous Bathchair-man stares at me and
wonders whether I should be a likely fare, but evidently gives it up. By the way, I own I should like
to ride round Brighton in a Bathchair. Why not?
Why should these extraordinary conveyances—
which I seriously incline to think never came from
Bath at all—be reserved for the halt and the
maimed? Why has no improvement been made in
their fashion and decoration? They are as obstin-
ately at a stand-still and behind the age as the
bathing machines. Where did the race of Bath-

chair-men spring from : that semi-clerical, semi-
nautical class of men with that peculiar kind of
walk only to be acquired by years of anxious and
hard dragging of Bathchairs ?　Is the office heredi-
tary ?　Have the same family dragged the same
chair for years ? or is it a matter of sudden inspiration ; and is a boy seized with a violent longing to
clutch the well-worn brass-bound handle, proudly
exclaiming at the same time 'And I, too, am a
Bathchair-man ! '　By the way, you never heard of
a Bathchair-boy, so I am inclined to think that it
is an office of some importance, not to be under-
taken before arriving at a sober maturity.

A pretty fresh-coloured light-haired damsel
rides by in a tight-fitting habit, ' the tint of a night
in the still summer weather,' which a certain enthusiastic versifier has raved about.　She has a
lovely figure, and sits her horse admirably.　There
is some question about the handling of the bridle,
and the riding-master positively ventures to clasp
her daintily-gauntleted little hand and adjust her
fingers.　Upon my word, it is too bad.　That
riding-master is no fool, and has a pleasant jest and
a lively anecdote to tell àpropos of everything.　I
hate riding-masters though, and that riding-master
especially from the bottom of my heart.　I wish I
knew the address of that young lady's papa, and I
would call upon him and whisper a word of warning
in his ear.　But why should I trouble myself in the
matter, why should I seethe into indignation on the
subject, for what does it matter after all ?

A sour ascetic-looking old young lady in a
skimping black gown, who has been to an early

service at an ultra Ritualistic church passes by.
She looks mortified and cross, and as if she
wanted her breakfast. She is followed by a
stalwart-looking gentleman in a cheviot suit, just
returning from Brill's: this gentleman's nose is
very red indeed, but I am inclined to attribute
this nasal rubicundity rather to the action of
sunshine and saline breezes than to any undue
indulgence in alcoholic drinks. Shall I run after
him and ask him which it is, or would he resent
such pardonable curiosity as an impertinence?
Shall I go and tell him that his coat does not fit,
for I can see it is two inches too big at the back?
No, I will not; for he might get irate and punch
my head, especially as I see he is evidently well
satisfied with his costume. Why should I disturb
his serenity, and throw myself into a profuse perspiration?

There are the pretty girls from next door going
out. I know they are going out without turning
my head round by the ripples of silvery laughter
that break upon my ear. They have got new morning muslins on,—I can tell by the ' cruckle ' they
make as they go down the steps. They look in at
my window, but I take up my opera-glass and apparently am intently occupied with gazing far out
to sea, and pretend I do not see them, for as they
disturb my peace of mind I prefer to treat them
with cynical indifference, though there is one grey-
eyed, brown-haired, dimpled damsel amongst them
who would melt the heart of a stoic.

There is a goat-chaise passing along just by the
railings, with a bonny little child in it, drawn by

such an evil-looking old goat, with a terrific pair
of horns. I wonder whether those horns are real
or tied on! I have heard they are occasionally tied
on. Think the boy would let me pull them if I
went across and gave him sixpence? Supposing
he did, and they turned out not to be false ones,
and the goat butted me furiously in the waistcoat.
The very idea makes me warm. No, I am better
where I am.

Who is this pulling up before the door? Ah,
I know the brown face and the yellow beard of a
particular friend of my own, who is accompanied
with a nice sister of his own. Particular friend
says,

'What, not out yet, old fellow!'

'Will you come for a drive, Mr Lazy?' says
nice sister, with an impudent toss of her head.
'I'm going to drive Fred down as far as Brill's.
Will you come?'

'Suit me admirably, thanks,' say I, and take a
seat by side of nice sister, and am whirled too
quickly down to Brill's, thinking all the while
what a curious anomaly it is that 'mooning' can
be carried on so much better in the broiling sunshine than under the cooling influence of lunar
rays.

BUNS.

'ONE a penny bun, two a penny bun; one a penny, two a penny, hot cross bun, all 'ot!' This simple chaunt, which used to disturb the slumbers of Londoners at the earliest hour on the morning of Good Friday, will, I fancy, in a few years' time be numbered with the oracular speeches of the ancient watchman, and become lost in the limbo of the street-cries of the past. The vendors of hot cross buns are, I venture to think, becoming fewer, as the belief in buns grows more limited and the desire for their consumption wanes. I am sorry to say that I have come to the conclusion that bun-worship is a thing of the past, and the disciples who still bow down before the shrine of bundom are very limited in number. Easter is— or was—the buniferous period of the year. In the days of my youth we believed emphatically in buns, and looked forward to Good Friday, as a Great Bun Festival—with a capital G, a capital B, and a capital F — and prepared our minds and our stomachs accordingly. If my recollection serves me we had stacks of buns sent in from the baker's the day before, we rose early in the morning and purchased halfpenny buns from the small itinerant vendors who awakened us with the chaunt above quoted; we had hot buns for breakfast, plain,

toasted and buttered.   We had them for luncheon :
we took them to church with us and crumbled
them and munched them furtively during the most
moving part of the sermon.   We had them before
dinner, during dinner, and after dinner : we tried
to eat some more at tea time, made another effort
at supper time, and finally took one to bed with us,
and dropped off to slumber amongst the crumbs.
I once knew a boy who ate twenty-one buns before
luncheon on Good Friday.   Not small buns mind
you, but good substantial extensive penny hot
cross buns.   He came to no untimely end, he still
lives, and is a very clever and influential member
of society.   This excessive bunolatry, no doubt,
had some effect upon his physical conformation at
the time : his face assumed a bunesque character,
from which his eyes peered like two glittering
currants.   I have not seen him since the days of
my youth, but I hear he has grown up to be a very
handsome man.

In the days to which I allude you might venture
to treat school-boys to buns, and you would be
literally astonished at the number they would put
away if you gave them *carte blanche*.   It was a
very inexpensive treat, for with two shillingsworth
or so of buns, and with three or four bottles or so
of ginger-beer to wash them down with, you might
successfully satisfy the somewhat rapacious appetite
of the school-boy by rendering it physically impossible for him to consume any more.   I should like to
know anybody who would venture to treat a school-
boy to buns in the present day.   I know I should
not dare to propose anything of the kind to him.

I might ask him to dine at my club, and even then
I should give particular orders to the *chef* that
he must take every possible pains with the
dinner, and caution the butler that he must be
more that usually careful with regard to the selection of the wines. But I would no more dare ask
him into a pastry-cook's shop and offer him unbounded buns and unlimited ginger-beer than I
would venture to take my ancient maiden aunt to
a *ballet* ball. If you attempted to inveigle him into
a pastry-cook's, under the pretence of doing the
magnificent, I fancy you would be utterly crushed
by the way he would inform you that 'Sweetstuff
was all very well for women and children, but he
didn't care much about it, th-h-anks.' Possibly
it is the case that bun-eating is mostly confined to
women and children and serious people in the present day. I believe the quantity of buns that
are flattened in pious pockets and crushed in re-
ligious reticules during the May Meetings at Exeter
Hall is something prodigious. You see a bun will
bear a great deal of ill-usage before its nutritious
and sustaining qualities are altogether extinguished.
It will bear doubling up, and crushing, and folding,
and. sitting upon. You can wear it in your coat
pocket, or your hat, or put it inside a bundle of
tracts. It is as emphatically the food of the good
folk at Exeter Hall as the unctuous muffin is the
staple edible of serious tea-fights.

When I come to think how few bun shops
there are in propinquity to Exeter Hall I am very
much astonished. There are plenty of sly taverns,
a large quantity of seductive bars and naughty

fish shops, but, alas, and alas, the 'bunneries' are few. How is this ? We also know that the Jews have especially bakers and butchers of their own. Possibly the leading orators at Exeter Hall have their own particular bunsters, and supply all the members of especial congregations at a reduced rate, so that everybody arrives padded with buns and enabled to hold out during the lengthiest discussion or the most exhausting oration. Perhaps those people who subscribe to the Pongo Mission do so under the express understanding that they may take it out in buns. I am sure I am unable to say how this may be. Perchance, in the lowermost depths of Exeter Hall, in the mysterious labyrinth of passages in which we sometimes used to get lost when we took a wrong turning in coming away from the Sacred Harmonic, is a private bunnery, presided over by ancient maiden ladies who supply with buns and lukewarm milk-and-water the good people who attend the May Meetings. I should like very much indeed to know if this is the case. If it is not, I know that the whole affair is an inscrutable mystery. There is no doubt more buns are consumed during the May Meetings than at any other period in the year, and yet there do not seem to be a sufficient number of shops in the neighbourhood of Exeter Hall capable of supplying the demand.

Albert Smith used to say that a good deal of surreptitious bun-eating went on at the Zoological Gardens. He informed us that people said they must ' buy a bag o' buns for the poor bears,' but he averred that they ate all the buns themselves and that the 'poor bears' never had a crumb. From personal observation at the Zoo I am sure this is perfectly true. It only shows to what hopeless degradation the unbridled bun-eater may be in time reduced. He—as a matter of fact, I believe it is she—will even rob a dumb innocent animal in ordor that his terrible and unhealthy craving for buns may be gratified. Upon my word, I think that it is high time we had a licensing bill for bun shops, with very stringent regulations for their government. I think if the British public were to hear the opinion of an eminent physician with regard to buns on the brain they would be very much astonished. It is scarcely my purpose to go into the finer theories of bunnal excess in this present paper. I propose to make it rather descriptive than analytical : to treat rather of facts than of speculations. I have no desire to read a homily with regard to the vagaries of the Good Bunsters, neither do I wish to discuss the truth of Dr Johnson's dogmatic assertion, that 'A man who would eat a bun would pick a pocket.'

Some day I mean to read a paper at the Royal Society, entitled ' The Influence of Bun on Mankind,' in which I propose to go into all the deeper questions relative to this matter. Till then I wish to confine myself to a few reminiscences with regard to my early bunhood. There were seven distinct specimens that I can call to mind—the hot cross bun, the ordinary penny bun, the common halfpenny bun, the oval bun with plums in it, the Chelsea bun, the Bath bun, and a peculiar square variety of the Bath bun, which was only to be obtained at Streeter's at Brighton. Of these varieties the oval plum bun, the Chelsea bun, and the common halfpenny bun have, I fancy, altogether passed away. The luxurious character of the age has probably led to the gradual extinction of the halfpenny bun. The oval plum bun always had a parvenu air about it. It assumed a plum-cakishness though it had it not : there was no honest bunly pride about it whatever : this circumstance, I fancy, must have led to its ultimate disestablishment and downfall. The Chelsea bun has perished, I fancy, because the old Chelsea bun-house has been removed, and possibly people could not fancy any bun equally good that came from any other house. There were some horrible tales in connection with the hospital, circulated by some jealous rival baker with regard to the manufacture of these buns, but no respectable person in Chelsea, in those days, believed them for an instant.

In the days of my early bunhood I resided for a long while in Chelsea, in a good old house, in a rare old row of red-brick houses, a house that was panelled from top to bottom, and had not a square inch of paper on any part of the walls. A house with a queer little fore-court, with massive gate posts surmounted by vast globes with high railings in front, and with a gate that was a perfect puzzle of elaborate ironwork. A queer old many-cupboarded, white window-sashed, high-roofed house it was ; I only wish I lived in such a house now. On one side there was a ladies' school, and on the other a mysterious individual resided, whose chief delight seemed to be to never have his windows cleaned, and who had the reputation of being a miser. He never gave any money away, and organ-grinders never invaded his fore-court. I believe the reason he never gave any money away was simply that he had none to give. And the reason why he was called a miser was only that he was very poor. The ladies' school next door was altogether another affair. A greater contrast could hardly be found than the miser's garden and that which the young ladies used as a sort of play-ground on the other side. The one was carefully ordered and trimly kept, the other was overgrown, dank, deserted, and weed-covered. Very gay were some of these fine old back gardens: especially fine were the lilacs and laburnums. I never smell the scent of the lilac, but it recalls vividly to my mind this quaint row of houses.

And what has all this to do with buns? I think you will ask. Well, it has everything to do with buns, and it has especial reference to those of the peculiar make known as ' Chelsea.' Here I first enjoyed my Chelsea bun. I believe that now-a-days the real Chelsea bun has altogether vanished. I fancy it is a bread stuff entirely unknown to the rising generation. Therefore a man who has tasted a Chelsea bun—a real genuine Chelsea bun, mind you—is an individual to be treated with respect, but he who has had his fill of these cakes of the past, he who has wallowed in them, so to speak, ought to command unbounded admiration. I remember on great occasions there were especial expeditions organized to get us supplies from the Old Chelsea Bun House. If my recollection serves

me this was not the actual Old Chelsea Bun House,
but it was its successor, and it had a sufficient flavour of antiquity to impress my youthful mind very
much indeed. There was a peculiarity about its
architecture which was very different to that of the
ordinary pastry-cooks, and the vast green dishes
in which the buns were exposed for sale struck
me as being very much out of the common. The
ladies who served in the shop had none of the
flightiness or weak prettiness of the ordinary run
of confectioners' young ladies. They had a sad and
aristocratic air: they looked as if they might have
been the faded widows of reduced rural deans. The
expedition to the Old Chelsea Bun House was one
of considerable excitement in more ways than one.
On our way thither we frequently looked in and saw
the young gentlemen at the Duke of York's School
—it was the desire of my life then to be a distinguished performer in their band—and on our return
we used to take our way through the Hospital and
have a chat with one or two ancient pensioners who
were our especial favourites. The bag of buns
generally remained intact till we returned home,
for we did not give the Duke of York's boys the
chance of seeing them, and our ancient Waterloo
heroes did not hanker after them. Indeed, I am
inclined to believe they valued more highly the sixpence or the screw of tobacco that we occasionally
took them.

I believe I am perfectly right in stating that the
Old Chelsea Bun House has been entirely swept
away. Whether the manufacture of Chelsea buns
is still carried on in the neighbourhood I am

unable to say. I do not think there would be an
equal charm about this peculiar breadstuff unless it
were purchased at that old-fashioned shop and sold
by those sad faded widows of reduced rural deans.
Vast changes have taken place in Chelsea since the
time I speak of. I fancy the row of quaint, old-
fashioned houses still exists, but the neighbourhood
is much changed. It is still changing, and will
change still more. But I am forgetting all about
the buns. When we got our cargo home we not
infrequently distributed it to our especial pets
next door. And we found the pinafored, pig-
tailed, short-frocked, frill-trousered young ladies
liked Chelsea buns as well as we did. I do not
know that this has anything to do with the bearing
of my discourse, but it is all connected with the
legends and anecdotes of bundom, a very useful
book which I propose to compile one of these fine
days.

A PARADISE FOR THE BRIEFLESS.

I AM if you please at Locarno. I am sitting in
my bed-room at the Albergo della Corona, and
just thinking it is time I was in bed. How nice it
is to write *Albergo!* It makes one think one really
must be in Italy at last. I have had an excellent
supper, I have been smoking a quiet pipe in the balcony, and I have been gazing on the bright moon
shedding a silvern glory over the waters of the Lago
Maggiore, and I have almost come to the conclusion
that Locarno must be a very nice place indeed.
Almost, I say, for since I came in from my dream
on the balcony I have done what all well-regulated
English travellers are expected to do—I have
picked up *Murray* and read the following terrible
intelligence. He says :—'The criminal statistics
of the district around Locarno show a large amount
of crime in proportion to the number of its inhabitants. The neighbouring valley of Verzasca is in
evil repute for the number of assassinations com-
mitted in it. Bonstetten, who travelled through it
in 1795, says they all wear at their girdle behind,
a knife a foot long, called *falciuolo*, to kill one
another. He states that the average number of
lawsuits among a population of 17,000 souls was

1,000 yearly.' That is one lawsuit per year to every seventeen individuals. Well, the year 1795 is so long ago that let us hope it is not true. But it goes on to say :—'In 1855 one of the richest men in the town, leader of one party, was deliberately murdered by two brothers, leaders of the other party. The two brothers have been sentenced to perpetual imprisonment.' This however is quite in our own time, and much too near to be pleasant. I am not sure that I consider this place altogether so delightful as I did. Supposing those two handsome, honest peasants—as I thought them a moment ago—who were looking at me as I lounged over the balcony, were at this present time waiting for me under the piazza of the hotel, each armed with a terrible *falciuolo* and ready to whip it into me, if I dared to venture out. I am very tired, so I will not give them a chance. Yesterday I ascended the Reuss; and to-day I descended the Ticino : that is to say, I traced the first river to its source, and I followed the second to where it empties itself into the Lago Maggiore. In plain English, I have crossed over the St Gothard pass. It is by no means the first time I have come this way to Italy, and I hold, as I always have held, that the ascent from the Swiss side is rather wearisome, and the endless repetition of hopeless granite rocks and stern grey mountains becomes in time very tiresome. It is very grand, but there is too much of the same kind of grandeur.

The descent is a different matter altogether. Directly you pass that icy cold lake near the summit and leave the hotel and the Hospice behind

you, you begin to take a little interest in your
journey.   You find change every minute, and you
have a rapid transition from sterility to fruitfulness,
from stern granite to luxuriant vegetation, from
snow to sunshine, from Switzerland to Italy, which
is very remarkable.   More remarkable than anything else is the trot down the series of zig-zags
cut in the face of the rock before you reach the
comparatively level ground in the Val Tremola.
There is very seldom an accident here, but if a pole
were to break, or a horse shy or stumble, I would
not give much for the lives of the passengers in the
carriages.   Whenever I go down this pass I am
always thinking if the linch-pins of the wheels are
secure.   As we skim round a corner I say to myself 'linch-pins:' as we just shave by a post I again
ejaculate 'linch-pins;' and I think if one little
linch-pin were to come out I might find myself
standing on my head in the road that I can distinctly see a thousand feet below me.   The drivers
are generally very careful, but there was an accident
that happened the day I came up that might have
been terrible in its consequences.   Near the upper
side of the Devil's Bridge a carriage, containing a
lady and gentleman, two maids, and three children,
was turned off the road, fell down the cliff and
alighted on the only bit of grass in that neighbourhood.   Strange to say, although the carriage
was smashed to pieces, the occupants, though, of
course, a good deal bruised and shaken, were not
seriously hurt, neither were the horses.   Had it
not been for the patch of soft grass, every one
would, probably, have been smashed to atoms.

Such accidents as this, however, occur but seldom. It takes a good deal of careful driving, I can tell you, to get a carriage safely down the Italian side of the St Gothard Pass. I thought this morning how I should like to see a few members of the Four-in-Hand Club tool their coaches down this steep and elaborate incline. I should like to see that accomplished whip, Sir George Wombwell, drive down this pass. It would pleasure me hugely to see Mr Adrian Hope, Lord Londesborough, or Lord Macduff try their powers on this circuitous road. It would be quite a new sensation for a few members of the Four-in-Hand and the Coaching Club to try this.

As we drive onwards we find the luxuriance of the country increases even more rapidly than one would expect. We pass from granite to grass, from grass to pine trees, from pine trees to rich pastures by the time we reach Airolo, a quaint little village with an Italian name and a good many Italian characteristics at the foot of the St Gothard pass. A little further on we find chestnut trees, and soon after passing Faido we begin to see vines. At Faido the confusion of tongues and the muddle of nationalities seems to be *in excelsis*. At the Prince of Wales's Hotel you will see inscriptions on the front of it in English, in French, in German, and in Italian. Not, mind you, the same information conveyed in four different languages, but a sort of patchwork, as if the landlord did not know which nation he belonged to, or as if his house-painter had been a cosmopolitan lunatic. Talking of vines, every one who comes this way for the first

time will be struck by the difference in the training
of the vines in Italy to that of the scrubby little
perky shrubs you see on the Rhine. It is true the
Italian wine may not be so good as the Rhenish,
but the manner in which the plants are arranged is
infinitely more effective. Long alleys, arcades, and
arbours, with vines supported on their granite pillars, may be seen attached to the poorest houses.
A man can not only sit under the shadow of his own
vine, but he can run races, play at bowls, give dinner parties, hang out the family washing—in short
do anything beneath it he pleases. Still passing on
you find the vines increasing in extent and the black
clusters becoming more and more plentiful. Patches
of maize now appear with long flag-like leaves and
feathery tops; you may occasionally see fig trees,
and there are apple and pear trees in plenty. The
language changes, too, quite as rapidly as the
scenery. We have passed from French, German,
German-French, and Swiss *patois*—into Italian-
French, Italian-German, and a Lombardian *patois*,
even before we know it.

The peasants too have changed. The men
and the women you meet upon the road have
none of that hardy, dried-up, mummy-like appearance that betokens the dweller in mountain-
ous regions. The men look more swarthy and
sullen, the women become more picturesque in
their attire, and their eyes are larger, darker, and
more expressive. You see the architecture of the
houses change. You soon lose sight of the wooden
houses of Switzerland with their stone-weighted
roofs, and have in their stead dwellings of a daz-

zling white colour, with curious piazzas and porches, decorated here and there with some bright-coloured roughly-daubed picture of the Virgin Mary or some popular saint. You see such inscriptions as 'Si vende vino et si allogia,' 'Bigliardo,' &c., on the taverns, and all the names over the shops have an Italian smack, and when you rattle into that quaint little town with a mellifluous Italian name—Bellinzona—and note the dark piazzas, the propensity for keeping the windows shut, and the rooms as sombre as possible, the sleepy-eyed honest-looking oxen, apparently steered by a swarthy-looking man by a pole as if it were a ship's tiller, the peculiar smells, and the long curiously-coloured sausages that seem to be the staple food of the place, you begin to think you must indeed be in Italy. Still more do you think so when two hours later you arrive at the picturesque town from which I am writing this letter, but if you think so you will be mistaken, you are still in Switzerland and will not arrive in Italy till you get to Luino on the other side of the Lago Maggiore. Still this place with such an evil reputation is thoroughly Italian in every respect. I would warn travellers over the St Gothard not to be led away with the representations of people all along the route. Every one seems to make a dead set against Locarno, and tries to insist upon your staying at Bellinzona. It is impossible to make out the reason of this, for Locarno is a very much more picturesque place than Bellinzona ; it is situated on the lake close by steamers to all parts, the hotel is of the cleanest and most comfortable description, and the head-

waiter is one of the most polite and considerate I
have ever met.

There is a peculiarity about this place which is
well worth noting. If Thackeray had known of it
I think he would have written another chapter to
his inimitable 'Book of Snobs,' and I am sure the
town would have given as much pleasure to the
countess in Tom Robertson's 'Caste' as did the
Chronicles of Froissart. The little place is even
more snobbish, more particular as to matters of
caste, than is a small English town, and I am sure
I cannot say more. I am informed that there are
no less than seven grades, all declining to visit or
intermarry in this place. First come the *nobili*, then
the *borghesi*, then the *terrieri*, or old landholders.
After these come the *oriondi*, or settlers from the
villages, and the *sessini*, then the *quatrini* and
mensualisti, foreign settlers. It must be a terribly
difficult town to live in. If you visited with, say
the *borghesi*, you would be pretty sure to offend all
the other six sets. If you gave an evening party
and invited all the seven sets you would probably
have a free fight before the evening was over, and,
doubtless, the *falciuolo* would be freely plied by
your guests on their way home.

It is no wonder with all these sets everlastingly
sneering, backbiting, and quarrelling, that there
should be such an enormous quantity of lawsuits in
the course of the year. I know several young briefless barristers who, if they could only acquire a
perfect knowledge of the Italian tongue, and come
and reside at Locarno, might amass an immense
fortune. It certainly would be a paradise for the

briefless.   And I know one or two old ladies with
a vast capacity for making mischief, who would be
quite in their element if they could only live here
and set the whole seven sets by the ears.   I would
gladly give my mite towards a subscription for
paying the aforesaid old ladies' expenses, if they
would promise to come and live here and never
return to England any more.   I fear, however, it
will be difficult to secure them, but I certainly
think this place would be worth the serious attention of certain members of the bar with whom I
am acquainted.

Talking of barristers in connection with this
town, can it be possible they have already heard of
its reputation and are come to spy out the neighbourhood ?   I do not know how this may be, but I
certainly met a couple of barristers in the *sala* this
evening. They might not be briefless, but they certainly were barristers, because they told interminable circuit stories and fired off a collection of the
oldest 'Joe Millers' I have heard for a long time.
They belonged to a large party ; there were papa
and mama, two or three young ladies, and one or two
friends.   They had taken possession of the room
and organized a high tea after the most approved
English fashion.   These large English family parties are rather a nuisance to meet travelling on the
Continent.   They spoil the individuality of places
and double the prices.   Directly you see an inn
announced as 'where every English comfort may
be obtained' avoid it, for you will find the prices
are doubled, and you get a bad imitation of English food, and you might just as well stop at home

and go to a good London hotel. I know several hotels where you are not allowed to smoke after dinner because the ladies are going to have tea, and you are hunted away from the dinner-table by a portentous tea-urn and a bad imitation of muffins. The very thing you travel for is to get rid of English food and English customs for a time, and people who cannot travel without what they are pleased to call their ' English comforts ' had much better stay at home. They will be a long while, however, before they stamp the individuality out of the Albergo della Corona. It is a thoroughly Italian inn, with vast suites of rooms, with a court-yard with galleries running round it, with large balconies, with curiously painted walls and ceilings. These family parties are certainly a nuisance, and the one I speak of was no exception to the rule. They read extracts from *Murray* to one another; they audited their accounts in public; they gushed terribly; they talked ' Alpine club '; they played on the piano and they sang! Ye gods, how they played and sang. We had all sorts of music played in the most extraordinary fashion. We had selections from 'Masaniello': we had the 'Burlesque Galop': we had the *gendarmes'* song from 'Gene-viève de Brabant': we had the 'Mandolinata,' and the 'Conspirators' Chorus,' from La Fille de Madame Angot. We had nigger songs with a tremendous chorus, in which each seemed to have his own idea with regard to time and tune, and in which each seemed to be at variance with his companions: and, worse than all, we had the ' Little Wee Dog.' To think that I should have come

all the way from London to Locarno to hear the
'Little Wee Dog' indifferently played upon a
piano very much out of tune. I was driven away
at last, and I think I am much better employed
in my own room in lounging on the balcony and
enjoying the superb view and writing by fits and
starts.

Whilst I am writing the music is still going on.
It does not make much difference to me, for I can
write in the midst of any amount of noise, but I
should think it must be a prodigious nuisance to
quiet folks who are stopping in the hotel. I can
smell the cigars of the barristers who are smoking
in the balcony below, and through the music fine
old crusted 'Joes' and lengthy circuit stories,
come wafted on the breeze. At last the young
lady has stopped playing the 'Little Wee Dog.' I
hear the piano shut. Presently the barristers, who
have talked themselves hoarse, give over and go to
bed: there is a closing of shutters; there is the
rattle of boots as they are put outside the bed-room
doors, and in a few minutes all is silent.

I light my penultimate pipe and I go out on
the balcony. The moon is still glinting gloriously
on the water: there is not a ripple on the lake:
there is not a soul about the street: there is no
sound to be heard but the whirr of the grass-
hopper. The serrated edge of the mountain range
opposite cuts sharp against the clear starlit sky. I
watch a light iu a little *châlet* high up the hill on
the other side of the lake for a long time as I
smoke. I wonder who lives there, and why that
one light—that single light in so large a tract of

country—is burning so late.   At last my friend in
the *châlet* puts his light out and puts an end to
my speculation.

With regret I retire from the balcony and put
my light out and creep into bed, thinking that
after eighteen hours' hard work I shall sleep so
soundly that I shall not even dream of the terrible
falciuolo.

OLD-FASHIONED PEOPLE.

IT has been the desire of my life to give a party composed exclusively of old-fashioned people.

But I do not know exactly how I can carry out my project. There are plenty of old-fashioned people, but the difficulty is to find out where they reside. They are usually chance acquaintances or persons that you only know by sight. Some days you meet a great number of old-fashioned people, and on other days you do not meet any. I have a theory of my own with regard to this. I have an idea they all reside in one vast asylum, a sort of living Madame Tussaud's or an animated Jarley's, and that the days when you see them in such numbers is on the occasion of a holiday or a festival at the asylum. I have often tried to run an old-fashioned person to earth, I have followed him and endeavoured to track him to this limbo, but he has always given me the slip, and I have never yet been able to satisfactorily determine his dwelling-place. Are these old-fashioned people merely ghosts, are they reflected on the atmosphere from some strange influence of long ago, do they appear for a moment and then vanish into thin air only to return again, when circumstances may be propitious, in as sudden and as unsatisfactory a manner? Do they lurk about those places that they frequented

years ago, and do they return to their old haunts
long after they have actually ceased to exist ?
Many of these curious specimens of humanity do
not strike you at the time : you look at them without noticing anything particular about them, and
it is frequently only when they have vanished that
you say ' Dear me, what an old-fashioned person ! '
After all, I am inclined to think they are not ghosts ;
that they have an actual and substantial existence ;
that they have inherited their ' old fashion ' just as
they have inherited the colour of their eyes or their
hair, or some family deformity or eccentricity.
And when I say old-fashioned people, I do not
mean, mind you, extremely *old* people.   Why,
bless you, I know school-girls and school-boys,
and even babies, who have old fashion in every line
of their face and stitch of their clothes.   Old
fashion seems to be a condition frequently independent of age or period.   The varieties of old-
fashioned people are something extraordinary :
they exist in every phase and condition of life :
they are to be found in every profession and trade.

Have you never been at the theatre and been
suddenly struck by an individual sitting close by
you who, though he has not spoken a word, at once
causes you to say to yourself ' The Kembles and
the elder Kean, Sir ! '   This is the old-fashioned
actor : you can tell him at a glance.   He is closely
shaven, his face is rather red, his cheeks are very
blue, and he wears a light juvenile but unmistakable
wig.   He has a high stock, rather frayed at the
edges, and the least bit of shirt collar showing
above it.   He never has an overcoat : it is gener-

ally a cloak, one that used, I believe, to be called
a camlet-cloak, and it is fasteued round his neck
by a very cruel arrangement of chains and hooks,
which is very difficult to fasten, and once fastened
it is almost impossible to undo. You may find him
in the pit of Drury Lane on a great night, and
occasionally he will be fluttering about the upper
boxes. He does not think much of the young
school of actors, and altogether pooh-poohs the
modern *jeunes premiers*. 'Mere clothes-horses,
mere clothes-horses, take my word for it, sir!' he
will tell you. He takes snuff prodigiously, his
snuff-box was given to him by some young blood
who was the lion of the green-rooms long ago, and
he manipulates it with all the elaboration and
finish of a careful bit of stage business. He is
quiet, polite, and gentlemanly: he wears the most
curly brimmed of hats: he resides somewhere off
the Waterloo Road: nobody knows how he lives,
for though he calls himself and is known as an
actor, he never has an engagement. To behold him
in his glory, you should go to a certain theatrical
tavern in Drury Lane on some especial night, and
when he has had his fourth pipe and his third glass
of gin-and-water his opinion on Mr Fechter's
Hamlet, is, I can assure you, worth hearing. He
never, except when he goes home, strays away
from Covent Garden. The taverns in the neighbourhood are his clubs, and the Central Avenue is
his park. You may sometimes see him tottering
round the Piazza with all the dignity of an ancient
nobleman crawling along St James's Street on his
way to White's or Boodle's. He wears one ragged

glove and flourishes one still more ragged in the
other hand, and sports a high-comedy cane, with
vast tassels, and which cane you will find on inquiry
once belonged to a famous actor whose name is un-
familiar to you. The old-fashioned actor is said to
be descended from a noble family, or he once fought
a duel with a marquis, no one knows exactly which.
He cannot understand the success of such theatres
as the Prince of Wales's or the Gaiety, and looks
upon morning performances as something almost
impious. The toll-house keeper at Waterloo Bridge
touches his hat with profound respect every time
he passes through, for he has an idea that the old-
fashioned actor was a friend of the Duke of Wellington, and somehow or another rendered great
service at the battle of Waterloo, and is the author
of a farce entitled *Up, Guards, and at 'em.* The
old-fashioned actor is good-humoured and enjoys
life and his hallucinations thoroughly: he is always
on the look-out for an engagement, he believes
implicitly in Shakspere, and he pants for the
revival of lengthy terrible tragedies and fine old
standard comedies of the dullest description.

The old-fashioned artist is, perhaps, even more
remarkable. More remarkable because rarer. I met
two of this class the other day going round Fitzroy Square. They looked as if they had just stepped out of one of Mr Opie's picture-frames. They
were blithe young students many many years ago:
they were probably probationers at the time Mr
Fuseli was keeper at the Royal Academy, and,
doubtless, have a rare collection of anecdotes concerning that wild and eccentric genius. These

gentlemen believe implicitly in Sir Joshua; they
pooh-pooh Sir Thomas Lawrence, and they do not
know what to make of Mr Millais, Mr Leighton,
or Mr Sandys. They think the English school
of painting has been gradually decaying for the
last half-century, and their opinions, when they go
to the exhibition at Burlington House, are generally a treat to hear. However, they still look upon
the Royal Academy with the deferential respect
they would accord to the Queen, Lords, and Commons of England, and still talk of young Mr
Haydon as a clever crack-brained iconoclast. I
wonder how those two old gentlemen get their living, and whether they were ever fashionable portrait painters. Did they ever attempt to compete
with that admirable colourist, Mr Jackson? I can
fancy that at one time of their lives they must
have been intimate with Sir David Wilkie, and
have attended a certain life-school in St Martin's
Lane whereat Mr William Etty was the presiding
genius. The works of Mr Dante Gabriel Rossetti,
the water-colour drawings of Mr Burne Jones,
and the pictures of Mr Whistler, are all mysteries
to them. As for modern portrait painting, they
despise it altogether. They detest the delicacy,
the air, the daylight of the modern school of por-
traiture. What they like is the eyes in deep
shade, regulation triangular shadow under nose,
regulation high light on brow and nose, lamp-
light effect, hair mixed up with murky background;
coat also mixed up with murky background,
grimy-looking neckcloths, and no hands if they
can possibly be avoided. They do not care much

about landscape I fancy. If they do it is that hateful style of composition known as classic landscape, a branch of art in which a somewhat peevish and overrated artist Mr Richard Wilson used to excel. They would probably stickle for their 'brown tree' as *paysagistes* did in the days of Sir George Beaumont. They are great admirers of the works of Patrick Nasmyth, and become quite enthusiastic with regard to the pictures of 'Old Crome.' One, possibly, was a Gold Medalist, and the other had the Travelling Studentship at the Royal Academy many years ago, and it is not at all unlikely that their first efforts may have been exhibited at a time when Richard Cosway, Sir William Beechy, Charles Rossi, Joseph Farington, Joseph Nollekens, Northcote, James Ward, and Martin Archer Shee were Royal Academicians, Benjamin West president, and a certain landscape painter, Joseph Mallord William Turner by name, held the post of professor of perspective. All this, you know, is quite within the bounds of probability. I recollect more than a dozen years ago, when I used to attend the lectures at the Royal Academy of Arts, in Trafalgar Square, having a curious, grey-haired old gentleman pointed out to me as being the 'crack' student at the time Fuseli was keeper, and a favourite pupil of his. It appears that he never got much beyond his studentship, for his name as an artist is unknown to fame. He continued, however, to attend the lectures with as much assiduity as the most enthusiastic boy present, and I recollect one evening making a slight pencil memorandum of him in my sketch book. I became so interested in these two ' old-fashioned artists ' that I followed them round Fitzroy Square, and am ashamed to say I tried to listen to their conversation. They did not appear to be very loquacious, they were somewhat asthmatic and infirm : they made me feel melancholy and I pitied them sincerely. I was not sorry, then, when they suddenly melted into thin air, and I lost all trace of them, somewhere about the middle of Howland Street.

The old-fashioned mama is a type of character that you occasionally meet with in the present day. She flourishes to a greater extent in the country than in London. In town you may often find her in the best shops—for shopping, I should tell you, is a part of her *culte*—and she is to be seen in great force at the bazaars. She loved to pervade the Pantheon before it was turned into a wine store, but now her great joy is the Soho. You may frequently encounter her there in the present day ; she generally spends what she pleases to call ' a good long morning ' in flitting about this extraordinary emporium. You may know her at once : she is energetic, good-humoured, and somewhat inclined to *embonpoint*. She is well-dressed ; though her garments are very old-fashioned in cut they are of the most costly materials. If you inquire of the hall-porter you will possibly hear she arrived in that old-fashioned chariot which swings easily on its C springs, like a boat on the ocean. You will, perhaps, discover—if you get into conversation with her footman—that he has been in the family ever since he was a boy, and that the

coachman recollected the old-fashioned mama being brought home a blooming bride. I fancy
this lady resides somewhere about Russell Square,
that being the comfortable quarter peculiarly in
harmony with her old-fashioned ideas. She
generally has a large family. Frequently you
may see a bevy of bonny bouncing girls in short
frocks about with her. For she looks upon
children as children, and does not believe in the
' child of the period.' Her babies remain in the
nursery till they are well grown and sensible, and
her girls are not unfrequently married from the
school-room. She is somewhat strict in her family :
she will be obeyed by her children, but she is very
much beloved. Her daughters are in pinafores at
the time many young ladies are enjoying their
third or fourth flirtation. She has a horror of co-
operative societies, and always pays ready money
for everything. She rarely goes to the theatre,
except to take the children to a pantomime once a
year. She is a fair musician, though she scarcely
ever plays anything except the tunes fashionable
when she was a girl. She loves small dinner
parties, plays a fair rubber at whist, dances quad-
rilles, but has not quite made up her mind with
regard to the latest style of waltzing. She is a
staunch churchwoman; she is neither Low nor
Ritualistic, but believes in the pleasant unctuous
sermons of the old port-wine vicar school. She
goes to church twice on a Sunday, and insists that
her family and children shall do the same. In the
country she is the heartiest and most hospitable
lady of your acquaintance, and her daughters are

the bonniest girls in the neighbourhood. Indeed, as I have before hinted, you are much more likely to meet with favourable specimens of this comfortable class in the country than in town.

The old-fashioned clerk, too, deserves more than a passing notice. He has been well-nigh elbowed from his desk and chivied from his chop-house by the high-pressure commerce and the elaborate restaurants of the present day. And yet you encounter him occasionally. He has given up, for the last thirty years past, the cherished idea of marrying his master's daughter and becoming the ' Co.' in the great house he continues to serve. He plods steadily on a weary, dreary round from one year's end to the other. From nine in the morning till six at night the same monotonous occupation without a break or misfortune to vary it. His only variety is for an hour—from one to two—in the middle of the day, when he goes to take his dinner at his favourite chop-house. He avoids the modern luncheon-bar, for he loves quiet, and likes to sit down and read his newspaper as he eats. He likes to go somewhere where he is not worried by expensively-dressed men of business and blatant young brokers' clerks. Another thing, he prefers to go where he is known and where he is respected. There is a tradition at the Banjo, which he ' uses,' that he has seen better days. And here his threadbare coat and his somewhat over-brushed hat are treated with the greatest consideration. That dapper white-capped cook has heard something about his having lost money in the South Sea Bubble or the Railway Panic of

'41, he is not quite sure which, and there are some faint rumours that our old-fashioned clerk once came to the City in his carriage, had many clerks under him, was a magnate on 'Change, and was favourably mentioned in the Bank Parlour. No one knows whether these rumours are true or not, but every one thinks they are. So a particular corner is always reserved for the old gentleman; the cook puts by choice steaks and grills tempting little bits of fat for his especial delectation. The head-waiter asks him for news, and consults him with regard to the price of stocks and shares and the political aspect of Europe. Thus he enjoys just a little relaxation till his time is up; he buttons his old-fashioned threadbare coat—your old-fashioned clerk is the only person that wears ' swallow-tails ' in the present day—and goes back to his office and calculates, and enters, and ticks, and balances till it is time to go home.

When once you have called up an assemblage of old-fashioned people there is no end to them, and I begin to think it is rather a good thing there is no chance whatever of my giving that party I spoke of at the commencement of this article. The mention of one old-fashioned person calls to mind another. Each one brings such a vast number in his train that it is difficult to depict a tithe of the multitude that presents itself. There are a few specimens, however, that I cannot leave unde-scribed. First and foremost amongst these is the old-fashioned sailor. He is very rare in the pre-sent day, and is I fancy only to be met with occa-sionally at Portsmouth. The progress of education,

the building of ironclads, the advance of competitive examination, and the neglect of Dibdin's
songs by the Admiralty, have well-nigh swept him
out of existence. Still you may occasionally see
him. He is the same rollicking, hearty, reckless
being as of yore, and if he has any money to spend
you may be sure he will spend it as long as he is
on shore. He, however, has some idea with regard
to investments and has heard something about
' putting by for a rainy day.' I do not think he
takes his grog quite so strong nor quite so frequently as in the days when they wore pig-tails,
but he is quite as brave and as open-handed as he
was in those days. If he does not cook gold watches
in a frying-pan and eat bank notes between bread-
and-butter, it is not from any meanness or churlishness, but because he knows he can put his
watches and his bank notes to better use. He can
still spin as good a yarn and sing as jovial a song
as ever, but he feels a good deal of heart has been
taken out of him by the hideous ironclads and
turret-ships of the present day. I am inclined to
think the real old-fashioned sailor now can only be
met with in the person of some brown, kippered,
rugose old salt, who left the service long before
ironclads were introduced. Before Greenwich
Hospital was disestablished you might have seen
a score of such grand old fellows amongst the
pensioners.

The old-fashioned governess is still to be met
with, especially in some parts of the north of
England, and she is well worth studying. She
has a cordial hatred of school boards and ladies'

colleges. She will allow no lecturers nor professors
in her house; indeed, she has a wholesome horror
of introducing any male eagles within her dove-
cote. The dancing-master and the writing-master,
both the shady side of fifty, and married men with
large families, are the only privileged individuals.
Her learning is not very extensive, but what she
knows she knows thoroughly. She is prim, precise, and lady-like : she would like to introduce
the working of 'samplers' once more : she still
believes in the stocks and backboard. She is kind
and considerate : she chooses to be obeyed : she
will not be answered nor allow her pupils to argue
with her. She is averse to setting long tasks :
her discipline is decisive : she advocates such
primitive punishments as putting in the corner,
sending to bed in the middle of the day, and implicitly believes in the efficacy of 'a good sound
whipping'—as she is pleased to denominate it—
for naughty little girls. She insists upon seeing
all correspondence that comes to the school, and
will allow no newspapers or books to be read
without her sanction. She is very neat in her
dress; it is simple but expensive, and her caps all
marvels of handiwork. She has unlimited faith in
the vicar of the parish, and gets him to harangue
her lambs when they require it, and very often
when they do not. She is perhaps helped by her
sister : they have generally seen better days : they
have a pretty hard life of it, and frequently retire
with a very scanty income for the remainder of
their days. She does not think much of the modern

muscular maiden, and anything so 'unladylike'—
as she calls it—as gymnastics she abhors. The
very notion of Madame Brenner's graceful girls in
their Garibaldis and knickerbockers, and the idea
of the evolutions they go through, would strike
her with horror. She would call them all 'tomboys.' Anything that betokens any active muscular exertion she disapproves of. She often asks
in the severest tone of reproof, when some light-
hearted girl is running along at full speed or
romping tremendously, 'Miss Poppet : *Pray*, Miss
Poppet, are you a young lady, or *are* you a
tomboy ? ' In nine cases out of ten it will be
found that Miss Poppet would sooner be the
latter than the former. The old-fashioned governess is, after all, a lady. All her pupils turn out
ladies, or it is their own fault. Everything she
teaches she teaches thoroughly : her pupils may
not get a smattering of everything, but they
know a few things completely when they leave
her care. With all her faults and peculiarities,
most of her girls leave her establishment with
regret.

Perhaps rarer than the above class is the old-
fashioned landlord, the veritable Boniface, the
majestic 'mine host.' Railways have nearly done
for him, and palatial hotels, with limited companies
and limited comfort, have well-nigh chivied him
out of existence. I saw one or two fine specimens
of this class the last time I was up in Wensleydale ;
and, indeed, you are obliged to go out of the track
of railways before you can encounter them in all

their glory. And what a capital thing it is, and how thoroughly you appreciate a good country inn and an old-fashioned landlord in the present day. At your palatial hotel they do not care if they never see you again, and if they see you again even the next week they do not remember you. It is all one to them whether you come or go. How different it is with your old-fashioned landlord ! He knows you well. He recollects all about the last time you came, and who accompanied you : he inquires after everybody : he wishes to know if you would like the same room as you had last time : he recollects what were your favourite dishes, and he takes the greatest pride in getting up some of his choicest vintage for your delectation. What an excellent judge he is of ale, too ! What a pride he takes in pouring it out carefully and holding the glass up to the light, and informing you that it is 'as clear as sherry wine.' Then, how he takes a pleasure in seeing that everything is exactly as you like it, and with what a pride he does bear in the principal dishes himself. You always find there is something more than pounds, shillings, and pence between yourself and the old-fashioned landlord. Then there is the wife and daughter ; a wife, mind you, who knows how to cook, a daughter who knows how to look after the house. It is pleasant enough to have one to cook for you and the other to wait upon you, I can tell you. Late in the evening it is mighty enjoyable to be invited into the parlour, and later still to put yourself behind a solemn churchwarden pipe and partake of a bowl of punch which mine host takes the greatest pride in mixing. How, on these occasions, do you hear all about everybody, and how vastly well you are entertained with all the gossip of the place! In former times the landlord of the chief inn in a town was a man of considerable importance and vast influence; and the bar-parlour was a sort of social 'Change—a centre of gossip and news. Now-a-days an old-fashioned landlord is rarely to be seen. If you go to a gigantic hotel you find a number of head-waiters who *don't* attend to you, and possibly a magnificent secretary who snubs you if you venture to make a complaint. There is an absence of comfort, a want of welcome that has entirely departed since the inn has been changed to an hotel, and the old-fashioned landlord has been supplanted by the modern limited company. If you are fortunate enough to meet with an old-fashioned inn in some country village and a real old-fashioned landlord—and both these are to be' met with occasionally, even in the present degenerate days—you will be surprised what a length of time you will stay there, and how you will enjoy yourself. This is a matter that should be well considered by all proprietors of palatial hotels. They do not know how well it would *pay* to have a real live landlord who should be about all over the place, and whose mission should be especially to welcome and look after his guests, and to see that the servants did their duty.

Old-fashioned servants are becoming rarer and rarer. I do not know what becomes of them, whether they emigrate, or die out, or better themselves, but they become scarcer and scarcer every

23

day. What an air of stability do old retainers give to a house! The white-haired butler who knew your father when he was a schoolboy, and the magnificent housekeeper, who nursed your mother when she was a baby. The ancient groom who gave you your first lesson in riding, and the old keeper who showed you how to load your first gun. We have but too few of the old retainers in the present day. The class who would stick to a family through thick and thin—in adversity as well as prosperity—is every day becoming smaller and smaller. It is a matter of pounds, shillings, and pence with most people in the present day. But if the modern class of servants knew how little their kind of service *pays* in the long run I am inclined to think they would make some alteration. If you get one of the real old-fashioned servants he is invaluable; you respect and consider him just as he respects and considers you. He is well worth double the wage of the others, and you gladly pay it because you can trust him in everything, and do not have to waste your time in looking after him. The old-fashioned nurse is very rarely seen in the present day. She is generally substituted by a smart young lady, either of German or French origin, who passes her time in carrying on a flirtation with the footman and in neglecting her charges. The jovial old nurse, fat and merry, with plenty of quaint songs, funny nursery rhymes, and curious tales is rarely seen. I knew of such a one in the days of my youth. A marvellous nurse she was, and had the most wonderful relations in the world. Whenever she went to see them they sent her back literally padded with buns and laden with oranges, and with packets of the most delicious almond hard-bake ever tasted. Upon my word, I think that my nurse's relations must have belonged to the very best class of old-fashioned people.

DRIFTING HOME FROM HENLEY.

AFTER all, I am inclined to think that the day after Henley Regatta, when you are quietly drifting homewards, is the pleasantest period of the entire trip.

At the regatta itself, there is so much bustle, there is so much excitement, there is such a terrible clangour of church bells, such a banging of guns, such shouting and cheering, that it almost becomes tiresome. On both days of the regatta you meet such a number of your acquaintance, you are interested in so many races, you have to lunch with so many people, and you have so many people come to lunch with you, you are continually rowing some one over to the other side, or you are taking trips in somebody else's boat. You have to look in at the Red Lion, you are obliged to lounge on the lawn, you have appointments to keep at the Blasted Oak, or to assist at a pic-nic down Remenham way. You are so worried by the braying of the band, the shouting of singers, the comicality of the improvisatore, the thrumming of banjos, and the shrieking of vendors of fruit, and ' 'krect cards,' that you have no time to thoroughly enjoy yourself. There is a want of repose, there is a deficiency of that dreamy idlesse which is necessary to constitute perfect happiness. There is a deal of business to

be got through, and business always was, and ever
will be, inconsistent with pleasure in its finest and
most perfect sense.   The drifting home day is even
better than the day you row up.   For when you
are rowing up, though you may row in the laziest
fashion, you always have the idea that you must
get to Henley by a certain time.   You know the
races will commence on a certain day and at a
certain hour, and you feel well assured that if you
are not there at the time appointed the committee will not defer the races till your arrival.
I am not going to say anything about the regatta,
for the daily press always teems with graphic and
elaborate accounts of this pleasantest of aquatic
festivals.   It has been almost as much done to
death as the Derby, and indefatigable ' specials '
have said well-nigh all that is to be said on the
subject.

But still I have somewhat to say with regard
to our drifting home.   And I can assure you we
drifted home in most lazy fashion.   We did not
hurry ourselves in the least.   We stopped here
and we stopped there just as we pleased.   We did
not mind whether we reached home to-day or to-
morrow, or even the day after that.   We supposed
we should get home somehow, but when we arrived
was a matter of perfect indifference.   We dropped
quietly down just as the last race started on Friday
evening.   Just as dainty toilettes were beginning
to be scarce on the lawn, just as the pic-nic parties
were packing up their plates in the Remenham
meads, just as the pretty row of feminine boot soles
have walked themselves off from the banks on the

Berkshire side, just as people are preparing to see the prizes distributed, we watched the sparkling sperules drip from our oar-blades as we drifted down.

In the golden evening we drift down. We note the charmingly-appointed steam-yacht 'Isabel' just preparing to start: we see on board a number of exquisitely-costumed dainty damsels petting a grave, majestic mastiff, and it recalls to us John Leech's famous sketch of the 'St Bernard Dog at the Mont Blanc Lecture.' A gigantic silver tankard is being lazily passed round. Some one is humming the *barcarolle* from *Masaniello*: there is a sweet scent of sedges and of newly-mown hay borne on the breeze. And so, 'mid an exquisite harmony of pleasant sights, sound, and perfume, do we drift down.

With the golden evening paling and the grey twilight deepening, do we drift down. Past Fawley Court, past the Temple with its encampment of boating men, past Culham Court, not coming to a halt till we arrive at Hambledon Lock. Poor old broken-down, dilapidated Hambledon Lock! It is as picturesque as it is dilapidated. It has not yet been smoothed into churchwardenly respectability by a tasteless Thames Conservancy, and looks as if its gates might drop off their hinges, and all its battered timbers roll into the water at any moment. We find here a close pack of boats of all kinds on their way down to Medmenham and Marlow. So closely are they fitted in that it is a marvel how they ever will get out again. At regatta times this lock is often

crowded to excess. They are not particular enough
to close the gates when a certain number of boats
are in.   It has always been the case at this lock
during Henley week.   Many years ago I recollect
having occasion to address the custodian in very
impressive terms on the matter, because he would
permit a gigantic houseboat to enter the lock when
it was crowded with small boats.   The boats, however, and their occupants, behaved pretty well on
this occasion, all except an unwieldy boat with an
awning, which somebody christened the man-of-
war, and which got into awkward positions,
swung itself across the lock and got in everybody's way.

We notice a well-built brown-faced young
fellow sculling a light boat, and a sweet dimpled
damsel with short fair hair steering him.   Happy
youth to be steered by such a dainty maiden, and to
be able to read the 'inner light' of her lustrous eyes
in the gloaming.   The creaking, wheezy, dripping
gates groan and scroop as they slowly swing back,
and we pass out from the ruck and pull smartly
down to Medmenham Abbey.   There we land just
to have a look at the new hotel, for we have serious
thoughts of taking up our quarters there next year.
I always regret very much that the quaint little
tavern which formerly here existed has been pulled
down, and I have ever a prejudice against the
modern hotel on the banks of the Thames, but still
I think we might pass a fortnight very pleasantly
at the new hostelry.   All the arrangements seem
to be of the very best description.   Whilst we are
lounging on the lawn looking at the roses, the 'Grey-

hound,' that prettiest and swiftest of river-steamers, with our friends on board, comes noiselessly sweeping by. They signal to us to know if we are going down with them, or if we would like a tow. We shake our heads and try to look furiously muscular; there is a waving of hats and a fluttering of handkerchiefs, and the little vessel is soon out of sight. We sit down on the landing stage, and watch a group of romping damsels who are chasing and tickling one another to the sound of gladsome girlish laughter. Pleasant enough it is to watch these merry maidens dancing across the lawn, and we would like to stay here for some hours, but the twilight deepens, and it will be dark before we reach Marlow if we do not start soon. We pull away from the grand old abbey with regret, and hear the silvery voices ringing clearly through the still evening air as we take our way towards Hurley.

In the grey-green twilight do we drift down. Past the ancient garden of Lady Place, and under a wooden bridge. As we pass beneath it we catch a glimpse of dainty little boot tips, we have a vision of snowy frills and of petticoats pouting through the palings. We put on our best style, for from remarks which reach us, the beauties of the bridge are evidently no mean critics of the art of rowing. Hurley Lock is quite one of the old school that has not yet fallen a victim to the zeal of the Thames Conservancy. Here we find a racing-eight taking up the greater part of the pound. We are just able to get in in time. Our two young friends manage to get in at the same

time, and we think they look happier than ever,
and as the twilight deepens our brown-faced young
sculler is obliged to gaze closer and closer in order
that he may read the expression of those fathomless eyes. There are a good many people on the
banks and lounging about the timbers of the lock.
Indeed, Henley Regatta must be the only excitement of the year for the good people of Hurley.
It must be something like the Derby-day is to the
sober, serious, particular, tea-drinking, muffin-
eating, scandal-loving population of Clapham.
After we leave the lock we put on a sharp spurt
and pass a couple of pretty girls in most bewitching costumes rowing two lazy youths who are
languidly smoking. And uncommonly well did
these two young ladies pull. They pulled as if
they meant it; there was no playing at rowing with
them; there was a finish and a style about their
performance that was something remarkable, and
their boat sped along merrily. We encountered
them again in Temple Lock, they were not a bit
distressed or flushed : they were two of the clever-
est little *rameuses* I have seen on the Thames for
many a long day. Know ye Undine of the Temple
Lock, who takes your money, who tenders your
ticket, who trips across the lock gates, who winds
up the sluice with such grace and dexterity, 'charming each heart and delighting each eye' ? If ye
know not Undine of the Temple Lock with her
coquettish hat and her pleasant smile, you have a
pleasure to come. And, let me whisper it very
softly, and she has the neatest ankles in the parish
of Bisham.

It is getting almost dark beneath the over-hanging trees in Temple Lock—the boat contain-ing our two young friends is alongside us again. Miss Dimples is singing a dreamy little song to herself, but I think her cavalier seems to under-stand it. There are looks of intelligence pass between them, and her dimples come and go more than ever. ' O so white ! O so soft ! O so sweet is she !' I cannot help saying to myself, for it so exactly describes the little lady. We pass by Bisham Abbey and Bisham Church, run beneath Marlow Suspension Bridge, and get down to the ' Complete Angler' when it is dark. We are by no means in a hurry, so we rest here for the night. I will merely mention that we had our customary *douche* under the weir and subsequent header, the glories of which I have elsewhere described. We are off in good time the next morning for we have fixed to lunch and to dine on the road, and we mean to be lazier than ever.

In the sparkling sunshine, mid the soft summer breezes, do we drift down. We are through Marlow Lock before the ruck of boats have started. There is only one boat going through with us, and in it we re-cognize the coxswain and number two of the Oxford crew. Passing by Quarry Woods, we drift slowly down till we halt at a cottage on the opposite side, to see some old friends of ours. This cottage we first took shelter in during a heavy shower coming up to Henley a dozen years ago, and we have called here ever since whenever we have passed. The good man and his wife and his numerous family always look for us as regularly as Henley Regatta comes round. Here then we pull up, and are received in state by the family on the little wharf. One of our crew, who is a most crafty compounder of cups, begins to be very busy with champagne and soda water, with lemon, and strawberries, and cucumbers, and curaçoa, and ice, and various other ingredients : he finally makes a superb cup, which is passed round to the family and appears to afford them unbounded satisfaction.

We bid them good-bye, we leave them frantically waving adieux to us on the bank, and we pull steadily on till we reach the cut leading to Cookham Lock. We pass under the foot bridge, the word is given ' easy all.' We happen to look up at the bridge, and we see, half-sitting, half-lounging, on the parapet, a fair girl with wonderful chestnut hair rippling over her shoulders, with ripe round lips that seem formed for kissing purposes, and nothing else. She was biting those red lips of hers and pouting : she was shaking those pretty plump shoulders. In the background I could see mama, who was looking very stern and severe about something. There was evidently some difference of opinion between them, and I am afraid my pet with the chestnut is a naughty girl. I should like to get out of the boat and inquire into the matter, but perhaps I might get myself into trouble. I protest I dote upon naughty girls, and this damsel, with her red lips, her wilful shoulders, her big tearful eyes, was something delicious.

In Cookham Lock we encounter a large boat filled with a number of people, who are evidently going on a pic-nic somewhere down the river. A wonderfully jovial party they are. There are several bonny girls amongst them, some hearty gentlemen, and a superb colley-dog named Toby, who is rapturously kissed—I suppose on the same principle that ladies kiss babies before gentlemen—by the prettiest girl of the party. Going up to Henley so many years I am continually seeing the same people, and noting the changes that take place from year to year. Do you recollect my seeing three sisters at this lock some time ago? Troublesome Thirteen, Bashful Fifteen, and Sweet Seventeen. Well, there are those three sisters again. However, there are changes. There is a gentleman in a light suit, who is paying very great attention to Sweet Seventeen, Bashful Fifteen is looking prettier and more womanly than she did, and Troublesome Thirteen is as troublesome as ever; she is climbing about all over the place like the bonny tom-boy she is. She has, however, shot up, and will soon be too big for short frocks and frilled pantalettes. If I go up to Henley a few years hence, I may probably find all three sisters married. Who knows?

Under the glorious woods of Cliefden do we slowly drift down. Here our indefatigable friend thinks it would be a good opportunity to manufacture another cup. He accordingly commences diving into hampers, and rummaging in baskets, popping corks, tasting, shaking his head, and becoming generally mysterious. By the time we reach Boulten Lock—perhaps the most picturesque lock on the river—he has a magnificent cup ready. Pleasant it is to rest for a while as the water is sinking, to loll back in your boat, gaze up at the blue sky, and bask in the sunshine or to gaze into the depth of the 'two handled dew-clouded chalice,' and take deep draughts of clear amber liquid, and let lumps of ice bob against your lips, and rosy strawberries float into your mouth.   Pleasant, mighty pleasant is this, but there are other boats coming down, we can hear wild shouts of 'Lock! Lock!' up stream. The pound must be filled again, and we must pass out.

On we go, then.   Past the Ray Mead Hotel, past Sir Roger Palmer's house, which is now becoming charmingly embowered in trees, and settling down into pleasant harmony with the surrounding scenery.   Past a lot of new buildings on the right bank, which are spoiling and vulgarizing this part of the Thames.   We do not even pause at Skindle's the well beloved, we shoot under grey picturesque little Maidenhead Bridge, we go through Bray Lock, and we land at last at Amerden Bank.   Here we have luncheon.   Despite our mooning and our laziness we begin to feel ravenously hungry, and the sight of a marvellous bit of cold roast beef, a large salad, and bright tankards of ale is by no means displeasing.

We spend a good deal of time in this pleasant hostelry, and after luncheon we sit outside in the shady garden and smoke long pipes and enjoy ourselves prodigiously.   I think some of us went to sleep.   I know everything seemed to be delicious and dreamy.   No one had any desire to move, and had it not been that we were engaged to dine with our excellent friend, the crafty compounder of cups, at Datchet, I think it is very probable we should be at Amerden Bank at the present moment.

And so we drifted home from Henley.

BRIGHTON GHOSTS.

IT seems absurd to connect 'kind, cheerful, merry Doctor Brighton' with anything so dismal as ghosts, and the ordinary visitor to this most popular of all sea-side resorts would have some difficulty in discovering them. They are not to be found in the morning, when the Light Brigade is pattering up and down the cliff, or the pretty walking advertisements of young ladies' schools are passing to and fro; neither are they to be encountered in the afternoon, when the pavement is crowded with loungers, and the roadway is blocked with carriages. It is not till long after the sun has set, and the Light Brigade have assumed their evening dresses, and the school-girls, clad in innocence and pretty frilled night-dresses, have retired to their warm white nests and taken a large instalment of beauty sleep; it is not even till the illuminations have become faint in the gigantic hotels, and the lamps along the Parade are burning pale, that the ghosts at Brighton begin to flit about.

Then, when the streets are silent and deserted, when no sound is to be heard but the tramp of an occasional policeman and the moan of the wind, when the sea drawing back the shingle seems to speak clearly, and then breaks and runs up in a confused chorus, reminding one of the reading of psalms by priest and congregation in some secluded country church, then I can assure you the ghosts come out very strong indeed. You cannot stir a step without meeting some kind of spirit of the past—of the present century or the previous one, of long ago or only yesterday; they come one by one, they come linked together, they come in groups, they come in legions, and the only way one can lay them is to pass them thoroughly in review. Come with me then, O reader, wrap thy Ulster coat around thee, draw thy sealskin cap over thine ears, and stick a gigantic Cabana between thy lips, link thine arm in mine, and I will take thee for a trip in Brighton ghost-land. It is just the period for our expedition, they are just closing the billiard rooms, the Grand Hotel is beginning to look sombre, the wind is moaning dismally, and the sea appears to be playing at priest and congregation more than ever, and reciting the psalms with greater energy than usual.

This particular part is always haunted by ghosts of the garrison. At this very part was the most important fortification Brighton ever possessed. Most middle-aged people can remember it well. It was called the Battery, and it mounted six forty-two pounders, which the garrison were always afraid to fire, for fear of bursting the guns, or breaking the windows, or hurting themselves. The Battery, the small house—which occupied a portion of the site of the Grand Hotel—and the garrison was generally comprehensively alluded to as the Artillery; whether the title applied to the pieces

of ordnance, the barracks, or the garrison, no one
was rash enough to determine. I own I should
like to know what position in the British Army
the garrison occupied. They wore an unaccountable uniform, something between a Chelsea pen-
sioner and a Russian policeman. We used to call
them the Brighton Toddlers. I have a sort of idea
that they were a band of veterans, and that the
youngest drummer-boy of the corps exhibited a
Waterloo medal with considerable pride, and ac-
knowledged to the age of sixty-seven. In connection with this military establishment do I see a
queer little man with a closely cropped white beard,
with a curiously shapen cap on his head, and with
his face turned well up, as if he were trying to read
an inscription in the sky. This is the Star Gazer.
If you watch him you will see he is careful to close
all the gates he sees open, and you may track him
all along the road by the clangour of gates. Do
you see that jolly-looking gentleman in a Bath-
chair ? He is certainly a hopeless invalid, but
evidently makes the best of his position. He is
devouring a dozen or two of oysters at the present
time, and presently his attendant will bring him
out a pot of stout. When he has finished this he
will gravely light a long churchwarden-pipe, and
sit and puff solemnly before all the fashionable
passers-by. This is the individual we used to call
the Hardened Sinner. But we must move on, for
we have lots of work before us this night.

Let us turn up West Street. How silent and
deserted it seems to be. Stay, do you not notice
a handsome face looking out of the tavern window,

on the left ? Do you not recognize the laughing
eyes, the flowing ringlets, the cavalier moustachios
and imperial. Take off your hat, it looks very
much like his most gracious Majesty King Charles
the Second. What talking and laughter is going
on at the little house opposite ! Surely that ponderous voice is familiar. No one could thunder out
' No, sir ! ' with such vehemence, unless it were the
lexicographical bear. Let us peep through the
half-drawn curtains. Yes, there is Dr Johnson,
with his wig very much awry, and his face very
red. Sitting close to him is James Boswell, apparently making a memorandum on the back of
a letter. Mrs Thrale, the accomplished hostess, is
laughing merrily, and Miss Fanny Burney is very
much amused by something Mr Foote, the come-
dian, has just said. That pretty maid-servant who
has just entered the room with a tray of glasses is
the one whom Dr Johnson gets to pump on his
head in the morning, when he has taken too much
wine the preceding night. Judging from present
appearances, I should think the Doctor will require a good deal of pumping on to-morrow
morning.

Let us pass on. Let us mount the hill, take
our way through St Nicholas churchyard. How
quaint the old church looks in the dead of night,
and what an orgie of ghosts we might hold here
were we so minded ! See, here is Captain Nicholas
Tettersel, in his picturesque costume, looking like
a stage pirate. Would you not like to have a chat
with him about the king, and ask him whether he
did not deserve to have a peerage conferred upon

him? What a history, too, could Phœbe Hessel
relate. Far greater were her exploits than the
young lady who 'follered arter' Mr William
Taylor, 'under the name of William Carr,' and
her reward was less. Mr Taylor's lover was made
captain of the 'gallant Thunderbomb,' whereas
the lady love of one of 'Kirke's Lambs,' and who
herself fought at the battle of Fontenoy, was allowed but half-a-guinea a week from royal bounty.
Would you not like a little quiet conversation with
that rugose kippered individual Mr Smoaker Miles,
and hear all about his saving the Prince of Wales
from a watery grave, or gossip with that ancient
mermaid Martha Gunn, concerning the beauties
she has dipped in her time, or exchange a few
words with the beautiful Mrs Anna Maria Crouch?
All this would be really entertaining, but I cannot
allow you to linger.

I am anxious to take you up a little, narrow,
bleak, side street, not far distant. Does it recall
anything to your mind? There is a bright light
in the lower window, and the reflection of
serpent-like plants and spiky creatures on the
blind; there is a faint illumination in the upper
window, and occasionally the shadows of figures
pass across it. Cannot you fancy Mrs Pipchin
is taking her warm sweet-bread in the lower room,
and that Florence is poring over Paul's lessons in
the chamber above? Do not all the inhabitants of
the 'castle of the ogress' at once crowd upon
your imagination, Miss Pankey, Master Bither-
stone, and Berry, Wickham, and Susan Nipper?
We could linger here for a long while, as we just

catch the cadence of the sea in the distance, and ponder o'er that wondrous prose poem of 'what the waves were always saying.'

We get into an entirely different atmosphere when we reach the Steyne. Here we drift into an assemblage of the beginning of the century. Just coming out of the new club-house do we see Mrs Fitzherbert, looking very beautiful, talking to her friend Miss Seymour, and the finest gentleman in Europe, in a plum-coloured coat and a brown hat, is in close attendance. That mysterious-looking person who has just passed is Colonel Hanger; and those three lively individuals leaning against the railings are known as Hellgate, Cripplegate, and Newgate. That comical-looking man in green pantaloons, green coat, and green neck-tie, with powdered hair and a cocked hat, is a harmless maniac; his name is Cope, but he usually goes by the title of the Green Man. That fat man, who has just taken off his hat to the Prince, is General Dalrymple, and the one behind him, in quaint militia uniform, is Earl Berkeley. Colonel Bloomfield is in attendance on the Prince, and the melancholy-looking gentleman who has just dropped his cane is Mr Day, who seems to have well earned his *sobriquet* of Gloomy Day. Do not you wonder who that gentlemanly-looking individual in the costume of the middle of the last century, who is evidently searching for something in front of the Albion Hotel, may be? That is Dr Richard Russell, the actual founder of Brighton, who first recommended the place as a health resort more than a century ago. He is evidently looking for his statue. He used to live on the site of the Albion. Why have not the Brightonians erected a statue to his memory years ago? Those two gentlemen in white coats, with voluminous capes, are two of the most noted whips of the day; the one is Sir John Lade and the other is Mr Mellish; and talking to them is Mr Crampton, the famous jumper. What a crowd there is to be sure! Here comes Lord Sefton, talking to the Bishop of St Asaph; there are the Duke of Grafton and Earl Craven, the Countess of Barrymore, the Countess of Jersey, and Mr Sheridan. There are all these ghosts, and a great many more, start up every moment; they worry us with their everlasting change and their perpetual chatter. Let us flee from them, and drift into a quieter neighbourhood.

I certainly feel more at home here. Do not you? I thought I could not be mistaken in this particular house. This is the very spot in 'Steyne Gardens' occupied by Miss Honeyman, and here that kind little lady, assisted by Hannah and Sally, look after the welfare of their lodgers. It must surely have been to that first floor, with the quaint little balcony, that Lady Ann Newcome, recommended by Dr Goodenough, brought her invalid boy Alfred. Here came Ethel, too, and Miss Quigley, and the invaluable Mr Kuhn; and it must have been in that room down-stairs that the dignified little Duchess regaled the courteous courier with some of that especial Madeira. Hither frequently came dear old Colonel Newcome, and Master Clive was by no means an infrequent visitor. Mighty pleasant are the ghosts that

haunt 'Steyne Gardens' and the joyous recollections they bring back. Cannot you call to mind
Clive making sketches for his little cousins in
these very rooms ? Have you forgotten a certain
journey by rail that Clive and Ethel made to
Brighton in after years, and what transpired on
the road ? Do you remember the meeting in
this unpretending little mansion between Clive
and the most noble the Marquis of Farintosh ?
What a debt of gratitude we owe to those kindly
magicians who invest commonplace neighbourhoods with such delightful ghosts !

Let us take flight as far as Castle Square. It
is silent and deserted. Perhaps we are too early,
for surely there should be the roll of ghostly
wheels and the crack of ghostly whips. If we
only wait long enough, we ought to see a phantom
Bellerophon come lumbering in, or the wraith of
the Quicksilver flash past. We may perhaps see
the whole place change like a scene at the pantomime, the shutters of the shops fall down and
become suddenly converted into the Age, Blue,
Red, and Snow's coach offices, and the square may
become once more crowded, and we may look in
wonder as we see the Times, the Royal Clarence,
the Comet, the Union, the Rocket, the Red Rover,
the Economist, and twenty others whirl noiselessly
past, and vanish into the darkness. Does Sir
John Lade ever come back in the dead of night
and perform those wondrous feats with a phantom
four-in-hand through the narrow streets that made
him so famous in the days of the Regency ?

We ponder this in our minds as we take our

way down Ship Street, one of the quaintest bits of old Brighton yet remaining. We halt opposite the Old Ship Assembly Rooms, and gaze upon the old-fashioned entrance and bow window, and half expect to see the roadway blocked with sedan chairs, and to hear the clamour of noisy linkmen. I wonder whether the guests at the Old Ship are ever disturbed by the sound of dancing and weird music, in the middle of the night. Do the disembodied spirits of Mr Yart, Mr William Wade, Mr J. S. Forth, and Lieutenant-Colonel Eld, ever come back and institute ' assemblies ' at the witching hour ? and is 'Lady Montgomery's Reel,' and such like bygone terpsichorean vagaries, ever executed by a pale courtly company in powder and patches ?

Once more along the cliff; the night is getting chilly, and it looks very black out at sea. Still the priest keeps clearly enunciating his verse, and the congregation almost trip him up in their anxiety to say theirs; they become almost angry in their eagerness. We shall have a wet rough night, but still we feel scarcely inclined to go home yet awhile. It is a most fascinating pursuit, this ghost hunting. We pause before a quaint comfortless house, a prim mansion that looks as if its footman could floor you with a classical quotation, and as if its housemaid were thoroughly acquainted with the first book of Euclid. A hopelessly classical and irremediably cold house. Without doubt this is Dr Blimber's; here Mrs Blimber lamented she had not had the pleasure of knowing Cicero, here came little Paul to school, and here was Cornelia adjured to 'bring him on.' Everybody is gone to bed, and the house is so still now, that one can hear a chain jingling in the back yard, and the measured strident tick of a clock in the hall. We cannot help wondering whether that is Diogenes dragging at his chain, and half fancy that the clock is making the inquiry, 'How is, my, lit, tle, friend?' We should not be at all surprised to hear a pompous voice say in its sleep, 'Gentlemen, we will resume our studies at seven to-morrow morning.' Surely that window up above, that small window to the left, must be where Paul waited and watched for his sister Florence. The ghosts of fiction are pleasanter than those of fact: they even seem more real, and we believe in them more implicitly. Again I say, what do we not owe to those kindly wizards, who invest common streets, ordinary modern bricks and mortar, with an everlasting romance, and an undying interest?

The wind is increasing in violence, we have to struggle against it, the street lamps flicker violently, the sea has begun to roar; the priest has been entirely overcome by the congregation, and they are having it all their own way. They appear to be quarrelling amongst themselves, and are making a prodigious noise over the matter. An occasional scud of spray drifts across the Parade—the rain is beginning to pelt down in good earnest, we have no umbrellas, so cannot at present pursue any further our researches in Brighton ghost-land.

MYSTERIOUS SHOPS.

DURING a long course of wandering about this great world of London, I have been an enthusiastic student of shops. For many years past I have so constantly flattened my nose against their window panes, that it is a wonder that it does not represent the nose of a Hottentot after he has been passed through a rolling-mill, rather than the elegant, aristocratic, and well-shapen organ that at present decorates the figure-head of the good ship Tiny Traveller. I do not know that shopkeepers have benefited much by my studies, for my observations are confined generally to the exterior of their establishments, and I think that if the proprietors had their way they would frequently call in the services of an energetic policeman and insist upon my moving on. As they have no power to do this, I look upon the entire shop world throughout the length and breadth of the metropolis as one vast exhibition, open to me from one year's end to the other; an exhibition to which I never have to pay a shilling for admission, or sixpence for the catalogue; an exhibition of which I may have just as much or just as little as I please; an exhibition that I can enjoy in the open air, where I can ride when I feel tired, eat when I am anhungred, or drink when I am athirst. Mr Jonas

Chuzzlewit was perfectly right when he stated the exhibitions that cost nothing are the best in London, and most assuredly, of all the gratuitous exhibitions in London, that of the shops is the cheapest and the most filling at the price.

Looking at the shops has been a passion with me from my youth up : so much so, that I rarely, if ever, walk decorously down one side of a street. I am perpetually tacking, or vandyking from one side to another, to view some pet window, or to note if some particular article that I have been hankering after for many months past is still on sale. This pastime, however, like all pastimes, has its drawbacks; occasionally, in the course of my travels, I come upon mysterious shops that I cannot understand at all. These shops seem to have no ostensible means of getting a living; they sell things that no one is likely to want, or if they sell things that people are likely to want, you never see any customer inside their doors. And yet their proprietors seem to do well : they appear to be happy and well-to-do, they laugh and grow fat. Sometimes these shops cluster together, as if they did trade amongst themselves, but mostly they stand alone in their mystery, and you discover them in neighbourhoods where you would least expect to see them. These solitary shops generally manage to deposit themselves in localities where there is likely to be the very least demand for the wares they are supposed to sell.

I know of a mysterious chemist's shop, which by daylight and in fine weather is one of the most depressing and dismal you could wish to behold.

Although you see such inscriptions as '*Teeth extracted,*' and '*Prescriptions carefully prepared,*' in its window, its door is rarely opened, and the serenity of the extractor of teeth and the careful preparer of prescriptions seldom disturbed. It is, however, a Tapleyan shop, and it only 'comes out strong' under the most untoward circumstances. On a wet night it becomes particularly jovial, and if a man happens to be run over at the corner and brought in with a dislocated collar-bone and a couple of broken legs, it becomes absolutely hilarious. When the streets are sopping and glassy, when every light gets reflected in the pavement and the roadway, when the very puddles become gay with a thousand will-o'-the-wisps, my chemist has a pyrotechnic display of the quietest but at the same time most brilliant nature. The best of it is it lasts longer than any other description of fireworks, it is not a bang, and a fizz, and a sputter— cheered by the awe-struck 'O-o-o-o-h!' of a thousand spectators. It lasts all the evening. You may take a reserved seat on the kerb-stone at seven o'clock, and you may enjoy your fireworks until half-past. Then you may go away, make a call upon a friend and return at nine o'clock, enjoy half an hour's more fireworks, which you will find will give you a tremendous appetite for a dozen of oysters at a snug little shop hard by. All the time your fireworks will go on, the weather will make no difference whatever, indeed, in wet weather they appear to rather greater advantage than when it is fine. On these occasions the shop almost loses the character of a pyrotechnic exhibition : it gets bolder in its brilliancy and more demoniacal in its demonstration. It looks as if the proprietor had caught a lot of fiery-dragons and one-eyed jelly-fishes, and had shut them up together and given them wood-engraver's glass globes, 'port' and 'starboard' ships' lanterns, and 'caution' and 'danger' railway lamps to play with. And what a lark they are having with their playthings to be sure! What a game of diabolical pitch and toss seems to be going on! How they kick the 'port' lanterns into the 'starboard,' and shiver the danger-signal into a thousand pieces. If you look closely you will see an apoplectic jelly-fish get inside the 'caution' railway lamp and wink. It is one of the most terrible sights you can ever wish to behold. A demoniacal gelatinous wink in the railway interest is something fearful.

Once I recollect going close to the window, when there was a particularly jovial street accident, and the proprietor of the shop was in better spirits than usual. I was startled at beholding the head of the chemist himself—a most respectable man, a licentiate of the Apothecary's Society, a member of the Pharmaceutical Society, a churchwarden, a subscriber to Mudie's, the father of a family, the husband of a wife, and altogether a most respectable member of Society, and greatly looked up to in the neighbourhood—through one of his own green glass bottles. I think I never saw anything so truly horrible in my life before. My respectable chemist was upside down, his decorous well-conducted countenance looked like one of those horrible toys made of Indian rubber, which

were so popular amongst children some time ago,
and appeared as if it had been seized by the ears
and stretched out until it was oval the wrong way.
And then that respectable man's mouth! Ye gods,
his mouth! I never shall forget it! It seemed to
go all round the bottle and back again, and when
he smiled it was something fearful. It was as if a
chevaux de frise of white ivory were bristling all
over the bottle, or as if a porcupine with his quills
turned perfectly white by grief had been suddenly
frightened. Altogether, this mysterious chemist's
shop, when it chooses to come out strong, is one of
the most delightful exhibitions you could wish to
behold.

It is not often that you meet with a congeries of
mysterious shops, but when you do the result is
very terrible; they seem to egg one another on in
mystery, and conspire together to keep the public
in low spirits. The Arcade of the Melancholy
Mad Bootmakers, which existed in London some
years ago, was most depressing to the spirits.
It was long, very narrow, and badly lighted,
having shops, or rather cells, on one side of it.
You rarely saw any one walking about, and to find
a person in any one of the shops was a still greater
novelty. The majority of the tenants of this dismal tunnel were bootmakers. There was an hypo-
chondriacal chemist's—the very coloured bottles in
whose window appeared to be in the lowest possible
spirits, and failed to wink and blink at the passers-by
after the ordinary sportive custom of such bottles
in general. There was a hair-dresser's shop with a
Brobdignagian shaving-brush in the window, which

looked a likely sort of place to get your head shaved
preparatory to paying a visit to the tailor's hard
by for the purpose of purchasing a strait waistcoat. There was also an agency office, whose
window was screened by a large dusky wire
blind, lamentably suggestive of insolvency and the
Bankruptcy Court, which impression was further
strengthened by a padlock on the door and a large
bill announcing the premises were to let. Besides
the shops already enumerated was a mysterious
wine merchant's with a shabby red curtain, a dusty
comatose-looking shop for the sale of fishing tackle
and where you might hire opera-glasses. And
with these were exhausted all the resources of this
melancholy tunnel. What did the inhabitants with
themselves after business hours? Had they any
homes to go to? Or did they sleep in those little
entresols over the shop, or under the counter, or
roll about in wild agony the whole night long
among their own boots?

The above, however, was a rare instance; as a
general rule shops must be alone in their mystery
or they cease to be mysterious. I recollect not
very long ago there existed a very mysterious little
curiosity shop in a lane leading out of the Walworth Road. Now the Walworth Road is not a
very likely place for a hunter of *bric à brac* to visit,
is it? Nevertheless, there this shop was, a little
bow-windowed shop which looked like an alderman
who had been sat upon : the window was crammed
so full of curiosities that you could not see beyond
it. The place was a circulating library too : there
was a library but it did not circulate, and the same

novels—lively works of forgotten authors of about the year 1811—remained flattened against the window panes at the same thrilling part of the story as long as I knew the shop. All the children of the neighbourhood knew these fragments by heart, but they never had the coin to pay for the hire of the work, much less the money to leave as a deposit, the consequence was that they all finished the tales according to their own ideas, and frequently in a manner 'that would very much have astonished the author could he have heard it. These books never altered their position from one year's end to the other. They kept their place as if they were fixtures. So did the old china, the Hindoo gods, the Caffre spears, the Malay creases, the bows and arrows of the South Sea Islander, the shark's teeth, the spiky uncomfortable-looking shells, the million geological specimens, the cowries, the wood carvings, the shattered Roman pots, the rusty ironwork, the ancient coins, the mouldy walking-sticks and canes, and the useless collection of old fowling-pieces, horse-pistols, and rusty cutlasses. All these things were never moved; they never changed in any respect save that they became rustier and dirtier every day. Nobody ever bought anything and nobody was expected to buy anything.

The shop was kept by a most amiable old lady, who, according to her own account, was quite a middle-aged woman when the Princess Charlotte died. She was a short, stout, jovial old lady; she had become in figure like unto her shop, and her mind was crammed with a quantity of odd recol-

lections and useless curiosities in the way of anecdote also like unto her shop. She would talk
about the Princess Charlotte, and would take great
pride in a little picture of the princess, when about
five years of age, and her royal mother, engraved by
Mr S. W. Reynolds from a painting by Mrs Maria
Cosway, and she would recite you certain 'lines'
on Chalon's Portrait of the Princess Charlotte on
the smallest provocation. The old lady was fond
of gossiping: she, assisted by her two daughters—
one was somewhat of an invalid—would talk to
you as long as ever you pleased to stay.

If you made any purchases, they always
seemed to feel aggrieved, as if by removing the
article you bought you entirely threw their little
museum out of order. It was a small house:
the old lady and her daughters had scarcely
room to live, and yet the largest and best room
on the first floor was fitted up as a sort of show-
room into which no one ever went. This room
was set out with odd cups and saucers, cracked
jars, ancient paste shoe-buckles, faded miniatures
painted after the manner of that most coxcomb-
ical of Royal Academicians, Mr Richard Cosway,
lidless snuff-boxes, and boxless lids, fans of peacock's feathers, cracked little mirrors, faded finery,
tarnished gold lace, and soiled brocade. And,
as a melancholy commentary on all this, a lute
with a very large rift in it, with its strings broken:
a flageolet with its mouthpiece broken, a flute
with its middle joint missing, and a brass figure
of Time, unlacquered, black and disconsolate,
with his scythe broken in two. It is impossible to

describe all the curious, useless, unsaleable, dilapidated things there were in this room.   Round the
walls were hung engravings in red by Bartolozzi
after Cipriani, with black margins and mouldy-
looking gilt frames.   Over the chimney-piece was
a convex mirror with candle branches.   One of the
candle branches was broken off short, and from the
other hung one of those old-fashioned coral neck-
laces with gold clasps that school-girls used to wear
many years ago.   I often used to wonder whether
it belonged to the Princess Charlotte when she was
a baby, but I never liked to ask for fear of provoking a flood of recollections.   The window curtains were of faded chintz, of a pattern that could
not be matched in the present day, and the plump-
est, sleekest cat with a brass collar kept watch and
ward over this unaccountable little room.

Sometimes I used to discover the old lady
having a ' dish of tea ' in the little parlour behind
the shop.   There was a courtliness about her, and
she gave a flavour of stiff brocade to her faded print
dress and a dash of old English point to her muslin
cap.   I always fancied that when my old friend
was a slim young girl that she could dance the
Minuet de la Cour to perfection.   I could fancy
that at one time she had been quite the belle of her
circle, and an adept in the use of the fan.   But the
shop, the curiosity shop, the emporium for *bric à
brac*, the circulating library that did not circulate,
but was within the roar of the Peckham omnibuses
and within sight of the Clapham conductors, was
the great mystery to me.   I called at this house so
often that I became pretty well acquainted with its

internal economy. I found that the old lady and her daughters were by no means overdone with this world's goods : that they were obliged to live somewhat poorly : that they had to pinch and to save, to pare and to contrive, in order that they might get along decently. And yet they did not seem to care to make money by the sale of the goods in the window, or the circulation of books in their library.

If I ever wanted to buy anything they generally let me name my own price, and I always felt they were granting me a personal favour in allowing me to remove it. Was this old lady, I thought often to myself, a duchess in disguise, and had she some particular reason for living in this eccentric fashion ? Were all these curiosities but remnants of her former greatness—mouldy heirlooms that cost her a deep pang to part with ? I could never understand it. All the dirty children round the neighbourhood treated her with profound respect when she took her walks abroad ; the ragged boys left off their game of pitch-penny and touched their hats ; the roystering, shock-headed girls left off their game of hopscotch and dropped a curtesy. It was very rarely that she ventured out of her shop, however : she seemed out of her place walking in the streets. A luxurious sedan-chair, and a couple of powdered footmen for bearers, and a half-a-dozen more with flambeaux and stout silver-headed canes to clear the way, would have been more in harmony with her style of locomotion. The old lady never had her windows broken by tip-cats, nor did the rude boys ever attempt to 'chivy' her sleek well-fed cat. Indeed, this cat was about the only being on the establishment that did not look as if it had seen better days. There was no element of decay, no suspicion of departed grandeur, about this sleek old tabby as he rolled over the faded novels and picked his way gingerly amongst the curiosities. I sometimes used to think that this sleek tabby was the presiding genius of the place, and that everything was sacrificed in order that he might be made comfortable. The mystery of the whole establishment worried me. Sometimes I fancied that it might be a cloak for some other trade. That there might be a private entrance to some smuggler's cave under the counter, and that bold outlaws might bring cargoes of brandy up the Surrey Canal by night and take them up a dark passage to this curious little shop, whence they could be taken away in the daytime by mild-looking gentlemen in long cloaks disguised as antiquarians.

Another idea subsequently struck me. I had noticed the vast amount of information the old lady had acquired relative to the Princess Charlotte, and also the faultless accent with which she pronounced French words when she had occasion to make use of them. It struck me that she might, at one time of her life, have been governess to the princess, or, if not governess, nurse. I resolved not long ago that I would make another call and unravel the mystery. I found not without some difficulty — for the neighbourhood has greatly changed within the last few years—the lane off the Walworth Road, and I discovered the shop. But its aspect had entirely changed. New tenants had taken possession : another race who knew not the Tiny Traveller had arisen. A dirty, impudent young man, in the ironmongery line, who was singing 'p'raps she's on the railway, p'raps she's on the sea, p'raps she's .gone to Brigham Young a Mormonite to be,' gave me an evasive answer when I made inquiries, and my courtly old lady and her daughters had departed no one knew whither.

MY PRIVATE PICTURE GALLERY.

THERE is, perhaps, nothing in the world so delightful as a quiet stroll round a private picture gallery. If you go to the Royal Academy you are crushed and crowded; you find a mob round the favourite pictures, and you are only able to get glimpses of their beauties by instalments,—between hats, chignons, and bonnets moving before them. The exhibition at Burlington House is a pleasant lounging ground, it is a good gossiping saloon, it is a favourite flirting gallery, but as for people going there to enjoy the pictures, it is simply absurd. It can only be accomplished by going very early in the morning, and even then it can only be achieved in a limited degree; there are too many works of art to be seen, too many rooms to be 'done' in a given time, to make the inspection of pictures anything more than a wearisome labour and a matter of duty. When once a thing becomes a matter of duty it resolves itself into a painful performance. The foregoing remarks apply equally to the well-lighted galleries at South Kensington, the National Gallery, the Louvre and the Salon in Paris—indeed, any galleries that are popular and public all the world over. You come away with a confused kaleidoscope of all the pictures mixed together, with a clear recollection of no single one of

them, and with probably the very worst headache
you ever had in your life.

It is altogether a different matter if you get into
a private picture gallery.   If you are turned loose,
so to speak, among the pictures; if you are not
worried by a garrulous housekeeper, nor pestered
by an ignorant *cicerone;* if the proprietor has such
confidence in your honesty that he knows you will
not slip a silver sconce or two in your pocket, and
such implicit belief in your good behaviour that he
knows you will not take advantage of his absence
to job your umbrella through his favourite Guido;
in short, if he permits you to behave 'like a bee,'
to quote Mrs Blimber, 'about to plunge into a
garden of the choicest flowers, and sip the sweets
for the first time,' and buzz about his picture gallery whithersoever you list, you will be able to
enjoy pictures in a way you never enjoyed them
before.   What delightful mornings I have passed
in the quaint galleries of Knole in this wise.   How
I have mooned over the pictures by Sir Joshua and
Gainsborough, with no sound to be heard but the
rustle of the leaves outside.   I have wandered and
pondered and dreamed in these pleasant art-pas-
tures, till I have almost peopled the place once
more with the bright-eyed beauties and the gallant
gentlemen that these accomplished artists painted.
I have half fancied there was a film of hair-powder
floating in the rooms, an odour of lavender, a rattle
of sword hilts, and the *frou-frou* of stiff brocade
over the polished oaken floors.

What glorious mornings I have passed in old
Venetian palaces, with no one to speak to me, no

one to worry me, and no interruption save the sharp splash of the water outside, and the fierce 'Ah ! y—ee !' of the gondolier as he urges his craft forward. How I have gloated over the glories of Paolo Veronese, steeped myself in the mysteries of Tintoretto, and revelled in the superb sunshine of Tiziano Vecelli. Surely this is the right way to study pictures. When all the surroundings are in harmony with their period. When if they were to suddenly come to life, and step out of their frames, they would find themselves as much at home as they would have been more than three hundred years ago. It is true that if they went down-stairs they might discover a *Gazzetta d' Italia* that they could not quite understand ; if they went out of doors, the railway station, the steamers flitting about the lagoon, the crowds of strange people at Danieli's, might cause them to wonder ; but if they kept inside their *palazzo* they would be just as comfortable as ever they were. How one drifts entirely out of the nineteenth century in some of these quaint old places !

And yet all these delights of quiet galleries at home and abroad pale before the enjoyment that I derive from the inspection of my own private picture gallery. Perhaps you did not know that I had one. Nevertheless, it is true enough. And so have you, my dear madam, and so have you, my dear sir ; you have one also, my dear young lady, who are just out, and you, my dear young gentleman, who are now keeping your first term at Oxford. School boys at Eton, pets in pantalettes at Miss Demure's at Brighton, babies in arms, all have

their private picture galleries, of which they keep
the key, and of which they alone can understand
the catalogue.   I am not going to attempt to describe the galleries of any of these good people,
simply because I do not happen to be provided
with a key to unlock the door, and because the
catalogue is written in a language with which I am
by no means familiar ; but with my own it is altogether a different matter, and I can tell you a great
deal about it.   It is a favourite amusement of mine,
when I have nothing to do—and very often when
I am busier than usual—to sit down by the side of
the fire, and go for a tour of inspection round my
little gallery.   Lovingly gazing on many a charming picture, looking at it through the magnifying
glass of age, and polishing it up with the silk hand-
kerchief of recollection.   There is always a variety.
I generally seem to go round my gallery a different
way, or the pictures are not arranged in the same
fashion.   Some pictures I lose sight of for years ;
there are some that I can never escape seeing when
once I open the door of my gallery.   It often, I
fancy, depends upon the weather, my state of health
or temper, as to what pictures happen to catch my
eye.   Sometimes I care to look at nothing but
those that are bright and brilliant ; at others I gaze
exclusively at grey and sombre pictures, and paint-
ings in a very low key of colour ; but more often it
is, as on the occasion of this present visit, I see
pictures of every variety.

Here is something very pretty !   Two girls
beating up against the wind along a rugged stone
pier.   Over the sea wall you can see the bright

dashing sea, the grey sky with the gulls flashing
white against it.   You will notice the crisp, merry
breakers far out at sea, and a spirtle of spray occa--
sionally dashing over the wall.   What two bonny
girls bravely breasting the breeze are these!—the
one dark, and the other fair.   They are evidently
sisters, and about two years difference between
them. The younger has blue-grey eyes of wondrous
eloquence ; her face is of that delicious tint that
fair girls often acquire by exposure to the sea and
sun :

> 'Her cheeks so kist by ardent sunny ray,
>   That bright carnation blushes through the brown,'

to quote the lines of a certain modern songster.
She has a torrent of fair hair of a rare tint and
wonderful luxuriance, which is rippling over her
pretty plump shoulders, which is blown over her
eyes, and twisted and turned in every way at once
by Mr Boreas, who seems to be having the friskiest
of games with these two damsels. The tresses of
the elder sister are massed closely round her head,
and imprisoned in a net ; but you see what superb
dark tresses they are, and what coils of real hair
would come falling about her if Mr Boreas ventured
to pull away the net. What a pretty contrast these
two bright, laughing, blooming sisters are!   Do
you notice what excellent figures they have ?   Mr
Boreas has as much an eye for a good figure as a
sculptor, and if a girl receives a certificate of good
figurehood from this critical gentleman she has
nothing to fear.   But I beg you to notice how well
these young ladies, with their pretty holland dresses.

wrapped tightly round them—like the drapery of
the Venus of Milo—pass through the ordeal. What
round, girlish figures they have! What exquisite
grace there is in every line, and what a superb
study of flying drapery it is! You may see the
evidence of gentle ladies in the exquisite little
boots, the dainty artfully-tucked petticoats, the
dazzling white stockings, and snowy frills, that are
from time to time revealed. What a sparkling
sunshine, what joyous laughter, what bright, breezy
briskness, what life, beauty, and youth there is
about this scene! One feels all the better, and
younger, and fresher for looking at it. I think
this picture must have been drawn by John Leech.

The next that catches my eye is a most remarkable little work. It is framed, as it were, in the
black doorway of a gondola, which gives extraordinary value to the marvellous colour beyond it.
In the immediate foreground are a pair of uumis-
takable English boots, which look out of all proportion to the rest of the picture. Beyond them
is a tawny gondolier asleep, and then comes the
prow of the gondola glittering in the sunshine. It
is, perhaps, merely as a study of colour this work
should be viewed, for the figures are very small,
and scarcely affect the composition in any way.
But what colour it is! What mellowness, what
harmony, what variety! You can look at it for a
week, and find a fresh beauty every minute. Do
you note the mouldy walls, with their scaly surface,
with their fungoid growth, their shattered masonry,
as if they were suffering from a cutaneous disease,
and a red brick rash had broken out here and there.

Do you see the reflection of the prows of passing
gondolas on the damp walls—the queer windows,
securely barred by an ornate tangle of ironmongery; the dilapidated doors and water-worn
steps? Then how picturesque is that group of
stripen mooring-posts, with their quaintly-fashioned
heads; how well do those weather-beaten green
shutters repeat the colours of the water under the
low bridge, and what value there is in that bit of
yellow drapery drooping from the quaintly-carven
stone balcony on the left! What excellent effect
there is in the mass of warm shadow just beyond,
and how well does the crumbling tracery of a glorious old grey church in the extreme distance finish
the picture! The blue-faced clock, with its faded
golden figures, you think almost too positive in
colour till you raise your eyes and see the deep
blue sky against which all the roofs, spires, and
chimneys stand out with an almost photographic
distinctness. There are plenty of figures—and picturesque figures too—on the bridges, leaning from
windows, lounging in balconies, and lolling in gondolas. But they are of secondary consideration—
they serve as bits of colour in exactly the right place,
to conduce to one grand harmony. I have a strong
idea that this lovely study of colour must have
been painted by James Holland.

Another Italian scene, but one of a very different kind, I cannot refrain from giving a passing
glance at. A terrace in a garden by the Lago
Lugano. You can see what a lovely night it is;
the moon is almost at its full, and is glinting superbly on the waters. There are one or two boats
flitting about the lake, as you can see by tiny glow-

worm lights, or when they drift with their un-
covered awning frames, looking like the skeletons
of some huge lake fish, across the path of the
moonlight. A little group of lights of the faintest yellow marks a village on the other side of
the lake. A couple of boats with lamps almost
close to the shore, repeat the colour in an orange
tone. It is again repeated almost to redness in the
incandescent tips of the cigars of some loungers to
the extreme left, and it culminates in bright vermil-
lion in a cigar held by one of the principal figures
in the immediate foreground. A handsome young
fellow he is without his hat ; his face is almost in
shadow, but you get a sort of silhouette against
the moonlight, which shows its handsome outline
distinctly. Do not you fancy you can almost hear
the mournful plash of the little ripples on the shore,
and almost smell the dainty perfume that is wafted
on the soft evening air ? The second figure too,
how charming that is ! You can see her face ex-
cellently as it is upwards turned in the moonlight.
What eloquent, pleading, large eyes ! what a pouting kissable mouth ! What faith, what hope, what
exquisite tone there is in the whole expression !
How admirable is the pose of the young girl, with
her two hands clasped round the arm of her lover !
How well the curling blue vapour from his cigar
brings his head away from the background of oleanders, whose magnificent bunches of pink bloom
you can even distinguish in the cold moonlight.
I do not think anybody but John Phillip could have
so cleverly arranged such a contrast of hot and cold
colour, nor could any one have painted the pink
tint of that oleander in moonlight so skilfully.

Next to this comes a study of a young girl in a simple white dress, seated on a bank, amidst pure English woodland scenery. The dress is diaphanous, and has no decoration save a few *céladon* ribbons; you can see her warm white bosom and exquisitely-shapen arms through the thin gauze of muslin. She has an innocent little straw hat on, underneath which her closely cropped silken hair curls luxuriantly. She has fathomless brown eyes that are very lovely, and she has a lap full of wild flowers. The face is bent forward, and is in shadow, save the tip of her delicately-rounded chin, and she is holding a scarlet pimpernel to her lips. How lovely are the pearly grey shadows on her soft skin, and how daring is the introduction of the bright red flower. Pray note how well rendered is every turn of her girlish figure and how skilfully indicated through the drapery! By her side sits a noble St Bernard dog—brindled, with a white blaze on his chest. His head is magnificent, and his limbs are something enormous. The young lady is decorating his collar with wild flowers, which he endures patiently with a sort of grim humour, as if he were saying to himself, ' See what fools these pretty little pets make of us big, strong, superior animals ! ' A wonderful contrast this picture presents between the pretty, tender, soft girl, and the magnificent, powerful brute. I am inclined to think this must be the work of two artists. I feel confident that nobody but Mr George Leslie could have painted the beauty ; and I am certain no one less skilful than Sir Edwin Landseer could have done justice to the beast.

Would you please to look at this long sea-scape?

There is nothing much in it, perhaps you will think. Yet how true to nature you find it. It has a low horizon, and you see a great deal more sky than sea : it is getting towards evening, the breeze is freshening, the tide is rising, and the waves seem to be chasing one another on to the sand. What grand grey clouds are those, and what an angry-looking sunset it is ! The more you look at this picture, the more interested you become. You presently become conscious of the figure of a young fellow in the right-hand corner. You see he has stopped and is gazing down on the sand. You then see there is the print of tiny boot soles extending right along the hard yellow sand in the foreground, and just at the point where he has stopped they have been joined by the print of boots of a larger and more masculine nature. The young fellow looks as startled as did Robinson Crusoe when he discovered the print of the foot of his man Friday. Of course he is a minor part of the picture, but it serves to give a human interest to the superb sky, the chasing billows, and the approaching storm. It looks very like the clever work of Mr Henry Moore.

I have in these few brief notes just given you a peep at a few of the pleasantest works in my private picture gallery. There are other pictures in it which I keep perpetually curtained, and there are some whose faces I would gladly turn to the wall. Some day, perhaps, I may discourse on these ; but, as I said in the beginning of this article, the real way to study and thoroughly enjoy pictures is to see only a few at a time

COMING BACK.

A CERTAIN disreputable unprincipled cynic of my acquaintance once said, 'The next most delightful thing to falling in love is falling out of it.' This man had evidently a most ill-regulated mind, and I was obliged to warn several mamas with large families of marriageable daughters against him. I have no doubt he eventually came to a bad end. Let us hope he is by this time married to a very strong-minded woman who keeps a very sharp eye upon him. Let us hope he is very much married, and now that he cannot help himself he has seen the error of his ways. I do not wish to enlarge on this subject, though I could do so to the extent of a dozen pages or more. I have no desire, however, to discourse on love, or marriage, or Shakspere, or the musical-glasses, in this paper. I simply quoted the saying of my cynical friend because it bore some resemblance to a remark I was about to make relative to returning to town after a holiday. I really think, and I am quite certain there are very many will agree with me, that the next pleasantest thing to starting for your autumn holiday is coming home again. The whole affair after all bears some analogy to being engaged to be married and eventually backing out of your engagement by mutual consent. You start for your trip in the highest spirits and look forward with bright hope and anticipation of the joyous time you will have : you are busy getting your travelling kit together, saying good-bye to your friends, getting your passport *visé :* you have no time to calculate whether you will enjoy yourself or not on your trip : you take it for granted you will : you are all hurry and excitement and anxious to be off and away : the idea of your outing proving a failure, or your being bored in the least, never enters into your calculations for a moment.

It is just the same with being engaged to be married. Say you are engaged to a pretty girl : you thoroughly believe in her, you trust her in everything, you think she is as true as steel and there is none like unto her. All this you will swear to in the first flush of your engagement. You are so pleased with your conquest : your vanity is so tickled by having not only the hand but the heart of a pretty girl for your own that you do not question her sincerity for a moment. But after the first excitement of your betrothal has died away, and you find the girl is false at heart, that you can place no dependence on her, that her charming artlessness was all assumed, and that absolutely you could trust the most distinguished liar of your acquaintance—most of us are acquainted with distinguished liars, I am quite sure that I know half a dozen—more than you could trust her. Then, my brethren, would ye not find it a mightily pleasant thing to fall out of love ? Then would not the returning of presents and letters, the getting back to your bachelor haunts, your distinguished liars, your easy-going ways, your club, your residence among men and things you could trust, be as charming as the return to town after a pleasant holiday at the sea-side, the country, or the Continent? I think there is no doubt whatever but that it would be so.

One of the most pleasant things in coming back is coming back to your necessities and finding them luxuries. Why, bless your heart, a man who spends all his life in London has not the least idea what a life of luxury he leads from one end of the year to the other. He has his *Times* and his *Daily Telegraph* damp from the press every morning at eight o'clock, and if he happens to be awake and tolerably sensible by ten he is posted up in all the news of the day. He does not look upon this in the light of a luxury. Not he! But let him be away from England, and never see an English paper till it is four days old, and sometimes missing that, and not seeing another for a fortnight, and won't he just appreciate the morning papers that arrive before he is out of bed, though a goodly portion of them were in manuscript when he retired to rest. He will then be able to realize what a life of luxury he has been leading for so many years past without knowing it. How one enjoys, too, especially if one has been pottering about in out-of-the-way Continental towns, the glorious luxury of one's own tub. Possibly one has had to memorialize landlords, issue manifestoes to waiters, send protocols to chambermaids, enter into diplomatic relations with ' bootses,' in order to secure some kind of apparatus commensurate with an Englishman's idea of washing. Perhaps, after ringing all the bells in the hotel, bawling yourself black in the face, nearly being involved in a free fight,

and upsetting the entire establishment, you have
been able to obtain a couple of pie-dishes, and a
milk-jug full of water, and towels about the size
and substance of cheap pocket-handkerchiefs.
Then to come back to one's own tub, is indeed a
luxury. You never looked upon it in that light
before, but now you do. To find it there when
you wake in the morning—and not to have to ring
violently for it, as if you were going to commit
suicide, and if it did not come quickly you were
afraid you would change your mind—to find it
waiting for you to tumble into, to find your large
sponge, and your vast Baden towel, is something
that you highly appreciate. To come back to
one's own bed-room and one's own bed, after the
musty-fusty chambers and the hard uncomfortable
couches one has experienced, is very charming.
After travelling about with one's shirts mixed with
one's boots, and hair-brushes sprinkled with tooth-
powder, it is very delicious to find everything in
its proper place, that you need not trouble about
sending things to the wash, and if you should require an extra shirt or two you will know where to
put your hand on them. It is a great pleasure to
find all the little contrivances, which have grown
imperceptibly with the occupation of your own
bed-room, have so increased in value; and it is an
inestimable blessing not to be obliged to look after
your night-shirt. After having lost six night-
shirts in eight days, it is very comforting to
know, if you do not pack it up, you will find
it there just the same when you go to bed in the
evening.

26

How pleasant it is to see your own familiar bits
of furniture blinking in the firelight, your favourite pictures looking down upon you with their old
expression, and your thousand and one little nick-
nacks and household gods giving you a silent welcome. To fancy your old clock even ticks faster
and chimes in a more hilarious fashion, and your
looking-glass glistens more than heretofore, as it
reflects such a brown, brown master, and wel-
comes him back again. And then your books!
After being confined to Continental *Bradshaw*, a
Murray, and a torn *Baedeker* for the last six weeks,
you will find your own modest bookshelves seem
like unto an unlimited Bodleian. You had no idea
that you had so many books, or that they were
half so interesting. You positively gloat over
your own little collection. You treat yourself to a
tasting order in your special poetical bin. You dip
into your favourite vintage; you 'draw samples'
of your Swinburne, your Tennyson, your Marston,
your Rossetti, your Praed, your Leigh, your Locker,
and your Mortimer Collins. You spend a long
time in the Thackeray cellars, and find it difficult
indeed to tear yourself away from those of
Dickens.

Again, you find it is a great joy to be back
again at your own writing-table, and to wallow
once more amongst comfortable writing materials.
After being compelled to use the thinnest of
foreign post, so thin that if you become at all
earnest or enthusiastic you will send the point of
your pen through at least a quire and a half, it is
a blessing to come back to decent paper and a
capacious blotting-pad. After the miserable rusty

nibs, splodgy quills, and pale, muddy ink of foreign hotels, you find your own carefully-chosen implements and materials to be very enjoyable. To be able to begin to write at once, directly after breakfast if you like, without having to clear a space on the table, make innumerable preparations, and go on a foraging expedition in search of writing materials, is joy indeed. What a mine of valuable knowledge, what a wealth' of learned information, do your books of reference appear to be now, and how you value their accuracy after being obliged to trust to your memory for a quotation, and ' draw on your imagination for your facts,' for so many weeks past! In short, how highly you value the little world—the tiny world so important to you, but so utterly insignificant to the rest of the universe—that is contained within your four walls. You did not think much of it when you left town a couple of weeks ago. You thought it was rather a silly little world, and, as a world, somewhat of a failure. It was not the complete little place that you intended it should have been. Indeed, you were rather disgusted with it altogether, and would have at once disestablished it had it been in your power. But now you have changed your opinion altogether, and you consider it is the most complete and well-organized little world you ever saw in the whole course of your life.

It is in the month of October that wet days at any of the holiday resorts become a serious matter. Rainy weather just at this period is bad for lodging-house keepers, fly drivers, bathing-machine proprietors, donkey boys, and shrimp vendors, and the whole class who feed and fatten on the summer visitors to the sea-side. Rainy weather at this time decides whether the season is to be long or short. A few prolonged showers at the beginning of October will do many hundreds of pounds damage to a popular watering-place. People begin to turn their faces homeward in this month, and the popular sea-side towns lose a large portion of their surplus population :—

> ' Home come the beauties from Ramsgate and Margate—
>   Sad is the wavelet, the summer breeze sighs—
> *Blasées* with using man's heart as a target,
>   Only for shafts from their fathomless eyes!
> Whitby is silent and Filey deserted,
>   Sirens are scarce upon Scarborough sands ;
> Flown are the fairies that fearlessly flirted,
>   Mute is the braying of Teutonic bands.
> Cold blows the blast round the sweet Isle of Thanet,
>   Beating its headlands with billows of snow ;
> Lovers grow cold 'neath the silver-orbed planet,
>   The season is over, 'tis better to go.'

It only requires a few wet days to show you how hopelessly uncomfortable the best of lodgings may become, how hard up you may be for amusement, how utterly weary you grow of the whole place, and how glad you are of any excuse to run away from it altogether. Being in sea-side lodgings during long, dull, wet autumn evenings is positively the most detestable state of existence. You cannot stir out, there is no amusement worth seeing in the town, and if there were you would be wet through before you got there. You think it is scarcely cold enough to have a fire, and so it is not lighted, and you sit staring at the hideous grate bedizened with its detestable paper fripperies and tinsel tomfoolery. You have not any books, you have read everything in the library, and you have gone through to-day's papers steadily. You have read them, advertisements and all, upside down, inside out, and hindside before: you gape till it is time to go to bed, and when you go to bed you cannot sleep. You are thoroughly miserable, and right glad are you when your holiday is at an end and you are obliged to pack up your traps and spin off to town.

It is curious, too, how you find how admirably things have gone on in your absence ; indeed, I think more matters of importance happen when you are away from town than at any other time. If you want sensations to come about, if you require novelties, wonderful accidents, startling marriages, extraordinary inventions to be brought out, just go away for a month, and you will be astonished at the variety of unaccountable affairs that have come to pass in your absence. People seem to take advantage of your being away. Directly your back is turned, one of your most intimate friends gets married, or commits suicide, or goes mad, or becomes bankrupt. You feel perfectly certain that if you had remained in town for a year in the expectation of seeing either or all of these events come off, they would not have taken place.

I am inclined to think that London never appears to such advantage as when people are gradually getting back after the autumn holidays. There seems to be something so cozy and genial about it. You love to sit over your fire of an evening, to light the gas directly it begins to get dusk, and you hear the muffin-man ringing his bell round the square. You enjoy people dropping in of an evening, and chatting over their holiday experiences, and if you feel inclined to turn out, you will find the club smoking-room is tolerably full, it is brilliant and jovial, there is none of that hopeless greyness that you experienced when you looked in just before you started on your trip. Then the theatres are beginning to wake up, the managers are getting somewhat hopeful, and we are commencing to speculate on new pieces. We are already talking about the Cattle Show, and have visions of those country cousins of whom I have already spoken. We are beginning to chat about the pantomimes, and some of the knowing ones amongst us talk in mysterious fashion, and could, if we were so minded, divulge what are to be the titles of those at the principal houses. People may say what they like, I hold that October and November are two of the pleasantest months in London. Those months when, amidst the short days and the gloom, you can thoroughly appreciate the brilliancy of gas and the glow of the fire.

'No nation,' said Albert Smith, 'makes such a fuss about its "tea-kettle" comforts as the English. No people is more notoriously anxious to get away from them.' And having got away from them, I would add, no people is more unfeignedly thankful to return to them. Possibly even the laziest of loungers who has done me the honour to accompany me in these Tiny Travels, may feel some satisfaction in returning to the Land of Nod. Who knows?

THE END.

JOHN CHILDS AND SON, PRINTERS.

BY THE AUTHOR OF 'TINY TRAVELS.'

Now ready, one vol. crown 8vo, handsomely bound, 7s. 6d.

THE SECOND EDITION OF

THE SHUTTLECOCK PAPERS:

A BOOK FOR AN IDLE HOUR.

By J. ASHBY-STERRY.

CONTENTS :—1. The Den. 2. Hot Coals in the Land of Nod. 3. Lost on the Lagoon. 4. Round the Tower Ditch. 5. Sun Pictures. 6. The Sported Oak. 7. La Reine de la Bretagne. 8. With Hooky Dockly. 9. The Child of the Period. 10. Under the Shadow of Bleak House. 11. With an Order. 12. On the Road to France. 13. Mid-Channel Miseries. 14. Beyond the Bounds of Probability. 15. The Rows of Great Yarmouth. 16. Grey November. 17. Ninety in the Shade. 18. Over the Roofs. 19. Bathing at Portrush. 20. In Search of a Church. 21. A Cruise upon Soles. 22. Pickled Egg Walk. 23. A Quiet Evening and a Little Music. 24. Firelight Fancies. 25. Still Summer Night. 26. Nothing in the City. 27. Warm Weather Wishes. 28. An Uninteresting Walk. 29. On the Motive Power in Inanimate Objects. 30. Roasted Chestnuts. 31. Railway Readings. 32. On the Bridge. 33. The Big Pike of Constance. 34. Spring's Delights. 35. Taken in Tow. 36. Hunting the Hare. 37. The Demolition of the Den.

OPINIONS OF THE PRESS :—

Morning Post.

'It is above all in the geniality of this book—in the author's power to establish a sort of confidential relationship with his readers—that its great charm is to be found. A keen relish and perception of what is characteristic in men and things, at times full of minuteness and finesse, at times bold and vivid ; a light of fancy which generally enhances instead of diminishing the accuracy of detail, and which only breaks into a glow of hyperbole when the writer's high spirits or earnestness carry him away, for which you like him all the better. These qualities, combined with an artist's sense of colour and attitude, show the mental resources of the essays ; but all these merits derive their intensity, and some of them their existence, from the sympathetic nature that applies them.'

Morning Advertiser.

'A gem that ought almost to entitle its author to take a permanent position in the rank of such essayists as Addison, Steele, Goldsmith, and Lamb.'

Standard.

'The book is full of sunshine, and there is not a page in it that cannot be read with interest.'

Daily News.

'Everywhere Mr Sterry carries with him an observant eye, a light and graphic pencil, and an abundant and tolerant good nature.'

Hour.

'There is a sense of languor about Mr Sterry's writing that renders it delicious to idlers ; the very pages seem redolent of summer flowers, or to be softly stirring with the wooing of the zephyr, inviting dreamy repose, laziness, and meditation. . . . It is written in easy, graceful English, and does not contain a dull page from cover to cover.'

Pall Mall Gazette.

'These light and lively papers, in the form of travelling sketches, essays on familiar subjects, and descriptions of every-day scenes, range in tone from the sentimental to the burlesque, but hover, for the most part, be-tween these two extremes. Their character, indeed, is sufficiently indicated by the name. A shuttlecock is made of cork and feathers ; and, properly feathered, a shuttlecock will fly at the least touch in any direction.'

Globe.

' 'Some of them are graphically descriptive of mountain scenery and London streets ; some tell of adventure by sea and land ; and some assume a mock air of philosophic teaching worthy of a Yankee pen.'

The Graphic.

'Mr Ashby-Sterry does not profess to penetrate very deeply into any-thing ; but in a series of bright, lively, amusing essays, he skims gracefully over the surface of many familiar scenes and ideas. The keen observation which he displays, and his habit of regarding his subjects from a Londoner's point of view, recall the writings of the late Albert Smith. . . Wherever he goes the author evidently keeps his eyes open to good purpose, and his book is just the volume we should choose to take down with us to the sea-margin when the holidays begin.'

Spectator.

'The very lightest reading we were ever entertained with. . . *Sensa-tions* are the things with which the author seems most commonly imbued, and which he is great in describing with a picturesque and humorous vivid-ness. . . . It is mixed sense and nonsense from a mind full of pleasur-able recollections, too lazy during the prattle to be morbid about truth, intensely sensitive to comfort or discomfort, but refined by poetic feeling and an appreciation of beauty, and fired occasionally by a manly impulse towards exertion. . . . His perception is quick and delicate, his humour lively, his experience in travel not inconsiderable.'

Court Journal.

' These papers will reveal to the reading public an essayist of rare quiet humour, a sort of mixture of the style of the "Spectator" and "Tatler" writers, and the best modern American essayists.'

Court Circular.

'Mr Ashby-Sterry expresses a hope that his book will be a favourite travelling companion during a summer ramble, but we can assure him it deserves a fairer fate—a place of honour on the bookshelves of those who love the lively chat and pleasant fancies of an accomplished essayist.'

Weekly Dispatch.

'If man, woman, or child requires a book of harmless amusement and a thoroughly enjoyable volume to read at any time and in any place, on a rainy day at home, on a sunny day at the sea-side, on a journey either by land or water—anywhere, in fact, except in church—the best thing to be done is at once to invest in the "Shuttlecock Papers."'

Land and Water.

' As Mendelssohn's "Songs without Words" suggest by music thoughts which fit the imagination of every hearer, so each of these refined sketches suggests to the mind's eye of the reader a picture done in type and printer's ink. . . It is just the book to tranquillize the brain after a hard day's work, to smooth out wrinkles, and send one to bed with a smile on one's tired face. The reader finds his thoughts and recollections of scenes he has visited laid before him without trouble to himself, and feels inclined to appropriate the ideas as his own.'

Hornet.

'The man who amuses and entertains his fellows does a great service to poor humanity ; the author of a smile is a good fellow ; and Mr Sterry is more than that, for there is a wreath of smiles—genial, spontaneous, un-affected smiles—in his pleasant, lazy, happy book.'

Figaro.

'Surely this is the sort of writing we want. Anything to make life pleasanter ; anything to throw a glamour over the hard matter-of-fact ex-

istence of the present day ; anything to make us feel we have a heart ;
anything to stir our slumbering sympathies and latent tastes,—should be
welcomed ; especially when it is in itself perfectly pure, and leaves no sting
nor disagreeable after-taste behind.'

Fun.

' Fun, freshness, and fancy.'

Judy.

' The easiest of easy reading surely is this bright green volume for phi-
losophers on their backs, and stay-at-home travellers in easy-chairs by open
windows.'

John Bull.

' Under a light style and considerable humour there is concealed a good
deal of useful instruction and high principle.'

City Press.

' In these days of high pretences it is really refreshing to meet with an
author who does not consider that he has a special mission to fulfil, and is
content to amuse his readers without seeking to pour stores of information
upon them on the sly ; and for this reason, if for no other, we are inclined
to welcome Mr Ashby-Sterry's handsome volume.'

Church Times.

' Nothing can well exceed its miscellaneousness, and people must be hard
indeed to please that can find nothing in it to their taste. It seems exactly
the sort of volume to take to the sea-side when the weather is too hot for
serious reading, but when absolute *far niente* is not to be thought of.'

Civil Service Gazette.

' It is a book for the far-off sea-side and the home fire-side, for the railway
and the steamboat, for the morning and the evening, for brief intervals
from business and more lengthy periods of recreation. The young, the
middle-aged, or old, the erudite philosopher or the simple clodhopper, will
alike find it a genial companion, a desirable friend, to be courted and sought
after as a newly-discovered pleasure.'

School Board Chronicle.

' For an hour after study, after dinner, or in the evening, on board a
steamer, or lying lazily in a nook by the Thames, Mr Ashby-Sterry's book is
one of the best volumes we have seen for many a day. . . . A companion
not exactly for an idle hour, but for intellectual rest.'

Mirror.

' Open where he may, the reader is at once engaged by its easy, graphic
descriptions, and the rippling humour which seems to bubble in every line.
It is the very champagne of " special reporting," and yet there is in it more
suggestion than usually belongs to that popular branch of modern literature
— a power of concentration ; a happy faculty of intensity even in its lightest
passages ; and a certain concentrated habit of observation which, combined
with the ability to touch in lights and shadows, somehow indicates the art
of the painter combined with that of the author.'

Illustrated Review.

' He might, indeed, have called his book "Jottings from the Journal of a
modern Mark Tapley," though the comparison does not hold good in every
point, for the opportunity of being jolly under circumstances that would
make it creditable to be jolly, though it was unaccountably denied to Mark
Tapley, was at times vouchsafed to Mr Sterry, and it is only bare justice to
him to allow that on these occasions he did indeed " come out strong."'

South London Press.

' It is a book not to read and straightway return to a circulating library,
but to be retained on our shelves to dip into when we are disposed for a
pleasantly-employed hour—certainly not an " idle " one—with an instructive
and agreeable companion.'